It only takes me a minute now to locate the request form for Idaho and the county I was born in. I fill it out and use my emergency credit card to pay for the processing fee. But my finger hovers over the mouse before I confirm the order. Waiting. Excited. Scared. A little guilty, maybe, because I don't know how my parents would feel about this, and they've got so much to deal with right now.

But they don't have to know.

I bite my lip. Close my eyes. Take a breath. And click confirm.

I only want to find out her name, I tell myself. Because I always think about my birth mother on my birthday. It'd be nice if I could put a name to that hazy image of her in my mind, that teenage girl, who maybe looks like me.

I wonder if she thinks about me, too.

THE HOW

&

THE WHY

Cynthia Hand

HARPER TEEN
An Imprint of HarperCollinsPublishers

HarperTeen is an imprint of HarperCollins Publishers.

The How & the Why
Copyright © 2019 by Cynthia Hand
Emoji art supplied by EmojiOne
All rights reserved. Printed in the United States of America. No part of this book may be used
or reproduced in any manner whatsoever without written permission except in the case of brief
quotations embodied in critical articles and reviews. For information address HarperCollins
Children's Books, a division of HarperCollins Publishers, 195 Broadway, New York, NY 10007.
www.epicreads.com

Library of Congress Control Number: 2019939428
ISBN 978-0-06-269317-4

Typography by Ellice M. Lee
21 22 23 24 25   PC/LSCH   10 9 8 7 6 5 4 3 2 1
❖
First paperback edition, 2021

For Mom and Dad, who didn't ask for a refund
even though I was clearly a faulty baby.
And for the anonymous girl who put me into their arms.

Thank you.

I love you because the entire universe conspired to help me find you.

—Paulo Coelho

Dear X,

Today Melly has us writing letters to our babies.

I'm not keeping you, so this felt like cruel and unusual punishment. There are fifty girls at this school, and only a few of us are choosing adoption, and most of those are open adoptions, where everyone knows each other's names and you send emails back and forth to the new parents and get pictures and an update every month or something. But I'm not doing that, either.

So I said I'd like to opt out of this assignment.

Melly said fine, I could opt out if I wanted to, but then she said that there's a program where you write a letter to your baby, which they can request when they turn eighteen. So if there's something you want to say that can't be done by checking a box or writing down your blood type, here's your chance.

"You can write whatever you want," Melly said. "Anything."

"But it's optional, right?" I asked.

"Yes."

"Which means I don't have to do it."

"Okay," Melly said. "You just sit here and chill."

Then she passed around some yellow notepads, like legal ones (which seems kind of old school if you ask me) and she gave one to me, too. "Just in case," she said. Sneaky Melly.

The other girls started scribbling away. Apparently they all have important things to tell their babies.

Not me. No offense, but I don't even know you that well.

To me, you're still sort of intangible. I know you're in there, but you're not obvious yet.

You're tight pants.

You're heartburn.

You're the space alien slowly taking over my body.

You're X.

I can't imagine you as an actual baby, let alone an eighteen-year-old person reading this letter. I'm not even eighteen yet myself.

So what could I possibly have to say to you? I don't have any great wisdom to pass along that couldn't be summed up by the words <u>use birth control, girls</u>. But that's complicated, because if I'd done that, you wouldn't exist. I'm sure you prefer existing.

Some things are better left unsaid, was my thinking. So I sat there, chilling. Not writing a letter.

But obviously I changed my mind.

I started to consider you, I guess. If I were an adopted kid, I'd want there to be a letter for me. Because I'd want to find out the things that aren't in the paperwork. I'd be curious. I'd want to know.

2

So . . . hi. I'm your birth mother, aka the person who lugged you around inside of me for nine months.

I have blue eyes and brown hair and I'm a Libra, if you're the kind of person who's interested in signs. There's not much more to tell about me, I'm afraid. I'm solidly average—sorry, I wish I could report that I'm a genius or gorgeous or spectacularly gifted at the piano or chess. But I'm just typical. My grades aren't fantastic. I don't know what I want to be when I grow up. I'm not a cheerleader. I don't do sports.

I am into music. I collect old vinyl records. I go to concerts, music festivals, that kind of thing. I follow some of the local bands.

Right now I'm living at Booth Memorial, a place where pregnant teens go to finish high school. It's a school, but it's also a group home—like in those days when girls used to disappear for months and their parents would tell everybody they were "visiting an aunt." Most of the homes for unwed mothers around the country have closed, since having a baby out of wedlock isn't the super shocking thing it used to be. This place is mainly a school now. A few of us live here, but the majority of the students live at home, and, like I said, they're keeping their babies. There's a daycare on campus where they can bring them after they give birth.

I guess you must be wondering why I'm not keeping you. The simplest answer is this: I'm not cut out to be a mother.

Not that I'm a terrible person. But I'm sixteen years old. I don't think anybody is exactly qualified to be a mother at sixteen. I'm trying not to be judgmental, but the girls around here, the ones who are keeping their babies and who look at me like I'm some kind of monster because I'm not keeping mine, they think it's going to be sharing clothes and braiding each other's hair and being BFFs. But that's not the real world.

The real world. God, I sound like my father. He would not approve of this letter-writing thing. Dad's a believer in the clean-slate philosophy.

3

"After this, you can start over," he keeps telling me. "You can wipe the slate clean."

What he doesn't say, but I hear anyway, is, "And then nobody will have to know."

So here I am, hiding out like it's the fifties. At school—at my old school, I mean—nobody knows about my predicament except my best friend. I'm sure people are asking her where I am. I don't know what she tells them. But maybe it's easier being here than parading my pregnant belly through the halls of BHS. It's less to deal with, anyway.

The point is, I hope you get it—the why of the whole thing. I hope you have a good life—a boring, no-drama, no-real-problems kind of life.

Good luck, X. I wish you the best.

Your host body,

S

1

"Happy birthday, Cass," says Nyla.

"Thanks." I dunk a chip into the salsa and eye the mariachi band singing in the corner of the restaurant. I hope Nyla didn't tell them it's my birthday.

"So how does it feel," she asks, "the great one eight?"

I shrug. "It's not a big deal."

"Not a big deal?" she scoffs. "But now you can buy cigarettes."

"Ew." I crunch the chip. "Like I would ever."

"Agreed—ew—but you can do so much now," she elaborates. "You can purchase lottery tickets. You can open your very own bank account, or get a tattoo. You can drink alcohol in Europe."

"Yeah, I'll get right on that."

"My point is, now you're a grown-up." She leans forward across the table, like she's about to impart some secret of the universe. "You're an adult," she whispers.

I lean forward, too. "I kind of liked being a kid."

She sighs and sits back. "Boo. You're no fun."

"You're just jealous because you're not going to be eighteen for another twenty-nine days." I love lording it over Nyla that I'm exactly one month older than she is. And therefore wiser.

She scoffs. "When we're forty you're going to wish you were the younger one."

"When we're forty, I definitely will." I grin. "But right now I'm happy to be your elder."

She sticks her tongue out at me.

"Hey, now. Respect your elders," I scold her, and she rolls her eyes.

I check my watch. It's seven thirty. Still time to sneak in to see Mom. "We should get going," I start to say, but at that moment the mariachi guys show up to serenade me with "Happy Birthday" in Spanish. Nyla sings along as I glare at her. The waitress plops a giant serving of fried ice cream down in front of me, a single candle burning in the middle.

Everyone in Garcia's turns to look.

"Oh wow . . . thank you . . . so much." I blow out the candle and push the bowl of melty ice cream into the middle of the table so Nyla can share. "I hate you, by the way."

"No, you don't." She licks ice cream off her spoon. "I'm pretty sure you love me."

"Fine, I love you," I grumble. I notice that the elderly couple at the next table over is not-so-subtly staring at Nyla. It happens. Occasionally people in this white-bread Idaho town act surprised when they see a black person. It's what Nyla calls the unicorn effect. People see her and stare like she's some rare and magical creature that they've only heard about in storybooks. Which is weird for Nyla, because she was raised by a white family in a white town and doesn't totally identify as American Black.

We ignore the gawkers and polish off the rest of the ice cream. Nyla gestures at the waitress for the bill. Which she pays. She always pays, birthday or not. I try not to feel guilty about it.

"Dinner was *excelente*," I say as we walk out to Bernice, Nyla's car. "*Gracias, señorita*."

"*De nada*," Nyla replies. Yay for three years of middle school Spanish. This is unfortunately about the collective sum of our ability in that language.

We climb into the car. "Seat belts," Nyla says primly, and we're off.

I get the sensation that we're sailing instead of driving, which is normal. Bernice is a boat. She's named after Nyla's grandma, because she's a total grandma car—silvery blue and enormous and built like a tank. But Bernice always gets us where we need to go.

"On the road again," Nyla sings as we're cruising along through Idaho Falls.

"Just can't wait to get on the road again," I join in.

I check my watch. Seven forty. Still time. Then I realize we're heading in the opposite direction of home. "Hey, where are we going?"

"Oh, I thought we could take a drive," Nyla says mysteriously.

Like this is something people do: take drives. "A drive where?" I ask as we turn onto Hitt Road. Hitt Road, I think for more than the hundredth time, is an epically bad name for a road. Why not call it Smash Street? Insurance Claim Lane?

Nyla glances in the rearview mirror. "To Thunder Ridge."

"Um . . . why?" Thunder Ridge is a hill that overlooks the city. As far as I know, making out is about all people do there.

"It has a nice view," Nyla says. "I thought we could hang out a bit. Talk."

"We've been talking all day. That's practically all we do, is talk."

"Cass."

"Nyla." I give her a look. "What's going on?"

"Nothing. Can't a girl take her bestie to a quiet spot to contemplate the meaning of life and birthdays?"

"I guess, but you know my dad has that birthday tradition where he tells me the story of the day they got me, and we look at my baby book, and there's me in a bunch of frilly pink dresses, and I want to vomit, but I also kind of love it? I don't want to miss that."

"You won't miss it." She's got her phone out now. She's driving and texting. She knows I loathe driving and texting. I hate texting, period, especially when you're supposed to be having real time with someone. It's important to be present, my mom always says. And, come to think of it, Nyla was texting all through dinner. Which is not normal Nyla behavior.

"Ny, come on," I say. "What's going on?"

"Nothing," she says, and then suddenly changes her mind: "You're right. Thunder Ridge is a silly idea. I'll take you home."

She pulls into a subdivision and then flips a U at the entrance and turns us around.

We drive back toward our part of town.

"Country roads, take me home, to the place I belong," Nyla sings.

I don't sing along this time. I'm confused. I feel like I'm failing at some kind of crucial friend test. We stop at a light, and Nyla finishes singing John Denver. She looks at her phone. Touches up her lipstick in the mirror. Checks her phone again.

"Is there something you specifically want to talk about?" I ask. "Because I can talk."

"Nah, I'm good," she says. But obviously she's still being weird.

"I do love our meaning-of-life conversations."

She smiles. "Me too."

"I'm here for you."

"I know."

"So . . . you can talk if you need to talk. I'm listening. I swear."

She seems to consider this for a minute, and then she says, "I can't think of anything to say. Besides, we're almost there."

We are. Bernice veers off into my neighborhood. There are a bunch of cars parked along the street in front of my house. Nyla has to park a little ways down.

"You want to come in for a minute?" I ask. "We could—I don't know—*talk*?"

She smiles. "Did you know that now you're eligible for jury duty? You can be called upon anytime, and you have to do it."

And yay, we're back on the subject of being eighteen again. I make a face. "Excellent."

"Plus, now you can *vote*."

"I can't wait."

"You can enlist in the army," she adds as we make our way up the sidewalk and onto my front porch.

"No, thank you." I gaze at my house. The windows are dark—the living room curtains drawn. I wonder if Dad's already at the hospital.

"You can buy fireworks," Nyla continues. "Or go skydiving. Or go to real-people jail." She gasps and grabs my arm. "You can get married without the permission of your parents!"

I arch an eyebrow at her. "That's great news, Ny. Too bad I'm single." She knows this. She also knows that I don't plan to get married until I'm at least twenty-five. "Though speaking of which, there is one thing I do want to do," I say as I fumble with my keys at the front door. "Now that I'm officially eighteen."

"Oh yeah?" Nyla cocks her head at me, her curly hair like a dark halo around her head. "Don't tell me you want to get your belly button pierced. Because I do not approve."

"Ouch. No." The lock clicks and the door swings open, but I stop and turn to face Nyla. "I want to have sex," I announce. "I think it's time. I'm ready."

I don't know why I say it like that. It's not really the sex part I'm ready for, exactly. It's the boyfriend part. I'm eighteen now, and I've never had a real boyfriend. I've gone on a few dates here and there, kissed a guy or two, made out a little, but I've never been in love, never felt *that way* about anybody. But somehow it's easier to talk about sex than it is to confess that I want to fall in love, which sounds cheesy. It's also fun to say something shocking to Nyla every now and then. Which totally worked; she's frowning, staring past me over my shoulder into the dark house like she wants to go inside. "Uh, Cass—"

"I mean, obviously I don't want to have sex just for the sake of having sex," I clarify. "That's stupid. I know. I want to be a responsible adult now that I'm actually an adult. I would want it to be with the right guy. And maybe the right guy won't come along this year, because—come on, do we know any guys who are, like, boyfriend material? Not really, right? And I'm okay with that."

"Okay. . ." Nyla still looks super uncomfortable.

"All I'm saying is, if the right guy *does* come along, I'm open to the idea of having sex."

That said, I turn to go into the house and almost run smack into my dad inside the doorway. He's wearing a paper party hat. Holding a flaming birthday cake. Surrounded by my grandma and my uncle Pete and, like, ten of my friends.

"Surprise?" my dad whispers.

"Oh my God."

"Yeah," he says. "Yeah, I know."

"You were all standing here."

He gives a painful smile. "We were."

"I say go for it, honey," says Grandma. "Seize the day."

"I'm a big no on this one," says Uncle Pete. "No sex for you. Possibly ever."

"Wait, how am I not considered boyfriend material?" says my friend Bender. "I'm, like, hot."

"Does this mean I'm going to need a shotgun?" asks Dad.

I'm humiliated for all of five seconds. But then Nyla starts giggling, which makes me start giggling, and then we're all outright laughing, then singing, and then I blow out the eighteen candles on the cake.

2

"Was it a good cake?" Mom asks later, at the hospital.

"It was grocery store cake." I sit on the edge of the bed and rub her feet under the covers. Even through the blankets they feel like blocks of ice. "Dad can't make himself go to the shop."

"I miss it." Mom sighs. "I miss everything."

I nod. "I used to think the shop was actual magic."

"It was," Mom agrees, but then she does that thing where she makes a conscious choice not to dwell on what she's lost. "So. Happy birthday. I'm sorry I couldn't be there for your party."

"It was no big deal," I say, and actually I'm glad this time that she wasn't at my party, so she didn't get to hear my embarrassing announcement regarding boys. Which I'm pretty sure no one else is ever going to let me live down.

She reaches over to the bedside table, where there is a small package wrapped in blue paper. "Here."

I unwrap it. It's a ring box. Inside is a silver ring with a circle of stars around the circumference.

"It's a copy of a sixteenth-century English ring in the British Museum," Mom explains. "It's called a poesy ring."

I get an instant lump in my throat. Do not, I think, under any circumstances, cry in front of your sick mother.

Mom takes the ring and reads the inscription on the inside: "*Many are the starrs I see, but in my eye no starr like thee.*"

"It's perfect." I slide the ring onto the middle finger of my right hand, where it fits, well, perfectly.

"You've always been my star." Mom opens her arms for a hug. "Happy birthday, darling girl."

"I'll never take it off," I promise into her bony shoulder. "Never ever."

She lies back against the bed again, her face pale. "I can't believe you're eighteen," she murmurs. "It feels like I blinked, and you went from being a baby to being all grown up. How did that happen?"

"You fed me," I answer. "I think that's how it works."

Mom laughs. "You used to cry from ten o'clock at night to a little past two in the morning, every single night until you were almost six months old. No matter what we tried."

"It's amazing you didn't send me back and ask for a refund. I was clearly a faulty baby."

Mom shakes her head. "We were thrilled to have you. We didn't care about the crying."

This is a familiar scene between us. Mom always says, "You were the most gorgeous baby. I couldn't believe it, the first time I saw you."

Then I say, "You were the most gorgeous mom."

And then Mom says something like: "I would have been happy with a boring, regular baby. That's all I was thinking about—that I wanted a baby. Any baby would do. But you've always been extraordinary. So smart. So funny. So beautiful. I could never have imagined in a million years that I'd be so lucky to end up with a daughter like you."

And I say, "Okay, Mom, stop. You're making me blush."

I wait for it, but this time Mom doesn't go into any of that. She's quiet.

"Are you okay?" I ask. Mom's always been a talker. Silence is usually a bad sign.

"I'm so tired of being here," she says.

My breath catches. It's been more than a year since that night in the movie theater when she had the heart attack. One minute she was munching popcorn and laughing at Chewbacca, and the next she said it felt like an elephant was sitting on her chest. We called an ambulance immediately and rushed her straight to the hospital. She spent hours in surgery and months in a state of touch and go. For a while she got to come home, hooked up to a machine that pumps her blood for her, but a few months ago she had to go back to the hospital full-time.

She needs a transplant. I'm choosing to believe that she's going to get a new heart. Soon. I hope.

But here's the thing: through all the ups and the downs of this past year, my mother has never complained. It's an unspoken rule we have. For my sake, Mom tries not to show me how painful and exhausting it is now just to make it from one day to the next. And I, in return, try not to show her how terrified I am of losing her. And so we go on pretending that life is basically normal. I act like a standard-issue teenager—I keep my grades up and keep performing in plays for the high school theater and keep talking about boys and the drama club and how gross the cafeteria food is, and my parents act like Mom's stay at the hospital is a minor inconvenience, a temporary thing.

Normalcy. That's our goal. We've gotten really good at acting like everything's fine.

But now Mom said she's tired of being here, and I don't know if she's being literal or figurative. And I don't know what to say.

"I'm sorry," I go with finally. "I know this sucks."

She closes her eyes and smiles faintly. "The universe unfolds as it should," she murmurs. This, too, is what she always says. She's not religious, but she believes in this greater force: the universe. Which somehow, in her mind, anyway, makes her heart problems part of some bigger picture. She has faith in that.

Her leg jerks slightly, her hand relaxing in mine. Her breath becomes even and deep. She's fallen asleep. She does that a lot—conks out mid-conversation. I tuck her in, being careful not to tangle the covers in the hand with her IV. Then I sit watching the rise and fall of her chest, trying to commit every part of her face to memory. The gentle curve of her eyebrows. Her nose. The shape of her ears.

People who don't know I'm adopted always tell me I look like her. I choose to take it as a compliment. Mom has long blond hair and gorgeous hazel eyes that are this perfect mix of green and brown. I don't resemble her at all, really. But everyone keeps saying I'm the spitting image of my mother, unless they don't know her, in which case they tell me I look like my redheaded, green-eyed, freckle-faced dad. Whom I resemble even less.

I turn her words over in my head: *the universe unfolds as it should*. If that's true, then I have issues with the universe, because it's not fair. My mom has the best heart, and it's failing her.

Screw you, universe, I think. But I also kind of think: *Please help?*

I stand up and turn off the light, waiting in the dark, listening as the vitals monitor beeps and beeps, a steady, comforting sound, because it means she's still here.

"Good night, Mom," I whisper, and then I sneak out and close the door.

3

Dad's up grading papers when I get home. He's a fifth-grade teacher, the cool kind that all the kids wish was their dad. He works ridiculously hard, long hours for terrible pay, but he loves it.

"How is she?" he asks when I pop my head into the spare room he uses as an office.

"She seemed kind of low," I report.

He nods. "She hates missing out on special occasions."

"I know."

"Speaking of special occasions, I've got something extra special for you." He puts down his pencil and goes to the closet, where he pulls out another wrapped gift, which turns out to be a shirt for Boise State University, because it's Dad's lifelong dream that I attend BSU (like my father before me, he always says—a Star Wars joke) and watch football games on the famous blue "Smurf Turf." Even though no one in my family is really into football.

"Oh, Dad, come on," I groan.

"I know," he agrees. "But I happen to think you look particularly good in blue and orange." He waggles his eyebrows at me. "It's almost time to start applying. I don't want to pressure you, or to rush you, sweetie. But now's the time to spread your wings, if you know what I mean."

"I know, I know." I hug the shirt to my chest. "Thanks, Dad." I try to keep my expression neutral, which frankly is a big test of my acting ability. Not that there's anything wrong with Boise State. It just feels so . . . small potatoes. So Idaho. I have dreams, bigger dreams than Boise State, wild, improbable dreams, and I'm not ready to wake up and face reality yet. Plus, it's hard to even think about going to college right now, what with Mom in the hospital. So I change the subject. "Thanks for the party, too, by the way. It was fun."

"It was . . . illuminating. Do we need to talk about sex?"

"Um, no. We already did that." It was like five years ago when my parents sat me down and explained sex to me, in detail, with props like a banana and a condom. It was informative, but not something I'd ever want to hear again. Like, ever.

"Do you need me to get you a prescription for anything?" he asks now.

"There's no boy, Dad," I explain. "I don't know why I said all that earlier. I didn't know you were . . . I didn't mean it."

"It's fine if you did mean it," he says. "But I want you to be safe."

And this is why Dad can be mortifying, but also kind of great. He has no shame about letting me know how things are (my parents are both prone to grand, inspirational speeches from time to time, usually about how very "special" I am—it's embarrassing), but then Dad always steps back and lets me decide the best course of action for

18

myself. He calls it "respecting my autonomy." So I know Dad's opinion, but what I do is up to me.

"I . . . I was thinking it would be nice to finally have a boyfriend," I confess. "That's all."

He nods. "I can see that. You've had a lot going on over the last year."

I bite my lip. "You don't think it's too much? That I'm just a meat bag full of hormones, and I should wait until . . . until things settle down . . . before adding boys to everything else?"

He snorts. "Aren't we all just meat bags full of hormones?" He ruffles my bangs. "In my experience, which, yes, I understand is going to be totally different from your experience, big life events happen when they're ready to happen, no matter what you've already got going on."

"The universe unfolds as it should," I murmur.

He nods a bit sadly, because now he's thinking of Mom. "So be careful, sure. Try to make good choices. Be kind. Be aware that feelings are just that—feelings. Feelings can be fickle. But be open to the possibilities."

And that's the inspirational speech for today. "Fine," I sigh dramatically. "Consider me open to the possibilities."

His eyebrows come together. "But there's no *actual* boy right now? You're only talking about a theoretical boy?"

"Yes. A theoretical boy."

"Right." He cringes. "I would never threaten anybody with a shotgun. That was a joke, earlier."

"I know."

"I find the whole shotgun thing totally patronizing."

"And you don't own a shotgun," I remind him.

"Good point."

I give him a quick hug. "I'm going to bed now, Dad. Night."

He presses a kiss to the top of my head. "Good night, Boo. I hope you had a decent birthday. There's leftover cake in the kitchen. But it's not the best cake, is it?"

"It's definitely subpar," I agree.

I get a slice anyway and go to my room and sit at my desk for a while, picking off the frosting and wasting time on my laptop. Then I get ready for bed and spend like an hour staring up at the ceiling and twisting my new ring around and around on my finger, pondering the meaning of life, birthdays, college, and the existence of theoretical boys, which seems more than silly now, considering that my life is firmly in this bubble of high school and theater and hospital, and it's unlikely that I'm going to randomly bump into a new guy. And that gets me contemplating the overall will of the universe.

This weird unreliable universe.

Which gets me thinking about my birth mother.

I always think about her on my birthday. Probably because it's the one thing I definitely know about my birth mother: that on September seventeenth, eighteen years ago, a sixteen-year-old girl had a baby, and that baby was me.

It was just one of the facts I grew up knowing about myself: I have blue eyes, my favorite color is purple, I like pizza, and I'm adopted. When I was little my parents told me they picked me out of a cabbage patch. As I got older my dad started to claim that I was left in the backyard by an alien spacecraft. Those were meant to be jokes, but there was a real story there, too, one they told me again and again, about a lonely couple who desperately desired a child, and a brave young woman who wanted to give a better life to her baby. It's always felt like a fairy tale written specifically about me. One where I was the happy ending.

But that's the thing, I think, frowning up at the ceiling. I'm the ending of the story. I don't even know the beginning.

And I'm eighteen now. I'm an adult. Legally, anyway.

I get up and go to the doorway of my room, peering down the hall, where I can see Dad's finally gone to bed. Then I close my door, lock it, and open my laptop again.

Like I said, I think about my birth mother. When I was six and went to vacation Bible school with my friend Alice, and they told us the story of Moses and his mother weaving a basket out of reeds and setting him afloat on the Nile, hoping to save his life. Or at dinner at another friend's house when I was eight, when I looked around the table and noticed that every single member of her family had the same nose. Or when my mom took me to a Broadway show when I was twelve, and little orphan Annie sang this song about her parents, wondering if they were far away or close by, wondering if her mother played piano, if she collected art, if she sewed. And suddenly my chest felt tight.

"Betcha they're good," Annie sang out into the darkness. "Why shouldn't they be? Their one mistake was giving up me."

That was when it really hit me. My birth mother was out there, somewhere. Then I looked at my actual mother sitting next to me with this pained look on her face, but also like she was trying to be brave, for me, and I dashed away the tears that had filled my eyes. I smiled. Because I didn't want her to feel like that's how I saw her and Dad—like a place my birth parents had dumped me.

After that I thought about my birth mother more often. On birthdays. Or those times that inevitably your friends start talking about the things they inherited from their parents that they wished they hadn't—a cleft chin or double-jointed elbows or nearsightedness. It always kind of bugs me, how much I don't know about that kind of thing—what's lurking in my genes—how there's this entire set of information that I am totally clueless about. So a couple years ago curiosity finally got the better of me, and I went online and did a few internet searches, not to find my birth mother, exactly, but to discover who she was. Who she is.

And maybe, by extension, who I am.

I didn't find anything. But I remember that there was something about being eighteen and requesting my official birth certificate—not the one they issued to my parents, with their names listed and my name as the one they gave me, but the original. The one with my birth mother's name.

It only takes me a minute now to locate the request form for Idaho and the county I was born in. I fill it out and use my emergency credit card to pay for the processing fee. But my finger hovers over the mouse before I confirm the order. Waiting. Excited. Scared. A little guilty, maybe, because I don't know how my parents would feel about this, and they've got so much to deal with right now.

But they don't have to know.

I bite my lip. Close my eyes. Take a breath. And click confirm.

I only want to find out her name, I tell myself. Because I always think about my birth mother on my birthday. It'd be nice if I could put a name to that hazy image of her in my mind, that teenage girl, who maybe looks like me.

I wonder if she thinks about me, too.

Dear X,

Me again. Who else, right? Last night after dinner the girls in the dorm somehow got to talking about the letters. Then Brit had the idea that we should all read one another's. I protested, but I was outvoted. So this is peer pressure, really. Take note. Peer pressure is not only about drinking beer.

Brit's letter was the longest—she tried to write out her entire life story and every tiny detail about who she is and how she ended up here. Her baby's a girl. If it weren't for the unfortunate circumstances—she's thirteen, and the father is a married volleyball coach; she's right out of a daytime talk show, Brit—she'd keep her baby, she says. She has this idea that when the girl turns eighteen she'll find her again, and they'll simply pick up where they left off, mother and daughter, happily ever after.

She's clearly not a fan of reality. But I didn't say anything. She's just a kid.

Teresa's letter was like a confession—she wrote about God and her sins and how she hopes her baby can grow up without shame. Which made us all go quiet for a while.

Out of the four of us who are currently living here at Booth, Heather's letter was the best. She talked about the better life she wants for her baby, and she listed some things that it would be helpful to know, like that blushing runs in the family and not to be embarrassed if he/she turns out to be one of those people who blush easily, because somewhere in the world she's out there blushing, too. She was bright red the whole time we were reading the letters. It was sweet.

My letter was the shortest, and everyone agreed that it was terrible. Impersonal. Unhelpful. In other words, I got it all wrong.

"You didn't say anything that will help the baby get to know you," Brit complained.

"Because I don't want to be known," I said. No offense, X, but I think that's for the best. You go your way. I'll go mine.

Brit looked at me all full of pity. Like _she_ felt sorry for _me_.

"You're a good writer," Heather piped up, blushing, of course. "But . . ."

They all think I should rewrite my letter.

I told them to mind their own business and went to bed. I wasn't going to write anything else. I don't owe you my life story or any real explanations for anything. That's not how this process works. I am giving you freedom and a chance to start fresh. A clean slate for both of us, really. I don't want to mess that up with my baggage.

But today I had some downtime in my room, and I kept thinking about the other girls' letters. If I were Brit's baby, I'd read that long, detailed letter, and I'd understand so much. Maybe more than I'd want to know. But it got me thinking again that I'd want to. Know, I mean. I'd want to know more about where I came from. The how and the why. The story.

I don't want you to feel shame, like Teresa wrote about. I don't want to label you a mistake, but you aren't my brightest shining moment, either. That's not your fault. You're a good thing. You shouldn't have to feel ashamed of the way you ended up in this world.

And Heather was right in what she wrote about blushing in her family. I'm sure there will be connections between us, like blushing, like how easily we get cavities, that sort of thing, that are always going to be there, invisible but also unerasable. It makes me wonder about you. The ways you will turn out like me, and we won't even know it. The pieces we will share.

So I might owe you something, after all.

A beginning.

You see, when a man and a woman love each other very, very much . . .

Ha-ha. Well, that's not my job, telling you about that. You're eighteen. If you don't know this stuff already, I'm not going to be the one to tell you.

If I were you, though, I'd be curious about the guy who spawned you—the sperm donor, so to speak. He's never going to be your father in any real sense of the word, the same way I'm never going to be your mother, but you should know something more about him than what the paperwork will tell you—that he's nineteen years old and 6'1" and he's got green eyes and blond hair.

Yep, I fell for the older guy. I'm an idiot. I think we've established that.

I'm going to call him Dawson. That's not his real name. There's a TV

25

show I used to love that you've probably never heard of, and he looks a little bit like the guy on that show. Tall. Blond. But the TV Dawson was into movies, and my Dawson is into music.

This was all because of the music.

So last November I went to a Pearl Jam concert at the Idaho Center Arena. Don't judge me if Pearl Jam is washed-up by the time you're reading this. I love them. I will always love them—I will go to my grave loving Pearl Jam. I love them so much I paid out the nose for a seat near the stage. So I'm there, and there's an empty seat next to me. I notice this blond guy skulking around in the aisle, and I can tell by looking at him that he's trying to find a better seat than the one he's got. He keeps eyeballing the seat next to mine, but he waits, he waits until the opening band starts up. He waits until we're all screaming—Matt Cameron is sliding behind the drums, Eddie Vedder taking the stage, and Mike McCready and Stone Gossard strapping on their guitars—and the blond guy makes his move and scoots in next to me.

Usually I wouldn't care. But I paid a lot for my seat. I stood in a ridiculously long line to get it. I had to plead with my dad. I had to promise not to smoke pot, which is what my dad assumes is all that happens at Pearl Jam concerts, I guess. I had to be a committed fan to get this seat. So I turn to the guy.

"Hey, can I see your ticket?" I ask him. "I don't think this is your seat."

It's loud. The stage lights have all gone red. The band's playing. Eddie's starting in on "Of the Girl." People are screaming and cheering and jumping up and down, hands raised.

The blond guy doesn't hear me. Or at least he acts like he doesn't.

"Hey! You! That's not your seat!" I grab his shoulder.

He turns. Smiles.

"Heavy the fall, quarter to four," he sings along, like it's right to me, *"fills his mind with the thought of a girl."* He looks into my eyes. As if I'm the girl in the song. As if I'm the point of him being here.

I know. I shouldn't have fallen for it. But he's hot—I hope you end up looking like him, because frankly, he's a specimen. The biting words I had planned—the scathing condemnation of this jerk-off taking someone else's hard-earned seat—die on my lips. The guy's still smiling, still singing, and he knows the words by heart. The lights change blue. Eddie's voice wraps itself around us like a seductive serpent of alternative goodness. I become aware that I'm still hanging on to the guy's shoulder. He's warm under my fingers. I let go. The guy angles back toward the stage, still singing. I can't hear his voice over Eddie's, but it's like I can feel it, and I start singing, too, waving my hands in the air, and that's how it goes, the entire concert. We sing. We move to the rhythm. We stare up at Eddie Vedder, so close we can see the beads of sweat on his forehead, we sing and sing, we sway, we forget about everything else, we let the music take us.

Then, hours later, it's over. I feel like I'm waking up from a dream. The band leaves the stage. The lights come up.

The guy turns to me again. He tells me his name. I tell him mine.

"There's a band you should listen to," he says like he knows me, as we're walking out. "You'd love their sound. They're playing here." He writes an address down for me on a scrap of paper. "Next Saturday night. The Sub. Nine o'clock."

The Sub must be a bar or something, I think. I'm not old enough to go to bars.

"Okay." I wait for him to ask me to go with him to said bar to listen to said band. But he doesn't. He smiles, and his eyes are green, I notice again, and he smells good, like sandalwood and pot smoke, maybe—don't tell my dad, and don't smoke pot, kid, cuz blah blah blah, just say *no—and that's it. That's how I became acquainted with the person who contributed to half of your DNA.*

Pearl Jam.

So now you know how your story started. With a guy I randomly met at a concert.

I hope that's enough.

S

4

"Don't look," whispers Nyla into my ear, "but there's a new guy over there."

It's a Saturday morning, and we're sitting in the house of the Bonneville High School auditorium, waiting to audition for *Into the Woods*, a musical that's all the fairy tales put together. Ny and I both adore this show, and we're desperate to be in it. I'm feeling sick to my stomach, which is business as usual. This is, like, the twentieth audition I've done, but I'm still a bundle of nerves.

I glance around, but I don't spot anyone unfamiliar. "Guy?" I repeat. "What guy?"

"I said *don't* look." She tries to point with her head.

I follow the gesture, trying to look without looking like I'm looking, and sure enough, sitting in the second row with his green Converse sneakers propped up on the seat in front of him is a boy I've never seen before. I don't know why I had to try to be subtle about it. Everybody in the theater is blatantly staring at him, gossip-whispering. The Bonneville High School theater scene is made up of a small, tight-knit group of the same students, performing play after play together, semester after semester, year after year, so anyone new among us is whisper-worthy. But this guy seems oblivious to the attention he's getting. He's focused on filling out the audition form, bent over his paper writing furiously like it's an application to Juilliard.

"Hey, he may even be cute," I observe, although from this angle it's hard to be sure. I'm mostly seeing him from the back, but he has a nicely shaped head. Dark, careless hair. Skinny jeans. Good shoes.

"More importantly, he's male," Nyla says.

"Amen to that." It's a curse of high school theater that there are, like, three girls for every boy. Nyla and I have both done our share of playing male characters because there simply weren't enough boys to fill the roles. Hopefully this new guy is more than cute. Hopefully he can act. And, for the purposes of this production, as it's a Sondheim musical and the music is really freaking hard, hopefully he can also carry a tune.

The chatter in the house goes quiet as our drama teacher—Joanna Golden, but we call her Mama Jo—glides down the aisle and up onto the stage.

I blow out a shaky breath.

"Don't be nervous," Nyla commands me sternly in a whisper. "If you're nervous, I'll be nervous. And if I'm nervous, I won't hit the high notes."

"I'm not nervous," I whisper back. "I'm completely relaxed. See?" I give her a terrified gritted-teeth type smile.

"Right. Well, don't forget: I got you, babe," she says.

"I got you." This is part of our preperformance support ritual. We bump fists.

"Good morning," Mama Jo says warmly. "I'm thrilled to see so many of you. This is a large-scale production and we're going to need a big cast, so be patient; we've got a lot to get through today. Make sure Sarah the stage manager has your audition form—raise your hand, Sarah, everybody see Sarah?—and then sit tight and wait to be called up. First I want to hear the musical auditions you've prepared. Only one song per person, please. And after I've listened to everybody, we'll break for lunch, and then come back and have you read for some of the roles. Sound good?"

There's a weak chorus of yeses. Everyone, it seems, is equally nervous. I find this comforting. We're all in the same queasy boat.

"Good," says Mama Jo. "Let's get started." She jogs over to sit next to Sarah in the house, who hands her the first form on the pile, which of course belongs to:

"Nyla Henderson," she calls out loudly.

I feel Nyla tense beside me. "You got this," I say as she stands up and brushes past me.

"Hi, Nyla," Mama Jo says when Nyla's up at center stage. "It's good to see you."

Nyla smiles. "Hi. It's good to be seen." Nyla and I have performed, like, seven plays on this stage, all the way back to when we were freshmen. Mama Jo knows us both very well. Which takes some of the pressure off, I guess.

"What will you be singing for us today?" Mama Jo asks.

"'Memory,'" Nyla answers. "From *Cats*."

The music gets cued up, and Nyla begins to sing. At first her voice is soft—nervous, in spite of her swagger—but then her shoulders relax and she really starts to belt out the song, hitting every note solidly, the lows and the highs. And she doesn't just sing. So many people, they get up there and they just sing, but Nyla becomes the character. She fills the lines with emotion. She believes it, and makes us believe it, too.

The song's the perfect choice for this audition. I should know. I helped Nyla choose it, and we've been practicing for weeks. But even though I've heard her sing it, like, fifty times, I can't help but hold my breath as she reaches the final note, a waver of tears in her voice. Then the music fades and everyone listening sits back, quietly stunned.

"Wow, thank you, Nyla," says Mama Jo after a few seconds. There are sporadic claps and hoots, my own included. Nyla sashays back to her seat like her total awesomeness is no biggie.

"Show-off," I fake grumble as she plops down beside me. Mama Jo calls up someone else, and I can breathe for a few seconds. "How am I supposed to follow *that* up?"

"Not my problem," Nyla says, but then grins and puts her arm around me. "You're going to slay it, too. You know you are."

I wish I was as sure as she is about that, but whatever. Nyla's amazing. If I'm being honest: she's better than me. She always has been. I try not to feel competitive with her, but it happens. Sometimes she gets the part I want. Sometimes I get the part she wants. We've learned to navigate the envy, "the green monster" we call it, and simply try to be there for each other. Through thick and thin. Through everything.

We listen to, like, ten more songs from the other students—all good, no bombs. Everyone has apparently brought their A game. That'd be fantastic, if I weren't competing with all of them for a part. Every time Mama Jo calls someone up who's not me I tense up even more.

"Breathe," Nyla whispers.

"I wish I'd gone first. How did you get so lucky? Who did you bribe?"

"Relax, Cass. You're going to be fine."

"You're only saying that because you went first, and now you're off the hook. You're already fine. You're—wait."

Mama Jo has called out a name I don't know.

It's the new guy. He ambles up the stairs and onto the stage like he's been here a million times. He tells Mama Jo he's going to sing "Stars" from *Les Misérables*, a challenging song to say the least, but one of my all-time faves. He takes a minute to stretch—raises his arms above his head, drops them, rolls his head from side to side, shakes out his hands. And then the music begins.

"Whoa," says Nyla after a minute. "New guy can sing."

I stare at him. He's not a big person—he's maybe five nine, and slender—but he's got this huge voice. He gets his notes to the back of the theater with ease. The song starts low, but his low notes don't get lost the way they sometimes can. He practically purrs the song out, and he knows how to act, too. As we're watching it's like he stops being a high school–aged boy and becomes this bitter, weathered police inspector, determined to catch the runaway prisoner he's been hunting for years. Then he shifts and sings in his upper register, this Adam Levine–like falsetto that makes goose bumps jump up along my arms. I've never had that happen before—goose bumps, without being cold. He's that good.

"Holy crap," breathes Nyla. "New guy can *sing*. What did she say his name was again?"

"Sebastian," I answer. "Sebastian Banks."

"This I swear by the stars!" sings Sebastian Banks, holding the last note long and steady and perfect. Then the high school–aged boy reappears, gives a little nod, and walks swiftly off the stage.

Nyla whistles. "Dang. Good thing he's not auditioning for any of the female roles."

I shake my head in wonder. "I'd hate to follow that up."

"Cassandra McMurtrey?" Mama Jo calls.

I close my eyes. "Well, crap." Another, better word bubbles up in my brain, but I always try not to swear in front of Nyla, who never swears if she can help it. My throat feels tight. This is bad. I don't know how I'm going to get any notes out.

"Um, you got this?" Nyla offers.

"I got this," I repeat, and then I take a deep breath and head up onto the stage.

5

"You killed it," Nyla informs me five minutes later, when I wobble back to my seat.

"Thanks." I hope she means this in the positive sense. I don't know how I did. I always go into this white space when I'm up there, a kind of fugue state. But it went all right, I think. Maybe I wasn't a showstopper like Sebastian, or a catch-your-breath performance like Nyla. But I was good. Good enough. I hope.

We must be done with the singing part of the audition, because Mama Jo's on the stage again. "All right, ladies and gentlemen, I'll see you back here at two o'clock, ready to read."

Nyla nods to a few of our friends like, "Lucy's?" and they nod back like, "Of course, meet you there," and she gathers up her jacket and her bag. "Shall we do lunch?"

"Wait," I tell her. "I want to talk to the new guy."

She follows me as I make a beeline toward the front row, where Sebastian Banks is bending over, tying the laces on one of those green Converse. I wait awkwardly for him to stand up. Then I flash him a smile. "Hi."

"Hello," he says, smiling back a bit shyly.

"Sebastian, right?"

"Call me Bastian. And you're . . ." He's staring at my face like he's trying to place me. ". . . Cassandra."

"Call me Cass."

He glances at Nyla.

"Oh, I'm Nyla," she explains. "Call me Nyla." I'm the only one allowed to call her Ny. She says it's lazy when other people shorten her name, like they can't be bothered to pronounce more than one syllable, but I get away with it.

"Cass and Nyla." Bastian gives a little bow. "Nice to meet you."

And just like that—bam—I've met a new guy.

"You're awesome," I blurt out. "I mean, you did awesome. Up there. Earlier."

"Yes, we're impressed," Nyla agrees.

"Thanks." He's still staring at me. It's a little intense.

"You're new here," I say, but of course he knows that. "I mean, you're new to us. Here. At this theater."

He nods. "Yeah, I've done some plays before, at my old school, so I thought I'd give it a try here. Besides, I love *Into the Woods*. I couldn't resist."

I'm nodding so much I'm going to give myself whiplash. "Me too. I'd kill to be in this show. Well, not literally kill, but . . . you know. Metaphorically kill."

Nyla is also staring at me now, but like I've lost my mind.

36

"Anyway," she says slowly, "great to talk to you, Bastian. We should probably get—"

"Do you like pizza?" I ask him. "A bunch of us are going to Lucy's for lunch. Would you like to come with us?"

"Um, sure. Why not?" he says.

Nyla gives me a sharp look as we're going up the aisle out to the parking lot. She loves pizza, probably more than she loves me, honestly, but I asked this guy out with us without running it by her first. Which breaks a sacred rule between us: friends before mens.

"Are you kidding me?" she whispers as we—me, Nyla, and Bastian—pile into Bernice. "What just happened?"

"Sorry," I whisper back. "I should have asked."

"It's fine, I guess," she says, but she starts humming the melody of "Jesus, Take the Wheel" to herself on the way to Lucy's.

"This is a fantastic car," Bastian observes from the back seat as we cruise along. "What model is it?"

"A Buick Regal," Nyla says, warming up to him slightly because even she can't resist any flattery aimed at her precious car. Good call, new guy. Good call.

"Does your car have a name?" he asks, grinning. "Tell me it has a name."

Nyla's chin lifts slightly. "Her name," she says grandly, "is Bernice."

We meet up with Ronnie, Bender, and Alice at Lucy's and eat the aforementioned pizza, and then drive over to a nearby Starbucks for some mandatory coffee (except Nyla, who doesn't do coffee for religious reasons) and by the time that's over, we've learned that Bastian lives on the west side of Idaho Falls (whereas we all live on the east side), that he's a senior but new to Bonneville (before he went to Skyline High School, across town), he's an aficionado of classic movie musicals, he owns three pairs of Converse sneakers in different colors, and he's a sucker for pumpkin spice lattes.

And he's still staring at me.

"Do I have something on my face?" I ask finally.

He shakes his head, laughs. "No. I'm trying to figure out where I know you from."

"Oh." So he was staring because he thought he recognized me. Or maybe that's some kind of flirty line. I kind of hope it is.

"Maybe you've seen her in a play," Ronnie suggests. All through lunch she was smiling and breathy when it came to Bastian, practically fluttering her eyelashes at him.

"I haven't seen any Bonneville plays," Bastian says.

"She also does community theater," Bender adds helpfully. "Cass was Anne in *Anne of Green Gables* this summer. Her hair was bright red. It was something to behold."

"I didn't see it," Bastian admits, "although now I wish I had."

I push a strand of my newly-dark-brown hair behind my ear and try to think of a clever reply, but nothing comes out except, "Yeah, that would have been . . . cool."

Who even uses the word *cool* anymore? My dad, maybe. Ugh.

Bastian's still staring. "Seriously, I swear I've seen you somewhere before."

I shrug. "Maybe I have one of those familiar faces."

"Do you do state drama?" Nyla jumps in. "Cass and I do a scene for that every year. We're the reigning champions, as a matter of fact."

She and I fist bump.

Bastian laughs. "No, sorry. I've never been to the state drama competition."

"You should totally go," Alice says, her voice even higher pitched than usual. It's embarrassing, the way we're all totally fawning over the new guy. We're such a bunch of hormonal meat bags. "They give out this awesome scholarship to one deserving senior," she tells him. "Ten thousand dollars a year to the college of your choice."

His eyes widen. "I'll definitely look into that. Paying for college is at the top of my to-do list lately."

"Me too," says Alice.

"Definitely," giggles Ronnie.

"So what about you?" I ask to change the subject. "I mean, what shows have you done?"

"Let's see." He props his chin in his hand. "Last spring I was in *Charlotte's Web*. I played a pig."

I laugh. "Isn't the pig the starring role?"

"Yeah," he admits. "And it was kind of great, actually, doing a show for kids. I loved making them laugh."

"What else have you been in?" Ronnie asks.

He takes a sip of his latte and thinks a minute. "I was Joseph in *Joseph and the Amazing Technicolor Dreamcoat*. And Biff in *Death of a Salesman*. And Tony in *West Side Story*."

"Shut up. I was Maria in *West Side Story*," Nyla gasps.

"She was amazing," I add.

"I was," Ny says.

She was.

"I believe it," he says. "You've got a luminous voice."

I glance at Nyla. Just last week she told me that, even though people are constantly praising her for what an amazing voice she has, they always seem to imply that she's talented because of her color. "It's like, of course *she* can sing," she said. "Like we're all expected to be

Aretha Franklin." One of the many reasons that Nyla is determined to go to college somewhere big and diverse and get the heck out of small-town Idaho.

But this is an entirely different kind of compliment. Even Nyla gets a bit flustered over this one. He just said her voice was *luminous*. Wow. "Thanks," she says softly.

Bastian glances around the table. "So who do you want to be in *Into the Woods*. What parts do you want?"

"Red Riding Hood," says Alice.

"Rapunzel," says Ronnie.

"The baker," says Bender.

"Cinderella," Nyla and I say at the same time.

He looks back and forth between us. "Uh-oh."

"Nah, we're fine," Nyla says.

"We're good with whatever happens," I agree. "What part do you want?"

"Cinderella's prince," he admits with a laugh.

"You should be Jack, with a voice like yours." Ronnie cocks her head to one side. "Jack's the best singing role."

"I do like Jack. *There are giants in the sky*," he sings, loudly enough that people seated around us shoot us some strange looks. "But no, I want the prince. The prince is fun, and trust me, I can rock a pair of tights."

No doubt. I smile. At this point I'd smile at pretty much anything he says. I'm clearly not doing any better than Ronnie and Alice when it comes to Bastian. He's undeniably cute, from the front, even. He's got the great voice. The sense of humor. He's a fellow theater nerd. And he's not staring at Ronnie or Alice right now, is he?

No. He's staring at me.

He's interested (or at least I *think* he's interested, if I'm reading him right) in little old *me*.

I was just saying I was ready to find myself a boyfriend, and then plop. Sebastian Banks practically falls out of the sky.

Um, thank you, universe?

"Gotta love a man in tights," I twitter.

Nyla's not having it, though, luminous or not. She gives me the subtlest of eye rolls and turns to Bastian, all business. "So why did you change schools?"

He stares at her. "What?"

"You were at Skyline, but now you're at Bonneville. Why?"

He glances away. "Oh. It's a long, boring story, trust me. There was a thing."

"A thing," she repeats.

"At school. I—" He sighs. "It's a long story."

"Wow, that's incredibly nonspecific," Ny says.

I nudge her with my leg under the table. Nyla's always direct, and most of the time I find this refreshing, but right now I'm finding it rude. Who cares why Bastian changed schools? That's certainly none of Nyla's business. We just met the guy.

"Hey, look at the time." Bastian pretends to look at his watch, like her sudden interrogation is a joke. "Maybe we should get back to the theater?"

Bender checks his phone. "Yeah, actually, we should go."

"It's time to kick butt and take names." Nyla rolls her head from side to side like she's preparing for a fight. And maybe she is.

Bastian stifles a smile at her casual substitution of the word *butt*.

It's funny, I know, the way Nyla switches out swear words. Sometimes it's easy to forget she's Mormon, and then she'll say something like *dang* or *frick* to remind me. But it's part of what I love about her—the weird combination of good girl and badass.

"Yeah, come on." I take a final swig of coffee as we all jump to our feet. "Let's go kick some butt."

The afternoon goes by in a blur. We read for the different parts, and sing with the piano, and get up and down from the stage so often it's hard to keep track of who's doing what. Then the audition's over and Nyla and I hang out for a while (just the two of us this time) in the Barnes & Noble at the mall, where Nyla gives me a hard time about Bastian.

"You're so predictable," she says as we walk between the bookshelves. "You're not even playing the romantic lead with this guy—not yet, anyway—and you're already crushing on him."

"I am not," I protest. "There's no crushing. Ronnie and Alice were crushing—I mean, did you see how they were drooling all over him? Not me. I have a thing called dignity."

Nyla folds her arms. "Uh-huh. Right. But you always fall for the leading man."

"I do not." I feel like a broken record here. "Not . . . always."

She gives me her no-nonsense face and starts to tick examples off on her fingers. "Gilbert in *Anne of Green Gables*. Mike in *Wait Until Dark*. Elwood P. Dowd in *Harvey*, which was epically poor judgment on your part, I feel, because that guy smoked. And now . . ." She heaves a melodramatic sigh and bats her eyelashes. "*Bastian*."

"Hey. I only just met Bastian," I say. "He could turn out to be a total jerk face."

"Good. I'm glad you're being sensible about this." Ny picks up a book and flips it over to read the back. "Judge not a book by its hot, hot cover, Cass. That's in the Bible somewhere."

"So you agree that he's hot."

"He's not . . . terrible-looking," she says lightly.

She finds him attractive, too, is what I take from that. Which only means she's not blind. But Nyla's Mormon, and Bastian's not, at least judging by his rampant coffee consumption at lunch. So he's off-limits. Nyla doesn't date outside her church pool. Or much at all, really. She always says she's too busy for boys.

My phone chirps, and then Nyla's does, too, and we glance at each other nervously. It's got to be the email with the cast list. Our fates decided.

"I got you," Nyla says.

"I got you," I reply, and take a deep breath.

We unlock our phones at the same time.

Nyla's name is the first listed.

She got Cinderella. The green monster instantly rolls out of bed like, WHAT? I push past him and keep scanning the email, relieved to see my name listed farther down.

I'm the baker's wife, it turns out.

"That's an awesome part," Nyla says quickly. "I love the baker's wife. Some would even say she's the female lead."

"There are no real leads in this play," I reply. "It's a total ensemble. And I'm glad you got Cinderella. That's a great singing role, and you have the best singing voice."

"The baker's wife is onstage for most of the show," Nyla insists. "Well, she does get killed off in the second act. But she has that awesome solo. And she comes back as a kind of ghost."

"I know."

"Are you . . ." She makes a scared face. ". . . disappointed?"

A little. "No," I say without a second's hesitation. "I like the baker's wife."

"So we're good?"

"We're good. And hey—look at this—Ronnie's Rapunzel, Bender's the baker, and Alice is Little Red. All is officially right with the world," I report.

"How about the new guy?" Nyla asks. "What'd he get?"

I lift my phone again to check. "Ah ha! Cinderella's prince. And he's also been cast as the wolf. I think those roles are always played by the same actor."

"Oh," Nyla says in an odd tone.

I'm not sure what her problem is. "That's the part he wanted, right?"

"Uh-huh." She's gone weirdly quiet, especially since she landed her desired role. Then I put the obvious two and two together: Nyla's going to be Cinderella, and Bastian is going to be Cinderella's prince.

They're going to be romantic leads.

The green monster swivels around to sneer at me. It's not pretty. But I try to ignore the stab of jealousy. Be the better person, here, Cass. See it from Nyla's point of view. And she's probably freaking out because kissing scenes are awkward. Even if you like the guy. I would know; my first-ever kiss was for a play. It was *super* awkward. But does Cinderella actually kiss the prince? I try to remember. "I don't think you have to smooch him, Ny. It's fine."

She snorts. "It's not *me* who has to kiss him."

Wait. What? I gasp and clap my hand to my forehead. "Wait. Wait wait wait. The baker's wife has an affair with Cinderella's prince!"

6

"How did it go?" Dad asks when I get home. "Your mother has called me no less than three times wanting to know what happened with your audition."

Interesting fact: *Into the Woods* happens to be my mother's favorite play. I mean, any show where one of the main characters is a *baker* is going to earn major points with my mom. She literally squealed with delight when I told her what the fall musical was going to be. She even said this show is going to be the highlight of her year or something. No pressure.

"She could have called *me*," I point out to Dad. "I do have a phone, you know."

"She doesn't want to pester you. But she has no problem, obviously, pestering me." He holds out his hands like he expects me to fill them with something. "So how'd it go?"

I smile triumphantly. "I got the part of the baker's wife."

"Yep," she says softly, popping the *p* sound.

I clutch my head. *"I'm* going to have to kiss Bastian! I'm going to have to practically make out with him. Onstage. In front of everybody."

She raises her eyebrows. "I know. Good thing you're not crushing on him, right?"

I feel a bunch of things all at once: terror, exhilaration, the urge to laugh, the urge to buy myself some quality lip balm. I remind myself that this is only a play. It's not real life. But it feels awfully real in the moment. Me and the hot new guy. Sitting in a tree. K-I-S-S-I-N-G.

"Just remember," Nyla says, wagging a finger at me. "Friends before mens."

"I thought you wanted Cinderella." His eyebrows bunch together.

"Cinderella's good." I don't even know why Nyla wanted Cinderella, if I'm being honest. The witch has the best singing part, and is all badass and stuff—definitely Nyla territory, but that also could be a kind of stereotype, I guess. Nyla wanted Cinderella, and Mama Jo always takes what we want into account. "But the baker's wife is the female lead," I inform Dad lightly.

"Well, then," he says. "I'm proud of you, Boo."

"Thanks, Pops." I give him a hug.

He rests his chin on the top of my head for a minute, then pulls back and looks down at me.

"And Nyla? How'd that work out?" He cringes. "Did *she* get Cinderella?"

"She did. I'm totally cool with it. She had a killer audition."

"I'm glad." He must think I'm disappointed and putting on a brave face, so he drops the subject. I love him for that. "You hungry? I could whip something up."

"I ate earlier. I need to crash. I've been on an adrenaline high all day."

"Go," he instructs me. "I will check in later for signs of life."

I start trudging toward my bedroom, but then he calls after me, "Oh, honey, this came for you in the mail today."

I turn. He's holding out a large envelope.

I know what it is the instant I see it. It's from the Idaho Department of Health and Welfare.

My birth certificate. I'd almost forgotten I'd requested it.

"Oh. Right. Thanks," I murmur hoarsely as I walk back to retrieve it.

"What is this, by the way?" he asks, reading the envelope. "It's official-looking."

Cue panic. "It's my birth certificate. I requested a copy."

He frowns. "Why do you need your birth certificate?"

My mind spins. I think about the way Dad's face will look if I tell him the truth—that I'm interested in finding out who my birth mother is. That the envelope in his hand holds the answer. And then he'll almost certainly tell Mom.

I can't even imagine Mom's face.

So I lie.

"It's for college applications," I stammer—the first thing that comes to mind.

My stomach twists. This is the only out-and-out falsehood I've ever told my dad, outside of that one time when I was like two and told him it was my rubber duck who pooped in the bathtub, a story my parents will never let die.

He grins. "So you're finally applying, huh? Thank God. I thought I was going to have to write your entrance essay myself. And I'm a terrible speller."

More stomach twisting. Even my high school guidance counselor has been on me about this lately. "Come by, Cassandra, and I'll give you some pamphlets!" she keeps calling out at me whenever I pass by the front office this semester. "You've got to make some big decisions. Soon."

"Well, I'm getting ready to apply," I say to Dad. "The deadlines aren't until November or December, but I want to get a jump on it. Nyla and I are working out what we're going to do for our audition videos." This is all true, kind of. I mean, I *should* be preparing to apply for college. I plan to apply for college. Nyla has been talking about audition videos. And it's possible that I might be required to provide a copy of my birth certificate.

"Where do you want to apply?" Dad asks, grinning. "I want to hear the list, of course, but what's your first choice?"

"Uh . . ." I know he wants me to say Boise State, but I can't bring myself to smile and nod about it this time. So I go with the real answer. It kind of slips out. "Juilliard."

"Right," Dad says after a long pause. "Right. You've always liked Juilliard." He calls up a wooden smile. "In New York City. That Juilliard."

"There's only one Juilliard, Dad."

"Right. Well. Good for you, Boo. You go . . . You go conquer the world." He hands me the envelope. "Get some sleep." He heads off to the kitchen.

I go into my room and quietly close the door. I don't want to lock it, because Dad might hear me lock it, and then he'd know something was up. I put the envelope on my desk and stare at it like I could somehow read what's inside without opening it. Opening it feels like a betrayal of the people who love me.

I am who I am, after all. A name's not going to change that.

Her name.

Maybe my name—the original one, anyway, the one I had before my parents named me.

I sigh and pick up the envelope. It's heavier than I would have expected.

It's only paper, I tell myself. Paper and ink.

But it's also an answer, to a question I've been silently asking my whole life.

I open the envelope, careful not to tear it, and slide the certificate from between the layers of cardboard it's been packed in.

Then I take a deep breath and try to call up the courage to read what's there.

49

Dear X,

Melly acted surprised when I gave her the second letter. I explained that the first letter sucked, so the second one was like a P.S., and she looked startled but then she said she guessed that'd be okay. There isn't a rule that there can only be one letter. She said I could write as many letters as I wanted.

I said, "No, thanks. I'm good with the two."

Clean slate, right?

But I've got some free time at the moment. And there's not much else to do.

Heather's gone. That's the big news around Booth.

Her seat is right next to mine in algebra. We don't have desks here, because it would be tough to squeeze our bulging bellies behind them, but we sit at a series of folding tables, two or three girls to a table, usually.

And every day for first period, which is Algebra II for me, I sit next to Heather.

Except today.

"Where's Heather?" I asked when it became clear that she wasn't going to show up.

"What are you supposed to do when you have a question?" Miss Cavendish said. She's not a bad teacher, just the shy, baby-faced type who thinks she can only keep her authority if she's a stickler for the rules. This is her first year teaching, and it's obvious.

I raised my hand.

"Yes, dear?"

"Where's Heather?"

"She's gone to St. Luke's. Her water broke early this morning. She might have even delivered by now," Miss Cavendish reported. "Isn't that wonderful?"

I don't know what it is, but wonderful doesn't seem like the right word for it.

Of course the other girls instantly started talking amongst themselves. It's always a huge deal whenever one of us gives birth. We want to know all the details: When did she start having labor pains? How bad were they? But how bad, <u>really</u>? On a scale of one being stubbing your toe and ten being like having your foot chopped off, how bad was it? Did she have an epidural or try to be a hero? Did she end up with a C-section? Will she have a huge scar now? Did she have a male doctor or a female? How long was she in labor? How long did she push? Did she poop on the table? Did she have to have stitches, after? Did she scream and cry? No, really, how bad was the pain?

We don't usually get the answers to these all-important questions until much later, of course. Each girl is given a two-week maternity leave after giving birth before we have to return to school. More, if it's a C-section. But we like to speculate. It passes the time.

So Miss Cavendish went back to explaining functions and the rest of the class kept whispering about Heather. I was thinking that my room is right next to Heather's, and I didn't hear a peep out of her this morning. Not a groan or a cry or heavy breathing or any of it. It must have happened early. And I must have really been out.

But then I heard this girl Amber say something rude.

Now, first off, I never liked Amber. She's one of those girls who act like they should get a medal for being here. And she's always talking about her plans. She's keeping the baby, and after it's born she's going to get her stylist's license or whatever and cut people's hair until she can save up enough money to go to college, and then she's going to become an accountant. Because there's always going to be a need for accountants. Which okay, yeah, is not the worst plan I've ever heard. Good for Amber, right? Go be an accountant. Live your dream.

Except I have algebra with her, and the girl is flat-out terrible at math. The day Amber becomes an accountant, I'm going to be a rocket scientist. Which is to say, never.

And this girl won't. Stop. Talking.

About how she's going to be mother of the year: cloth diapers, organic butt paste—the works.

About how she could never have even considered giving her baby up for adoption. Not even for a second. Oh no.

About her "support system" of her obviously awesome parents and grandparents and friends, who are all going to help her raise said baby. It takes a village, right?

About the benefits of breast milk and the newest industrial-grade breast pump.

In other words, Amber's annoying. Even on good days it takes a lot of restraint for me not to punch Amber in the nose.

So she was sitting there, not listening to Miss Cavendish lecture about math, babbling on about Heather, and she said, and I quote:

"I wonder if Heather will even want to hold her baby? Or maybe she'll ask the nurses to take it away the minute it's born."

I clenched my teeth.

She wasn't done. "I mean, how could you hold your baby and then ever let it go? That's the thing I can't understand. It's your baby. It's part of you. I could never do that."

I counted back from ten. Melly's been trying to get me to count as a way of keeping my temper. I can be hotheaded at times, and being pregnant doesn't help. But this time the counting didn't work. I kept thinking about Heather's letter and how much she obviously cared about her baby. The blushing thing. The way she wrote about a better life.

"It's so selfish," Amber continued. "She's going to give her baby to a stranger, all so she can go back to her old life and, like, get wasted at parties and act like it didn't happen."

Okay, secondly, I can't picture Heather at a party. She plays the flute in the school band. Not that flutists can't party, but I can't imagine her sloshing around with a red cup in her hand, laughing at some guy's tasteless joke. Heather's got this layer of . . . I don't know . . . dignity about her. Heather's not the type of girl who goes to wild parties.

I should know. I am the type of girl who goes to wild parties.

"Do me a favor, Amber," I said quietly.

She looked startled. I don't usually talk to her. "What?"

"Shut the hell up."

Everything went completely, blessedly silent for about five seconds. I thought maybe that was it. Maybe she'd shut up.

"What is your problem?" Amber said then, still half whispering.

"Why do you have to talk smack about Heather?" I countered. "You don't even know her."

"Oh, and you do?"

Well, no. I mean, we aren't friends, Heather and I. Not really. But I've lived next door to her for the past couple of months. I know her well enough to know the term selfish should not be applied.

A throat cleared timidly. Miss Cavendish had turned around and was attempting to glare us into submission. "No talking, girls. Focus, please. Now, are there any questions about the function of functions?"

Amber smirked at me. Like she got the last word.

I raised my hand.

"Yes, dear?"

"Can you please tell Amber to shut the hell up?"

"Oh my God." Amber raised her hand, too. "Can you ask her why she has to be a bitch all the time?"

Thirdly: I do not like being called a bitch. Why do people always jump to that word? It's so unimaginative. Plus, I like dogs. On behalf of canines everywhere, I take offense. I mean, I don't like Amber, but I wouldn't call her a bitch. I'd say she's more of a dunderheaded douche canoe.

"Why am I the bitch when you're the one bitching?" I fired off. Which I thought was pretty good.

Amber got up. Her belly is enormous, so it took her a minute. She's also a bigger girl than me. Six inches taller. Meaty shoulders. I honestly can't picture her as an accountant. (Actually, that's unfair. I guess accountants can come in all shapes and sizes.)

"Bitch," she said again, which got some hoots from the rest of the girls.

Well, shit, I thought. I can't sit here and take it. I stood up, too. "Mucus plug," I said. A little pregnancy insult there.

"Girls!" Miss Cavendish looked back and forth between us. There was a quiver in her voice. "Girls, stop it."

"You think you're special, don't you?" Amber said coolly. "Living here, but acting like you're above it all. We all know about you. Your dad, the big politician. Your mom, the beauty queen. Your brother, the football star."

"She's not my mom," I clarified. "She's my stepmom. Get your facts straight, at least."

Miss Cavendish clapped her hands together. "That's enough."

"So they're hiding you here." Amber waddled up to get right into my face. "You know why? Because they might be all rich and fancy, but you're trash."

"Shut. Up."

"It doesn't surprise me that you're going to abandon your baby."

Oh man, I was going to have to hit her.

"Do you even know who the father is?"

That's when I punched Amber in the nose.

I shouldn't have. I'll admit that. But in my defense, she was really egging me on. And I didn't hit her too hard. I didn't break her nose, for instance. That's something. It must have looked kind of funny, though, that whole scenario, two pregnant chicks facing off. I punch her—she pulls my hair, all the other preggo girls jump up and start yelling or crying. Like a weird form of sumo wrestling.

So yeah. I'm currently in detention. Which at Booth means in the chapel. I'm in here with a bunch of Holy Bibles and the exercise mats they use for the Lamaze classes and the trusty yellow legal pads where I've been writing these letters. Writing another goddamn letter.

And here's the thing I want to know. Do you think I'm selfish?

I still stand by what I said in the first letter: I'm not meant to be a mother. Not now, anyway. Maybe not ever. I just used the word *goddamn* in a letter to my unborn child. I'm not really the nurturing type, and that's unlikely to change.

If I kept you, I'd only screw you up. I don't have some master plan for my life. I can tell you that I'm definitely not going to be an accountant. Or a rocket scientist. I don't have wonderful, supportive parents who would help. They'd only screw you up worse—trust me on that one. They did a number on me. You deserve to be raised by grown-ups. People who get along. Who love each other, even.

But does any of that matter? Are you going to think I was selfish, no matter what the reason? Are you going to think I abandoned you?

I hope not, X. I really hope not.

S

7

Cassandra Rose McMurtrey. That's what was on the birth certificate.

My name.

Born to Catherine Elaine McMurtrey (mother) and William Patrick McMurtrey (father) on September seventeenth, eighteen years ago. Looking at that high-quality piece of paper, you'd never know it wasn't my original birth certificate—it's got the official signatures and the state seal and a watermark and everything—except that it's signed and dated in November of that year. A couple months late.

Idaho, the internet rather snarkily informed me when I looked into it more closely, is a closed-record state. As in, they'll never give me my original birth certificate, no matter how old I am. I'd have to get a court order. And to get a court order, I'd have to have a good reason. Like a medical reason. A legally sound reason.

Curiosity, it turns out, is not enough.

So this is who I am: Cassandra Rose McMurtrey. That's my answer.

"You're quiet tonight," Mom remarks.

I blink up from my phone, where I was supposed to be finding this funny cat meme I wanted to show my grandma but was actually spacing out. "I'm fine," I mutter, because I am. Fine, that is. It was an impulsive thing, requesting my birth certificate, and nothing came of it, and that's okay.

I'm fine.

"You're too skinny." Grandma pokes me in the ribs. "Isn't your father feeding you? I swear that man thinks a person can survive on bark and pine nuts."

I put a hand up like I'm swearing on an invisible Bible. "I'm eating three square meals a day, I promise."

"Well, you should eat more," she pronounces.

"Mama, back off about her being skinny." From the hospital bed, Mom smiles at me. "My daughter is practically perfect in every way."

"Well, I suppose that's true." Grandma doesn't get the reference to *Mary Poppins*. She lifts Mom's legs one by one and rolls a thick sock onto each foot, then unfolds a blanket and tucks it around Mom's hips. After that she goes out to refill Mom's water. Comes back with the water. Adjusts my mother's straw in the water. Then disappears again; I don't know where. That's how she is when she's here. Grandma likes to have tasks to accomplish.

"Don't mind her," Mom says after Grandma bustles out of the room.

"I don't mind her." I adore Grandma. She says what she thinks, but she's still kind and generous and an all-around good person. I want to be exactly like her when I'm an old lady.

"How's school?" Mom asks.

"Fine. I got a B-plus on my chemistry test, which I consider a minor victory."

"Congratulations. And how's the play going? Off to a good start?"

I smile. "We did a table read yesterday, and we're going to start blocking act one tomorrow." Just saying the lines out loud for the make-out scene between the baker's wife and Cinderella's prince gave me butterflies. Bastian was so funny at the reading, making everybody laugh because of how totally into the prince's role he was.

"I was raised to be charming, not sincere," was his best line, and he said it so deadpan that the entire cast cracked up for like five minutes.

But when we read the kissing part between the prince and the baker's wife, he didn't look directly at me. He was shy. It was kind of adorable.

"I still can't believe you're doing *Into the Woods*," Mom sighs. "My favorite musical."

"It's going to be great," I tell her. "I can't wait for you to see it."

The actual performance is months away, though. I try not to think about how there's a possibility that she might not see it. I force myself to believe that she will. She'll be in the front row. With Dad.

Mom gives me a weak smile. "And there's a new boy, right? What's his name again?" Ugh, she's too darn perceptive for her own good. I wonder if she's been talking to Nyla, who comes by on her own to visit her sometimes. She always brings daisies, Mom's favorite flower. I glance around. Sure enough, there's a fresh vase full of daisies next to the window.

"Bastian," I say to answer Mom's question. "He's, um, fine."

"Fine as in fine? Or fine as in *fine*?" Mom wags her eyebrows up and down. I can't help but laugh.

"He's reasonably attractive," I admit.

"And . . . ?"

"And what?"

"Well, dear, you know you always get a crush on the leading man."

I gasp in fake outrage. "I do not." Dangit, Nyla.

Mom wrinkles up her nose. "So you don't actually like this new boy."

I don't answer right away. It feels like some kind of trap, and it seems weird, sitting here in a hospital with my dy—my sick mother, and she wants to talk boys. But I also know if we were a normal family, a regular old mother and daughter, we'd talk about boys. So I decide to give in and play it up for her a little.

"I don't know," I confess. "Bastian is kind of perfect."

Her eyebrows lift. "Perfect?"

"He's cute. Funny. He seems nice, too. And he's a theater person," I say. "So yes, okay, fine, let's just say I'm open to wherever the universe decides to take me, romance-wise."

"Excellent." Mom seems pleased that I've picked up on her philosophy. She sighs wistfully. "I had a boyfriend in high school. His name was Justin Irish. He was six two and had red hair and was completely dreamy."

"You obviously have a thing for tall gingers," I laugh. Because Dad.

"Indeed." She grins. "And you have a thing for the leading man."

"I do n—" I throw up my hands. "Bastian is not even the leading man in this play. He's . . . Prince Charming."

"I see." Mom taps a contemplative finger to her chin. "Is this why you're being so quiet? Because you think I might not approve of you dating someone? Because, believe me, I am fine with it, honey. You haven't had a boyfriend yet, and that's okay, of course. But maybe that's a little bit my fault."

I glance up, startled. This conversation is swiftly crossing into the no-fly zone. Like we're actually going to act like Mom's heart thing happened, and it was a big fricking deal.

She pats my hand. "You should take a chance on love anytime you can. So go for it—go out with this guy, if you decide you like him. Don't feel like you have to spend all your free time waiting here with me for my new heart to show up. Live your life. That's what I want for you. And then you can come back and tell me all about it."

And now we've returned to our regularly scheduled program of "acting like everything's normal." I swallow. "Okay."

"You're still being quiet," Mom observes.

"I'm fine. I have a lot going on right now, is all, without even adding dating to the mix. School. The play. College plans. There's so much happening."

Mom gets an expression on her face I can't quite read, like she's waiting for something unpleasant to happen. Or like she's scared. She glances at the door.

"Hey, what's the matter?" I ask.

She sighs. "Your father told me you got your birth certificate."

And here we go. I'm busted. Crap. "Yes," I say slowly.

"He said you needed it to apply to Juilliard."

That's the thing about lies. They're like boomerangs. You think you've gotten away with something, you throw the lie as far away from you as you can, but it always comes hurtling back.

"Yes," I say again.

Her heart rate monitor picks up speed. *Beep beep beep*, it goes, like the beat of a fast song at the school dance. I sit down next to her. "Mom?"

She closes her eyes for a few seconds. Takes a breath. "You can't go to Juilliard. With the medical bills and the second mortgage and all that, we don't have the funds to send you. I know you've been dreaming about going there since you were a little girl. And I know we told you that there was a mutual fund we set up for your college education, but. . ." She looks away, toward the door again. "That money's all gone now. I'm so sorry, honey."

For a few minutes I can't say anything. I'm shocked. I wasn't even being that serious when I said Juilliard to Dad. In the back of my brain I know it's a pipe dream, really, but to hear Mom say I can't go—it packs an unexpected punch. I shouldn't be this surprised. I might not have known all the details, but I've been paying attention this past year. I know that my parents had decent health insurance through my dad's job before my mom's heart thing happened, but even with good health insurance the medical bills decimated my parents' savings, gobbled up their retirement, the cake shop, the second car we used to own. Nyla's been silently paying for me all year, slipping a twenty into my hand when we go to the movies and telling me to buy our tickets, paying for lunch, for the cute shirt she saw me eyeing at the mall, for last weekend's pizza. Because my family's broke.

Finally I nod. "I know."

Mom squeezes my hand. "Your father and I do want you to go to college. You're so smart, and you're so talented I know you'll get scholarships, and we'll make it work. Somehow, we will make college happen. But we can't afford Juilliard."

"I don't want to go to Juilliard," I blurt out.

She frowns. "You don't?"

"No. I mean, I did. Juilliard was the dream. But only five percent of the actors who apply to Juilliard get in. I'm good, but I don't know if I'm top five percent good," I confess. "So even if we could afford it, I probably wouldn't get in."

"Oh, honey."

"And the tuition is really high," I say quickly before she launches into some speech about how very much she believes in me. "But then on top of that I'd have to live in New York City. Which is wildly expensive, too. Honestly, I don't know how anybody affords to go to Juilliard."

"There must be scholarships."

"Which I'd have to compete for, with the five percent. Which means I'd have to be like in the top one percent."

"Sweetie . . ." Mom's still got that wounded look on her face, like it's her future that's dying by the wayside here, instead of mine.

"Lately I've been thinking that it's good to have smaller dreams, too. Backup dreams."

"Backup dreams," she repeats faintly.

"Like maybe I'll become a teacher, like Dad. He loves it. I probably would love it, too. Teaching runs in the family, right? So I could be a high school drama teacher, and then I'd get to plan and direct like two or three shows a year, and I'd be the boss of everybody, the undisputed theater queen, which sounds like the best thing ever, and then I'd get my summers off to have fun and do community theater."

Mom's trying to read my expression. "You've given this some thought, haven't you?"

Actually, I'm kind of making it all up on the spot. My improv skills at their finest. But I keep going. "My point is, I don't want to apply to Juilliard. Because I don't want to go to Juilliard. Because I have a different dream now."

She's looking way happier already. "Okay, so maybe . . . Boise State, then?" she suggests slyly.

I can't hold back the groan. "Not you, too! It's bad enough with Dad. Did you know he gave me a BSU shirt for my birthday?"

She smiles. "Well, can you blame us? That's where we met. That's where the magic happened, my dear."

I hold up my hand. "I don't need details."

"I know BSU is your dad's dream, not your dream," she says with a sigh. "But it's an excellent school, and it's an affordable option, and I think you should give it a chance. Go visit it, anyway. Maybe you'll like what you find there. Maybe it can be part of your backup dream, like you said."

She's right, I tell myself. She's right. Of course she is.

"Okay," I murmur.

"Okay?"

"I'll go see it. Sometime. Soon," I add.

She claps her hands together. "Your father will be thrilled. You want to be a teacher. And you'll consider going to Boise State."

For some reason this makes a lump pop up in my throat. "Go, Broncos?" I offer up weakly.

She beams. "Go, Broncos."

Without warning Grandma blasts back into the room. "They've got green Jell-O today," she says loudly, holding up a plastic bowl covered in plastic wrap. "I tried to barter for something better, like raspberry, but they told me no can do. Who in the world ever liked green Jell-O?"

She put the Jell-O on the little table next to Mom's bed. "What'd I miss?"

I look at Mom, waiting for the boomerang to come back around and smack me in the head.

"Cass met a new boy," Mom says instead of bringing up the college stuff. For which I am grateful. "An attractive boy, it turns out."

"Oh dear." Grandma shakes her head. "Is this about the sex?"

Now it's my turn to gasp. "Grandma!"

"I was at the birthday party," she reminds me. "You said you wanted to have sex. With the right boy. Do you think this boy is the right boy?"

"I didn't mean what I said on my birthday," I stammer.

"I know I said you should go for it." Grandma keeps talking like she doesn't even hear me. Which is entirely possible. "But honestly, if you want my opinion, now's not the time for romance. Not at your age. You should simply enjoy being young. Don't waste your time getting serious with anybody."

"Mama, you got married when you were seventeen," Mom points out.

"Look, I just met this guy," I say, exasperated. "I don't even know him."

"I may have gotten married young, but no one ever claimed that was a good idea." Grandma folds her arms across her chest. "I was in the family way. That's what you did back then."

Mom knows all about the "family way" thing—she was born about seven months after Grandma and Grandpa got married, and she could do the math. Grandpa died of a stroke when I was seven. But before that, from what I can remember, Grandma and Grandpa seemed happy together. So the family way thing worked out for everyone.

"You should get her some birth control pills," Grandma adds

65

sagely. "Or that thingy they insert up in there. No sense repeating the sins of the past."

Oh my God. The worst thing is that I can't tell if she means her past, with the shotgun marriage, or mine—with the irresponsible sixteen-year-old birth mother.

"We'll get her some birth control pills," Mom says. "I don't have a problem with that."

"Look, I don't need—"

"And that vaccination for girls. And condoms," Grandma adds. "Because there are so many diseases out there nowadays."

That's it. "I'm not having sex!" I yell right as the nurse walks in to take Mom's vitals.

The nurse's mouth opens, then closes. Then she turns on her heel and goes out again.

"Now see what you did," Mom says to Grandma.

"Me? I wasn't the one screaming about sex."

I drag my hand down the front of my face. Then I burst out laughing. After a few seconds Mom and Grandma join in. It was too funny, the strangled look on that nurse's face.

"Never a dull moment with you two," Mom says, and she seems so much lighter than she did during the college talk. She seems relieved, like me saying I don't want to go to Juilliard has lifted a weight off her chest. Which is how I know it was the right thing to do.

Grandma turns to me. "Well, aren't you even going to tell me this boy's name?"

"No, Grandma," I say, still giggling. "I'm not."

8

"She actually said that?" Nyla gasps. "Sins of the past?"

"I know, right?" It's the next morning, and we're standing on the empty stage in the Bonneville auditorium before the bell rings for first period. Nyla got me up this freakishly early by telling me she wanted to practice for the state drama competition. But it turns out that she actually wants to get a jump on the college audition tapes.

"Your granny is something else." Nyla finishes screwing her video camera to the top of a tripod and steps back, looks at it critically, then adjusts it slightly to one side. "And why, exactly, did you decide to discuss sex with your grandmother?"

I cross my arms. "It's your fault, now that I think about it. You told Mom about Bastian. And Mom told Grandma. And hence Grandma took it on herself to give me advice in the romance department. See? Your fault."

Nyla nods. "Okay, yeah, sorry. My bad. But when I visit your mom—and come on, she's practically my mom, too, Cass—she asks me questions about you. And she keeps asking until I give her something juicy. She's like a cuddly, sweet version of the Spanish Inquisition."

I give a fake gasp. "No one expects the Spanish Inquisition. Her chief weapon is surprise. Surprise and fear."

"Two," Nyla amends, holding up two fingers. "Two chief elements. Surprise, fear, and a ruthless efficiency."

"Three. Three chief elements."

And we're off on a Monty Python riff. My dad would be so proud that he's indoctrinated us so thoroughly into a British comedy show from fifty years ago.

"All right, fine," I say when I finish geeking out. "But try to resist my mother's questioning when it comes to my love life, okay? Friends before mens. And, er, moms."

"Okay," Nyla agrees reluctantly. "He did keep staring at you yesterday when you weren't looking," she informs me, going back to messing with the video camera. "It's creepy."

"Who?"

She gives me a don't-be-stupid look. "I gotta say, I'm with Grandma on this one. We don't have time for boys." She steps back and brushes off her hands. "Let's audition for some colleges."

"Do we have to? Can't we just practice for state drama?"

"No more avoidance, my friend," she says. "We're making audition tapes. Early-admission deadlines are coming up fast. We've got to strike." She pushes me to the center of the stage and retreats behind the camera. "And action," she calls.

I give her a tired look. "Why do I have to go first?"

"And . . . action!" she says again, louder. The video camera makes a beeping noise.

I sigh and take a few seconds to compose myself, staring at the floor. Then I lift my head and try to channel Beatrice from Shakespeare's *Much Ado About Nothing*. "*O! that I were a man for his sake! Or that I had any friend would be a man for my sake! But manhood is melted into curtsies, valor into compliment, and men are only turned into tongue, and trim ones too: he is now as valiant as Hercules that only tells a lie and swears it. I cannot be a man with wishing, therefore I will die a woman with grieving.*"

The camera beeps as Nyla stops recording. "That's, uh, great, Cass." She gives me what's meant to be an encouraging smile, but I know her too well to be truly encouraged. She thought I sucked. Because I did, in fact, suck. I was kind of phoning it in.

"So that was decent, but let's try it again," she suggests. "This time give it everything you've got. Believe the ever-living shiz out of it."

"Maybe I should do the Juliet monologue instead." I heave my wistful Juliet sigh. "*And when he shall die, take him and cut him out in little stars, and he shall make the face of heaven so fine that all the world will be in love with night.*"

For some reason this makes me think of Bastian. I can immediately see us onstage together. My Juliet to his Romeo.

"No," Nyla says flatly.

"But—"

"You should play one of Shakespeare's strong women. This is your chance to show them you have the acting chops to be Kate. Rosaline. Lady Macbeth." Nyla lifts her face to an invisible spotlight. "*Oh, that I were a man!*" she cries. "*I would eat his heart out in the marketplace!*"

Sigh. She's good. She's better than me.

"So do it one more time," she says again. "Blow the socks completely off those folks at Juilliard."

Ah, Juilliard. As Shakespeare would say: *there's the rub.*

But I suck it up and try the monologue one more time. It doesn't go any better.

Nyla shuts the camera off. "What is wrong with you? Did something else happen last night?"

We can joke about my mom, but the Spanish Inquisition's got nothing on Nyla, not when she knows something's up, so I sit at the edge of the stage and tell her about my new and improved college plans, i.e., not going to Juilliard.

Nyla slings an arm around me when I'm done talking. "I'm so sorry, Cass. That's . . ."

"Not awesome," I finish for her.

"Yeah."

We're quiet for a minute, letting it sink in. Because here's the thing: I've been dreaming of Juilliard since middle school. I know I'm probably like every other drama nerd in the country—we all think we're going to be stars. But I really did. For years I've haunted the Juilliard website, scouring everything I could dig up about their proud history, the plays they perform every year, the famous directors and actors who graduated from there to go on to total greatness. I've watched the video tour of the school an embarrassing amount of times, and I can so easily picture myself in those airy white rooms, taking acting lessons, voice, movement, singing, stage combat, all that Juilliard has to offer. From there it isn't hard to picture myself walking the streets of New York City, strolling down Broadway, and looking up to see my own name on the marquee of a Broadway theater.

CASS MCMURTREY. Juilliard graduate. Winner of the Tony Award. (applause applause)

But that's only a dream. I'm becoming more aware lately that I don't live in a dream. I'm a resident of cold, hard reality.

"I mean, I guess I always knew it wasn't going to happen," I say. "Like I might as well apply to go to college on the moon."

"Maybe you could—" Nyla says after a while, but I stop her. No time for wallowing. I jump to my feet.

"Let's do yours," I say.

Nyla frowns—but the theater is only going to be empty to film auditions for a few more minutes. So she pops up and blasts out this amazing monologue from *Antigone*. And then a bit from *Chicago*, and Emily from *Our Town*. She makes it look easy. Deep down I know that she would totally have a shot at Juilliard, if she wanted to go to Juilliard. But Nyla wants to go to USC. She pictures herself in Hollywood, strolling along Sunset Boulevard, her face on a movie poster at the bus stop. I can picture it, too. And Nyla never has to worry about money. Her family is loaded. Her dad is literally a brain surgeon. You could fit most of my house inside the great room of her house.

"Okay, now you again," she says when she's finished with her audition pieces.

"I think I'm done for today."

She puts a hand to her hip. "Do you need me to give you a kick in the pants?"

"No, thank you."

She turns the camera off again. "Cass. You want to go to Juilliard. You have to at least try."

"Actually, I don't. I'm not going to. Because I'll either a) not get

71

in or b) get in and not be able to afford it," I say. "Neither of those options sounds like fun. But here's the thing: I think that's okay."

I tell her about this wildly new concept of becoming a drama teacher and going somewhere more local. The backup dream.

"Oh my gosh." She grabs my arm. "Are you actually considering going to Boise State?"

"Maybe."

Her eyes widen. "That's so—" She can't even finish the sentence. I know she's remembering all those nights we stayed up talking about how we were going to leave Idaho someday. See the world. Be part of something big and different and new.

"I know," I whisper.

"Your dad is going to be *so*—"

"I *know*."

She bites her lip. Nyla's always had this idea that we should always try for the big things, the awesome things, the extraordinary. Probably because she started out in life in an orphanage in Liberia, and now she's here. Her entire life is a freaking miracle. She's probably so disappointed in me right now. I can tell she wants to give me a pep talk about believing in the improbable. Try, try again. Reach for the stars.

But I don't want to hear it. "Anyway, I told my mom I might possibly consider *maybe* taking a look at Boise State. Like, go visit it sometime. See if it grows on me."

"I'll go with you for moral support," Nyla says immediately. "Just say the word. I'm there."

"Thanks. But it's possible that I won't even go to college next year. Maybe I'll postpone."

It feels like a betrayal to say this, because that's me looking into the future and thinking I'll have to postpone, because maybe my mom will—

"Okay, so let's make a tape for Boise State," Nyla says.

The bell rings.

I shrug. "We should go."

The door of the theater bursts open and a bunch of freshmen start to trickle down the aisle. Nyla and I make for the exit. We stop at our respective lockers, then walk together to the staircase, where I have chemistry downstairs and Nyla goes upstairs for French. Nyla's quiet the whole way to class, but I can practically hear her mind going a mile a minute. Trying to figure out how she can help me.

"Wait," she says, right before we go our separate ways. "I think that Boise State could be . . . good."

I find myself nodding. "I could come home and see my parents on the weekends. Do my laundry. Get Dad to make me some down-home vegetarian meals."

"And you'd be a big fish," Nyla says.

"Excuse me?"

"If you went to somewhere huge and expensive, you'd be a little fish in a big pond. But at Boise State, you'd be a big fish in a smaller pond."

"I think Boise State has like twenty thousand students, Ny. It's not like it's a community college. Not that there's anything wrong with community college."

She makes a frustrated noise in the back of her throat. "What I mean is, you'd be the obvious talent. You'd get better, bigger roles, way sooner than you would at Juilliard."

I hadn't thought of that before. "I guess so."

"It could be good," she says again.

"Yeah."

We stand there for a second, students milling around us.

"I gotta—" I point downstairs.

She nods. "Me too. And I have to make up a test during breakfast break. So I'll see you at lunch. Lucy's?"

"Sure." It's been so great this year that seniors are allowed to go off campus for lunch. And so great that I have Nyla, who has never blinked an eye at paying for my lunch, and she's never tried to make me feel like I owe her.

She really is the best bestie a girl could ask for.

I will never be able to pay her back, I realize in this moment, watching her walk away. I'm probably always going to have less than she has. Which doesn't make me feel mad or jealous or anything. It's simply the way things are. The truth. Whatever.

That's apparently what the universe has in store for me.

9

I'm in an off mood all day, trudging through on a kind of autopilot until I literally bump into Sebastian Banks in the hall outside the choir room.

"Hey, watch where you're going," he says to me, but he's smiling. He has a dimple in his left cheek, I notice. Dang. This guy could not get any more perfect.

He just said something funny, it occurs to me. I should say something funny back.

"You're not in choir" is what comes out of my mouth.

Total fail.

He presses a hand to his chest. "I do believe that I have recently signed up for this class. So yes, I am in choir."

"Oh, good," I say. "We could use you."

He arches an eyebrow. "Okay."

"I mean, we could use your voice. We're painfully thin in the baritone section."

"Well, I am here to help." He makes a show of holding the door open for me, and we saunter in together. People stop talking to stare at us—well, at Bastian, really, as I am old news. I glance around—Nyla's not here yet. I wonder if she's going to be pleased or annoyed that Bastian is joining our class.

"Boys are over there," I say, gesturing to the right side of the room.

"Thanks." He doesn't go, though. And I don't go to my section.

"So I'll see you at rehearsal after?" I try to remember if he was on the schedule for today. The baker's wife and the prince don't have a lot of real interaction in act one, which is what we've been blocking all week. My mouth gets dry and my chest gets all fluttery if I allow myself to think about act two. The very extremely kissy act two. I wonder if Bastian gets nervous thinking about it, too.

"I'll be there," Bastian says, but then he touches my arm before I can leave. "Hey, I was wondering if you'd do me a favor."

Yes, please, I think. "Yes?"

"I just found out about this state drama competition. And how there's this amazing scholarship for seniors?"

"Yes?" I mean, I was there when he found out about it. So I don't know what he's getting at.

He smiles. Hopefully he thinks my utter stupidity is cute because otherwise I'm bombing. "Is that a question?"

"No." I try to snap out of it. "I mean, yes, there is a scholarship for seniors. I've never really paid much attention to it before because, well, I haven't been a senior until now, but there is one. It's like ten thousand dollars a year, even. To the school of your choice."

"Right, so I was thinking I should do the drama competition this year," he says.

"You should."

"And I was wondering, would you be my partner? I'm not in the drama class this semester, because I was late enrolling, and anyway, that's all complicated, but the short version is that I know you have to have a partner to compete, and I thought I'd ask you."

I stare at him, completely dumbfounded for several seconds. My knee-jerk reaction is to say, *Why yes, Bastian, of course I'd be your partner in the drama competition. I'd love to. We can rehearse at my house. When would you like to start? Tonight?*

But then I think, *Down, girl.*

Because I remember Nyla. I am always partners with Nyla for the state drama competition. We've won in our age group every single year for the past three years. We've already picked out our scene for this year. We're already rehearsing. It's going to be epic.

And I think, *Friends before mens.*

"So what do you say?" Bastian asks, because I'm just standing there looking stricken. "The suspense is kind of killing me."

"I can't. Be your partner. Because I already have a partner. So I can't." God, how am I this inarticulate around him?

"Oh." He sounds genuinely disappointed. "Can you maybe direct me to someone who might need a partner?"

Normally everyone's already paired up by this point in the semester. But I happen to know that Ben Monahan had to drop out last week. Who was doing that scene from *Barefoot in the Park* with . . .

"Alice," I say.

"Alice," he repeats.

"Alice Hastings. Tiny blond, green eyes. She was at lunch with us the other day, remember? She needs a partner."

"Right. I know Alice," he says more brightly. Of course he knows Alice. He plays the wolf in the musical, and Alice is Little Red. "Great. I'll ask her tonight at play practice."

"Great." The bell rings, and we both take our seats in the correct sections. Nyla slips in beside me at the last second before our teacher comes to the front to start our warm-up scales.

"What's up?" Nyla asks as the room fills with the sound of "me me me me me me me me meeeeeeee," and then "moo moo moo moo moo moo moo moo mooooooo."

"Nothing," I say. Which is true. Things are exactly the same for me right now as they were ten minutes ago. But Bastian did ask me for a favor, and I helped him. I mean, sure, I may have just directed him into the arms of another girl who also happens to think he's hot. But he at least seemed grateful. And he wanted to ask me, specifically.

That's good news, on the Cass-gets-a-boyfriend front, anyway. I think.

At this point I'll take all the good news I can get.

Dear X,

I'm just going to lean into the letter thing. I hope that's okay. I mean, if it isn't, I guess you could stop reading these. If you even are reading these, assuming they're not sitting in a dusty box somewhere. I don't know.

What I do know is it's prom night tonight, and I'm thinking about all the girls at my old school with their dresses and their corsages and their dates, and that makes me think about Dawson. But I know I wouldn't have gone to prom with him, even if I hadn't ended up here.

I hate that I'm thinking about Dawson, obsessing about him even though things are so over between us. It feels weak.

Everyone's moping around here today. I don't know if it's prom or something in the water. People have been giving me a wider berth than usual since I punched Amber, and I'm fine with that. She got a black eye, and I did feel a little bad about that until I remembered the way she asked me if I even knew who the father of my baby was. Which makes me want to black her other eye.

Anyway. We're all kind of down. Heather's still gone. Brit's especially moody—I could hear her crying from pretty much anywhere in the dorms this morning. It's not her fault, though. This is not how she thought she'd end up. She bought into the myth where the prince comes and carries you off into the sunset. You grow up watching movies like *The Little Mermaid*, where Ariel is sixteen, and she's even an entirely different species from the prince, but it all works out for her anyway. Happily ever after. Love conquers all.

But here's good old reality: if you're in a relationship when you're sixteen, everything is probably not going to work out. There's too much _after_ when you're sixteen. Ever after really doesn't have a chance. Happily ever after is a joke.

I want to rewrite *Little Mermaid* so Ariel shows up on Eric's doorstep and says, "Hey, you know that time when you 'kissed the girl'? Well, I'm pregnant with our fish-tailed baby. So man up, Eric. My dad doesn't have a shotgun, but he has this huge trident, and he thinks we should get married." But then the next thing she knows, Eric's on the fastest ship out of town. Poor poor Ariel.

Clearly I'm jaded. I'm sitting here all knocked up, and there's no Prince Charming in sight.

Still, I want to emphasize: it's not your fault, either.

I went to the Sub that night. Bet you didn't see that coming, did you? It turned out (and I can't believe I didn't automatically get this) that SUB stood for the Student Union Building at a college. I showed up at nine thirty, so he wouldn't think I was too into it, and there were handmade signs directing me to the basement, where music was wafting up from a little theater. It was crowded—standing room only. I walked in and there he was, the blond guy from the Pearl Jam concert, sitting up on the stage with his guitar. His voice, which I didn't get to properly hear at Pearl Jam, instantly gave me goose bumps, this slightly smoky, half-whispered melody, like Dave Matthews with a touch of Eddie Vedder. He saw me right away, caught my eye, smiled. He has great lips—I'll give him that, this little smirk that once upon a time could make me weak in the knees.

I'd had boys look at me that way before. I am, like I told you before, fairly average in the looks department—average height, average weight, kind of flat up top but then I'm only sixteen, right? But I have nice eyes, or so I've been told. I wonder if you'll get my eyes or his. Like I said, you'd be better off if you end up looking like him. He's boy-beautiful. He knows it, too, he knows every time he's up there on the stage, crooning away, smiling that little smile, and he brushes the hair out of his eyes and glances out at some girl in the back of the room, she's going to swoon.

I wasn't any different. My breath caught every time he met my eyes.

The music was good. I wouldn't have fallen for him if the music wasn't good. At least I had some standards. And he was clever with the lyrics:

You think you know what I'm about.

You think you're going to ferret me out.

But you forget I'm the fox, girl, you're the hen.

From here it's only a matter of when.

You're probably thinking I should have known, right? He wasn't exactly trying to hide who he was or pretend he was something else. I liked that about him, actually. He seemed more mature than the high school boys I was surrounded by all day—more certain of himself. He seemed like he knew what he wanted.

And right then, it seemed like he wanted me.

I stood in the back and swayed to his music, smiled at him when he smiled at me.

After his set was done he came over and stood in front of me, grinning.

"Hi."

"Hi."

"You came."

"Obviously."

"You liked it, right?"

"You didn't tell me it was _your_ band." I didn't want to fawn all over him. I still had a shred of dignity. But I couldn't stop smiling. It was embarrassing, how much I was smiling. My cheeks hurt with it.

"Come on. You liked it."

"It was all right. You're . . ." I looked up at him. More goose bumps. "You're pretty good."

"You're pretty."

Damn. Nobody had ever talked like that to me before. It felt like being in a movie, like something that was already written out for us to say. I was pretty sure I was blushing. But I tried to be confident.

"You're pretty, too," I said. "And you can really sing, can't you?"

He took that in stride. "Among other things. You want to get out of here?"

"Okay."

He nodded to his drummer and took my hand, and the next thing I knew, we were back at his dorm room, where he told me he wanted to . . . listen to records.

"Records?" I repeated stupidly. "Like, vinyl?"

He laughed this husky laugh. "It's the best sound." He gestured to where, crammed between the bed and his desk, he had this little table with a record player on it.

That's when my obsession with vinyl officially started. That night. He had this amazing collection—not just the alternative stuff like Pearl Jam, Nirvana, the White Stripes, Radiohead, but classics like John Lennon and Jimi Hendrix and Billy Joel.

He was so hot. Sitting on his bed, listening to the music, he'd tilt his head back and sing along, and goose bumps would jump up again all along my arms.

Here was a person who loved music as much as I did. I'd never met anybody like that.

And, as I mentioned, he was hot.

So. At one point we were sitting on his bed, listening to Leonard Cohen's low, gravelly voice sing "Hallelujah," the sound so completely pure pouring out of the record player. He was right about the sound. I had my eyes closed, letting the song wash over me. Then I heard Dawson make this pained noise, this sigh, and when I opened my eyes he was so close I could see the blond tips of his eyelashes.

"Hi," I murmured.

"You have amazing eyes," he said. "They're so blue."

He kissed me. Then he kissed me again, harder, and kissed me again. And again. And again. He had this little bit of stubble, which was gold like his hair so you couldn't see it unless you were up close or the light hit his face a certain way, but that night we kissed so much that his stubble scratched up my chin. It was raw and red, after.

We didn't have sex, if you're wondering. Not that night. That night we listened to music. We talked, a little. He told me that he was a singer, yes, and he could play guitar (at one point he pulled a blue Stratocaster from underneath the bed and played me a bit of "Purple Rain") and he had dreams of making a record of his own someday, but he was also an actor, a painter, and he wanted to try writing a screenplay about his life.

Because his life so far was obviously interesting enough to base a movie on.

"You're a Renaissance man," I said, which he seemed to like.

I talked about concerts I'd been to. Because I couldn't think of anything else that was comparatively interesting.

But mostly we played records and made out. We might have gotten around to sex, actually, (it was getting hot and heavy) but at some point the door opened and another guy came in, an Asian guy with shaggy hair and a Star Wars shirt.

I have to admit, the first time I ever saw him, I wrote him off as classic nerd.

"Oh," the guy said, frowning the second he laid eyes on me. "Sorry. There's not like a sock on the door or anything."

Dawson sighed. "This is my roommate, Ted."

So no, no sex that night. I probably shouldn't tell you about the sex, anyway. No one wants to hear about their parents getting it on. Even if we're not your real parents. You know it happened. I know it happened. You're the proof.

It was my first time, though, that first time with Dawson. It was a few weeks later, on Christmas break, when most of the students were back home and the dorms were perfectly quiet. And we did use protection, that first time. Or at least I thought we did. I asked, "Uh, do you have a condom?" and he said, "Sure," like I'd asked him to get me a glass of lemonade or something, like he was being a good host, and then he put one on. But when it was over, the condom wasn't on anymore. And I was too busy trying to understand my own body, the way it had hurt (it hurt more than I expected it to, although my friends warned me it would hurt), how his bare chest felt against mine and the roughness of his hairy legs tangled with my legs, a whole new world of sensations, to ask him about the missing condom.

Sometimes now I want to drive over and ask him: Where was the condom?

I didn't ask him. I kept going to see him, week after week, and for a while we were what I'd call happy. Dawson was like a drug, and I couldn't stop taking him over and over. I went to one of his improv nights at the college, and he was the best actor on that stage—so clever, so quick on his feet. He snuck me into the art studio to see a painting he was working on. It was a self-portrait where there were two Dawsons, back-to-back, one painted in red and one in black. He wrote a song for me. It was called "Blue" and compared my eyes to the ocean and the sky when it storms and a chunk of turquoise and the wing of a mountain bluebird.

I thought he was so imaginative. So cool. So perfect.

I thought I was in love with him. I really did. I did that pathetic thing where I wrote our names together in the margins of my notebooks at school. I smiled when I thought about him. I started looking into applying to the same college, even though he'd be a senior when I was a freshman, but still. I wanted to be around him, however I could.

But, for all that, we never talked about what was going on between us. We didn't label ourselves. We didn't make commitments. We made out. And hung out. I thought that meant we were together. I was his girlfriend. At least I thought I was. Which felt special. Which felt right.

I had to pause to get lunch. Nothing sounds good these days. Sometimes even the idea of food makes me barf. I should be over the pukes by now, as I'm in week twenty-one of this sucktastic adventure called pregnancy, and morning sickness is supposed to peter off around week sixteen or so, according to the What to Expect book they gave me when I got here, but I still throw up pretty regularly. At home I stopped eating very much, but I can't do that now. The people around here check in all the time to make sure we've received the proper nourishment. And snacks. They are all about snacks here. Melly has this theory that the way to ward off morning sickness is to eat a grape like every ten minutes. "The trick is to never let your stomach get empty," she says. It worked when she was pregnant with her kids.

Anyway, Brit was crying in the lunch room. I grabbed an apple and a hard-boiled egg and went to hide in my room so I wouldn't have to deal with it. I wish I could help Brit. I do. Out of all of us, she's been screwed over the most. She's so young it's shocking that she's pregnant. I mean, when I was thirteen I didn't even know about sex. Her baby daddy is a grown man. A married man. Her coach. A pervert. He belongs in jail. These people—the adults: the coaches and mentors and tutors and parents, they're supposed to protect you. But they don't. They always seem to end up doing more harm than good.

It was quiet back at the dorms. The other girls were all at lunch.

Sometimes when I'm hanging out here by myself, I think about the way these rooms used to be forty or fifty years ago, crammed with pregnant girls. I try to imagine four girls in this little room, four beds squashed into this space where now there's only one lumpy twin bed and a built-in desk and a dresser. Four girls gathered around the little sink in the corner where I brush my teeth, which I hate doing lately, because my gums bleed. It's like a horror movie up in here every morning and night. Four girls would be pretty crowded. But there's strength in numbers, too.

So where was I? Oh yeah, Dawson. The missing condom. The days I thought I was falling in love with him. The regrettable song about how blue my eyes are. And now you.

Which brings me to about three months ago, when I sat in the hall outside his dorm room again, waiting for him to come back from play practice or choir or the art studio or wherever he was, because he was always out somewhere. It was the day after Valentine's Day, I remember, and I hadn't heard from Dawson in a couple weeks. I'd come to tell him about my little problem. Our little problem, I should say. I was leaning against his door, my knees tucked up to my chest, and every now and then I'd touch my stomach in complete disbelief, thinking about this weird little thing growing in there—this thing that was going to mess up everything. (No offense, X. I was pretty wigged.) And I thought, at least if he knows about it, we can decide what to do together.

Hours passed. He didn't come. It was like ten p.m., and this was a huge problem, because I had a newly imposed "oh my God you're PREGNANT, you obviously need boundaries" ten p.m. curfew on school nights, and I knew my stepmom was going to use me breaking the rules as yet one more reason I wasn't qualified to be a member of the family. That and I had to pee.

So I started to cry a little (I'm not a big crier, but the hormones were going strong, and things seemed bleak in the moment) and when I looked up again, there was that guy Ted staring at me.

I got to my feet. "Have you seen Dawson?" I mumbled, wiping at my face.

"I think he's doing a tech rehearsal for Hamlet. Uh . . . come in." Ted unlocked the door and gestured for me to go into their room. He was still looking at me like I was a grenade that had been tossed in his lap, like I was going to explode.

Maybe I was.

I went in. It was better than sitting out in the hall. As I passed the closet I caught sight of myself in the full-length mirror. I had raccoon eyes from the crying and the mascara. My face was all broken out. I looked about the same as I felt.

"Here." Ted handed me a tissue. I sat on Dawson's bed—where all the trouble had started—and blew my nose. Ted was messing around with an electric kettle and rustling through drawers, until the next time I looked up, and he was holding out a mug of what looked like tea.

"I don't have milk," he said. "Sorry."

For some reason I started laughing. I get like that when I'm upset, like when it's the worst possible time to laugh, it bubbles up from nowhere, and I can't stop. It's inappropriate—I mean, I laughed at my grandmother's funeral, and I loved my gran. This time was worse. This time I laughed so hard my sides hurt.

"Thanks," I said after I calmed down. I took the tea and drank deeply, the hot liquid warming all the way from my throat into my empty stomach. I clutched the mug in both hands, warming them, too.

"You want a Pop-Tart?" Ted asked.

"Yes."

"It's cherry."

"Okay."

I hadn't had a Pop-Tart in years. My stepmom didn't allow that kind of unhealthy shit in the house. It was delicious, coating my tongue with a sweet greasy cherry-flavored film. I wolfed it down.

Ted sat on his bed across the narrow room. He didn't seem to know what to say to me in this definitely-awkward situation.

"So he's in Hamlet?" I said after I was done stuffing my face. I brushed crumbs off Dawson's red-and-blue plaid bedspread and tried to wipe the mascara out from under my eyes.

"I guess so. It's all he talks about."

"Is he Hamlet?"

"No. Freshmen play the smaller roles, I think," Ted said. "He's like Rosencrantz or Guildenstern or one of those."

I nodded.

"Do you want to listen to some music?" He knew from his other encounters with me that I liked music. That was probably the only thing he knew about me.

"Sure."

He didn't try to play any of Dawson's records. He put on a Green Day CD that he played using his computer. I listened, more out of politeness than anything else. Green Day isn't my thing. But Ted was nice. He'd gotten a haircut since that first time I'd seen him. He was wearing a shirt that read Q: How many programmers does it take to change a light bulb?

I still don't know the answer to that question. I never read the back of his shirt.

"You're into computers?" I asked.

"I'm a double major—math and physics. But I want to work with computers. I'm good at code."

"Cool." I had no idea what code was, but okay.

"What do you want to do?" he said.

"I'm not in college," I said.

"You don't have to be in college to want to do something with your life," he said.

I threw up. I didn't really have any warning, so I just leaned down and barfed on the tile floor, trying to miss the comforter. Instead I got a pair of black Converse sneakers that'd been sitting next to the bed.

Ted jumped to his feet. He was gone for a few minutes and then back with a stack of brown paper towels from the bathroom. He got on his knees to clean up the puke, but I tried to stop him.

"You don't have to do that. I can—" The smell hit me, and I vomited again. Less, this time. But still. I wasn't making it better.

I sat back on the bed, sweating. Ted quickly wiped up the floor. It was mostly Pop-Tart. I don't think I'm ever going to eat another cherry Pop-Tart for as long as I live. He left again for a minute and came back with an actual mop and a bucket and mopped the floor.

He was so nice.

"You're so nice," I said. "You're like the nicest boy I've ever met."

"How many drinks have you had?"

"I'm not drunk." I shook my head as he started to make some more tea. "No, thanks." It might be a while before I drink tea again, too. "I'm okay."

"You don't seem okay," he observed.

No shit.

"I'm pregnant." I don't know why I came out with it like that. Maybe it seemed easier than making up an alternative explanation.

Ted sat down. "Oh."

"Yeah. I need to talk to Dawson."

"Oh."

"Yeah."

"You could go to the theater and find him. I could walk you."

"I don't want to interrupt him. It's kind of a big conversation to have. And I should do it in private, don't you think?"

"Right. Well, he could be back anytime. You can hang out and wait."

"Thank you," I murmured. I lay back on Dawson's bed and curled onto my side. Green Day was still playing. "Good Riddance."

"I hate this song," I breathed into Dawson's pillow, and then I was asleep.

When I woke up Dawson was there.

"What the hell happened to my shoes?" he wanted to know.

"Hi." I blinked up at him, disoriented. Ted was nowhere to be seen. The clock on the nightstand read past two in the morning. The parents were going to murder me. Or not, it occurred to me, as murdering me would also be murdering an unborn child, and that would be a PR nightmare. I smiled.

Dawson looked tired. He had dark circles under his eyes. But then I realized it was stage makeup.

"I don't usually come home to find girls in my bed," he said. "Not that I'm complaining."

He pulled his shirt over his head and made like he was going to get into bed with me. I scrambled to sit up.

"No, I—"

He kissed me, then pulled away and frowned.

"Was it you who puked on my shoes? Those are my lucky shoes. I was wearing those shoes the night of the Pearl Jam concert. When I met you."

"Maybe they're not so lucky," I said weakly.

"Oh my God, babe. Are you drunk?"

"I'm sixteen," I said. "Why does everyone assume I'm drunk?" There had been a few parties, maybe, a few instances where I was not my best self, and that was mostly to blow off steam and give the finger to my straight-laced parental units. But I didn't make a habit of it. I'm not a total lush.

Dawson shrugged. "I got drunk when I was sixteen."

"No, I'm . . ." I took a breath. This was big. What would he do? What would he say?

I was about to tell him, I swear. But as I was looking into his face— that perfect face that was staring at me so unknowingly, so trustingly—I couldn't do it to him. I couldn't watch his expression when he realized how this was going to mess up everything. No offense, X. But it was. It kind of already had.

"I have to go," I mumbled. "I didn't mean to be here so long."

"What? I just got here. Why did you—"

"I thought we could hang out tonight. I didn't know about the dress rehearsal. And I didn't mean to fall asleep. I have to get home."

"Okay." He walked me to my car. He kissed me. It was the last time he'd ever kiss me. But I didn't know that then.

I got in the car and rolled down the driver's side window.

"I'll call you," I said.

He smiled. "Not if I call you first."

When I got home everybody was asleep. No one gave me a lecture or threatened my life or anything. The house was perfectly silent. I got into my pajamas and washed my tear- and mascara-streaked face and lay down in my bed. Then I mentally beat myself up for a while. Stuff like:

How could you not tell him?

What, you can spill the beans to the roommate, but not the actual guy who needs to know?

He deserved to know.

He had to know.

I had to tell him.

So I went to my desk and wrote him a letter. It wasn't a long letter. Not like this one is turning out to be. It basically said: "Sorry, I didn't tell you before, but I didn't know how. I'm pregnant. I think I'm having the baby, but we can talk about it. I'm sorry. I'm so sorry. Call me."

This letter writing thing's getting to be a habit.

I put the letter in an envelope I took out of my dad's office, addressed it to Dawson's college mailbox, stole a stamp, and stuck it in the morning's outgoing mail.

Can you guess what happened next?

He didn't call me.

Shocking, right?

I got the message, though. He didn't want to have anything to do with me. Or you. We are on our own.

I guess that's going to be a lot for you to process. Maybe you don't want to know any of it. Maybe you want to stay out of it, too. And I couldn't blame you for that. But now you know the story of your not-parents' star-crossed love affair.

In with a bang, out with a whimper.

Did he break my heart? A little. Yes. But that's how it goes. You live, you learn. Better to have loved and . . .

Whatever.

Peace out, X.

Yours truly,

S

10

"Cassandra McMurtrey to the front office, please," calls the speaker next to the ceiling in my first-period chemistry class. "Cassandra McMurtrey to the front office."

My heart starts beating fast. Anytime I get called to the office I think: this could be about Mom. The doctors could have found a donor—a new heart packed in dry ice in a cooler right now, in a helicopter, shooting through the air toward the hospital. Everything could go back to the way it was before.

Or it could be an entirely different kind of call. My dad could be waiting at the office with his brave face on. He could tell me that Mom is gone. Which makes me want to hide. Like if I don't show up to receive the news, it won't be true.

But I go. Of course I go. And instead of my dad, there's Nyla outside the front office, leaning against the wall with her backpack at her feet, grinning at me.

"What's going on?" I ask warily.

"Just go in there and get checked out," she says. "Roll with it, babes."

I go into the office.

"Oh, hi, Cass," says the front office lady. "How are you?"

"You sent for me?"

"Yes. I understand that you need to be excused for the day."

"Um . . ."

"And tomorrow, too, correct?"

"Um . . . yeah. I guess."

"Oh, don't worry. Your father called and okayed it." She beams. "I think your dad's terrific. My boy Aidan's in his class right now, and he's never loved a teacher so much. And your mother . . ." She gives me sympathy face. "I've been so sorry to hear about her health troubles."

"Thank you."

"Okay then, fill this out." She passes me a binder with the sign-out sheet in it.

In thirty seconds I'm back in the hall with Nyla.

"You ready?" She could not look more pleased with herself.

"What am I supposed to be ready for, exactly?"

"You'll see." She slings an arm around my shoulders and walks me toward the front door.

In the parking lot, there's my dad in his beat-up Honda, windows rolled down, grinning from ear to ear like we've won some kind of lottery.

I try not to laugh. Dad must have sent Nyla in to get me because he didn't want to freak me out by calling me to the office himself, because he knows what I would think. That's the cool thing about Dad—he's a type A personality, although you wouldn't know it from the ponytail and the way he never tucks in his shirts. He's the planner of the family. And he always seems to think two steps ahead.

"You all packed, Nyles?" he asks Nyla.

"Yes, sir." She lifts her backpack. I guess she's coming with us.

"I call shotgun," I say, and hop into the passenger's seat. Nyla slides into the back.

"Where are we going?" But I already know. We're going to Boise State. Of course we are.

"I want to go check out some Idaho colleges," Dad says. Bingo. "So it technically doesn't count as playing hooky from school, because I'm going to take you to multiple schools. I got a substitute for the next couple days. Packed you a bag. I picked a few outfits out of your closet, and they could be terrible. I'm warning you now." He pumps a fist in the air and hoots like he's at a concert. "Road trip! We're going on a road trip!"

"Road trip!" Nyla joins in. "Woo!"

I shake my head. "You guys are weird, you know that?"

"Thank you," Dad replies, like this is a compliment. "So both girls in the car? Check. Seat belts on? Check. You ready to go?"

"Check," I say a bit breathlessly. "I'm ready."

Dad floors it out of the parking lot. Five minutes later we're speeding down the Yellowstone Highway to connect to the freeway. We pass the familiar little white brick building by the railroad tracks next to the bowling alley. It still has the original sign—"The Sugar Shell," it reads in big yellow and blue letters across the front. The parking lot is empty. I can't ever remember the parking lot being empty, not even for a minute, when my mom was running the shop.

"So Mom set this up, right?" I ask quietly.

"We all did—your mother and Nyla and me." Dad takes one

hand off the wheel to pat my shoulder. Then he looks at me all serious for a second. "We want you to have everything you deserve, Cass. Your best life possible. And it'd be nice if your best life included going to college. Preferably somewhere close by. And affordable."

"Right," I say hoarsely. Like not Juilliard. Like Boise State.

I can feel Nyla watching me. I crane my neck around to look at her. "How are you doing back there, traitor? How long have you known about this little plan?"

"Only a few days," she says like it's no big deal.

"You could have told me, you know."

"But you love surprises, Cass. And I'm so glad I get to come along."

"When Nyla told us that she's interested in checking out the Idaho schools, too," Dad says, "we knew that this weekend would be the perfect opportunity for both of you."

I glance at Nyla again. "Wait. You're considering Idaho schools? When did this happen?"

She smiles, though it's her fake smile. "Of course I want to consider all of the options."

"Uh-huh." She is up to something, methinks. Something beyond moral support. I guess I'll find out what soon enough.

"Here we go!" Dad steers us onto the freeway entrance and accelerates. My heart's still beating fast—it hasn't slowed down since they called my name over the school intercom. The trip suddenly feels big. Important. Like this is when the course of my life is going to get decided.

Right here. Right now.

I swallow nervously. I don't know if I'm ready, maybe I'm not ready for all of this, but we're on the freeway now, doing seventy-five miles per hour, speeding toward the future.

11

Dad brought school supplies. Of *course* he did. He's got the entire trip planned out to like the minute, all written down in this blue notebook (a *college-ruled* notebook—a Dad joke) with a page for each institution of higher learning that we're going to visit, divided into two columns: pros and cons. We start at Idaho State University, which is in Pocatello (Dad calls it Poca-toilet-hole—a kind of mean Idaho Falls joke) and then we head west to the College of Southern Idaho in Twin Falls. Both places are nice, fully equipped with the standard college stuff: classrooms, dorms, libraries, bleary-eyed students.

I can't picture myself as one of them. It's been hard for me to imagine going to college at all, ever since Mom said I couldn't go to Juilliard. But I'm giving it the old college try (lamest joke ever).

Dad's calling this our "Idaho college trip," and we're touring a bunch of Idaho colleges, but it becomes clear almost immediately that, for my father, at least, I'm still supposed to end up at Boise State. I'm not surprised by this, obviously. On the four-hour drive west we basically have the same conversation about five times:

Dad says, "So Boise is not so far away from home that you can't come back for the weekends. But it's not so close that your family might pop in unexpectedly. You can feel like you've gone somewhere. Like you have your independence."

And I nod but say, "I wouldn't mind being close. Maybe I could go to Idaho State and live at home. Commute. It's only an hour. That'd be the cheapest option."

And Dad shakes his head. "We don't have much money, but your mother and I both want you to get the full college experience. Live on campus. Get stuck with an epically bad roommate."

"Okay. Well, maybe we can go look at University of Idaho . . ." That's like ten hours away, in the northern part of the state. "I've heard it's beautiful up there."

But Dad shakes his head again. No way. "Too far. Boise State, however—now that's the perfect distance away."

And he keeps on talking up Boise, Boise, Boise.

We get there around six in the evening—too late, Dad says, to properly scout the place out, so we'll do that tomorrow. In the meantime Nyla wants to have dinner at Big Jud's, this place that serves hamburgers the size of dinner plates. Dad and I still don't eat meat, but we go along with it. Because Tater Tots.

"So after breakfast tomorrow, we'll head over to BSU and hang out a little," Dad says, checking the notebook with the schedule. "But our official appointment doesn't start until one o'clock. I am psyched to see it all again. I'll show you where your mother and I had our first kiss."

"That sounds . . . great," Nyla pipes up. "But actually, there's somewhere else I wanted to go tomorrow morning." She pulls a brochure out of her purse and slaps it down on the table. "College of Idaho."

Dad and I both stare at her for a second. I grab the brochure and pull it toward me.

"It's a smaller college," Nyla explains, "only about a thousand students, but it has a good reputation. I thought we'd at least check it out. Since that's what we're here to do."

I've never heard of College of Idaho. But okay.

Dad nods. "Sounds like a plan, and of course this is your trip, too, Nyles."

"Thanks," she says. "I'm pretty interested in this place." She gives me a secret smile.

Dad grins. "And then we'll head over to BSU. Where they'll give us the grand tour."

I smile and nod. I'm woozy from being in the car so long, and ever since we saw the white dome of the state capitol building against the rolling foothills behind them, the trees all orange and red and gorgeous with fall, my brain's gone fuzzy. I'm happy to have Dad and Nyla steering me around where I need to go.

We resume eating and planning.

"Yum, this is amazing," Nyla says around a mouthful of Big Jud burger. "You two should reconsider meat. This is the best thing ever."

"How'd you even know about this place?" I nibble on a Tot, which is a little dry, unfortunately. I've only been to Boise a few times, ever. The last time I came here was when my Girl Scout troop did a project on the Oregon Trail. That was pre-Nyla. I don't remember much about that trip, except that it kept freaking me out that I was born here.

This is it. Boise. My place of origin.

I could be brushing shoulders with people who are related to me, I remember thinking back then. My birth mother could be the woman at the next table. Or the waitress. Or that lady riding her bike on the street outside the window.

Nyla takes a sip of her strawberry milkshake and sighs a happy sigh. "I used to come over all the time. There weren't hair salons for black hair in I.F. when I was a kid. It was a problem."

"And there are now?" Dad asks, like he's surprised we've progressed that far.

"Now there's Nelo's House of Fades and Braids." She pats her curls. "My mom doesn't have to drive me across the state to get my hair done anymore. Although that drive used to be our best bonding time. I miss it."

I adore Nyla's mother—Elizabeth is her name, but I call her Mama Liz the way Nyla calls my mom Mama Cat, and we call Ronnie's mom Mama Sue, and we all call Miss Golden Mama Jo. We each have a list of backup mothers. Mama Liz is like super mom—she can whip up a batch of organic gluten-free chocolate chip cookies faster than a speeding bullet. She's also the busiest lady I know. Nyla has ten-year-old twin sisters who were adopted from China and a six-year-old brother from Russia. Mama Liz is therefore constantly driving one of Nyla's siblings to dance class or karate or piano or whatever else.

"Time really is like sand in the hourglass." Dad sighs heavily. "It seems like yesterday you girls had only just met. Little seventh graders. And now you're going off to college." He gives a loud sniffle. "You're abandoning me," he fake cries.

"Aw. But look on the bright side. You can finally turn my room into that home gym you've always wanted." I pat him on the back. "You're going to be fine, Dad."

He laughs at the home gym idea and pretends to wipe his tears.

But then he gives a real sigh. And I realize, I don't know if what I said is true.

I don't know if he's going to be fine. If I leave for college. If Mom—

But for now we'll do what we always do: carry on. Pretend that we're a normal family. Even though that's never accurately described the kind of family that we are.

I wake up the next morning strangely calm. Today's the day, I think, that I'm going to figure out my life. And my parents will be happy, and I will be happy. And I'll look back years from now and laugh about how I used to imagine Juilliard. And I'll think about this trip as the turning point. And I'll be glad. Like everything's already been decided for me, somehow, and all I have to do is sit back and watch myself decide to go to Boise State.

But first we drive out to the College of Idaho, that place Nyla wants to look at. Which is in a town called Caldwell, about thirty minutes from Boise.

And that's when everything changes.

The funny thing is, I can't even really explain why.

It starts like the other colleges. First we meet the admissions people, and they walk us around telling us all the wonderful things about C of I, beaming like the college is a close personal friend of theirs they'd like me to meet. They're bursting with pride about C of I's small class size, the eleven-to-one student-teacher ratio, the professors, the way the college keeps getting listed as one of America's top colleges or best value colleges or home to America's happiest students. They walk us through the charming old buildings—it's the oldest college in Idaho, didn't you know?

I did not know. Because I didn't know this place existed until yesterday.

They show us the gorgeous, brand-new library. The rows of desks each with their own USB ports and electrical outlets. The quiet study spaces. The sheer number of books.

It's all very nice, but it's not exactly life-altering, until we're walking along this pretty tree-lined sidewalk down the center of the campus, the wind stirring the leaves in the trees, and a strange feeling washes over me. It's like a backward sense of déjà vu. Like suddenly I hear a voice inside telling me, with absolute certainty:

This is where you belong.

At the end of the sidewalk is a fountain, and the building behind the fountain is where the art and music and theater departments are located. We go in. We meet the main theater professor, who makes me laugh so much it's kind of embarrassing, and then he takes us into the studio theater, where most of the student productions happen.

I fall hard for this theater, total instalove.

It's an average-sized space with movable seating, so the setup can be flexible: you could arrange it as a traditional stage and have the seats all face it, in one direction. Or you could turn the seats in a box and do theater in the round. It's fairly basic, like I said, nothing particularly high tech or cutting edge about it. It's just a theater. But it feels . . . right.

"There's a larger auditorium, but we don't use that much. It's too big for us," the professor explains. "There's also another little black box in the basement of the SUB. The students do improv and put on the one-act plays they write there."

"Cool," Dad says.

I stand in the center of the empty stage, and goose bumps jump up along my arms. I want to be performing in this spot. Standing under these lights. Right here.

This.

This is where you belong.

"Awesome," Nyla says quietly.

I rub my arms. "Cool."

Dad doesn't seem to notice that I float through our afternoon tour of Boise State in a total daze. I try to pay attention to what the BSU admissions people are telling me, but my mind keeps wandering back to that theater at College of Idaho. To the tree-lined walkway that leads there, which I would take every day on my way to rehearsals. To the honors dorm with its cute little nooks at the ends of the halls, which they call stubbies. And for the first time, the idea of college-but-not-Juilliard feels doable to me.

College of Idaho, I think to myself as we're having dinner at the end of the day, this time at a Thai place that has vegetarian options. Those three words seem to echo in my brain over and over. College. Of. Idaho. I munch on my pad thai with fried tofu, and I think about how C of I's mascot is a howling wolf—no, a coyote, I correct myself. They're the Yotes. I smile. Go, Yotes.

"Weren't you impressed by the size of that big theater? Enormous!" Dad gushes to Nyla and me. But he's still talking Boise State.

"Right," I murmur, trying to focus on my noodles and not break my father's already fractured heart by telling him I'm not into his blue-and-orange dream for me. "It was a big theater."

"BSU has a great faculty, too," Nyla adds, although she's been unusually silent today. She didn't say more than three sentences the entire time we were at C of I, even though she was supposedly interested in going there. She's just been walking along next to me. Watching me. Keeping my dad entertained. "Lots of really good professors."

"Yes!" Dad says enthusiastically, nodding. He's been nodding all day, like he's ready to give his final answer. College? Yes yes. Boise State? Yes yes yes. "You'd get a good, balanced education in theater going to BSU."

"Right," I say.

He says "Yes," and I say "Right," and round and round we go.

But he is. Right, I mean. Boise State's clearly a good school. I had almost given in to the idea, actually, when he was trying to sell me on it yesterday. I was forcing myself to imagine cruising around that campus. Going to the football games with the blue turf. If I was going to go to college anywhere, I thought, or at least go to college somewhere that wasn't Juilliard, it might as well be Boise State.

But that was before we visited College of Idaho.

College of Idaho. It has a ring to it.

"I think it's the one, don't you?" Dad's practically glowing. "It's the right price. The right location. The right school."

"Right," I say softly.

12

We're late getting back. Nyla's sleeping in the back seat, so for the last two or so hours of the return trip to I.F. it's just Dad and me sitting in the dark, staring ahead at the mostly empty freeway and the sweep of the occasional oncoming headlights.

Nyla starts to snore.

Dad turns off the radio.

I'm trying to figure out a way to tell Dad I want to go to College of Idaho, to let him down gently, but I can't find the words.

Besides, Dad's back to thinking about how the passage of time works.

"It really does feel like yesterday," he muses, "when your mom and I were making this drive back with you for the first time." He laughs like he still can't believe it. "I drove the whole way about ten miles under the speed limit, and I couldn't stop looking in the rearview mirror, because I was sure they were going to decide it was a mistake, and we couldn't keep you after all."

"But you did get to keep me," I say.

He smiles. "You were so tiny. And loud."

I snort back a laugh. "Thanks."

"I sure do love you, Boo." He reaches over to ruffle my hair.

"I love you, too, Dad. Thank you for taking me on this trip. I am, honestly, really glad we did this."

"Thank you for being so patient with our current situation. I know it's not what you were expecting. You're the best kid I could have asked for. Really. How did we get so lucky?"

"We both got lucky." This is how I always respond when my parents say things like that. How fortunate we all were to find each other.

We drive in silence for a while. Nyla's stopped snoring, I notice. For now.

And suddenly I'm thinking about my origins again.

"So when you picked me up in Boise, when I was a baby, did you see . . ." I hesitate. We've talked about my adoption plenty over the years—it's hardly been a taboo subject—but we haven't gotten into the finer details. "Did you meet . . . my birth mother?"

He takes a sharp breath. "No," he says abruptly. "No, it was a closed adoption, so we didn't meet her. You were given to us by a social worker. You were wearing an orange jumper with little white ghosts on it. Because it was Halloween."

I've heard this part of the story before. That's why Dad calls me Boo.

I bite my lip, but then decide to keep going along this line of questioning. "But you know things about my birth mother. Like she was sixteen, and she had blue eyes, that kind of thing. Did someone tell you?"

"Sort of," he answers. "It was in the paperwork they gave us."

"Paperwork?" I've never heard them talk about any paperwork before.

Again, silence. This time it's Dad who breaks it.

"So . . . why all the questions suddenly, about your birth mother?"

"I just wonder, sometimes. Who she was. How I might be like her, if I am."

"I don't know if you're like her," he says. "But I know that you're awesome."

"Dad."

"I think you're a lot like your mother, actually. I mean—"

"I know what you mean." Cat McMurtrey. My mother. "You and Mom are my real parents," I say.

He glances over at me and smiles that half smile of his. "I'm glad you think so, too. I'd hate to think I was your fake dad."

"No, I mean, sometimes, when people find out I'm adopted, they ask me, do I even know who my real mother is?"

Dad shifts, changes hands on the steering wheel, then scratches underneath his ponytail. "Those super sensitive people, huh?"

I scoff. "Yeah. Sensitive. Why do they always say it like that? My *real* parents. It's so annoying. Sometimes it's on TV, too, when we find out a character has a secret past or something, like when Superman finds out he's not originally from Earth."

"I'll tell you this right now." Dad is a comic book nerd through and through. This is serious business. "Martha Kent is Superman's real mother. I'd beat up anybody who said otherwise."

I chuckle at the thought of my dad beating someone up. He's a total pacifist. "I always knew that was wrong, when they said it like that. Anyway." I stare at my hands where they're folded in my lap. "You're my real dad, Dad."

"Thanks, Supergirl," he says.

I punch him lightly in the arm over the Supergirl thing.

"Ow!" he cries out in fake pain. "Be gentle. You don't know your own strength."

We reach Idaho Falls after midnight, so late that we decide Nyla should sleep over at our house, which is a pretty common occurrence anyway, and besides, we have rehearsal in the morning, so we can go in together. We text Mama Liz, who gives her okay, and then we get all decked out in our pajamas with our hair combed and/or wrapped and teeth brushed, and settle in for the night, curled up next to each other in my double bed.

I'm almost asleep when Nyla says, "You want to go to College of Idaho, don't you?"

I'm instantly wide awake. I turn toward her. "Yes! How did you know?"

"I thought you'd like it. My mom took me there to see *The Nutcracker* on one of our Boise hair trips, and I thought it was pretty." She laughs. "Your face is such an open book sometimes. You were so into it this morning. You would have moved in today if they'd have let you."

I swallow. "Too bad my dad didn't seem to notice."

"Your dad was preoccupied with his overwhelming infatuation with all things Boise State."

"I know." I sigh. "I wanted to tell him, but . . ."

"You should tell him. He might be disappointed. But he wouldn't have taken us to the other colleges if he wasn't open to the idea of you picking the one you want. So tell him, Cass. He'll want you to go where you want to go."

Nyla's always so smart. She has a high emotional intelligence, my mother always says.

"Okay. I'll tell him," I promise.

She flips over onto her back and stares up at the ceiling. Then after a few seconds she turns her head toward me again and says, "Are you going to search for your birth mother?"

I gasp and sit up. "You faker! You were supposed to be asleep!"

She sits up, too. "I was asleep, until I wasn't, but then you two were in this intensely personal conversation, and I didn't want to interrupt to say, 'Hey, guess what, I'm awake!'"

I laugh. "Right. How much did you hear?"

"Enough. So are you? Going to search for your birth mother?"

"I didn't say I was, did I?"

"No. But it sounded like you were curious."

"I am curious," I admit. "But . . ."

"I don't think you should do it," she says.

I'm surprised and weirdly hurt by this. "Why?"

"I think you could be opening up a can of worms. You have a great family, Cass. The best family. And you don't know what your birth parents might be like, but they can't be better than the family you've got now. Let sleeping dogs lie."

"You think my birth mother is a sleeping dog?"

She doesn't answer my question.

"I wouldn't be searching for another family, Ny," I say carefully. "You're right. I already have the best family."

"Good."

"I want to find out more about my birth mother because . . ." I take a breath. "I guess I'm searching for myself."

"Okay. If that's what you feel like you need to do." She frowns and flops down again. I lie down, too, wondering if she'll tell me what she's thinking about now, but she doesn't say anything. She obviously doesn't get how I feel. Which is hard, because Nyla usually gets the adoption thing more than anybody else.

It's been different for Nyla, though. All my life people have been telling me how I look like my adopted parents—they assume I'm their biological child—and all Nyla's life she's been practically walking around with a neon sign flashing over her head that says ADOPTED.

So I guess it makes sense that we'd have different feelings on the subject.

I didn't even tell Nyla I was adopted until we'd been friends for like a year. The topic came up one afternoon at the Hendersons'. Mama Liz was making an enormous pot of palm butter soup—about once a month she tried to have a "culture night" and make Liberian food so that Nyla would feel connected to the place she'd originally come from. I could never tell if Nyla liked this attempt to under- stand her "African roots," as Mama Liz called it, or if she hated it, but she always ate the food without complaint. Anyway, Nyla and I were sitting at the big oak table in the kitchen, the air around us full of unfamiliar spices, and we were talking about how we'd done this blood typing experiment at school, and I'd discovered that my mom had this rare blood type. Which would turn out to be part of why it's been difficult to find a donor.

"I've never even known anybody with AB negative blood." Mama

Liz turned to me. "Do you have it, too? What's your blood type, sweetie?"

"O positive, I think."

"So your father is O pos. That's lucky."

"Actually, I think my dad's B positive."

Nyla and Mama Liz both looked at me like *That makes no sense.*

"I'm adopted," I explained.

"Oh my goodness!" exclaimed Mama Liz. "I did not know that. Well, doesn't our Heavenly Father work in mysterious ways?" She beamed. "It's another thing you and my Nyla have in common."

Nyla didn't say anything to me about it until later, when we were supposed to be asleep, sort of like now. I was stretched out on her trundle mattress, thinking about how my mom and me had like opposite blood types, and what did that even mean, when Nyla's voice cut through the dark.

"I was three," she said. It took me a second to understand what she was talking about.

"I was six weeks old," I answered.

Then we both sat up and told each other everything, every detail we knew about our lives before we'd come to Idaho Falls. I told her that my birth mother had brown hair and blue eyes, like me. The stuff my parents had passed along. Which apparently came from a form.

Nyla told me that her birth mother's name was Bindu, but she didn't remember what she looked like, exactly. She didn't remember much of anything before her relatively happy life here in Idaho. She also told me that culture night, with the fried eggplant Mama Liz cooked up and the spicy chicken gravy, sweet potato greens, and fufu—a kind of bread—didn't make her remember Liberia any more clearly. But she liked the food.

"It's awkward," I remember she told me. "They expect me to connect with my heritage and all that, and I don't know if I can. But I guess it's better than them acting like I came from nowhere. At least they try. They care."

We stayed up talking until two in the morning, and we didn't bring up our adoptions much after that. But it felt like something changed between us that night. Our friendship deepened. There was a new layer of connection that we shared. We'd both been lost, in a way. And then we'd both been found.

Dear X,

So that last letter might have been out of line. Just a smidge. I know. I tried to get it back, actually, after I gave it to Melly, but she said she'd already turned it in. Sorry if it was TMI.

I don't know what the hell I'm doing, if that's not obvious. Maybe the ultimate effect of these letters is that you'll be really glad I gave you up. Maybe you'll read all of this and think, wow, did I ever dodge a bullet with this girl.

I can't disagree.

"Seems like you have something to say, after all," Melly said this morning as she was driving me in for my checkup. "Writing all these letters."

She was smiling like, I told you so.

"I'm bored," I said.

"Sure."

"I am."

"Okay. That makes total sense. You're writing to your baby because you're bored. But why not write letters to someone else, then? Or write in a diary? Why the baby?"

To be honest, I don't know. It's not like I'm changing my mind about the adoption. It's not like I'm bonding with you.

"There are things I want the kid to know," I said to Melly.

"About you?"

"Yeah, and about other things."

"What other things?"

But that's none of her business, is it? "Hey, can you stop being a social worker for like five seconds?" I asked.

"Sure. What should I be, then?" Melly said. "What role can I play for you today?"

"Maybe a chauffeur. Preferably a quiet one."

I thought that was pretty funny. And the upside was, Melly didn't talk to me again for the rest of the drive.

I hate these visits to the doctor. First there's the waiting room, which is always filled with couples looking so out-of-control excited about being parents, or couples with their baby looking so completely thrilled to show everyone, like it's some big accomplishment, having a baby.

Getting pregnant is not that hard. Trust me. People do it every day. Every second, even. There's probably been like five hundred babies born in the two minutes that you've been reading this letter.

But back to the waiting room. There's this look everyone else gives me in there, this judgmental gaze, which starts at my clearly teenage face and moves to my belly and finally travels to my naked ring finger. Which *always makes me want to show them a different finger. And the one time I did that Melly went all red-faced like she was the one who was embarrassed.*

And then there's the weigh-in. No girl anywhere ever liked a weigh-in.

After that they ask me a bunch of questions about how I'm feeling and take my blood pressure and poke and prod me and make me pee in a cup. And then we listen to the heartbeat. That's always the weirdest part. There's my heart going all slow and steady and then suddenly I can hear yours, this quick-quick-quick sound, and the doctor smiles and Melly smiles and the nurse smiles, and one of them inevitably says, "That's your baby."

But all that time, I'm usually thinking, That's not my baby. You don't belong to me. I'm thinking about you in there, the size of a mango, they say, and growing bigger every second, and you can hear things now, they say, like my voice, like a dog barking, like a vacuum, and your lungs are developing this week and your fingers aren't webbed anymore.

See. You're an alien, X. That's how it always makes me feel.

So today, I got to skip the pee thing. Which was pretty awesome. But after all the other stuff was done, I started to sit up, to get my clothes back on and whatnot, and the doctor said, "Wait a minute. We haven't gotten to the best part."

"The best part?" Uh-oh. I had no idea what that could be.

"The ultrasound. Don't you want to see your baby?"

It turns out that wasn't a real question. I couldn't say no, I mean. They had to like count the chambers in your heart or something.

I told them I had to pee. Which I did. I always have to pee these days.

They told me it was better if my bladder was full. It would push you up a little so they could get a better picture. This is why they didn't make me pee earlier.

116

I had an ultrasound before, but it was months ago, and I couldn't really tell what I was looking at. But this time it was different. No offense, X, but your head was gigantic in comparison with the rest of your body. I could see your skull, and your eye sockets were huge. You absolutely did look like an alien, like one of those aliens in the abduction shows, the gray ones with the big black eyes.

The doctor moved around so we could see all the little white bones in your spine. Your leg bones. Your feet. At one point you stretched so we could see like a perfect footprint, and that was the weirdest thing ever, because you had the feet.

Everyone on my dad's side of the family has the same feet. My grandfather, my dad, me, my older brother, all of us. My mom used to call them "duck feet" because they're narrow at the heel but wide at the toe, and all the toes except the pinky are basically the same length across. The second toe is as long as the big toe, the third toe as long as the second, the fourth only slightly shorter.

So I was on my back staring up at this blackness on the screen and suddenly I saw a duck foot. The square toes.

I'm so sorry about the weird feet.

Then the doctor said, "Would you like to know the sex?"

And I said, "Huh? I already know about the sex, thanks. Obviously."

"No, no." He laughed. "I mean, the gender of the baby?"

"Oh." My first instinct was to say no. I try to keep it light, you know? I try not to get too . . . involved. I think it's better if you're an alien.

But then I was curious, and I said okay.

"It's a girl," he said.

"You're sure?" Melly asked.

"Well, it's not as easy to identify as it would be if it were a boy. But yes. I'm ninety percent positive. There's a baby girl in there."

I stared at the screen. I couldn't see the feet anymore. I couldn't see anything.

The doctor moved around again, so we were looking at your head. A side view this time. I could see your nose. I think you might have Dawson's nose, this little ski jump kind of nose.

"Is she sucking her thumb?" asked Melly.

"Yes," the doctor said, and then I could see it, too. You were totally sucking your thumb in there.

"We believe thumb sucking is genetic," the doctor said. "Did you suck your thumb as a child?"

"Nope," I said, but that wasn't true. I don't know why I lied. I guess I didn't want to go into it. I sucked my thumb all the way up until kindergarten. It messed up my teeth. It was because of the thumb sucking that I ended up having to wear braces for a period back in junior high that I'd prefer to forget.

This time I was the one who was quiet on the way back to Booth. Thinking. Feeling you moving around. I'd felt you move before, but it always felt like gas, or like a goldfish swimming around in my belly. Not a person. Not even an alien.

But you're not an alien.

You're a girl.

The doctor printed me a picture of you. Some of the other girls here—the ones who are keeping their babies, anyway—post these pictures on the inside of their lockers, or frame them, even. Heather had hers taped onto her headboard, so she could look at it while she was in bed.

I'm going to give this to you, though. Like a pre-baby picture. It can be the only picture that exists of the two of us together.

S

13

"I must leave you," Bastian says, his face hovering above mine.

We're finally blocking the make-out scene. I have a feeling it's going to be my favorite. There are five kisses between us in this part of the show. Five. Then he lifts me into his arms and carries me off. And now we're at the part where we roll, making out, from upstage to downstage.

It's a funny scene, and it's fun, too, but it's mildly terrifying. At least we don't have to actually kiss yet. When we get to the part in the script where it says we kiss, we both kind of lean forward toward each other, like we're going to kiss. But then we don't. Because we're high school students, and this is a Mormon town, and so we're encouraged to keep the actual kissing down to a minimum. The real kissing will happen later, like a week or two before the performance, later. Which is still a few weeks away.

"Let's try that again," says Mama Jo from where she's standing in the front row of the house. She's got that pursed-lip expression she gets when she's trying to articulate what she needs us to do. "I want three rolls, and then Bastian, you end up on top."

Awkward. Bastian and I go back to our starting position, then drop down onto the stage floor and put our arms around each other again. He doesn't know where to put his hands. I don't know what to do with my legs.

So: awkward.

"I should have brought breath mints," he whispers.

"Oh. Uh, sorry."

His dark eyes widen. "For me. I meant for me. Not for you."

He's so completely and utterly attractive in every way. It's hard to ignore from this vantage point.

"Okay, go," Mama Jo commands, and the music starts up.

Bastian and I hold on to each other and begin to roll downstage. It's difficult to control, but we manage one rotation, and then another, and another, and then we stop and Bastian lifts his head.

"I must leave you," he says again in the prince voice, which is deep and hilarious, and I can't help but laugh.

"That's great," Mama Jo says, laughing, too. "But I think we should try to get the roll a bit more smoothly."

"Do people actually do that?" Bastian asks quietly, just for me. "Do they roll when they're making out?"

"I don't know. I haven't." I'm blushing, I'm pretty sure. He's still on top of me, resting his weight on his arms so he doesn't squash me. Mama Jo hasn't told us to try it again yet or to move on. She's having a deep discussion with the stage manager about the logistics of the rolling. Or maybe we shouldn't roll, even, because that's, um, suggestive. Maybe we should be standing up instead and spin onto the stage.

"Spinning's not going to be easier," I whisper. I'm liking the rolling, truth be told.

"You have great lips," Bastian says.

My breath catches. His face is inches from mine. His breath smells like Italian salad dressing, which isn't bad at all. And he's staring at my lips.

"They're like a perfect bow," he says.

I'm definitely blushing now, aware of our legs all tangled up together. I should say something about *his* lips, shouldn't I? Just to be polite? Or his eyes, which are a very dark brown and reflecting the points of light around us in a way that makes them seem like they're sparkling. But what could I say: "You have great eyes?" Could I pull off that level of obvious flirtation? Am I ready to make my move? I mean, we've known each other for a few weeks. By now Bastian's been seamlessly integrated into our little theater-nerd group. We eat lunch together most days, joke around in choir, hang out before and after rehearsals. He doesn't stare at me anymore, that I can tell, but he still seems interested.

Maybe he's waiting for me to make the first move. I should totally make the first move.

"All right, let's stick with the roll, so try it one more time and then keep going," Mama Jo calls out before I get a chance to say anything at all.

Bastian helps me to my feet. We walk ten paces upstage, then lie down again. The music starts, and we roll. Roll. Roll.

"I must leave you," Bastian says, and jumps up, brushes off his pants. Then he starts talking about the giant he still has to slay, and I ask if we'll ever find each other again in the woods, and he tells me that this was "just a moment in the woods." That he'll never forget me. That I made him feel so alive. And then he's off, and it's time for my big solo. After which I will die.

I cock my head slightly to one side. "What was *that*?"

Mama Jo laughs at my delivery. "Good," she says. "Carry on."

"You're awesome," Bastian tells me as we're breaking for lunch.

I feel my cheeks going hot. It's weird and embarrassing. I don't generally have trouble talking to boys. I open my mouth. Words come out. It's easy. Sometimes with Bastian I feel like in this strange way I'm acting out a scene in a play, but it's my life. This is my scene with Bastian Banks, already written down, and we're performing it together. The Cass and Bastian show. In which Bastian just told Cass that he thought she was awesome.

"Why thank you, kind sir," I reply, because that's good writing right there.

"Do you like pie?"

"Huh?" Or maybe not so good writing.

"Pie. Like pumpkin. Cherry. Lemon meringue. I could go on, but—"

"Oh, that pie. Well. Who doesn't like pie?" I'm more of a cake person, but I can be flexible.

"I'm going to Perkins for lunch. Would you like to come?"

"Yes." Oh my God he's asking me out, isn't he, sort of, maybe, finally? But then I remember that I already have plans with Nyla. I wince and close my eyes for a few seconds.

"Are you okay?"

I nod. "I mean, I'd like to come, but—"

He nods, too, and then turns and hollers across the theater. "Hey, Nyla! You want to go for pie?"

"Uh, okay?" she calls back.

I beam at him. He wanted to ask me out—but he also knew that he should invite Nyla. He really is perfect.

He turns back to me. "So?"

I laugh and nod. "Let there be pie."

"We missed you two at rehearsal Thursday," Bastian says about an hour later around a huge mouthful of chocolate cream pie. "What happened?"

"We were on a road trip," Nyla says.

"Fun! Why didn't I get to come?" Bastian says. "I love road trips."

"With my dad," I clarify.

He snorts. "With your dad? How was that?"

"It was fun, actually." Nyla casts me a meaningful look. "It was quality parental time. Time for good conversation. You know. About the things we *want* in life."

I shake my head slightly. No, I still haven't told my dad that I don't want to go to BSU. I mean, it's only been a few days. I'm working up to it.

Bastian's eyebrows rumple. "I can't even get my dad off the couch most of the time." He shakes his head. "Where'd you go on this amazing road trip?"

"Boise," I answer. "We were checking out Idaho colleges."

Bastian nods. "Time to start applying soon."

"Yep. I need to be doing that. Now, I guess. Or, according to my guidance counselor, like yesterday."

"And?"

"And what?" I'm not sure what he's asking.

"And which colleges did you decide you want to apply to?"

"Oh . . . I don't know."

Nyla scoffs. "Come on, Cass. You do know." She smiles at Bastian. "I would like to go to USC. That's my first choice. But I'm also applying to California Institute of the Arts, DePaul, Northwestern, Carnegie Mellon, the New School, Pace, Rutgers, Brown, and . . ." She looks away from me. "Juilliard."

What? The green monster rears its ugly head at once. But . . . but Nyla always said she didn't want to go to Juilliard.

"Well, Juilliard's the dream for every actor, obviously," Bastian says. "So not Idaho for you, huh, Nyles?"

She gives me a slightly guilty, sympathetic pout. "Not Idaho. How about you? Are you planning to go to college and be a theater major?"

"Yes," he says with a determined look in his eyes. "But I already know where."

"Oh, really? Do tell," I say.

"I'm going to College of Idaho."

Nyla and I exchange thunderstruck glances. Oh, come on, universe. Seriously?

"College of Idaho?" I get out after about a minute of sputtering.

"Yeah. I've always wanted to go there." He starts talking up the class size, small, so you really get to know the professors. The honors dorm. The SUB with its little black box space in the basement.

"But did you see the main theater? The one with the white marble lobby?" I'm leaning forward across the table. I can't help myself.

"Yeah, that's Langroise Hall," he says. "That theater's pretty damn sexy. There's something about it."

"Totally sexy," I breathe. "I know."

"Oh my gosh, I can't decide if I need to leave you two alone or drive you to Caldwell right now," Nyla says with a roll of her eyes.

Bastian laughs. "So I take it you want to go to C of I, too, Cass?"

"I do." I sigh. "I really do." It's a little embarrassing, how completely in love I am now with C of I, when only a week ago I had such deep feelings for Juilliard. But that's life, I guess. You fall in love with a place. You get your heart broken. You move on.

"Now she has to break it to her father," Nyla adds.

I prop my chin on my hand. "My dad has a thing for Boise State."

"Ah." Bastian nods. Sighs. "My parents, too. They don't trust any college with the word 'liberal' in the description."

"Did you explain what 'liberal arts' actually means?"

"They don't care."

"Cass's dad isn't like that," Nyla points out. "He's going to be absolutely fine with Cass going to C of I. Provided that Cass ever tells him that's where she wants to go."

"I'm going to tell him, Ny," I say, frowning. "I just haven't had the right opportunity."

"Uh-huh."

I shoot her my "back off" look.

"How's your state drama scene with Alice going?" Nyla asks Bastian, seamlessly pivoting the conversation. I want to laugh at her, because she's asking all nonchalantly like she doesn't care, she's only curious, but I can tell she's sizing him up as competition. "It's only like a week away, now. The pressure's on."

"Oh, we're doing great," he says. "Alice is hilarious, and I adore Neil Simon plays. It's like the perfect scene for us—we're a married couple having our first big fight. It's super funny. What are you two doing?"

"The—"

"It's a secret," Nyla interrupts before I can spill the beans. "A secretive secret type of secret that we can't tell anybody, under penalty of death."

Way to be melodramatic, Ny, I think. She's way too competitive for her own good. And it's not like she wants to win because of the scholarship, which she obviously doesn't need.

Bastian looks suitably impressed at her pronouncement. "Oh. I see. Well, I'm sure you're going to be amazing."

"Darned right we're going to be amazing," Nyla says.

"But you're amazing, too," I say to Bastian. "I mean, you're going to be amazing."

"Let's all be amazing," he says wisely.

Indeed.

The check comes, and Nyla pays for my pie and hers, saying, "It's my turn, right?" so Bastian won't know it's always her turn, and we gather up our stuff. A blast of cold air hits us when we come out the door. Fall is about to give in to winter, any second now.

I shiver, and Bastian throws his arm around me as we traverse the parking lot. He pulls me into his chest. My heart starts to gallop.

"You're going to College of Idaho," he sings.

Dear God, I hope so.

"I'm also going to College of Idaho," he continues. "We're going to be in plays together. And have classes together. And hang out together all the time."

"Yes, I think that's what that means," says Nyla sharply.

"So it's destiny," he says, the sparkle coming back into his dark eyes. "We're going to be the best of friends."

Right, I think, staring at him. Friends.

14

"Hey, Boo," Dad says as I come into the house. He's standing at the stove, stirring his homemade marinara sauce. The house smells like basil. "How's it hanging, Supergirl?"

I march right up to him. I'm not going to wait. I'm going to tell him right fricking now. "Dad, we need to talk."

He stops stirring and looks vaguely worried. "Are you okay?"

"I'm fine."

"I wanted to talk to you, too," he says. "I've had something on my mind since our trip."

"Oh? Okay. Well, you go first, then."

"All right." He puts the wooden spoon down and goes to the office. He comes back holding an envelope.

What is it with my dad and mysterious envelopes?

"What's this?" I ask.

"In the car you were asking how I know the things I know about your birth mother."

My birth mother. Here we go. I suck in a breath. "Yeah?"

He hands me the envelope. It's a regular, business-sized envelope, but it's yellowed with age and stuffed with so much paper it's almost bursting. I've never seen it before. I open it and unfold the papers.

"Filing of Required Non-Identifying Health, Genetic, and Social Histories with the Idaho Adoption Registry," is what the top sheet says.

"It occurred to me," Dad says, "that we never let you read this yourself. I mean, at first you were too little to read anything, and then we kind of forgot about it, if I'm being honest. But it's yours. She filled it out. For you."

"Who filled it out?" I ask.

"Your birth mother."

I can't talk. I swallow, hard.

"That's everything we know about her," Dad says. "I think you deserve to know, too."

NON-IDENTIFYING INFORMATION
FOR ADOPTION REGISTRY

SOCIAL AND HEALTH HISTORY   ☒ Birth mother ☐ Birth father

The information in this report has been provided by the birth parent.
The Bureau of Vital Records is not responsible for the accuracy of this information.

DESCRIPTION OF SELF

Marital Status: ☒ Single ☐ Married ☐ Separated

☐ Divorced ☐ Widowed

If married or separated: ☐ Civil marriage ☐ Religious ceremony (specify)

Are you an enrolled member of a Native American tribe, Alaskan village, or affiliated with a tribe?   ☐ Yes ☒ No   If yes, what tribe?

Religion:

Christian

Ethnic background (e.g., English, German, etc.):

German, Irish, Italian

Country or state of birth:

Idaho

Race (e.g., Black, White, American Indian, Japanese, etc.):

White

Height:

5'3"

Weight:

115

Hair color and texture:

brown, straight

Eye color:

blue

Unique physical features (e.g., freckles, moles, etc.):

freckles

Complexion: ☒ Fair ☐ Medium ☐ Olive ☐ Dark

☐ Right-handed ☒ Left-handed

Physical build (e.g., big/small boned, long/short limbed, muscular, etc.):

average

Talents, hobbies, and other interests:

Music (listening to), movies, concerts. I tried being on the school newspaper staff this year but had to quit.

Which of the following describe your personality (check all that apply):

☐ Aggressive ☐ Emotional ☐ Happy ☒ Rebellious ☒ Shy

☐ Serious ☒ Calm ☐ Friendly ☒ Irresponsible ☐ Fun

☐ Temperamental ☐ Critical ☐ Outgoing ☒ Stubborn ☒ Unhappy

Comments:

EDUCATION

Last grade level completed:

10th

Average grade received or GPA:

C student

Presently in school: ☒ Yes ☐ No

Future plans for schooling:

Graduate from high school.

Subjects you are interested in:

Music?

Any school-related problems or challenges (tutoring, Special Ed, etc.):

Not really.

EMPLOYMENT HISTORY

Current occupation:

Military service: ☐ Yes ☒ No   If yes, branch of service:

Vocational training:

Work history:

I worked at Target last summer.

FAMILY HISTORY

Was anyone in your family adopted? ☐ Yes   ☒ No   If yes, who?

Your order of birth (e.g., 1st of 4):

2nd of 3?

Personal relationships with parents, siblings, or extended family members:

I live with my dad and stepmom. We don't get along very well. I see my mom and half sister once a year. I'm close with my older brother, but he's in college so I don't get to see him much.

Summarize adjustment to pregnancy. Include how you and your parents adjusted to the pregnancy, and if you had peer support:

My dad/stepmom suggested I go to Booth, so I wouldn't be embarrassed. <u>They</u> are embarrassed. My mom has been fairly supportive. I've had lots of peer support at school.

YOUR BIRTH PARENTS (child's grandparents)
FATHER

Age (if deceased, state age at time of death):

46

Health problems:

High blood pressure

Height/weight:

5'11", 200 lbs

Hair/eye color:

brown, brown

Build: ☐ Small ☒ Medium ☐ Large ☐ Extra large

Complexion: ☐ Fair ☒ Medium ☐ Olive ☐ Dark

Right-/left-handed:

right

Description of personality (e.g., happy, shy, stubborn, etc.):

outgoing, honest, critical

Talents, hobbies, interests:

politics, golf, skiing

Education:

college

Occupation:

lawyer

Number of siblings:

2

Race (Black, White, American Indian, etc.):

white

Ethnic background (e.g., German, English, etc.):

German/English

Religion:

Presbyterian

Marital status: ☐ Single ☒ Married ☐ Separated

☒ Divorced ☐ Widowed

Aware of this pregnancy? ☒ Yes ☐ No

MOTHER

Age (if deceased, state age at time of death):

44

Health problems:

Height/weight:

5'2", 100 lbs

Hair/eye color:

brown, blue

Build: ☒ Small ☐ Medium ☐ Large ☐ Extra large

Complexion: ☒ Fair ☐ Medium ☐ Olive ☐ Dark

Right-/left-handed:

left

Description of personality (e.g., happy, shy, stubborn, etc.):

hot-tempered but forgiving, energetic

Talents, hobbies, interests:

ballet, skiing, tennis

Education:

college

Occupation:

ballet teacher

Number of siblings:

0

Race (Black, White, American Indian, etc.):

white

Ethnic background (e.g., German, English, etc.):

Irish/Italian

Religion:

Agnostic

Marital status: ☐ Single ☒ Married ☐ Separated

☒ Divorced ☐ Widowed

Aware of this pregnancy? ☒ Yes ☐ No

YOUR BIRTH BROTHERS AND SISTERS (child's uncles and aunts)

1) ☒ BROTHER ☐ SISTER

Age (if deceased, state age at time of death):

22

Health problems:

Height/weight:

5'11", no idea

Hair/eye color:

brown, blue

Build: ☐ Small ☒ Medium ☐ Large ☐ Extra large

Complexion: ☐ Fair ☒ Medium ☐ Olive ☐ Dark

Right-/left-handed:

right

Talents, hobbies, interests:

football, wrestling, baseball

Education:

high school, some college

Occupation:

student

Religion:

Christian

Marital status: ☒ Single ☐ Married ☐ Separated
☐ Divorced ☐ Widowed

Aware of this pregnancy? ☐ Yes ☒ No

2) ☐ BROTHER ☒ SISTER

Age (if deceased, state age at time of death):

7

Health problems:

Height/weight:

4' or so, 60 lbs

Hair/eye color:

blond, blue

Build: ☒ Small   ☐ Medium   ☐ Large   ☐ Extra large

Complexion: ☒ Fair   ☐ Medium   ☐ Olive   ☐ Dark

Right-/left-handed:

left

Talents, hobbies, interests:

Candy Land, My Little Pony, Legos

Education:

grade school, kindergarten

Occupation:

kid

Religion:

Agnostic

Marital status: ☒ Single   ☐ Married   ☐ Separated

   ☐ Divorced   ☐ Widowed

Aware of this pregnancy? ☐ Yes   ☒ No

MEDICAL HISTORY

Please indicate "None" or "You" if you or any genetic relatives (i.e., your mother, father, sisters, brothers, grandparents, uncles, aunts, or any other children you have had) ever had or now has any of the medical conditions listed below. Please explain in the comments section.

Baldness:

Dad

Birth defects: *None*

Clubfoot: *None*

Cleft palate: *None*

Congenital heart disease: *None*

Cancer:

  Grandpa, bladder cancer

Other: *None*

ALLERGIES

Animals: *None*

Asthma: *None*

Eczema: *None*

Food:

  Sister. Allergic to peanuts.

Hay fever/Plants:

  Mom.

Hives: *None*

Medications:

  Dad. Blood pressure meds.

Other allergies: *None*

Other (specify): *None*

VISUAL IMPAIRMENT

Astigmatism:

  Mom. Wears glasses.

Blindness: *None*

Color blindness:

  Dad. Also my brother.

EMOTIONAL/MENTAL ILLNESS

Bipolar (manic depressive): *None*

Schizophrenia: *None*

Severe depression:

  Dad. After the divorce.

Suicide: *None*

Obsessive-compulsive disorder: *None*

Personality disorder: *None*

Alcoholism/drug addiction:

> *Dad. He also drank too much for a while.*

Other (specify): *None*

HEREDITARY DISEASES

Cystic fibrosis: *None*

Galactosemia: *None*

Hemophilia: *None*

Huntington's disease: *None*

Hypothyroidism or hyperthyroidism: *None*

CARDIOVASCULAR DISEASE

Heart attack:

> *Grandma. On my dad's side, in her 50s.*

Heart murmur: *None*

High blood pressure:

> *Dad*

Diabetes: *None*

SEXUALLY TRANSMITTED DISEASES

> *Gross. I really hope not!*

Chlamydia: *None*

Gonorrhea: *None*

Herpes: *None*

Syphilis: *None*

HIV/AIDS: *None*

Other (specify): *None*

NEUROLOGICAL DISORDERS

Cerebral palsy: *None*

Muscular dystrophy: *None*

Multiple sclerosis: *None*

Epilepsy: *None*

Stroke: *None*

Rheumatic fever: *None*

Other (specify): *None*

DEVELOPMENTAL DISORDERS

Learning disability / ADHD: *None*

Mental retardation (specify type): *None*

Down syndrome: *None*

Speech or hearing problems: *None*

Low birth weight: *None*

Other (specify): *None*

HISTORY OF DRUG USE

PRESCRIPTION:

Specify type (e.g., Prozac, Accutane, etc.)

☐ Before conception   ☐ After conception

OVER-THE-COUNTER:

Specify type (e.g., diet pills, antihistamine, etc.)

☐ Before conception   ☐ After conception

OTHER TYPES OF DRUGS USED:

Alcohol

Specify type:

  Beer, rum and Coke, vodka

Date of last use:

  Last year at a party.

☒ Before conception   ☐ After conception

Downers (i.e., sleeping pills, barbiturates, etc.)

Specify type:

Date of last use:

☐ Before conception ☐ After conception

Cocaine ("Crack")

By injection? ☐ Yes ☐ No

Date of last use:

☐ Before conception ☐ After conception

Heroin/pain killers

By injection? ☐ Yes ☐ No

Date of last use:

☐ Before conception ☐ After conception

Hallucinogens (i.e., LSD, Ecstasy, PCP, etc.)

Specify type:

Date of last use:

☐ Before conception ☐ After conception

Cigarettes

Specify type:

Date of last use:

☐ Before conception ☐ After conception

Marijuana

A couple times

Date of last use:

Last year

☒ Before conception ☐ After conception

Other

Specify type:

Date of last use:

☐ Before conception ☐ After conception

SOCIAL AND HEALTH HISTORY   ☒ Birth mother ☐ Birth father

If you wish, please add any additional information that will further describe you and your situation. (Consider your schooling, health, work, goals and hopes for the future, relationship history, religious or spiritual beliefs, challenges, strengths, etc.)

I'm an average student, but could probably do better if I put in more effort. I'm generally a healthy person—no major health problems, and I've tried to eat right during this pregnancy. I always seem to fall for the wrong guy, but that's why I'm here, I guess. I was raised Presbyterian, but I'm not religious.

I hope to be able to go on with my life after this. I don't know what I want to be when I grow up. I'm trying to focus on finishing high school.

I am only sixteen and I don't think I could give you the kind of life you deserve, so I'm doing this for both of us.

15

It's a lot.

I'm sitting at the breakfast table absentmindedly stirring my oatmeal and staring out the window at the big maple tree in front of our house. The leaves have all turned. Fallen. There's a cold, steady wind blowing, rattling the bare branches. The sun's peeking up. It's one of those quiet, pretty mornings, the kind where I like to walk to the bus stop even though it's cold.

But this morning I'm sitting here thinking. I'm sleep deprived. I was up half the night scouring the non-identifying information form Dad gave me. I read it like fifty times.

"You okay, Boo?" My dad appears in the doorway, dressed for school. He doesn't look like he slept much, either.

"Yeah, I'm . . . processing. Thanks for giving me that stuff," I manage.

"You're welcome."

I eat a bite of oatmeal. It's cold. This is why I don't do breakfast.

"You know the part I like the best?" he asks.

I blink up at him. "What?"

"The part with the sexually transmitted diseases."

"Uh, Dad. What?"

"For that section, she writes: 'Gross. I really hope not!' I can almost hear her voice when I read that. She's funny."

I have to admit, I didn't read that and come away with the notion that my birth mother had some great sense of humor. If I'm being honest, I'm disappointed in what she wrote. Especially that last part, where she was given the space to free write a little. She really didn't tell me anything important. It felt like a summary of all the boxes she'd checked. She had one page to fill, and she couldn't find anything meaningful to say.

Maybe she's not into writing, I tell myself. Not everybody communicates that way.

"Talk to me," Dad says. "Don't hold back."

"It's just . . . when I was little I used to picture my birth mother as a cartoon princess," I say. "She wore a purple dress and had long, flowing dark hair, and she was beautiful."

"Of course she was," he says. "Like you."

"Dad, please stop with the 'you're so special' talk." I give up on the oatmeal and take my bowl to the sink. "For some reason I always imagined my birth mother at the top of a white stone tower, locked away, and one day she lowered a basket down from the window, and inside that basket was me."

"Maybe we did make it sound too much like a fairy tale," Dad admits. "I liked the alien story better, myself."

"I wanted there to be a locket that she put around my neck, or a note, explaining how much I meant to her, but she had to let me go, because she was always going to be trapped in the tower. She had no other choice."

"She wanted you to have the life you deserve," Dad says. "That's what she wrote."

I shrug. "Well, that image of the girl in the tower is kind of clashing with the one of her at a party drinking vodka and smoking a joint."

Dad snorts and pours himself a bowl of cereal. "The thing is, your birth mother is a real person."

"Right," I murmur. "I know."

"She's got flaws. Like everybody else. She made mistakes. She's still out there, making mistakes, as we speak."

I flash back to the last page of the form.

I always seem to fall for the wrong guy, but that's why I'm here, I guess.

"Her mistakes aren't what defines her," Dad continues. "It's what she did with those mistakes, and she did something incredibly hard and incredibly giving and brave. And I'm always going to admire her for that, no matter what she did at some party when she was sixteen. And I'm going love her. Because she's part of you."

I feel tears coming on. I shake my head. I need to change the subject. I focus on giving my dad crap about his cereal choice instead. "Fruity Pebbles, Dad? Seriously? Mom would never let me eat that crap for breakfast. A snack, maybe. But not breakfast. It's pure sugar."

"While the cat's away—" he says, but his eyes get a little sad the way they do when he thinks about Mom being away from us. She's locked in her own version of a tower now. "Anyway. Give your bio mom some slack. She did the right thing. It worked out." He pats my shoulder. "You belong with us."

Dear X,

I got a call from my dear old dad today. Hip hip, hooray.

"How are you?" he asked me. This is what he always asks me. Even though he doesn't want to know the answer.

"Peachy," I said. "Can I come home now?"

I didn't mean it. I don't want to come home to that house with Dad and my stepmom and the white carpet and the dishes that chip so easily and being told every ten minutes to turn down my music. Plus Evelyn made it clear enough last time I set foot in that house that I'm a disgrace to the family. Evelyn—that's the name I've decided should be my stepmom's for the sake of these letters. She feels like an Evelyn. If you knew her, you'd agree.

Anyway, I didn't mean it when I asked to come home. I only did it to mess with my dad—to hear that terrified quiver in his voice when he said, "Oh, honey, I don't think that's a good idea. You're more comfortable there, aren't you? Around the other girls?"

I didn't mean it, but it also made me mad, hearing him scramble for a reason I shouldn't be there. Because I'm more "comfortable" here, like me and my ever-growing belly surely wouldn't fit in his big brick house on the hill. They told him about the fight with Amber, I'm sure, so he knows we're not all sitting around braiding each other's hair and singing hymns. And it made me mad that he was calling me instead of visiting me. Because he doesn't want to be seen visiting me. Because he's ashamed.

Clearly I have family issues. We put the "fun" in dysfunctional, if you know what I mean.

It's a good thing that you won't ever know these people. Trust me. You don't want to know my dad. Or Evelyn. Or my mom and her new husband, Brett, which is also a perfect name for that buttoned-up tightwad, or the Waspy grandparents. Really we're a family of assholes.

Except for my brother. He's all right. Of course, he moved across the country to go to college—as one does when you're trying to escape a family of assholes—and I never see him. He doesn't even know about you, X. And I'm probably not going to tell him.

I've been picturing you, ever since the ultrasound when I saw your feet and your nose, and was told of your status as a female pre–human being. I've been imagining a little girl with ponytails sitting at a kitchen counter eating breakfast. A breakfast her mom cooked for her. Like pancakes.

I try to remember. Was there ever a time when my family all sat around a table in the morning for bacon and waffles and talked about the weather and school and normal-family stuff?

The short answer is no: Even before the divorce, my mom never cooked. She could burn a hard-boiled egg—I'm not kidding. She's a hazard in anybody's kitchen. My stepmom is better at it, but she's also perpetually on a diet, and she works out in the mornings. She's not around for breakfast.

We're a cold cereal family.

Still, my parents' divorce was a good thing, because all I ever remember them doing before the divorce was screaming at each other. I tried to live with my mom initially, after the split, but then it was like she and I picked up screaming at each other where she and my dad left off. Bad habits die hard, I guess. So I moved in with Dad, who didn't talk to me much, but at least basically left me alone. Until Malibu Barbie came into the picture, anyway. And my mom married Brett and started screaming at him, too, but instead of divorcing him she had a kid: my half sister who I hardly know. But she's cute. Every time I'm over there, which is like once every couple months, she always wants to play Candy Land. It's a brainless game, and she never wants to play it just once. She wants to play like twelve times in a row. But I do it, because it feels like something normal to do: play a game with your little sister. I like it.

I wonder if you'll ever have a sister. Or a brother. I don't know the rules—do they let families adopt more than one kid? Do they let them adopt if they already have a kid? Nobody's really informed me about that stuff yet. I hope you do get to have a brother or sister someday. But then, I guess it's possible to be lonely in a family with lots of brothers and sisters. That's what I've learned. It's completely possible to be surrounded by people and still totally alone.

Anyway, be glad you don't have my family, is what I'm trying to say. I did think, in the beginning, anyway, that I might end up keeping you, and maybe my family would help me. I mean, it's supposed to be one of the options.

But that option went out the window the first day.

That morning—God, I'll never forget that morning—I sat on the toilet with the pregnancy test in my hand, watching the little indicator turn into a plus sign. Like, plus one. You plus one. Have a nice day.

And I thought, fuck. No offense, X, but FUCK.

Then I had to go to school, so I hid the test in the back of my underwear drawer and rode the bus and floated around from class to class, and I never stopped thinking about that plus sign, not even for a minute. It felt like a problem I should be able to solve, like if I concentrated hard enough, I could make it not true. I could tell myself it was a mistake. I could go home and take another test, and it would give me a different answer.

But when I got home my dad and my stepmom were sitting on the living room sofa waiting for me, and my stepmom was holding the test up with this triumphant expression on her face like AHA, I KNEW YOU WERE GOING TO SCREW UP and my dad was looking anywhere but at me.

My first thought was, Gross, I peed on that thing.

I said my second thought out loud: "You don't have any right to be messing with my stuff. That's my private business."

Evelyn snorted. "Oh, that's rich," she said. "You're PREGNANT, and you still want to be mad that we snooped in your room?"

"You did," Dad corrected her. "You snooped through her room."

She glared at him, and I took the opportunity to snatch the test out of her hand. Still a plus. Fuck. Then I stood there, fuming, because them knowing about it made it real. I couldn't change it now, or deny it, or even really take the time to let it sink in.

"Oh, no," my stepmom said as I was about to bail. "You stay right here, young lady."

I sighed. "What?"

"We're going to talk about this. We're going to make a plan."

For a second I felt a flash of hope, like the adults might be able to fix it. Maybe it would all be all right.

"Your father started his new job this week," my stepmom said.

"Yeah, I know."

"This could ruin everything he's worked for. He wants to be governor someday. Maybe more."

"So I guess I'm grounded then, huh?" I directed this to my dad, but he still wasn't looking at me. He didn't even seem like he heard me talking.

Evelyn made this disgusted sound. "You're a disgrace to this family," she said.

"I could have an abortion," I said. I'd never picked a side of this argument before. If anything, I would have considered myself pro-life before, the opinion that my parents had carefully instilled in me over the years, that abortion was murdering a baby. That all women who had abortions were going to hell, like the minute they died they'd get put down the eternal laundry chute straight into a fiery lake to burn for the rest of eternity. But in that moment I didn't think of you as a baby, X. You weren't one yet. You were like a pomegranate seed lodged behind my pelvic bone, or maybe not even that. You were a whisper. A rumor. A plus sign on a plastic test.

It seemed better if I could just erase you.

My dad was staring at me, and then he started to nod like he agreed with the abortion idea. But Evelyn gave a disbelieving laugh.

"She can't have an abortion," she said. "Someone would find out."

"No one would have to know," he said.

She shook her immaculate blond curls at him. "It always happens eventually—the things like this, they always get brought to light at the worst time. And that would ruin you, Rex."

(Okay, Rex is not my dad's real name, but I think it's hilarious so I'm keeping it.)

Anyway, she said, "Your daughter can't have an abortion. Ever. But especially not now."

There it is, X. You've got my wicked stepmother to thank. You're alive because it would have been a PR problem to get rid of you.

"So she'll have the kid," Dad said. "She's sixteen. How are the optics on that any better?"

"Well, she might be a slut, but she's not a murderer," Evelyn said.

"I'm right here," I reminded them. I don't like bitch as a term, as I've explained, but I hate slut even more.

"Who's the father?" Dad suddenly wanted to know.

He wouldn't like that Dawson was older than me. My mind whirled—something about statutory rape. Dawson could be arrested, charged with something, maybe even go to jail. Isn't that why they call it "jailbait"? And something about Evelyn calling me a slut set me off. So I shrugged. "Beats me. There are a few possibilities. Do you want me to pick one?"

Evelyn's mouth actually dropped open. It was super satisfying. Dad's mouth tightened into a line and his face got brick red.

"So there can't be a wedding," Evelyn said after a minute.

God, no. Even if Dawson was somehow okay with it, I didn't want to get married. I don't think I ever want to get married. I've seen what married life is like, and I don't want any part of it.

"It doesn't look good, no matter what we do," Dad said.

I turned to leave.

Evelyn made a noise like she was going to detain me again, remind me of whose house I was living in, that kind of bullshit, but Dad said, "Let her go."

The last thing I saw before I rounded the corner into the hallway was him dropping his head into his hands and her putting her arms around him.

"Don't worry," she said. "We'll think of something."

That's right, I thought. Comfort him. I'll just be over here pregnant.

It was a long night, that night. The longest. My brain kept turning circles, trying to find some way out. But there wasn't a way. There was only you.

In the morning, Evelyn tapped on my bedroom door.

"Your mother," she said, and handed me the phone.

"Hi," I said into the receiver.

"We still on for the weekend?"

"Yeah."

There was a long pause. Then Mom cleared her throat. "Evelyn told me that you're pregnant."

I hate Evelyn.

"I'm sorry," Mom said. That surprised me. Mom's a yeller, as we've established. I expected her to yell at me, tell me how stupid I was, how careless, what a disgrace to the family, right? Let's all agree. But instead she said, "Do you know what you want to do?"

"No," I answered. "I only just found out."

"When you're up here Saturday, we can get it taken care of," she said. "If that's what you decide you want."

"But Dad and Evelyn—"

"This is your life," she said. "Your father will simply have to deal with it."

"Okay," I said, swallowing hard. Mom can be a hard-ass sometimes, but this time she kind of came through. "Okay."

Well, obviously, X, I didn't have an abortion. I did go to Colorado. I played Candy Land with my sister. I ate pizza and threw it up again. I took walks in the snow. I pondered the meaning of life and contemplated the existence of heaven and hell. I may have even said a prayer. I wonder how many pregnant girls suddenly find themselves with a need to talk to God. But when it was time to drive to the clinic or whatever, I got in the car. No discussion. I got in, and we left.

We drove for a while in total silence.

"This is the right thing," she said finally.

I didn't answer. I didn't know if it was the right thing or if it was simply the easy thing or if I only wanted to do it because Evelyn said I couldn't.

None of it felt real, but I was going along with it.

Then the car started to slide. It was January—bitterly cold, icy roads. Mom has never been the greatest driver. She had just finished telling me that it was the right thing, and we hit a patch of black ice. The car swerved one way and then the other, and then we started to spin. Time slowed the way it does in these situations. I remember the grimace on Mom's face, the terror, the panic. I even remember the whiteness of her knuckles as she clutched the steering wheel. My stomach lurched. Snow and trees and lights whizzed by the windows. A horn blared at us. I screamed, and it was like the sound a deer makes when the mountain lion gets it.

Oh shit.

The car stopped. We both took a moment to catch our breath.

"Are you hurt?" Mom had her arm in front of me, like she could have kept me from going through the windshield.

I'd been wearing my seat belt. I was fine. We were both totally fine. The car hadn't collided with anything. We hadn't hit another car, even though there was traffic. We hadn't gone off the road. We hadn't flipped. We were stopped, having turned a perfect 180 degrees. We were facing the other way. Behind us, another car honked, because we were blocking the road.

Mom started driving, slowly pulling us into the correct lane. "Are you sure you're okay?"

I rolled down the window and threw up.

"All right," Mom said. She put on the turn signal to exit the road. To turn us back around. To be on our way to the clinic again.

I put my hand on hers on the steering wheel.

"Actually," I said. "Can you take me back to the house?"

I'm not a big believer in signs, X, and I didn't suddenly get a different opinion about abortion, not that I had a strong opinion about it in the first place. It came down to this: I was going in one direction, and then something happened to cause me to go the other way.

And here we are.

S

16

I give the envelope with the non-identifying information form to Nyla at school. Because even though she may have said that searching for my birth mother was a bad idea, she's the only person in my life outside of my parents who might understand what it feels like to read this form. And she's my best friend and I can't not share this with her. For better or worse.

So by the end of lunch she's read the whole thing and is officially ready to comment.

"Okay, first: whoa," she says as we get settled in one of our regular hangout spots on the floor in the Bonneville High School common room.

"Right?"

"How are you doing?"

"It's a lot," I say, crunching on my last carrot stick. "It's . . . a lot."

"But didn't you already know most of what's in here?" Nyla hands me back the envelope.

"Yeah." I put the envelope on the floor and stare at it. "My parents told me some of it. Like my birth mother enjoyed music, that kind of thing. But . . ."

But this . . . this is a whirlwind of specific details I didn't know before, like my aunt—I have an aunt, who's seven years older than I am—is allergic to peanuts, and my grandfather is a bald Presbyterian lawyer, and my birth mother apparently had freckles and worked summers at Target.

"But now you have people," Nyla says.

"Yeah." That's exactly it. Now, no matter how I try to look at it, it's like I have a hidden family out there, not only a biological mother and the necessary biological father, but aunts and uncles and grandparents and great-grandparents who each have lives and histories of their own. Suddenly, they're all real.

Nyla gets a wistful look, and I think, maybe I shouldn't have been so quick to share this with her. Maybe this is dredging up her own long-buried baggage.

But then she says, "I liked the part with the sexually transmitted diseases. Gross!"

"Wow, you too, huh?"

"So what are you going to do now?"

I stare at her. "What do you mean?"

"Are you going to search for her?"

"I thought you said that would be opening a can of worms."

She examines her fingernails. "Maybe I was wrong."

I scoff. "Who are you, and what have you done with my friend Nyla?"

She glances around us. It's loud in here. People are talking, eating, laughing. None of our other friends are nearby. No one's looking at us.

She scoots closer to me. "I have people, too," she says quietly. "I had a brother, once."

My mouth opens, but I don't know what to say. "Like . . . from . . ."

"Liberia," she whispers. "He was older, maybe ten or eleven when . . ." Her brow knits.

When her parents were killed. In the civil war there. Which is all I know about the situation. That's all Nyla's told me.

"I only remember him a little," she says. "Flashes. A joke he used to tell. I couldn't even repeat it to you now. I don't speak the language anymore. But I remember it was funny. And his name was Tegli."

"Oh, Ny," I breathe. It seems impossible that I have known her for so long, so many years, so many late nights up talking, and she's never said a word about having a brother.

"I was ten before I even told my mom about him. And then my parents discussed it, and they decided that they were going to look for him and make him part of our family, too, if they could find him. So they tried, and . . ." She stares off toward the lockers like she's seeing something far away. Something unpleasant. "Yeah. It didn't end well."

"I'm so sorry—" I begin.

She shakes her head. "The thing is—and I know this is going to come as a shock to you, Cass—but I've decided that you're not me. And I'm not you."

"Thank goodness, right?" I try to make this a joke, but it falls flat.

"I was being judgy about your birth mom," she says.

"You were?"

"My birth parents didn't choose to give me up. But your birth mother did. And I thought maybe that meant she wasn't—"

"—a good person," I finish for her. I get it. Other people have reacted that way, too, sometimes, when they hear I'm adopted. Like my adoption is a tragedy. Like I'm an abandoned baby who some heartless slutty girl left in a box on somebody's doorstep. A stray puppy in the rain.

Nyla touches the envelope, which is still on the floor between us. "But when I read this I could see I was wrong. She was just really young, right? She seems totally normal. And if I were you, I'd want to search for her."

I shrug. "I don't even know her name."

"There has to be something on the internet," she says. "Like a registry or something. And isn't there some information in this form you can use? Like clues?"

"Maybe. But there's nothing identifying about any of it," I say. "Which I think is the point."

Nyla nods thoughtfully.

"And—" I sigh. "I don't want to upset my parents."

"Your dad is the one who gave this to you," she points out.

"Not so I could search," I counter. "But so I'd know everything they know."

"You should ask him how he feels about it. Did you talk to him about—"

"I was going to, but I got sidetracked. I said I wanted to talk to him, but then he said *he* had something he wanted to talk about, and then he gave me this, and I—"

She folds her arms. "Cass!"

"I know. *I know.* Ease off, Captain Bossypants."

The bell rings. Lunch is officially over. People around us start to move toward class.

Suddenly Bastian appears before us.

"Hey, ladies, what's up?" He helps us get to our feet. "For the record, last night was amazing."

Last night with the kissing scene? I smile. "Yep. Totally amazing."

"Your song at the end," he says to Nyla, shaking his head like he still can't believe it. "You kill me, girl. I think I'm going to have to ask you to marry me in real life, even."

Hold on. He's going to ask *Nyla* to marry him? Because he liked *her* song at the end of act two? But . . . I'm the one with the big solo in act two.

"Yeah, good luck with that," she says, the tiniest hint of a smile appearing on her face. "But thanks. You weren't so bad yourself."

He turns to me, his brown eyes all warm and sparkly in a way that makes my heart beat faster. "And you, well, it should go without saying."

"Actually, I could do *with* saying."

He laughs. "Okay. Your solo is the shit, er, crap—" he amends for Nyla.

My solo is crap. "Gee, thanks."

"I'm surrounded by beautiful, talented women," he sighs. "How did I get so lucky?" His gaze falls on the big manila envelope in my hand. "What's that?"

Instinctively I pull it to my chest. I consider myself a pretty open person, really, but I don't go around telling people I'm adopted. It'd feel like I was trying to call attention to myself, and people tend not to get what it's like, anyway.

"Nothing," I say quickly, stuffing the envelope into my backpack. "Just some stuff for class."

"Speaking of class, we should probably scoot," Nyla says.

"Oh, very well. Goodbye, sweet ladies. Parting is such sweet sorrow," Bastian says, a line from *Romeo and Juliet*. Then he bows, blows us a kiss, and bounds off across the commons.

"He's such a drama nerd, he makes us seem like normal people." Nyla sighs, but she's smiling.

"He's perfect," I say.

"Yeah, he might be growing on me." She links her arm with mine as we walk. "Anyway, back to our conversation, before we were so charmingly interrupted. I will help you search for your birth mother, if you want me to. And for heaven's sake, talk to your dad, Cass. About the adoption stuff. And about C of I. Talk. To. Your father."

"I'll tell him," I promise. "I will. I *will*."

17

That afternoon I sit at the kitchen table waiting for my dad to get home from work. Then, partly because I'm bored and partly because that curious section of my brain will not shut up, I get out my laptop and type "adoption search" in the browser. And wonder if I'm opening a can of worms.

It immediately spits out a list of possible sites. There are a ton of adoption registries, actually, like "adoptionsearch" and "reunionfinders" and "reconnect.com." I pick the first one. It seems legit, and I can make my profile for free. I only have to answer the following questions:

Who are you trying to find?
    —my birth parent(s)
    —my adopted child
    —a sibling
    —a family member

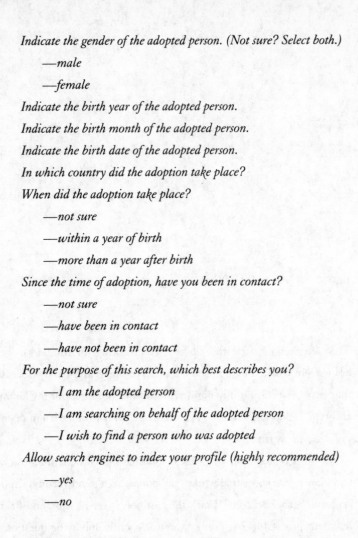

Indicate the gender of the adopted person. (Not sure? Select both.)

    —male

    —female

Indicate the birth year of the adopted person.

Indicate the birth month of the adopted person.

Indicate the birth date of the adopted person.

In which country did the adoption take place?

When did the adoption take place?

    —not sure

    —within a year of birth

    —more than a year after birth

Since the time of adoption, have you been in contact?

    —not sure

    —have been in contact

    —have not been in contact

For the purpose of this search, which best describes you?

    —I am the adopted person

    —I am searching on behalf of the adopted person

    —I wish to find a person who was adopted

Allow search engines to index your profile (highly recommended)

    —yes

    —no

It's the first question that stops me. *Who am I trying to find?*

I bite my lip. Am I trying to find her? Really? Am I seriously going to do this?

I have a mother, I tell myself firmly. A wonderful, loving, kind, talented, amazing mother, who is practically perfect in every way. I don't need another mother. I don't want one. I remind myself that

I don't actually think of my birth mother as a mother. I guess she's, like, thirty-four years old now, but I picture her as still being sixteen, bent over writing the word *gross* on the non-identifying form. In my mind, she's just a girl. Like me.

But the truth is, I feel something. A connection, to this person I don't know. But I still feel it. And whether she's sixteen or thirty-four, I want to know more about her.

I want to know who she is.

I return my attention to the website. It takes all of five minutes, and I have an official profile.

It reads:

Cassieintherye

I am searching for my birth parent(s).

I was born on September 17, 2000, in Boise, ID.

I was adopted in Idaho, USA, within a year of birth.

We have not been in contact since the time of adoption.

There's a place for me to upload a picture, but I go with the empty silhouette. There's also a section for a personal message I could leave, but I don't know what to say that doesn't feel obvious.

The screen reloads as it processes my profile.

View Matches?

My heartbeat speeds up. Are there actually matches? Would it ask me if I wanted to view my matches if there were no matches?

I press the button.

1 Member Found!

90% Match

My breath catches. It can't be this easy. My birth mother can't be looking for me. She can't be, can she?

I click on it.

Janet1222

I am searching for my daughter.

She was born in 2000.

She was adopted in the USA, more than a year after birth.

We have not been in contact since the time of the adoption.

No personal message has been entered.

I stare at the screen for a minute, my heart still pounding.

It's not me. That much I know for sure. I was adopted when I was six weeks old, not after a year.

I'm not who she's looking for.

But my eyes keep returning to the words *I am searching for my daughter.*

But she's not.

I shut my laptop and wait for my heart to return to its normal rhythm, which takes a while. And then there's the sound of my dad's key in the lock.

"Hi, Boo," he greets me as he comes in with an armload of groceries. "How was your—"

I jump up. "I don't want to go to Boise State." I say it quickly but clearly. Rip the Band-Aid off in one smooth motion, I'm thinking. Get it over with.

Dad's expression goes slack. "What?"

I help him put the groceries away and then guide him into the living room and onto the sofa, which is where we try to have all conversations deemed "serious" in our family.

"Is this about Juilliard?" he asks hoarsely.

"No." I laugh. "No, no, Dad. I want to go to College of Idaho."

His eyebrows lift so much they almost disappear into his hairline. "College of Idaho?"

I start talking. "There's something about it, Dad. It's like a feeling. And I know, I know, feelings are super unreliable, feelings can be fickle, like you say, feelings are nothing to base big decisions on, but I just really liked College of Idaho. I think it's the universe."

Down come the eyebrows. "The universe."

"I think something has been—er, directing me, to go to College of Idaho."

He frowns. "But Nyla was the one who wanted to visit College of Idaho."

"I know. It was Nyla, and destiny."

He scratches under his ponytail. "But you seemed so happy about BSU. I thought—"

"I was acting happy because you were happy. I want you to be happy, Dad. I do. But I also want to be happy, and College of Idaho, I think, would make me very happy. And well educated. So. Now you know."

I stop babbling and stare at him. Any second now he's going to burst out laughing and hug me and tell me of course he wants me to be happy.

"I need to look at my notebook." He goes off to his office. He stays there for like five minutes. I sit on the couch.

He finally returns, notebook in hand, and sits down again, gingerly, at the end of the sofa. He's got the notebook open to the C of I pros and cons page. He sighs.

"I don't think we can manage College of Idaho," he says after a minute.

"What?"

"It's too expensive."

What? I can already feel the tears coming, and it makes me feel immature, like I'm a toddler who wants to cry over not getting choc-olate milk. "How expensive?" I ask in a whisper, because I don't trust my voice not to break.

He angles the notebook toward me, so I can see what he's got listed in the cons column. The price of tuition.

I gasp. "That's almost Juilliard."

He nods grimly. "It's almost Juilliard."

I'm on my feet, pacing. My unspilled tears evaporate in a flash of anger. I feel stupid. I should have looked up all of the information about College of Idaho myself. Then I would have known. I've been stalking their website since our trip, looking at pictures, acquainting myself with the professors and the buildings and the food menus. Why didn't I look at the money stuff? I assumed since it was in Idaho we'd be able to afford it.

"I'm sorry, Boo," Dad says.

I turn on him. "Why did you even bring me to see other colleges, if I'm not allowed to go anywhere but Boise State?"

He looks pained, like root-canal kind of pain. "I wanted you to feel like you had choices."

"But I really don't?"

He shakes his head helplessly. "The other schools we went to—Idaho State, College of Southern Idaho—they aren't expensive. You could go to either of those."

I stop pacing. "I could take out loans."

"I don't think that's a great idea, but we can talk about it," he says, which is what he says when he's really saying no. "I don't want the start of your adult life to be under a mountain of debt."

"There are scholarships."

"True. But—"

"There are academic scholarships that I will definitely qualify for, and theater scholarships, and, and . . . the state drama competition next week!" I burst out.

He scratches at his cheek. "State drama?"

My mind whirls. "They award a scholarship to a senior who gives an outstanding performance in the competition. Ten thousand dollars a year, for four years, toward the college of your choice." It's the answer, I know it.

"Oh," he says. "Okay. Well . . . but that's not a for-sure thing, Cass."

"We've won it every single year. Every year, Dad." I grab his hand. "If I could get enough scholarships that C of I would cost the same as BSU, could I go to C of I then? Please, Dad?"

"Of course." He still looks mournful. "But . . . you're sure you don't like Boise State?"

"It's not that I don't like Boise State," I say carefully. "I can't explain it, Dad. But I don't feel like I belong there."

"And you feel like you belong at College of Idaho?"

I nod. "Yes."

He sighs. Then after the longest two minutes of my life, he says, "Well, I don't know how we'll pay for it, but I'll talk to your mother."

"You know what she's going to say," I venture.

He smiles and squeezes me on the shoulder. "Right. I guess I do."

"I had a high school friend who went to College of Idaho," Mom says later. She turns to Dad. "Dori was her name, remember, hon? We used to go and visit her sometimes. They'd have free movie nights in this old run-down theater near the college. We saw *The Cutting Edge* there."

"Oh yeah," he says, holding her hand. "Dori. She's a doctor now, right?"

"A history professor. She loved the college so much I think she went back to teach there after she got her doctorate," Mom says. "I should call her. See if she can give us some tips."

"So you're okay with it."

Mom frowns. "Okay with what?"

"With me going to C of I and not Boise State."

"Of course." She gives Dad a stern look. "If this is what you want, where you know, deep down, is the place you need to be, Cass, of course we're both going to support that."

I glance at Dad for confirmation. He nods distractedly. "But it's so expensive," I admit.

"The money will come," she says. "The universe unfolds as it should. I believe that."

"I want to believe that, too."

I can't help but notice that Dad's frowning, though. But then he notices me noticing, and gives me a wan smile. "Me too," he says softly. "So there you have it. College of Idaho is mother approved."

"Parent approved," Mom corrects him.

"Yes," Dad says.

"Thanks," I say, but I get the sinking feeling that we're all acting. A sense of dread has been building in my stomach since I got here. Like this is a scene in some play I'm performing in, and no more real than my former daydreams about Juilliard. I've been having this feeling a lot lately. Like what I'm living isn't really my life.

The nurse bustles in. "Time for the official business," she says, which is a version of what nurses always say when they want you to

166

leave so they can work on their patient. Dad and I hop up from our chairs.

"Stick around for dinner?" Mom says as we move toward the door. "I think it's going to be beef stroganoff tonight."

"Oh dear God," Dad says with a cringe. "Let's go find us some salad."

I shake my head. "I have play practice from seven to nine. I mean, I could get out of it."

Mom frowns. "No, no, go to rehearsal, sweetie. There's no sense sitting around here with us. We're just going to be watching the dust settle, aren't we, hon?"

Dad gives me that weird nod again. "Yeah. Go. I'll see you at home."

Dad waits outside Mom's room, but I head for the elevator. I call Mama Jo from the parking lot and beg out of rehearsal. We're working on the end of act two, and I only have a few lines because I'm dead. I'm tired. I'm processing a lot of new information right now. So I basically play the sick-mom card.

"Sure," Mama Jo says before I can even get out a full sentence. "Whatever you need."

"Thanks." So I go to Rumbi and sit eating their veggie teriyaki bowl, and try to unpack tonight's conversation in my mind.

My phone buzzes a few minutes later: a text from Nyla.

Nyla: You're not here. Why are you not here? Is Mama Cat doing okay?

Me: She's fine. I required a mental health night.

Nyla: Are YOU doing okay?

Me: I did a search on an adoption registry.

Nyla: !!! What happened???

Me: Nothing. There was nothing there. And then I told my dad about C of I.

Nyla: And?

Me: He's cool with it.

Nyla: Told you so.

Me: Yes, you did. You were right. It's annoying.

We text banter back and forth, and then she goes quiet for a while when it's her scenes she's rehearsing, and comes back about forty-five minutes later.

Nyla: What's up?

Me: Pineapple upside cake.

Nyla: Wow, so we're in THAT place. I thought you'd be happy about your dad being down with C of I.

Me: I am. But it turns out there are financial concerns. BIG financial concerns.

Nyla: How big?

I text her a screenshot of the tuition page.

Nyla: Frick.

Me: This might even call for a double frick, Ny. So we're definitely going to need to win the state drama competition and get that scholarship. Okay?

Nyla: You know it. We've got that in the bag. You want to come in early tomorrow and rehearse the crap out of it?

Me: 👍

Nyla: Excellent. K brb onstage for a while.

I head home when she's gone this time. I'm in my pajamas when she texts again.

Nyla: Okay, you're never allowed to skip rehearsal again.

Me: What happened?

Nyla: Alice is ticked off at Bastian. She had a meltdown in front of the entire cast.

Me: ☹ Why?

Nyla: He has to drop out of the state drama competition.

Me: Shut up. WHY?

Nyla: Something about his dad not letting him go on an over-night trip.

Me: Oh, wow. Wowwwwww.

Nyla: I know, right? He seemed really upset about it. I feel bad for him. He kept saying he was sorry, and Alice started crying, which only made him feel so much worse.

Me: It doesn't sound like it's Bastian's fault. It sounds like he's got dad problems.

Nyla: But Alice wanted a shot at that scholarship, too, and she can't compete alone.

I'd be upset, too, if I were Alice.

Nyla: I think I've finally decided about Bastian btw.

Me: ???

Nyla: I think I like him.

Me: WHAT? What do you mean, you like him?

Our earlier weird conversation with Bastian where he, I don't know, proposed marriage to Nyla, comes flooding back. The green monster lifts its head.

Nyla: I mean, I think he may be good people. As in, I approve of you liking him.

Me: O-kay. I approve of you approving of me liking him. Not that I've ever said I liked him. (But I do like him. Is it super obvious?)

Nyla: It's obvious.

Me: Do you think he likes me?

Nyla: He'd be a fool not to, and he doesn't seem like a fool. Anyway. You should ask him out. Now I have to get home if I'm going to rise at the crack of dawn to rehearse our scene tomorrow.

Me: Okay. Good night.

Nyla: Sleep tight.

Me: Don't let the bedbugs bite.

Nyla: You're a poet, and you don't even know it.

Me: Because I rhyme all the time?

Nyla: See, this is why I love you. But now that I think about it, if I had bedbugs, I would not be sleeping in my bed. I mean, obviously I'd need to get a new bed, if I had bedbugs.

Me: Or a new house. Ew.

Nyla: Seriously, how is that a saying?

Me: Right? How are you going to stop these supposed bedbugs from biting you? What, you just ask nicely? Use bug spray? And how exactly am I supposed to sleep tight? What does that even mean?

Nyla: That's it. I'm googling it.

Nyla: Oh my gosh never google it.

Me: 😄

Nyla: 🖤

Me: 😵

Dear X,

Today was the last day of school. Now all the other students are gone, and it's just me, Teresa, and Brit. Plus Melly, who works here year-round. And the Salvation Army people. It's like a ghost town. There's nothing good on TV. It's weirdly hot today, and Melly made us walk to the ice cream shop as our daily exercise, which is kind of funny. But, long story short: I'm bored. I'm bored and it's midnight and you keep squirming around in my belly so I can't sleep.

    Sometimes you're really a pain, X.

    Heather was back here last week, by the way. She must have had a C-section because she was gone way longer than the two-week maternity leave. I thought maybe we wouldn't see her again, but she's a senior and she wants to graduate, obviously, so she came back for the last week.

    Most of the girls come back here with their babies. They leave them at the daycare on campus and shuffle into class that first day with red eyes because they were crying because they hated to leave their babies, even one building away.

Heather's eyes were red, too, but for a different reason.

She didn't seem excited to tell her birth story, or to answer any questions the rest of us had about what it was like to squeeze something the size of a watermelon out of a hole the size of a lemon. She sat there in algebra reading the textbook, and then she started to work on some worksheets she'd missed. She did talk a little, though. She told me she'd missed me, although she might have been referring to my superior understanding of polynomials. She laughed at a joke I told. She raised her hand and asked Miss Cavendish a question.

She was better than I thought she'd be. She was keeping it together. An inspiration to us all, I'd say.

Then the daycare lady came in with a baby.

It wasn't Heather's baby, of course. It was this other girl Jennifer's baby. About three months old or so. A boy. The lady from the daycare walked in and passed the baby to Jennifer. So she could breastfeed. It's one of the benefits of going to school here. You can still breastfeed. In the middle of class. In the lunchroom. During PE. Whenever.

It took a while for me to get used to that. Breastfeeding is not something I've been exposed to much in my life, or, like, ever. And now at any given time of day, in comes the daycare ladies with the babies, and out come the boobs. They don't even try to cover up because, I think, they want it to seem normal or natural or whatever, and so the babies get their meals right out in the open. I was pretty uncomfortable with it the first few times it happened. It was hard not to stare. But it doesn't bother me anymore, so when Jennifer whipped out her breast to feed her baby, I kept doing my work. And then I happened to glance over at Heather.

Her face was red—completely beet-colored, starting from where her neck went into her shirt all the way up her cheeks and her ears to her hairline. She was staring at Jennifer. Well, she was staring at Jennifer's baby, at that fuzzy little head pressed into Jennifer's chest. There was this swirl on the back of his head. That's about all we could see from our table.

It got quiet. The other girls noticed Heather's face, too. We could all hear the sucking noises the baby was making, the little grunts and sighs, and the squeaks and scrapes of Miss Cavendish obliviously writing on the chalkboard.

Heather stared at the baby.

We all stared at Heather. We watched as her shoulders started to shake and then two big fat tears rolled down her cheeks.

"Hey," I said, reaching over, putting my hand over hers. "Hey. It's okay."

"I know," she said in this small voice.

I raised my hand. "Can Heather and I go to the chapel?"

Miss Cavendish spun around, annoyed. "What have I told you about raising your . . ." She looked from me to Heather. She followed Heather's gaze to Jennifer's baby. Then back to Heather's face. Then at me. "Yes," she said. "Go ahead."

In the chapel, Heather stopped crying. She seemed embarrassed at the fuss she'd made, which really hadn't been much of a fuss at all, if you asked me.

"I punched Amber last month," I told Heather.

"You didn't."

"I swear."

"How were you not expelled?" Heather asked.

"Because Amber was asking for it," I explained, but I don't go into details. "She provoked me."

173

Amber hadn't been in class today, I realized, and I was glad. The last thing Heather needed right now was to be told she's abandoned her baby so she could go party.

I patted Heather on the shoulder. "So a little crying's nothing to worry about. That happens like every day around here."

"I guess you're right." She wiped at her cheeks.

We were quiet again.

"It was a boy," she said after a while. "My baby."

"I know." We all knew. Every time a girl at the school had a baby there was a birth announcement posted to the front of the school bulletin board. Heather's baby was a boy, seven pounds, nine ounces.

"He had all this curly hair all over his head." She smiled at the thought.

"Did you hold him?" I asked. This had been Amber's question, but I really wanted to know.

"Yeah. For a few minutes," Heather answered. "They say that skin-to-skin contact is important right at first. And I . . ." Her voice wavers. "I fed him. The milk you produce right after you give birth is full of all this good stuff the baby needs. But after that I let his parents take him."

I squeezed her hand.

"They looked right together," she said.

"You did good." The door to the chapel swung open and I yelled "Go away!" to the startled face of the girl who was about to come in.

The door swung shut.

Heather laughed. "You're funny. You act like a tough girl, but you've got a soft chewy center."

"I do not," I said. "So I have to ask. Did it hurt?"

"Yes."

"Bad?"

"It was the worst pain I've ever felt in my life."

"Great." I stared down at my ever-expanding belly. "That's fantastic news. Couldn't you have lied to me?"

Heather looked serious again. "The labor pains were pretty bad, too."

That was about a week ago. Heather's gone home. I'm trying to picture her in her bedroom, playing the flute. Going to college, maybe even going to college parties. Going on dates. And I wonder if I'll ever see her again. Someday. If we'll ever be in the supermarket, say, wandering among the tomatoes, and I'll see her and say hi. And she'll say hi, too, and we'll go about our business, not revealing how we know each other, but smiling, because we remember that one day we had together in the chapel at Booth.

I had to take a little break from writing, because someone was knocking on the front door. It was after midnight and Melly's a sound sleeper, so she didn't answer. I went out in the hall and Teresa and Brit were already standing there, the three of us in our pajamas, listening to whoever it was knocking—pounding hard—on the door downstairs.

"We should call the police," Brit whispered.

"We should wake up Melly," Teresa said.

"We should see who it is." I went to the door and opened it.

It was Amber. She was dressed in pj bottoms and a big T-shirt that was ripped at one shoulder. But her eyes were the thing that immediately caught my attention—they were so dark that they looked like holes in her face, and there were two gleaming trails of tears down her cheeks. She was panting like she'd been running. She looked like a wild animal.

"Can I come in?" she gasped, and then looked behind her like someone was chasing her.

"Go wake up Melly," I told Brit. I pulled Amber inside and closed *and locked the door. Then I walked her to our living room area and sat her on the couch. She leaned back against the cushions and closed her eyes and put her hand on her swollen belly like she was glad it was still there.*

I turned on the lamp. Then I had to try not to look shocked.

There was a big purple bruise on Amber's neck, circling it like someone had tried to choke her. And another matching bruise blooming on her shoulder half hidden by the ripped shirt.

I didn't ask her if she was okay. The answer to that was obvious. And I didn't feel any kind of satisfaction that this girl who'd been so full of herself before was now brought so low. I just thought, well, shit happens to everyone, doesn't it?

Melly appeared in the doorway, hair a mess, wearing a robe but fully alert. Teresa and Brit trailed behind her.

"Are you okay?" she asked, sitting down next to Amber.

Amber shook her head. She lifted a hand to wipe at her nose, and her hands were shaking violently. "My dad kicked me out."

Melly's gaze went straight to the bruise on Amber's neck. She grabbed the blanket from the back of the couch and wrapped it around Amber's shoulders.

"Teresa," she said calmly. "Call the police."

Amber, out of all of us, had the best laid plans for her baby. But maybe all along she was telling us a story, a pretty fairy tale about her supportive family and her accepting friends and her perfect life.

I guess we're her village now.

S

18

"I've got you," says Nyla.

"I know." We're sitting in the hallway of the theater building at Boise State (oh, the irony!) waiting to be called in to our next round at the state drama competition. I'm extra nervous, for obvious reasons. We've made it through the first two rounds of the competition, last night and this morning. Bam. But now we're at the final round. The one that counts.

"Don't slap me so hard this time," Nyla says, moving her jaw around like it's sore. "You really clocked me last round."

There's a moment in the middle of our scene together where she slaps me in the face. And then I slap her back. And then she slaps me. And then I *really* slap her. It's stage slapping, or it's supposed to be. It's not supposed to hurt, but—

"I got carried away," I admit. "Think of it like Method acting, right? We're deep inside our characters. We're living the moment."

She gives me a look. "I'm not Method. I do a little thing called *acting*."

"Oh, right. Sorry, Mr. Olivier," I quip.

She rolls her neck from side to side. "So," she says, not for the first time today. "Do you think the world is ready for a black Anne Sullivan?"

She asks a version of this question almost every time we perform together, like when she was Hodel in *Fiddler on the Roof*, or when she was Emily in *Our Town*, and especially when she was Maria in *The Sound of Music*.

"They're going to be blown away by black Anne Sullivan. The judges in the last round were obviously impressed."

"And you're the best Helen Keller since Patty Duke. We're kicking butt," Nyla says.

"We're going to win this thing," I agree, more to myself than to her. We have to.

"And you're going to get that scholarship," she adds. "And go to College of Idaho."

I blow out a shaky breath. "Right."

"We won this last year," she reminds me. "We'll do it again. Easy peasy."

Last year we were hanging out in this exact same hallway, only that time we were dressed as nuns. We performed a scene from *Doubt*, and Nyla played tough old Sister Aloysius Beauvier, and I was Sister James, the young and naive one. It was awesome. I'm hoping this year the judges think we're even more awesome. Because this year my entire future is on the line.

No pressure.

"What do you want to do after?" Nyla asks. "We won't get the results until the closing ceremony, which is after dinner, so we've got like five hours to kill. Do you want to see a movie?"

"I don't know." Truthfully I can't think much past the way the next few hours could decide my whole future.

NO PRESSURE.

"I should get that Big Jud burger again," Nyla muses.

My stomach turns over at the thought of the giant hamburger.

"You're not going to puke, are you?" Nyla asks, eyeing me warily.

I take some deep breaths. "Have I ever yakked before a performance?"

"No."

"Well, I'm not about to start now."

A door down the hall opens and a judge sticks his head out. "Cass McMurtrey and Nyla Henderson?"

We jump up. "That's us."

"You're doing *The Miracle Worker*?"

"Yes, sir," I say.

"All right, come on in."

Nyla and I do our lucky fist bump. Then we follow the judge into the room, where they've already set up our makeshift set. A line of three judges is seated at a table.

I smile. The thing is: I'm always pretty good under pressure.

"Let's work some miracles," Nyla whispers as we take our places.

After that (and we did indeed kick butt) Mama Jo wants to take everyone to the mall, but Nyla and I decide to stay behind.

"I still can't believe Bastian didn't get to compete," Ny says as we watch the bus carrying the other girls pull out of the parking lot. Ronnie waves to us out the window, and we wave back. "That's the worst."

"And poor Alice," I muse. Because Alice should totally be on that bus.

"I saw them rehearse their scene during lunch last week. It was hilarious. It actually worried me a little," Nyla says.

And now we don't have to worry about competing with Alice and Bastian. This should be a good thing, but it feels wrong. "What is the deal with Bastian's dad, I wonder?"

"I don't know," Nyla answers. "What I do know is that I need something to seriously get my mind off this competition. I'm thinking IMAX." The Edwards theater here has one of those giant screens, which we don't have in Idaho Falls. But since last year with Mom, that horrible night at the movies when I almost lost her, even the smell of popcorn puts me on edge.

"Actually," I say slowly, "I want to walk somewhere. If that's okay."

"Ooh, a mystery," Nyla says, raising her eyebrows. "Even better. Count me in."

We stroll across the BSU campus.

"You sure you don't want to go here?" Nyla asks as we weave our way through the sea of Boise State students all bundled up in scarves and fingerless mitts and tall boots. It's cold, and the sky above us is gray and overcast, but the walk is still nice. The bare trees make a kind of lacy lattice against the horizon. The air smells crisp, like it's about to snow. The students around us are talking, laughing, chattering. They seem to be enjoying college life.

But nope, I still want to go to C of I.

And I have my own idea about how to get our minds off the competition.

"Come on." I veer toward the green belt that runs along the Boise

180

River, steering us downtown. In a few minutes we're standing in front of the redbrick building that's the Boise Public Library.

"I'm confused," says Nyla. "You want to go to the library?"

"I want to go to *this* library," I clarify. "Or . . . I think I do. Maybe it's a bad idea."

"What's up?" she asks.

"I looked into it: this library has the yearbooks from all the local high schools. So I was thinking, what if we search through the year before I was born?"

"And we'd be searching for what, exactly?"

"My birth mother."

Nyla's eyes widen. "You really want to?"

"Yeah. I think I do. Just to try to find out who she is, though. Anyway, you know how you asked me if there was anything on that non-identifying information form that might be useful?"

She nods.

"Well, it does say that Boise was my birth mother's place of residence at the time of my birth."

"Uh-huh?"

"And she wrote that she was on the newspaper staff that year, but had to quit. Probably because she got pregnant, right?"

Nyla gasps. "So you want to look at the school newspaper page in the high school yearbooks, because maybe there could be a picture of your biological mother in there."

"It's a long shot," I admit. "But it's all I've got to go on. And we're here in Boise, so I thought I should take the opportunity to—"

"Let's do it," Nyla says, obviously pumped up over the idea. "How can I help?'

In no time we're sitting at a table near the window with a meaty stack of high school yearbooks between us. I'm shocked by how many high schools there are in this area—more than seven, not even counting the private schools. It's way more than I expected.

Nyla literally rolls up her sleeves. She puts on her glasses, which always make her look like the world's most kick-ass librarian. "So what, we just go to the newspaper pages and look for someone who looks like you?"

Something in my throat squeezes. "She had brown hair and blue eyes, average height and weight, I think. And she would have been a sophomore or a junior." I grab the top yearbook—it's for Boise High School. It's red and black and has the words "Expanding Horizons" printed across the front with a rising sun graphic in the background.

"Okay," Nyla says, grabbing one, too. "I did say I wanted something to take my mind off the competition. This will do nicely."

My heart is beating fast again as I flip through the yearbook. Most of the pictures are in black and white. I pause on the drama page out of habit, taking note of what plays they performed that year. High schools are still mostly putting on the same shows, I notice. I move on quickly, past the sports, the chess club, and debate club and choir. Past the class photos. The teachers. The staff. Past the pictures of the prom. Finally I find the school newspaper page.

"In Search of the Story," it reads in big letters across the two-page spread. There's a picture of five students gathered around a table looking at something. Two girls, three boys. And another of twelve students standing in two rows—the official newspaper staff. Seven girls. Five boys.

My eyes roam over both photos, pausing on the girls. The pictures are in black and white, so they all look like they have brown hair, and there's no way to tell eye color. I look at their faces—lingering on their eyes and eyebrows and chins—but I don't see anything familiar.

Still, I take out a notebook and write the names of the girls on the newspaper staff: Kristi Henscheid, Melissa Bollinger, Melissa Stockham, Sandra Whit, Sarah Averett, Sonia Rutz, and Amy Yowell. Then I look up each of these girls and inspect all the pictures of them in the yearbook, from their official yearbook photo to any other random photo or group they were in.

It's harder than it might seem, looking for your own face in a bunch of old photos.

I don't see it. I don't find myself anywhere in here.

It's the same for the next three yearbooks. A list of girls who are possibly my birth mother. A blur of pictures. And nothing recognizable in any of them.

After a while Nyla takes off her glasses, rubs her eyes, and smiles her I'm-being-supportive-but-this-sucks smile.

"This is a bad idea," I sigh. "I'm never going to find her like this." I swallow down a wave of silly-yet-weirdly-crushing disappointment—I knew the yearbooks would be a long shot, but part of me expected to find my birth mother this way. Part of me thought she'd jump out at me, that fate would lead me where I needed to go. The universe and whatnot.

Clearly the universe is busy with someone else's life.

"I'm proud of you, Cass," Nyla says out of the blue. "This takes guts."

I scoff. "But I'm not really getting anything done. And maybe my birth mother didn't live in Boise—maybe she only came here to give birth. That was a pretty big assumption on my part. Or maybe she went to a private school. Or maybe she wrote that she worked on the school newspaper because she wanted me to think she had a hobby. Because otherwise she's pretty boring."

"Maybe," Nyla agrees thoughtfully. "But it's worth a try. Hold still." She lifts the yearbook she's been going through—Borah High School—and squints from me and then to the page and back again.

"We should go back," I say. "We should get some dinner. We've been here long enough."

"In a bit," Nyla says, waving her hand to brush off the suggestion. "We're more than halfway. Let's look at them all."

19

We don't find my birth mother in the yearbooks, but for a few hours it did get our minds off the impending awards ceremony and the fate of my college dreams.

Which is all I'm thinking about now.

Nyla and I dress up for the ceremony. Last year we were still wearing our nuns' habits when we won, and it was kind of embarrassing going up there. If you win first place you get to have your picture taken with your drama teacher, and that picture gets framed and put into a glass display case back at our high school, with all the baseball trophies and basketball jerseys, the pride of the school.

"The governor's here," Mama Jo whispers to us as we sit next to her in the auditorium where they're going to announce the winners. "See him?"

"The governor? Of Idaho?" I whisper back.

"No, silly, of Indiana," Nyla laughs. "Of course of Idaho. There he is." She cocks her head at the bald man in the suit sitting with the judges on the stage. He looks mildly uncomfortable, or bored, like he'd rather be somewhere else. I don't blame him.

I ask the obvious question: "Why is the governor of Idaho coming to the state drama awards?"

"Something to do with the scholarship," Mama Jo says. She smiles. "Good luck, girls. Not that you need it."

I need it.

We don't have to wait long. There are only a few categories, and each category has a third, second, and first place. They start with comedy. Then classical. Then musical. Then dramatic, which is us.

We don't win third. We don't win second. It's either all, then, or nothing.

I clutch Nyla's hand. I want it all.

"And first place in the dramatic category goes to Nyla Henderson and Cass McMurtrey for their stellar depiction of the famous struggle between Helen Keller and her teacher, Anne Sullivan, in *The Miracle Worker*."

I let out the breath I was holding. People are clapping. We stand up, and Nyla hugs me, and I hug her back, and we hug Mama Jo and wander up to the stage to collect our golden trophies and take a bow.

They're not Oscars, but they're pretty freaking good. And we don't have to give a speech, which is even better.

"Oh, stay here, girls," a judge tells us when we move to go back to our seats. He turns to the audience.

"We'd also like to announce a couple of special awards. Now every year, a sponsor has generously provided a scholarship to a deserving senior who performs in a spectacular way at the state competition. It's called the Excellence in Acting Award, and it is ten thousand dollars, per year, for four years, to be used toward the tuition of the college or university of the recipient's choice."

This is it. I'm holding the trophy in one hand and Nyla's hand in the other, and she is squeezing me tight. I feel dizzy. I feel sick. I really might throw up this time.

In the back of my mind I understand that Nyla could win this. We're both seniors. She's amazing as Annie. But I want to win so bad, and Nyla doesn't need this money, so I believe—deep down—that the scholarship will go to me.

"This year it was extraordinarily difficult to choose the deserving senior," the judge continues. "So difficult, in fact, that we were unable to come to a clear decision."

Um, what?

"So, in the face of this conundrum, the theater department at Boise State decided to step up and offer a second scholarship, of equal value, to a second deserving student."

Wait, I'm thinking. *There are two scholarships now?*

Nyla grins. She's almost laughing. I go weak with relief. It's happening. The universe unfolds as it—

"So I am pleased to announce that the Boise State scholarship will go to Cass McMurtrey." The judge gestures to me. Another judge hands me a piece of paper. Applause, applause.

"And the Excellence in Acting Award will go to Nyla Henderson."

Mama Jo is on her feet, cheering loudly. All the kids from our school are shouting and whistling and clapping.

Me, however, I'm looking at the paper they gave me.

Ten thousand dollars.

Per year.

For four years.

My eyes are blurry. I almost can't read the last line of the paper. Which says:

To go toward tuition and expenses at Boise State University.

Then Nyla and I have to get our picture taken with the governor. We stand on either side of him and he puts his arms out like he's got them around both of us, but he avoids touching us. His hands hover a few inches behind our backs, then drop the moment after the photo is taken.

"Congratulations," he says. Or I think that's what he says. I'm not really listening at this point.

"So where do you think you'll be using your scholarship?" he asks Nyla.

"I want to go to the University of Southern California," she answers, still beaming.

I try to match her smile.

"Fantastic," says the governor. He turns to me. "And Boise State is going to be lucky to have you, young lady."

"Thank you," I manage.

This is when Nyla realizes. "Wait. Hold on. What?"

"I guess I'm going to BSU," I murmur, and show her the paper.

The governor shakes our hands again and walks away. Nyla reads over the paper slowly, then turns to me. I've never seen this particular expression on her face before, this epic combination of horror and guilt. She could win an award solely on the basis of this singular expression.

"Oh crap," she says breathlessly. "Oh *shit*."

Yeah. That about sums it up.

I try to put on the it's-okay face, but I'm not that good of an actor.

But then Mama Jo is touching my shoulder, pulling me away, off the stage, not smiling anymore, not cheering, as somber as I've ever seen her. She says something about a phone call. I have to come with her now.

"It's about your mother," she says.

Dear X,

This week marks the beginning of the third trimester. It's the final inning of the least fun game ever, but at least the end's in sight, right? Lately Melly's been pushing me to get going on the adoption stuff. She's supposed to start processing things. We only have a couple months left. So this week, even though I'm not technically in school, I have homework.

Here's what I'm supposed to do by Friday:

Fill out the non-identifying information form. Yay. That sounds about as fun as a trip to the dentist. (More about dentists later.)

Start going through the potential adoptive parent files. These are the applications for the couples who want babies. Who want you.

In other words, I have to start picking your parents.

No pressure.

At first all the couples seemed exactly the same to me. There are no names attached to these people, just a sea of smiling photographs and the hopeful details they provided about their lives. Their dreams of parenthood laid right out there for me to see. Of course, they are all putting their best foot forward, so to speak. They all use the same kind of language, how much they would like to have a child, the joy that said child is going to bring into their lives, the incredible things they have to offer, the way that they're so ready to be parents. They all sound like amazing people. And I have to guess about what's left unsaid.

For instance, consider the following couple—the dad's a dentist and the mom's a hygienist. They clearly work in the same office. They own their home. They both grew up in the same town and went to the same high school. They were high school sweethearts, the form says. And they have a dog, a big beautiful golden retriever that there's a picture of in the file. In the picture, the dog is wearing a sweater and perfectly posing for the camera.

So I start mentally making a list of the pros and cons of giving you to this couple:

Pros:

You will have good teeth.

You will never be poor—since the world is always in need of dentists. You will be financially secure.

You will be raised in a stable environment.

You will have a dog friend. I like dogs. Evelyn's allergic to dogs, so I don't have one. But I like them.

And now for the cons:

This couple is boring with a capital B. I almost fell asleep reading their application. You're going to be so bored if I give you to them.

But then I think, what's so wrong with boring? Boring is safe.

Boring is like the opposite of half the other girls who go to this school, whose parents have problems with drugs or alcohol or are like Amber busting in here in the middle of night, almost strangled to death and kicked out of her house with nothing.

Amber's still here, by the way. She's been like a different person since she moved in. She's in Heather's old room. There's irony for you. At least I no longer feel the urge to punch her every time she talks. But then she's not talking a lot, either.

Anyway. Back to the cons of Team Dentist.

What if they're like cardboard people, X, who have never done anything exciting in life and never will? What if they're the type of people who hang out safely in their own little spearmint-scented bubble and take vacations to Hawaii once a year but otherwise don't feel the need to go anywhere or do anything fun?

I guess that brings us back to BORING.

The kicker is the dog. That poor dog in its sweater. The perfect dog in the perfect family, doing exactly what it's told. But in its eyes I can see the desperation. HELP ME—it's silently screaming.

You're the dog in this scenario, X.

So yeah, I put that application in the HELL NO pile.

This next potential dad—I kid you not—was a freaking brain surgeon. The mom was cool—she had a degree in music and there was something genuinely sweet about her answers. She seemed nice.

But they went in the NO pile, too. Because a) a brain surgeon? Really? Then he's probably never home, is he? And he probably thinks he's the smartest person ever. Who wants a dad like that?

And also, they're Mormon. I can't do that to you, X. I mean, no offense to the religion intended. There are a lot of Mormons in Idaho, *as you probably know, and they're good people. It wouldn't be the worst thing if you grew up Mormon. But I kind of want your religion to be your own choice, which I don't think it would be, if I gave you to them. But maybe that's true of every religion.*

And couple #3—the Hikers. This mom was a chef (pro: good food for you, X!) and the dad was an engineer (so probably financial security, also) but it seemed to me that they spent their every waking minute hiking or rock climbing or running marathons. And I thought, well, that's good, too, right? I mean, if those people were your parents, you'd be healthy. Well fed. Fit. And you wouldn't be bored, would you?

But you'd be tired. It exhausted me just reading their application. You'd probably be one of those kids who played three different sports at all times of the year and ate dinner in the car on the way to the next practice and possibly cracked your head open falling off the side of a mountain.

NO.

I realize I'm being overly critical. I'm looking for reasons to say no. But I don't know the whole story about these people, do I? What if I pick a couple who seems perfect, but the mom is secretly addicted to Xanax and the dad's a workaholic and they hardly speak to each other? Or what if I pick a couple who fight all the time and they're trying to adopt because they think you'll fix what's wrong with them? A fixer baby. That's what my little sister was to my mom and Brett, I'm pretty sure. And that's not fair to you.

I wish there was a way for them to be truly honest when they fill out these forms. I wish I could see not only their beautiful little dreams of a family, but their fears, too. Their flaws, instead of only their strengths. The truth. Not the polished up for-company version.

Anyway. I'll keep looking and hope I don't screw it up too badly.

Because that's why I'm doing this, right? This is exactly the point. I want you to have better parents than I could be to you. I want you to have a better life than I could give you.

But what if I pick wrong?

Of course, the grown-up version of you who's reading this letter already knows. I've already picked, on your side of things. And you're either happy about that or not.

I hope you're happy about who I chose for you. I hope you're happy, period.

That's what I want.

S

20

Mom's dying. Officially, this time. It apparently started yesterday morning with a low-grade fever and a cough, which developed, in the afternoon, into a massive fluid buildup in Mom's lungs, what the doctors call pleural edema. She was basically drowning. They tried to drain the fluid using a tube inserted into her chest, a fairly simple procedure except that it went wrong somehow, and her lung partially collapsed. Then she had to go into surgery, where she nearly bled out on the table. But they got her through.

She's still here. Still kicking, is how my grandma put it. Still fighting. Still alive.

But the doctors say she's in what they call a spiral. This is all way too much stress for her already stressed-out heart. They say she has six weeks, if that.

I try to wrap my head around it. Six weeks. I wonder how they come up with these numbers, like if there's a kind of handy chart somewhere where they can calculate the expiration dates for people. Because they can't really know, can they? But they always sound like they do.

Six more weeks with my mother.

If that.

"But there's a silver lining to this cloud," Dad says the next morning when we're all sitting around her bed at the hospital—me and Dad and Grandma and Uncle Pete, trying to act like this isn't the beginning of the end of our world. "She's been moved up to the top of the donor list."

"That's right," Grandma says. "Now we're going to get you a brand-new heart."

"A superhero heart," says Uncle Pete.

Right. I try to imagine then that there is a heart for my mom out there somewhere. A person walking around using that heart, unaware that disaster is about to befall them—a car crash or an aneurysm or a freak accident that will mean that person dies and my mom gets to live.

It feels wrong, hoping for it.

Mom squeezes my hand three times. When I was little that was the secret message she taught me: three hand squeezes = I love you. She'd do it when she dropped me off at swimming lessons, or at the doctor's office when I was about to get a shot, or when I accidentally dumped out the entire contents of my backpack in the middle of the hall at school one morning and a group of boys laughed at me. When she first had the heart attack there were a lot of times she couldn't talk for one reason or another, but she would squeeze my hand, so weakly sometimes I could barely feel it, but I'd hear the words loud and clear, and I'd squeeze back.

196

Squeeze squeeze squeeze. I love you.

"I'm sorry you had to rush home from the drama competition," she says when the rest of my family's gone home and we have a minute alone.

"It's fine. The competition was over. We won first place," I say, trying to smile.

For a second I plunge right back into that awful moment, the governor and Nyla and me and the realization that I am not going to go to C of I. I consider telling Mom about the epic fail regarding the scholarship situation. But then I don't. I don't want to put that on her.

"I wish I could have seen it," she says, with effort. "I feel like I'm missing everything good and exciting in your life."

"You aren't missing much of anything," I say, but what I think is, *But you will.* I know that's not her fault, but it still feels unfair. If she dies—and I force myself to think the word *if* and not *when*—there will be a giant Mom-shaped hole in the rest of my life.

She's quiet for a while, and I think she's gone to sleep. I stare at the oxygen tubes in her nose. Her face is the color of chalk, her lips, in spite of the oxygen, a weird mix of pink and gray.

"Don't you have rehearsal tonight?" she whispers.

"What? No. It's Sunday."

But of course I'm going to quit the play.

Her eyes open. "I need to tell you something."

I lean forward so I can hear her. "Tell me what, Mom?"

I brace for a goodbye, the "I'll always be with you, in your heart" speech you see in the movies. I swallow back my tears. "Maybe you shouldn't talk."

"There's a letter." She sits up a bit, clears her throat, and says it more loudly. "There's a letter for you."

"You wrote me a letter?"

"Not me," she says. "Your birth mother."

"What?"

"I know you're curious about her. Your dad told me you were asking questions."

"I was, but . . ." Right then I'm tempted to confess everything, the real reason I requested my birth certificate, the way I've been thinking about my birth mother so often these days, my conversations with Nyla, my unproductive search of an adoption registry, but I can't see how this information wouldn't upset my mom, and it's important for nothing to upset her right now. Better for her not to know that only yesterday I was at the Boise Public Library scouring the high school books, searching for my birth mother. "I don't think—"

"It's okay." Mom puts her hand over mine. "I want you to find her."

I'm so shocked it takes me a few minutes to form a one-word response. "What?"

"I've always thought about her, out there somewhere," Mom says. "I want to meet her. I have some things I'd like to say."

I sit back. "You want me to find my birth mother because *you* want to talk to her?"

"I want to know more about her. Don't you?"

"But you chose a closed adoption," I rasp out. "You were fine with not knowing who she was before, right?"

"Your dad and I were scared, especially in the beginning," she answers. "We didn't want to risk that someday she might want you back. We thought it'd be for the best if we didn't have contact. The other way seemed messy." She smiles faintly. "But you're eighteen now. And you have a right to know about this part of yourself."

She takes a minute to rest from all this talking.

I still can't catch my breath. "And Dad wants me to search for her, too?"

Her smile fades. "He's not in complete agreement, but he's okay with it. If you are."

My heart's beating fast, my palms suddenly sweaty.

"The day we got you"—Mom smooths the sheets down over her legs—"the social worker told me about a program they had, in the state of Idaho, where the birth mother could leave a letter for her baby."

"Wait, what?"

"And the social worker told me, even though I don't think she was supposed to, that there's a letter there for you. Your birth mother wrote you a letter."

I sink down at the edge of the bed again. Right. The letter. "She wrote me a letter."

"And the social worker said that when you turned eighteen you could request that the letter be given to you."

I've been eighteen for weeks, and she never said a word. "Why didn't you mention this before?"

"I don't know. I—maybe I didn't want to share you. But I'm thinking about things differently now." She tries to laugh, but it comes out as a cough. "Come here."

She hugs me, but she's so weak we both just kind of lean into each other.

"Are you sure?" I ask her, because my birth mother seems like the last thing we need to be thinking about right now.

"I'm sure, sweetie." She pulls back and tucks a loose piece of my hair behind my ear. "Get the letter," she says. "Then we'll go from there."

21

When Dad and I get back to the house we discover Ronnie, Bender, and Bastian sitting on the front porch. They jump up when they see us. "Hey, Cass."

It's Sunday afternoon. I've hardly slept. I haven't showered. I'm sure I smell like hospital. I was hoping to come home and clean up and maybe take a nap. "Hey?" I say blearily. "What are you all . . . doing here?"

"Nyla sent us," Ronnie explains. "She had church, but she thought maybe you could use some moral support. Like a group hug or something."

They give me a group hug. It's awkward, but good. Then they step back and consider also giving a hug to my dad, who looks so tired he's about to fall over.

"Hey, Papa Bill," says Bender.

"Hello, Mr. McMurtrey," Ronnie says at the same time. Dad was her teacher in fifth grade, and she's never been able to call him Papa Bill like the rest of my friends.

"Hello, kids," he manages, trying and failing to call up a smile. He glances around the group. "Ronnie, of course. Bender. And . . ." He frowns when he gets to Bastian.

"Bastian," Bastian provides. "I'm in the play."

For some reason the boy I like introducing himself to my father makes me blush. Which is so dumb I can't even. But then, I'm ridiculously tired.

"Right. The play," Dad murmurs. Because he also knows that of course I'm going to quit the play now.

"We brought pizza," says Bender helpfully. "And salad and bread and cheesecake from the grocery store."

"And flowers, for your mom," says Bastian, picking up a bouquet of daisies from the porch.

"That's so thoughtful of you," Dad says. "Come in."

We shuffle inside and force down some of the pizza, and then my dad disappears into his bedroom. I sit in the living room with my friends for a while, chatting about I don't even know what—my mom, a little, how great it is that she's been moved up on the donor list. How everyone's sure she'll get a new heart now. How much hospital life sucks. And then they talk about the play, which leads to how Alice is still ticked off at Bastian, and how that's problematic because Bastian is the wolf and Alice is Little Red Riding Hood, but they're just going to have to work together like professionals.

"She's right to be mad" is all Bastian has to say on the subject. And then everybody kind of stops talking. No one wants to discuss state drama, which is how I can tell they all know about the scholarship situation.

Nyla must have told them. I'm so exhausted I don't even know how I feel about Nyla telling my friends that I didn't get the scholarship. I mean, of course everyone was going to find out eventually, at school. But Nyla and I haven't even had a chance to talk about it. Not that I want to talk about it. Not that a stupid scholarship should mean anything to me right now.

My mom's what's important.

Eventually my friends get up to leave, but Bastian lingers.

"I know I haven't even met your mom," he says, "but I'm sorry."

I try to smile at him. "Thanks."

"I'm here for you, okay?" He gives me a long hug. It's warm and comforting and nice, and he smells really good. "You let me know if there's anything I can do for you," he says when he pulls back.

I think about it. I mean, he has a car.

So I say, "Actually, can you give me a ride?"

"Yeah. Anywhere," he says.

I bite my lip. "I need to take a shower first. Can you wait?"

"Absolutely. Take your time."

I leave him in the living room and hurry myself in and out of the shower. When I'm done I feel about 25 percent more human than I did this morning. And I look and smell a whole lot better.

Bastian stands up when I come back into the room. "Okay. You ready?"

I take a deep breath. "Yeah."

"Consider me your own personal Uber." He slings an arm around me. "Just tell me where."

When Nyla's family gets home from church, I'm the one sitting on their porch. Mama Liz rushes out of the car with her arms outstretched to hug me until I think my ribs might be bruised. Then I get hugs from Nyla's dad and all of her many siblings.

It's been a huggie day. It makes me feel like my mom's dead already. But I know everybody means well. All this hugging means that I am loved.

"Oh, you poor baby," Mama Liz keeps saying. "I'm so sorry, sweetie." She cries a little and hugs me again and asks me if I need anything to eat.

It's a while before I'm alone with Nyla, but finally we're in her room. The scholarship thing is still hanging in the air between us. I can't look directly at her, because even though I know it's not important, it still hurts in this weird way, so I wander around her room examining the posters on her bright yellow walls like I've never seen them before. I run my hand along the length of her dresser. I look out the window, where there is absolutely nothing interesting to see.

"Cass," Nyla says finally. "About state drama, I want to say—"

"Don't," I say quickly. "It's fine."

"But—"

"Please don't." I sigh. "I just need you to do something for me now, okay? Do you think you can cut school tomorrow?"

"Um, sure. Why?"

Get the letter. Then we'll go from there. "I have someplace I have to go," I say. "For Mom."

22

The Idaho Bureau of Vital Records and Health Statistics is located in a redbrick building in downtown Boise. My stomach sinks when I see all the people crowded into the waiting room. There's a machine where you take a number that they'll call when it's your turn.

My number is E145.

We're currently on E122.

Nyla sits next to me and starts knitting a pair of socks that I instinctively know is for my mom. My mom was the one who taught Nyla to knit, actually, a couple of years ago. She keeps offering to teach me, but I tried it a few times and I always end up with a mass of tangled yarn. I'm not crafty. But it would be nice to know how to knit at a time like this. It would at least give my hands something to do.

My leg's bouncing. Nyla puts her hand out to stop it. "You all right?"

"Not really."

Nyla's mouth twists. "Do you want to talk about the sch—"

"Nope." If I didn't want to talk about it on the four-hour drive over here, I for sure don't want to talk about it now. I'm think I'm good with never talking about it, ever again.

"Okay. But if you want to talk about it, I'm—"

"Still nope."

"Okay." She takes her hand away and resumes her knitting, humming her country music.

I pick up a three-year-old *People* magazine and try to steady my breathing. Get the letter, I remind myself, trying to stay focused on my mom in all this. Then we'll go from there.

I look at my watch every thirty seconds, so I know that Nyla and I wait approximately fifty-two minutes before my number is called.

"I got you," Nyla says quietly as I lumber to my feet.

"Yeah." I feel numb, like I'm floating out of my body and watching it all from above, like this isn't really my life, again—it's that scene where Cass gets the letter from her birth mother.

How do you even prepare for that kind of thing?

"How can I help you?" asks the clerk as I stumble up to the desk.

I hold out the appropriate piece of paper with a shaky hand. "I need to give you this form. I had it notarized."

The clerk takes the form. "Thank you." She looks it over. "All right. It's all in order." She stamps it, makes a copy, and hands it back to me. Then she leans forward to call out, "Next."

I'm confused. "That's it? But then don't I get—"

"You could have mailed the form in," the lady says cheerfully but also like she thinks I should have mailed the form in and therefore not wasted her precious time. "But it's good to bring it in person if you need a copy. Which I gave you."

"But now I get the letter, right?" I ask.

"Letter?" Now she's the one who's confused.

"The letter that my birth mother left for me."

The clerk's expression goes totally blank. "Who told you there'd be a letter?"

"My mom," I answer. "And then on the website for the Department of Health and Welfare I thought it said I had to come make a request for the letter in person. And I had to bring this form, signed by a notary."

The clerk turns around and calls into the back of the office. "Linda? Can you come here a second?"

A lady in a pink sweater—Linda, I presume—strolls up to the counter.

"This girl is asking about a letter written by her birth mother," says the clerk, loudly this time. Now everyone in the office—the people in the waiting room and the people working the desk—is staring at me with that look—the poor-adopted-you look. All except for Nyla, who just looks worried.

"Hi," I say awkwardly to Linda.

"Oh, yes, hello," Linda says apologetically. "There was a program— it ended about fifteen years ago, but there's an archive of these letters."

"Okay. I would like my letter, please," I say.

"They're in storage in another facility," Linda informs me.

I want to say *So get it*, but I know that would be rude.

"We hired someone last year to sort through them and handle the requests, but you see, unfortunately, there are fifteen years of requests that nobody has been taking care of until now. So there's a significant backlog," Linda says.

It sounds like I'm not getting the letter today.

"What does that mean?" I ask a bit hoarsely. "How long will I have to wait?"

She gives me a sympathetic smile. "It could be some time after you file your request that you receive the letter. It could be months. Maybe even years. I'm very sorry."

So I'm not getting the letter in the next six weeks.

I can feel my jaw tightening. "This is my life, you know." My voice sounds high and sharp and not like my voice at all. "This isn't just paperwork for me."

And now everybody is *really* staring. Out of the corner of my eye, I see Nyla stand up. I turn to leave.

"Do you still wish to file the waiver of confidentiality?" Linda asks.

I swivel back. "To get the letter? Yes. Right? That's why I'm here."

"No, the letter archive is a separate issue," she explains. "I'll put your name on the list for the letter archive right away." She copies down my name, my date of birth, and my contact information onto a yellow legal pad. There's not even an official form for the letter thing, apparently, which makes me think that this is never going to work, not if there are fifteen years of backlogged names on legal pads waiting for their letters.

"So wait, what's the waiver for, then?" I ask after that's done.

Linda looks at me with pity but also like I'm a moron. Because I obviously didn't read this thing I had a notary sign and everything. "It's if you wish to waive your right to confidentiality in the case of your adoption. We have a matching program, here. If the biological parents both submit a waiver of confidentiality, and the adopted child also submits a waiver, we can legally share the contact information between the involved parties."

"I bet there's a backlog for that, too." Okay, maybe I'm being a little rude.

Linda doesn't seem bothered, though. She works for the government and therefore deals with rude people all the time, apparently. "It's a careful process, and yes, it takes time."

It's all starting to sink in.

"So what you're saying is that if my birth mother wants to find me," I say slowly, "she can fill out this form, and if I also fill out the form, you'll give me her information and you'll give her my information."

"If the biological father also fills out a form, or if there's no way to locate him in a timely manner, then yes. That's how it works in the state of Idaho."

"Okay. Yes. I still would like to file the waiver." I let out the breath I feel like I've been holding since this morning. "And I'm not going to receive anything today," I say, just to be sure.

"That's all we can do for you today." Linda smiles patiently. The other clerk is helping someone else by now.

"Thank you." I shuffle like a zombie to the parking lot, Nyla trailing behind me. It's starting to snow, tiny light flakes that melt the second they touch my skin. A huge wave of relief and disappointment crashes over me, so strong my knees almost buckle with it.

"Are you okay?" Nyla asks.

I close my eyes and picture the way my face must have looked during that entire exchange with poor Linda. Then I start laughing, laughing so hard I double over and tears come to my eyes.

"All right. Definitely not okay," Nyla assesses.

I can't stop laughing. It's the weirdest thing.

When I finally look up, gasping for air, there's an old man standing in front of the building looking at me like I've lost my mind.
Which I'm pretty sure I have.

"Hi," I call out. "Nice weather we're having, isn't it?" I turn my
face up to the snow and take a deep, shuddering breath.

"Oh, good. Welcome back," Nyla says. "What do you want to do
now?"

"Nothing." I look around for where she parked Bernice. "Let's
go home."

Dear X,

    Melly has been basically yelling at me for the past two hours. She doesn't like the way I filled out the non-identifying information form. She says I can't turn it in the way I filled it out. I was too sarcastic in what I wrote, she said.

    "I was being honest," I told her. I think you deserve honest, don't you?

    "You need to remember that it's not only you who's choosing here," she said. "The adoptive parents have to choose you, too."

    Apparently she doesn't think they'd choose me, if I gave them the form this way, because if I'm sarcastic maybe they'd end up with a sarcastic baby. Can't have that, can we?

    So I did the form again. I was a good girl this time. I kept it to the basics. I was boring. Generic. I said what I'm expected to say, really, and nothing more. Maybe that's for the best. I do want them to choose me. To choose you, I mean.

But I'm going to include the original form here. The true one. So I can tell you how I really feel.

Melly also says I have to get the father to fill out the forms, too, because that's half of the information you need, isn't it? I'm not thrilled at the idea of talking to Dawson about it. I've been trying not to think about him at all. He still hasn't called. Not that I expected him to. He doesn't even know that I'm at Booth.

But I'll work on getting the form to him, because Melly's right. There's so much I don't know about Dawson. And so much you probably need to know.

S

NON-IDENTIFYING INFORMATION
FOR ADOPTION REGISTRY

SOCIAL AND HEALTH HISTORY ☒ Birth mother ☐ Birth father

The information in this report has been provided by the birth parent.
The Bureau of Vital Records is not responsible for the accuracy of this information.

DESCRIPTION OF SELF

Marital status: ☒ Single ☐ Married ☐ Separated

☐ Divorced ☐ Widowed

If married or separated: ☐ Civil marriage ☐ Religious ceremony

Are you an enrolled member of a Native American tribe, Alaskan village, or affiliated with a tribe? ☐ Yes ☒ No **If yes, what tribe?**

Religion:

I'm not religious. I can't remember the last time I went to church.

Ethnic background (e.g., English, German, etc.):

The same Chex mix of most people I know. European, with a dash of this or that. It's not going to explain why you like Mexican food.

Country or state of birth:

Idaho

Race (e.g., Black, White, American Indian, Japanese, etc.):

White and privileged and still in this mess.

Height:

5'3". Yeah, I'm a shorty.

Weight:

115. I assume they mean before pregnancy. And I'm still gonna lie. That's none of your business.

Hair color and texture:

Brown and boring. I've been trying to grow it out for two years but it never seems to get much past my shoulders.

Eye color:

Blue, like a pale, sky blue, I would say. My best feature easily.

Unique physical features (e.g., freckles, moles, etc.):

I have freckles across my nose that are "cute" is what the guys would say, and what I would consider to be the normal amount of moles.

Complexion: ☒ Fair ☐ Medium ☐ Olive ☐ Dark

Use sunscreen, okay? I freckle in the sun, like my mom, but my dad goes lobster red in like 10 minutes. We're a family of ghosts.

☐ **Right-handed** ☒ **Left-handed**

Yeah, and it's always been the biggest pain. I hope you're not left-handed. Even though that means I'm supposed to be creative or something.

Physical build (e.g., big/small boned, long/short limbed, muscular, etc.):

I'm average. I'm never going to be a supermodel.

Talents, hobbies, and other interests:

I'm into music. Some oldies, more indie, some alternative. I'm listening to "Kryptonite" by 3 Doors Down right now, and it is awesome. I also like writing, I'm finding out. More and more these days. I mean, I knew I liked it before. I tried working on the school newspaper for a while, and I did the yearbook this year. Mostly because my dad said I was required to have a school-related hobby. But that didn't last. Let's just say I'm not a fan of deadlines.

Which of the following describe your personality (check all that apply):

☒ Aggressive ☒ Emotional ☒ Happy ☒ Rebellious

☒ Shy ☒ Serious ☒ Calm ☒ Friendly ☒ Irresponsible ☒ Fun

☒ Temperamental ☒ Critical ☒ Outgoing ☒ Stubborn ☒ Unhappy

Comments:

Seriously? I'm "unhappy" that I'm being expected to categorize myself this way. What are you supposed to get out of this? I'm like checking all the boxes! How's that for stubborn? I'm seven months pregnant right now—I'm all of these things! I can't be summed up by a checked box.

EDUCATION

Last grade level completed:

10th

Average grade received or GPA:

C student, sorry

Presently in school: ☒ Yes ☐ No

Future plans for schooling:

I want to graduate and then get a job. I've never been great at school. Which is probably not what you want to hear. I did think about journalism (see above) but it seems like the newspaper business is dying fast and there's no way I'd want to be on TV.

Subjects you are interested in:

Music, but I don't play an instrument. History, but I don't want to be a history teacher and I can't remember dates very well. Art, but I can't draw. I'm okay at math but I hate it. You can see the pattern here.

Any school-related problems or challenges (tutoring, Special Ed, etc.):

Not really except that I don't like school and school has never really liked me.

EMPLOYMENT HISTORY

Current occupation:

Military service: ☐ Yes ☒ No **If yes, branch of service:**

Vocational training:

Work history:

I worked at Target last summer. It sucked, but there was a nice week where I built a bunch of bicycles out in the garden section. I liked putting together the bicycles—hey, maybe I'll be a mechanic!

That's it! This form has inspired me to fix my future.

FAMILY HISTORY

Was anyone in your family adopted? ☐ Yes ☒ No **If yes, who?**

If so, it's a deep dark secret.

Your order of birth (e.g., 1st of 4):

2nd of 3? Not sure how to answer when I have a half sister. I have an older brother and a younger half sister. Does that make me the wild middle child?

Personal relationships with parents, siblings, or extended family members:

I am a disgrace to the family, according to my stepmom. She's clearly very loving and supportive. My dad's the silent "leave her alone" type. Also super supportive, obviously. My brother is awesome, but he's also absent, which I can't blame him for. My mom is also largely absent, but that's fine. I'm more the independent sort.

Summarize adjustment to pregnancy. Include how you and your parents adjusted to the pregnancy, and if you had peer support:

My dad/stepmom basically forced me to go to Booth (a school/home for pregnant girls), so they wouldn't have to deal with me. My mom has been fairly supportive, although she was most supportive of the abortion idea, if I'm being honest. The teachers at the school are very helpful, though.

YOUR BIRTH PARENTS (child's grandparents)
FATHER
Age (if deceased, state age at time of death):

46

Health problems:

High blood pressure, because he's so uptight, I think.

Height/weight:

5'11", 200 lbs. He could stand to lose a few pounds.

Hair/eye color:

brown, brown

Build: ☐ Small ☒ Medium ☐ Large ☐ Extra large

Complexion: ☐ Fair ☒ Medium ☐ Olive ☐ Dark

Right-/left-handed:

right

Description of personality (e.g., happy, shy, stubborn, etc.):

He's a barrel of laughs. Ha ha, not really. But people seem to like him and look up to him.

Talents, hobbies, interests:

politics, golf, skiing

Education:

college

Occupation:

lawyer, and not the cool, trying-to-help-the-helpless kin

Number of siblings:

2

Race (Black, White, American Indian, etc.):

white

Ethnic background (e.g., German, English, etc.):

German/English, this may be where the uptight comes from.

Religion:

Presbyterian, or at least his butt warms a pew a couple Sundays every month.

Marital status: ☐ Single ☒ Married ☐ Separated

☒ Divorced ☐ Widowed

Aware of this pregnancy? ☒ Yes ☐ No

He wishes he wasn't.

MOTHER

Age (if deceased, state age at time of death):

44

Health problems:

Height/weight:

5'2", 100 lbs. She's basically skinny and perfect.

Hair/eye color:

brown, blue—we have the same eyes

Build: ☒ Small ☐ Medium ☐ Large ☐ Extra large

Complexion: ☒ Fair ☐ Medium ☐ Olive ☐ Dark

Right-/left-handed:

left

Description of personality (e.g., happy, shy, stubborn, etc.):

Around strangers she's the quiet type. She can get mad, but it blows over quickly.

Talents, hobbies, interests:

ballet, skiing, tennis—the skiing is the only thing I could tell they had in common

Education:

college

Occupation:

ballet teacher

Number of siblings:

0

Race (Black, White, American Indian, etc.):

white

Ethnic background (e.g., German, English, etc.):

Irish/Italian—I think this is where the yelling comes from.

Religion:

Agnostic—they used to fight about how she should go to church.

Marital status: ☐ Single ☒ Married ☐ Separated

☒ Divorced ☐ Widowed

They divorced each other and remarried.

Aware of this pregnancy? ☒ Yes ☐ No

YOUR BIRTH BROTHERS AND SISTERS (child's uncles and aunts)

1) ☒ BROTHER ☐ SISTER

Age (if deceased, state age at time of death):

22

Health problems:

Height/weight:

No idea, taller than me, average for a guy, I think.

Hair/eye color:

brown, blue

Build: ☐ Small ☒ Medium ☐ Large ☐ Extra large

Complexion: ☐ Fair ☒ Medium ☐ Olive ☐ Dark

Right-/left-handed:

right

Talents, hobbies, interests:

football, wrestling, baseball

Education:

High school, some college, although I think he might be majoring in beer and girls.

Occupation:

student

Religion:

Says he's Presbyterian to please our father.

Marital status: ☒ Single ☐ Married ☐ Separated

☐ Divorced ☐ Widowed

& loving it

Aware of this pregnancy? ☐ Yes ☒ No

2) ☐ BROTHER ☒ SISTER

Age (if deceased, state age at time of death):

7

Health problems:

Height/weight:

No idea, shorter than me and little.

Hair/eye color:

blond, blue—we all have my mom's eyes

Build: ☒ Small ☐ Medium ☐ Large ☐ Extra large

Complexion: ☒ Fair ☐ Medium ☐ Olive ☐ Dark

Right-/left-handed:

left, poor thing

Talents, hobbies, interests:

Candy Land, My Little Pony, Legos

Education:

Grade school, kindergarten, where she can already count to 100 and knows her colors!

Occupation:

kid

Religion:

Thinks of God the same way she thinks of Santa Claus.

Marital status: ☒ Single ☐ Married ☐ Separated
☐ Divorced ☐ Widowed

obviously

Aware of this pregnancy? ☐ Yes ☒ No

MEDICAL HISTORY

Please indicate "None" or "You" if you or any genetic relatives (i.e., your mother, father, sisters, brothers, grandparents, uncles, aunts, or any other children you have had) ever had or now has any of the medical conditions listed below. Please explain in the comments section.

Baldness:

Dad. Only on the top. He shaves his head though so people think it's intentional.

Birth defects: *None*

Clubfoot: *None*

Cleft palate: *None*

Congenital heart disease: *None*

Cancer:

Grandpa. Bladder cancer, I think. He died when I was little and no one seemed to like him very much before that.

Other: *None*

ALLERGIES

Animals: *None*

Asthma: *None*

Eczema: *None*

Food:

Sister. Allergic to everything, I think. There's something about kids today not getting enough exposure to germs.

Hay fever/plants:

>   *Mom. Every spring she could be a commercial for Benadryl.*

Hives: *None*

Medications: *Blood pressure meds, I think, and high-powered vitamins, and I did find Viagra in the medicine cabinet once, but no one wants to think about that.*

Other allergies: *None*

Other (specify): *None*

VISUAL IMPAIRMENT

Astigmatism:

>   *Mom. Wears glasses/contacts.*

Blindness: *None*

Color blindness:

>   *Dad. Also my brother, they have trouble matching socks.*

EMOTIONAL/MENTAL ILLNESS

Bipolar (manic depressive): *None*

Schizophrenia: *None*

Severe depression:

>   *Dad. After the divorce he went through a "phase" as he called it and started seeing a therapist, but he's better now.*

Suicide: *None*

Obsessive-compulsive disorder: *None*

Personality disorder: *None*

Alcoholism/drug addiction:

>   *Dad. He also drank too much after the divorce and crashed his car into our mailbox, but no one got hurt or arrested, so it's all good.*

Other (specify): *None*

HEREDITARY DISEASES

Cystic fibrosis: *None*

Galactosemia: *None*

Hemophilia: *None*

Huntington's disease: *None*

Hypothyroidism or hyperthyroidism: *None*

CARDIOVASCULAR DISEASE

Heart attack:

> *Grandma. On my dad's side, in her 50s.*

Heart murmur: *None*

High blood pressure:

> *Dad*

Diabetes: *None*

SEXUALLY TRANSMITTED DISEASES

> *Gross. This is a highly inappropriate question. Why is it important if your relatives got STDs? Ew. I refuse to answer on the sheer principle of the thing.*

Chlamydia: *Gross!*

Gonorrhea: *Ew!*

Herpes: *Double gross!*

Syphilis: *What is this, the 1890s?*

HIV/AIDS: *Nope.*

Other (specify): *None*

NEUROLOGICAL DISORDERS

Cerebral palsy: *None*

Muscular dystrophy: *None*

Multiple sclerosis:

> *None. I guess we've all been pretty lucky.*

Epilepsy: *None*

Stroke: *None*

Rheumatic fever: *None*

Other (specify): *None*

DEVELOPMENTAL DISORDERS

Learning disability / ADHD:

> *None. Again, either we're lucky or no one ever talks about it.*

Mental retardation (specify type): *None*

Down syndrome: *None*

Speech or hearing problems: *None*

Low birth weight: *None*

Other (specify): *None*

HISTORY OF DRUG USE

PRESCRIPTION:

Specify type (e.g., Prozac, Accutane, etc.)

☐ Before conception   ☐ After conception

OVER-THE-COUNTER:

Specify type (e.g., diet pills, antihistamine, etc.)

☐ Before conception   ☐ After conception

OTHER TYPES OF DRUGS USED:

Alcohol

> *At parties, mostly. I did replace some of my dad's liquor with water my sophomore year.*

Specify type:

> *Beer, rum and Coke, vodka, whatever is available. But I swear I'm not a lush. It's all social drinking.*

Date of last use:

> *Whenever the last party was. I can't even remember.*

☒ Before conception   ☐ After conception

I may like to have fun at parties but I haven't had a single drink since I found out I was pregnant. There may have been one party before I knew I was pregnant.

Downers (i.e., sleeping pills, barbiturates, etc.)

Specify type:

Date of last use:

☐ Before conception ☐ After conception

Cocaine ("Crack")

By injection? ☐ Yes ☐ No

Date of last use:

☐ Before conception ☐ After conception

Heroin/pain killers

By injection? ☐ Yes ☐ No

Date of last use:

☐ Before conception ☐ After conception

Hallucinogens (i.e., LSD, Ecstasy, PCP, etc.)

Specify type:

Date of last use:

☐ Before conception ☐ After conception

Cigarettes

I tried it once. Coughed until I threw up. Decided it wasn't for me.

Specify type:

I think that time it was Lucky Strike. Clearly not lucky.

Date of last use:

☒ Before conception ☐ After conception

Marijuana

Okay, a couple times. But I swear I didn't inhale.

Date of last use:

Last year at a party.

☒ Before conception   ☐ After conception

Other

Specify type:

Date of last use:

☐ Before conception   ☐ After conception

SOCIAL AND HEALTH HISTORY   ☒ **Birth mother** ☐ **Birth father**
If you wish, please add any additional information that will further
describe you and your situation. (Consider your schooling, health,
work, goals and hopes for the future, relationship history, religious or
spiritual beliefs, challenges, strengths, etc.)

*So I've been writing you a bunch of letters, which I hope you get,
and if you read those, you'll understand my situation pretty well. But if
for some reason this is the only thing you get from me, just know that I
care about you. The rest of it isn't that important in the big picture. I'm
healthy, and I'm trying to keep you healthy. I take my vitamins and eat
vegetables and try not to consume my weight in ice cream, which is tempt-
ing right now. It's been a hot summer. I'm trying to do the right thing here.*

*I know I'm supposed to say something inspiring, like God is in control
and He'll guide you to where you're supposed to be. But I don't think I
even believe in God anymore. Sorry. And I wish I could tell you that I
dream about seeing you again, someday, but I don't know if that would be
good for either of us. You're better off without me. I'm sorry, but you are.*

*I'm not happy. That's okay. We don't always have to be happy, right?
I am sixteen years old, and I got pregnant by a guy who's not in the picture
anymore, and I couldn't keep you or take care of you for a bunch of reasons
that would take pages to explain and probably still not really be the real
reasons. I've never lived in what you could describe as a happy home, and*

so if I keep you, you wouldn't either. Honestly, my life is a mess right now, and that's not your fault, but I need to fix it before I can be a mother. I hope you can understand. So right now I am trying to find you some parents who will be better. I want you to have a good life. I wish everything in the world for you, really.

I hope you get my letters.

Your trusty neighborhood biological mother,
S

23

So the letter thing turned out to be a total waste of time, but try telling that to my mother.

"We have to be patient," she says when I report back on my Boise adventure the next morning before school. Like always, she's determined to be optimistic. "We'll have to wait and see what happens."

But she knows. She's lying there hooked up to a machine that is functioning as her heart. Her lungs are slowly filling up with fluid again. Her other organs are strained and on the brink of shutting down. There's not a lot of time left. Not months, like the lady in the office said it could be before they get to my request in the backlog. Maybe not even weeks.

"Right. Wait and see," I agree, like I believe that's going to work.

"In the meantime," she says, "you could try another approach. It's easy to find people these days, with the internet and social media. There are search sites solely for adoptions. There are registries."

I sigh. "I know."

"Just think about it. Who knows? Your birth mother could already be looking for you."

"She's not," I say automatically.

Mom frowns. "She's not? How do you know?"

I swallow, hard. "I did a search . . . once."

"Oh." She's got hurt written all over her face. It's exactly what I was afraid of. "Why didn't you tell me?"

"Because I didn't want you to think . . ." I take a deep breath. "You're my mom. I didn't want you to think I wasn't happy, or I was looking for another family, or that you weren't enough."

"I would have understood," she says. "I *do* understand. I always assumed that someday, when the time was right, you'd search for her."

"You did?"

"It's what I'd do, if I were you," she says. "So what happened? What did you find?"

"Nothing," I confess.

She looks confused. "Nothing?"

I shrug. "All you have to do is put in your date of birth and the state you were born in, and if anyone from your biological family is looking for you, they'll get a match. It's easy. But there was no match."

"Which means?"

"She's not looking for me." I try to smile. "Which makes total sense. She picked a closed adoption, too, right?"

Mom squeezes my hand. "We don't know her story, or why she chose what she chose. But it's been eighteen years, Cass. She may think about things differently now."

"She's not looking."

Mom's lips flatten in that way she gets when she's made up her mind about something. "She might not know how to look."

"She's thirty-four," I point out. "She probably knows how to google."

"How long has it been since you did the search?" She looks around. "Where's your phone? We could look it up right now. It couldn't hurt to check."

"No." The word kind of bursts out of me. I can't imagine going on one of these sites with my mom watching over my shoulder. I remember how I cracked up in the parking lot yesterday, for a reason I still can't fully understand. "This is something I have to do by myself, okay? I can't explain why, it's just . . . weird and emotional and . . . private. And I don't think I want to anymore. If that's okay."

Her face goes serious. "All right," she says. "I understand."

The guy comes in with Mom's breakfast on a tray. She scoots over to make room and pats the space on the hospital bed beside her. The new drugs they put her on have at least perked her up a little. It's hard to believe, looking at her now, that a couple of days ago she was on death's door, and she's still dying. "Have you eaten breakfast?" she asks.

"You know I don't normally eat breakfast."

"You know I'm going to tell you it's the most important meal of the day." She pats the spot again.

"But . . . hospital food," I counter.

"True, but it's difficult even for a hospital to screw up breakfast. Let's give it a try."

Right on cue, my stomach rumbles. I haven't eaten since yesterday, and that was road trip food. I've had other things on my mind besides hunger.

My mom lifts the cover off her plate. "French toast," she whispers.

I sit down next to her. She pours out the little container of syrup and then proceeds to cut the French toast into small bites. Like I'm still three or something and she doesn't want me to choke.

"Eat up," she says. "You're a growing girl."

I stab a piece of scrambled eggs to be contrary. It's a mistake. They are cold and somewhat rubbery. I guess it is possible to mess up breakfast.

"You're the one who's supposed to be eating this," I point out.

"Oh, no. This is way too much food for me. I have to watch my girlish figure."

It's a joke. She's more of a stick figure these days. Before the heart attack she was a little chubby—not morbidly obese or anything, but carrying around a few extra pounds. She used to claim that she was in the wrong profession to be thin. "Nobody trusts a skinny baker," she always said.

I used to think that was funny.

She spears a piece of grayish sausage and holds it up. "This is probably terrible for my heart. And it's probably also terrible."

I lean over and take a bite out of it, which is directly against all of my vegetarian principles. It's horrible. "It's not too bad, actually. You should try it."

"Wait, who's force-feeding who here?" she says as I take the fork and attempt to airplane the bite of the sausage into her mouth.

"Drink your juice."

She takes a long sip of the orange juice, and then sits back and glances at the clock on the side table. "You better go to school. I think your dad's going to pick you up any second now. Will I see you later?"

"Of course. I'll be here right after school."

Her eyebrows furrow. "Don't you have rehearsal? Show time's getting close now. Only a few more weeks."

Six more, to be exact. Which might as well be forever.

"I . . ." I don't look at her. "I quit the musical."

Her mouth drops open. "What? No!"

"No, it's fine. I called Mama Jo last night. She understood. And hey, my understudy is super happy right now. I should be here. With you."

She shakes her head. "Cass. That's so sweet, and I appreciate it, but no. I want you to live your life, remember?"

"You're my life, right now."

"Oh, sweetie."

"Seriously, it's fine."

But her eyes have that steely look to them I know pretty well. "No. Call Miss Golden. She'll let you back in."

"Mom. The musical is not important."

"Of course it's important. I can't remember the last time you weren't in a play. It makes you happy. Plus this is my favorite musical. I want to see you up there on that stage, as the baker's wife," she says.

I stare at her.

"And I want to meet this boy you like, Bastian," she adds with a little laugh. "Your dad said he came to the house. I'm so jealous. And I want to see Nyla play Cinderella in the blue ball gown you told me about. And I want to give you all a standing ovation."

"But you can't," I say finally.

She meets my eyes. "I will."

"Mom. The doctors said we have six weeks. Less than that now, even. And how can I do anything but spend every minute of that time right here? How can I—"

"The doctors don't know everything." She lifts her chin. God, she's stubborn. "I'm going to get a new heart."

Something inside me kind of snaps, but I can't yell at her. But I can't go along with it all this time, either, so I say, quietly, "You don't know that."

"I do. The universe—"

"Maybe the universe doesn't work the way you think it does," I tell her, still working to keep my voice calm. "I can't keep pretending everything's okay. I just . . . can't."

She closes her eyes for a second, and then they snap open, bright with anger. "All right," she says in a clipped tone I associate with being in trouble. "*All right*. Fine. So let's say I'm dying."

I suck in a shocked breath.

"If I'm dying, if I'm going to waste away in this room, in this bed, I do not want you to be here."

It's like she punched me in the gut. "You don't want me here?"

"No," she rasps. She licks her lips. I give her the cup of water, and she takes a drink, hands it back, and carries on with the conversation. "I want you to be out there, living your life."

"Mom."

"Please," she says, and her voice softens. "Please, honey. When I got you, that first night you were in my arms, I made promises. I promised that I was going to give you the happiest, most beautiful life. That's why your birth mother gave you to me, because I was going to give you that life."

I sigh. "You can't promise my life is going to be happy, Mom."

232

"I'm going to do my best, because that was the promise I made. So if I'm dying, Cass, then this is my dying wish. Don't drop out of the play. Don't quit school. Don't stop hanging out with your friends. Live your beautiful life, every second that you can."

There's a quick knock on the door and Dad pops in. "Hey, sorry to interrupt, but I've got to get Boo to school . . ." His voice trails off. He looks from me to Mom and back again. "What's going on?"

"Okay, sweetie?" Mom asks, still looking at me. "That's what I want."

I'm crying, dangit, and I'm half furious, half devastated, but I'm not allowed to be mad at her right now and she's got me backed into a corner. I wipe at my face and nod once.

"Everybody okay here?" Dad asks.

"We're all peachy." My voice breaks on the word *peachy*. I dash my tears away. "Everything's totally normal, as usual. And apparently I have to do everything she wants."

"Yeah, welcome to the club," Dad says.

"Let's go," I tell him, grabbing my backpack. "I don't want to be late for school. I love you," I bark out to Mom. "I'm going. Bye."

"I love you, too," she says, and I'm out the door.

24

I go to school. I go to class. I go to gym class. I go to a meeting for the theater club. I go to class again. And then I go to lunch, where I sit at the same table where I sit every day, with the same people. But it doesn't feel like any kind of beautiful life.

"How's Mama Cat?" Nyla asks quietly.

"Infuriating. She won't let me quit the play."

"Wait, you want to quit the play?" Bastian asks.

I shrug. Right then Alice shows up. She gives Bastian a notably chilly look, but then she scoots in next to him at our table. "I'm over it," she announces.

"By which you mean . . . ," says Bender.

"The drama competition."

Dear God, please don't let us talk about the drama competition. Not now.

"I really am sorry," Bastian says earnestly.

Alice holds a hand up. "Over it, like I said. But now naturally I want to hear all about it."

Silence. Ronnie is trying to do something under the table—kick Alice, I think. But it doesn't work.

"What?" Alice asks. "Come on, spill it. I've been dying to know how it went all weekend, and then I was out yesterday with a cold, so maybe it was a good thing I didn't get to go. I could have gotten you all sick. Anyway, so . . . how was it?"

"We won second in the comedy category," Bender says quickly, and Ronnie nods and adds, "Hip hip, hooray!"

"Awesome." Alice swivels to Nyla and me. "And what about you two?"

"We won first," I report dutifully. "Hip hip, hooray."

Because I am an exceptionally talented actress. With a beautiful fricking life.

"Great!" Alice gasps. "Of course, that's not a surprise." She glances around the table nervously. She's finally catching on that something's not right, and then she thinks she knows what that is. "Oh, and Cass, I am so sorry. I heard about your mom. Everybody I know is sending your family prayers and healing thoughts."

"Oh, awesome," I say. "Thoughts and prayers."

Nyla looks at me like "*Stop*." "But the good news is, Cass's mom has been placed at the very top of the donor list now," she says. "So there's a lot to be hopeful about."

"That's great news," says Alice.

"Yeah, isn't it *awesome*?" I say brightly.

Alice can see that she needs to change the subject. "Okay, right, so, back to the drama competition. What about the scholarship? I really wanted to try for it myself, but—"

"I'm sorry," mumbles Bastian.

"I'm over it," she says. "But tell me about that. Who won?"

My teeth grind together. My brain feels like it's full of cotton balls. It's too much. Mom dying. Mom wanting me to find my birth mother because she's dying. Mom not wanting me to be there when she's dying. Mom missing my whole life, but maybe that's okay, because my life is not going the way it was supposed to, even though it's supposed to be beautiful and perfect and awesome. And the cherry on top is the f-ing scholarship.

"It's no big deal," Nyla says finally. "I—"

"Oh, but it *is* a big deal," I argue. "Nyla won. Nyla gets to go to the school of her choice. Of course she was already going to do that."

"Hey," Bastian says, reaching for my hand, but I pull away.

"So let's all congratulate Nyla. Hooray for Nyla." I know I'm being a brat, but I can't seem to stop—my rage over what's happening with Mom and the green monster suddenly converge into one giant fire-breathing dragon. "And she's such a freaking saint, too."

Nyla stands up slowly. "I'm sorry, Cass."

"Yeah, that makes it all better."

"Whoa," says Ronnie. "Let's all calm down, okay?"

"Yeah, let's breathe for a minute," Bender says.

"I don't need to breathe," I snap. "I am breathing."

"Hey, you won, too," Nyla reminds me hotly. "You got a scholarship—"

"To a place I don't want to go! And why don't I want to go there, Nyla? Oh, right, because *you* made me go look at College of Idaho. Because *you* knew I'd fall in love with it. And of course *you* didn't even consider how much it would cost!"

"I didn't know it was so expensive," Nyla shoots back.

"Because money is not a problem for you!"

"Wait. Cass got a scholarship, too?" asks Alice. "I'm confused."

"To Boise State," Nyla explains. "They gave Cass a scholarship to BSU, practically a full ride." She turns to me. "You get to go to college, right? Lots of people don't. Lots of people don't get to go to school at all."

"Oh boy, *lucky* me. Meanwhile, why don't you go to Juilliard, then, just to rub in how lucky I am?"

"Okay, you're upset," Nyla says slowly. "I know. But we'll figure this out. Maybe we can—"

I stand up. "*We* are not going to do anything. This isn't your problem, Ny. Stop acting like you're the one in charge of everything. Leave me alone."

And with that, I storm out of the cafeteria.

Nyla finds me ten minutes later in the second-floor ladies' room, fuming near the back window. Clearly she didn't understand the words *leave me alone*.

"Go away, Ny," I sigh.

She checks the stalls. There's no one else in here. She takes a deep breath. "I'm sorry about your mom. I'm also sorry about being the one who pitched you C of I without checking the cost first. And about the scholarship. I really am sorry, Cass."

She's trying to make nice. She's about three seconds from saying, "I got you." And I can't let her. I still want to wallow in my anger and this seemingly never-ending disappointment that feels like it's choking me. I'm so sick of being the good girl, of pretending that stuff doesn't bother me, of always thinking about other people instead of myself. So I go ahead and say the worst thing I can think of.

"I'm not, like, even surprised they gave it to you," I say softly. "Of course they gave *you* the scholarship."

Nyla goes completely still. "What's that supposed to mean?"

"It looks better for them to give the scholarship to you, even though playing Helen Keller is way harder than playing Annie Sullivan. They'll always give you the award, because . . ." I shrug.

She sucks in a breath. "Tell me you did not just make this about my color."

I don't answer. I know I've gone too far, but there's really no calling it back.

"So you think I won because I'm black." She stares at me. "You said that to me. You."

"I didn't say that." It sounds so ugly when she puts it that way. "Look, I'm sorry," I mumble.

She folds her arms. "Oh, don't do that. Don't say you're sorry if you're not sorry."

"I'm *sorry*, okay?"

She shakes her head. "You need to get over yourself. But I get it. You're having a bad day."

I let out a bitter laugh. "You think? Try a bad year."

"The point is," she says stiffly, "I get it."

But the green monster's still inside me puffing smoke. "No. That's just it," I argue. "You *don't* get it. You're still going to end up with everything you want. You dream about something, and you get it, Nyles. I mean, how many times have I heard your mom tell you that you can do anything you set your mind to. Anything, right? And you can. That's the absurd thing. You will."

Nyla scoffs. "We all have our problems, Cass. Don't act like you have the market cornered on hardships."

"What hardships do you have, exactly?"

Nyla flinches. "You not getting to go to the college you want is not the most tragic thing that could happen."

I throw my hands up in the air. "I know it's not!" I practically scream. "My mom's going to *die*, and *then* I won't go to the college I want. And then I don't even know. I'll probably end up as a drama teacher in a dumpy little apartment with a bunch of cats and no life, and meanwhile you'll go to USC or Juilliard or wherever else you'd like to hang out and be a movie star and live in a mansion on the beach and forget all about me." I turn away from her. "Go back to your charmed life and leave me alone."

"My life has not always been charmed. You know that."

"Oh, don't bring up Africa," I say. "That's not happening to you right now. You're fine."

She gets the face—the one I know means she's about to put the smack down. "I am not fine!" she says so loudly her voice reverberates off the bathroom tiles. "I lost my whole family! My language! My culture! That was my life! You. Don't. Know. Anything."

"Come on," I screech back. "You don't remember that stuff. You were a baby."

"That makes it worse!" she yells. "You selfish little—" Her fists clench like she's going to punch me but instead she presses one to her mouth, probably to hold in a swear. She makes a disgusted noise in the back her throat. "This is my fricking nightmare right here. I'm going to go."

I turn away, the word *selfish* still ringing in my ears. "You do that."

She stops at the door of the bathroom. "I'll be waiting for an apology from you when you start being yourself again. Unless this is yourself. In which case, don't bother."

Then she's gone.

I wilt down against the sink, exhausted, ashamed at my own reflection. Then I run and throw up in one of the toilets until I feel entirely empty. I wipe my mouth with a paper towel, feeling all-over sour. We've had fights before, Nyla and me. We've said things we didn't mean. We're both pretty emotional.

But not like this.

I'm losing everything, it seems. My dreams. My mom.

And I think I might have just lost my best friend.

25

The nice thing about having a total meltdown at school is that everyone leaves you alone for the rest of the day. Happily I make it through my remaining classes without puking or crying. I go to Mama Jo and ask to be in the play again, and she (*of course, whatever you need*) agrees. I rehearse diligently all evening, hitting every note, delivering every line perfectly, trying to ignore the whispering that's going on between my castmates and the deafening silence that's rolling off Nyla. And then I go home, slam my bedroom door because it feels like the only thing I can do at this point, put on my pajamas at like eight p.m., and sit on my bed, scrolling through past texts on my phone.

Don't let the bedbugs bite.

See, this is why I love you.

I'm sorry, I text Nyla at last. *I really am.*

It's okay. Don't worry about it, she types back almost immediately, which is not the reply I was hoping for. Because it doesn't mean she forgives me. But really, how could she forgive me? After what I said?

She doesn't text again.

There's a knock on my bedroom door. Dad. Who I assumed was still at the hospital.

"I come bearing soup." He's got a big bowl of minestrone on a tray with crackers, a glass of milk—which hasn't been my drink of choice for years, but okay—and a sliced apple. I move my legs so he can set the tray on my bed.

"I heard you had a rough day," he says. "And you know I'm a firm believer in the power of soup to make things better. So eat up."

"Who told you? Nyla?"

He scrunches up his eyebrows and looks mildly guilty. "No, uh, Ronnie's little sister is one of my students, and I saw her mother at pickup . . ."

I sigh. There are sixty thousand residents of the city of Idaho Falls. It's not a small town. But our part of it all at once feels very small and gossipy. "Oh, good. So everyone knows."

"Yep. I think so."

At least nobody else was there to hear the last part of my conversation with Nyla. The worst part. The part she's never going to forgive me for.

"Eat," orders Dad.

I take a bite of the soup. It's delicious. Mom always gets the credit for being the culinary genius in the family, but I forget sometimes that Dad also has mad skills in this area. The soup warms its way down into my stomach, and I do, weirdly, feel slightly better.

Dad sits down on the other end of my bed. "You want to talk about it?"

"Definitely not."

"I mean, I do know some of the story. Because you were apparently yelling in the middle of the cafeteria."

"I'm sorry."

"The way I hear it, I'm not the one you should apologize to."

"I apologized," I snap. "But okay, Dad. Take her side."

"There's no side. Cass. Honey. There isn't a competition, in life, for who gets to endure the most pain."

I take another bite. "I know. But if there was, I would totally win."

He leans back and looks at me, hard, like he's deciding what to say. "A while back, maybe three or four years ago, I had a conversation with Nyla's dad at a barbecue one night, and he told me about when Nyla first came to their family. There was a period there when things were pretty bad. Nyla didn't speak English. She cried all the time. She had terrible nightmares. She used to bite her parents, like hard enough to break the skin. And she'd hide sometimes, and it would take hours to find her. It wasn't easy."

Guilt tears at me. I didn't know any of that. She never told me.

Dad still has more to say. "The point is not that Nyla had it tough, although she did. It's that we all have it tough sometimes. Even those of us who seem on the outside like we're fine."

"What, like you?"

"I'm not fine." He stares down at the floor like there's some kind of message scrawled across my carpet. "I haven't been what you'd call fine in more than a year."

"Me, neither."

He scratches at his beard. "Before this, like way before this, there was a rough patch where your mom and I were trying to get pregnant, and we had two miscarriages. We blew our entire savings on fertility treatments that made your mom cranky and crazy, and then we lost the babies. So we decided to adopt, and we went with an open adoption at first, and we were matched with a birth mother, and we fixed up this room as a nursery, and we waited, so excited, and then that woman decided not to give us her baby, after all. And we were just . . . crushed."

"God, I'm sorry, Dad."

"It was a rough patch," he says. "This, right here, right now, this is a rough patch. And it could get rougher. It probably . . . it probably will."

A shiver goes down my spine at the thought of Mom actually being gone. Her casket. Her funeral. Her grave.

"So you're angry," he says. "That's fair."

"I'm sorry." Tears flood my eyes.

"Don't be sorry for how you feel. Feel what you need to feel. Own your feelings." He puts his arm around me. Sighs. "I'm mad, too. God, I'm mad. I had this perfect life, and now . . ." His lips twist unhappily. "But when you're going through a rough patch, you have to lean on the people who love you. Like Nyla. Like me. You can have your bad moments. You can even freak out on people. That's human. But you have to try to make it right, after. And you have to find your way through together. Got it?"

"Got it."

"Good."

I wipe at my eyes. "How'd you get so fricking wise?"

"Oh, I'm making stuff up," he admits. "I don't know anything except how to teach fifth graders about the scientific method."

I try to laugh a little. "Okay, Dad."

He stays there until I eat the rest of my dinner. And then he says, "With regard to the scholarship."

I sigh. "Do we have to talk about this?"

"Yes. We have to. As you know, I would be thrilled if you went to BSU."

"Dad—"

"But nobody's going to force you to go to Boise State, honey. We can still try with College of Idaho. I'll do my best. You do your best. And, who knows, maybe something will . . . change, with our financial situation." He hugs me. "What I mean to say is, go, Yotes."

I am the most spoiled, ungrateful person ever to walk the planet.

He gets up and goes to the door, then stops and stares at it for a second. "You've never slammed your door before," he says in this bewildered tone. "That was such teenage behavior I almost didn't know what to do. Would you like me to leave for the night so you can throw a secret kegger and wreck our house? Am I going to get a call from school telling me that you've been cutting school so you can ride around town with a boy on a motorcycle? I don't know if I can handle you being a regular teenager."

"I didn't even know you were home. Sorry."

He gives this sad little laugh. "You want to hang out with the old man?"

"Aren't you going to the hospital?" I should go back to the hospital. But Mom said she didn't want me there.

"She's with Uncle Pete tonight," Dad says. "They need some alone time, I think."

I wrap a blanket around my shoulders. "I suppose I could hang out, old man."

We head for the living room. When I was a kid we used to sneak in here sometimes after Mom was asleep and watch reality TV together. Dad and I both have a thing for *Million Dollar Listing* and

House Hunters International and *Flip This House*. Not that either one of us has ever shown any interest in renovating our own home.

"So, not to bring up another sore subject . . . ," he says after we've made popcorn and are sitting on the couch watching a married couple bicker as they bash through a possibly-load-bearing wall with a sledgehammer. He pauses the television. "How did your trip to the Bureau of Vital Records go?"

"You talked to Mom, right?"

"Correct."

"How did *she* say it went?"

He smooths down his beard. "She said you didn't get the letter."

"Yep."

It's quiet for a minute. Then Dad sighs and says, "She also wants you to keep searching."

"I know."

"Do *you* want to keep searching?" he asks.

I turn to look at him. "Yes . . . and no." I shrug.

He gives a pained smile. "Right. Well, I think your mom's great. I married her, after all."

"She is great," I agree. "The greatest."

"But I think she's wrong. I think she needs to butt out of this adoption stuff. It's not her life."

"But she said *she* wanted to meet—"

He shakes his head. "It's not her life. It's yours. And you need to do what's best for you."

I bite my lip.

"You got it?" Dad asks.

"I got it," I whisper.

He unpauses the television. We watch for a few minutes, but then I reach over and pause it again.

"Dad? Do *you* want me to search for my birth mother?"

"It doesn't matter what I want." But I can tell that he's doing the thing where he "respects my autonomy."

We go back to watching our shows until it's almost midnight. Then right as I get up to go to bed for real this time, he says, "Wait. Cass."

I sit back down.

He sighs. "The truth is, I don't want you to search for your birth mother. I mean, when your mom first brought it up, I hated the idea. I still do, really. I think it might be her worst idea ever. And she's had some doozies."

"You hate the idea," I repeat slowly.

He nods, not meeting my eyes. "It's like you said before. Your mom's your real mother. And maybe we need to focus on her right now."

I swallow, hard. "Okay."

He sighs and then changes his mind again. "But if you want to search, search. And if you don't, don't. It's your life. Say it with me."

"It's my life."

"That's my girl," he says.

But what I'm thinking in this moment is: none of us really get to have our own, separate lives. Our lives are always all horribly tangled up with the people around us. The people we love.

Dear X,

I had a dream about Ted. You remember, Dawson's roommate? (Also not his real name.) Geek poster boy? Skinny? Kind of grungy? Generally speaking, Ted's not my type, even if I was sure I had a type. I mean, if I was going to say I found a certain kind of guy attractive, I'd probably describe Dawson. Which is why I'm here.

    But I digress. It's not Dawson I had the dream about. Well, this particular dream did start out with Dawson. I dream about Dawson regularly. I'll go to his dorm to see him. Or I'll run into him somewhere—I've had dreams like that, where I happen upon Dawson by accident. Sometimes it feels like a good thing, and sometimes not.

    So earlier tonight I dreamed I was at the movies, and at some point I looked over, and there was Dawson, a few seats down and about a row up. He was sitting with another girl, a blonde, and from my vantage point, she was practically sitting in his lap. They were not watching the movie very closely, if you know what I mean. I could only tell that it was Dawson when they came up for air. So I was sitting there, in the dream, watching the guy I once thought I was in love with—the father of my child, I wanted to announce dramatically—pretty much doing it with someone else. And I felt jealous, sure. I could have ripped out the girl's pretty golden hair. I was mad, at him, though, for the most part. For forgetting me. But I also felt kind of, I don't know, accepting of the whole thing. Like it might not be a pleasant event to witness, Dawson and The Blonde, but it was all right. I don't own him.

And then someone touched the back of my hand, and I looked over, and, surprise!—I was sitting next to Ted.

"Hi," he whispered.

"Hi," I whispered back, and I instantly felt—good. Happy, even.

"Are you warm enough?" he asked.

"Actually," I said, "I'm hot."

"Oh, you've been hot for a while," he said, and leaned in to kiss me.

Ted! Kissing me! And I don't know how to put this delicately, but I was into it.

But that's when I woke up.

Let's psychoanalyze this, shall we? What is my subconscious trying to tell me with dreams like this? Here's what I think my brain is trying to share:

Don't fall for guys like Dawson.

Fall for guys like Ted.

Lesson learned, brain. Lesson learned. But maybe it's too little, too late.

It was the Fourth of July today. I mean, it's still the Fourth of July, as it's not midnight for another seventeen minutes. I always feel compelled to write you a letter on days that are out of the ordinary. I don't know why. This isn't a journal. At least that's what I keep telling myself.

I've never been big on the whole Independence Day thing. So we're a country. Big whoop. I guess that makes me less than patriotic. I just never thought it made sense to be full of pride for your country, simply because you happened to be born there. Why should I think America is the greatest country in the entire world? Because I was born in Denver, Colorado? But if I was born in say, Finland, would I still think the US was the greatest country? Nope, I'd think the greatest country is Finland. And I might be right. Finland does sound pretty cool.

It doesn't seem like a good enough reason to form such a strong opinion, is what I'm saying.

Anyway. We didn't do too much to celebrate the holiday here at Booth. They served us barbecue ribs and corn on the cob and potato salad and watermelon, and we totally pigged out. We're eating for eight, between the four of us.

And when it got dark, Melly popped some popcorn and put it in a huge bowl and we went out on the front step of the school, facing the street, and she produced a container full of little fireworks that she bought at Target.

And I thought, wait, Target doesn't sell actual fireworks. That I would know. I worked for Target last summer. Which was like the most boring three months of my life.

"Okay, pick one," Melly directed Brit. "Pick a good one."

Brit chose one of the columns. It turned out to be a smoke bomb. Its only trick was to make a large cloud of green smoke.

"Wow. That is truly awe-inspiring," I said.

"That is just so beautiful," added Amber.

We shared a smirk. Amber's growing on me. She does have a sense of humor when the occasion calls for it. I am beginning to feel sorry that I gave her that black eye that one time.

"Pick another one," Melly said, and held the box out to Amber.

She grabbed the biggest one.

"Prepare to have your socks blown off," she said.

That one was a smoke bomb, too. Pink smoke, this time, and a shrieking sound that made you squirm around inside me, X, but no colored sparks or patterns.

Melly handed the box to Teresa. She inspected each "firework" carefully.

"They are all smoke bombs," she announced.

"What? No!" Melly cried.

But they were. Told you Target doesn't sell fireworks.

All Melly had for us then was a few boxes of snaps. You know, the kind you throw on the ground to make a popping sound? We spent a few minutes throwing them at each other's feet and screaming and stepping on them to make them pop. It was funny, but it also left me feeling jumpy and irritable. But I guess everything lately makes me jumpy and irritable.

"I'm sorry, girls," Melly said when we were out of snaps. "I blew it this year."

"It's fine," I told her. "Pregnancy and real fireworks are probably not the smartest combination."

"Good point."

We went in and tried to go to bed. I don't know about the others, but I can't sleep much these days. It's too hot. There's a window box air conditioner in this room, but it doesn't work that well. And tonight there's so much noise outside. The whole city is blowing shit up. The sky outside my

251

window is going all different colors. Dogs are howling in terror. Patriotic country music is blasting from a house down the street. Finally I dozed for what felt like a minute and had that dream about Ted in the movie theater, and then I woke up all hot and bothered in a different way.

It's quiet now, though. That's nice.

I just put my hand on my stomach and felt you move in there again. I'm starting to feel your body parts, like your elbow or foot poking into my bladder, which is the weirdest. I can never picture how you're situated, though. I think I might be rubbing your head, but then Melly tells me I'm probably patting you on the butt.

I still have to talk to Dawson and try to make him fill out the non-identifying information form, and I'm guessing he's going to need to sign the other paperwork, too, for you to be adopted.

But school's out. I don't even know where to find him. I called his dorm room a few nights ago, and no one answered. Which makes sense because, like I said, school is out. I guess I'm going to have to wait for it to start up again. Maybe by then I'll have figured out what to say to him about you.

Ugh. Hold on for a minute, X. I have to pee.

Back. So I shuffled over to the bathroom and when I was out in the hall, I heard crying.

Goddamnit, I thought. Why can I never get a good night's sleep? What is it this time?

But it took a while to figure out, because whoever it was crying wasn't in the bathroom or the kitchen or the living room. She wasn't in Melly's room, where Melly was spread out like a starfish in the middle of her bed, snoring like a bear. She wasn't in Teresa's room, where Teresa sat up and said, "What's the matter?" in a worried voice, because she'd heard the crying, too, or in Amber's room, where Amber jerked awake when I opened the door.

That left Brit. Sure enough, her room was empty. Teresa and Amber and I stood at the foot of her bed staring at the pile of twisted blankets and the dark spread of water on the sheets.

Amber stated the obvious: "So Brit's in labor."

No shit. But where was she?

We went from room to room again, checking. No Brit. We wandered outside and started poking around behind bushes and looking in all the dark corners of the buildings. We must have been a strange sight, three heavily pregnant girls in the middle of the night searching the grounds like we were on some kind of Easter egg hunt. But we didn't find her outside.

"We should wake Melly," Teresa said when we came back inside.

"Wait." I held up my hand for us all to be quiet. We stood in the living room, holding our breath, until there was a noise. Not a crying sound this time so much as a heavy groaning. I moved toward where the sound was coming from, which turned out to be a corner behind the couch. Brit wasn't there, either. But there was a heating vent. I struggled to get down next to it, listening.

The groaning came again.

I straightened. "Is there a boiler room? Somewhere that feeds to the furnace?"

None of us knew, but we went around checking doors, until we found one in the back of the kitchen that led down a set of stairs. When we opened that door we could hear the noise more clearly. She was definitely down there.

We should have woken Melly. I don't know why we didn't wake her right away, once we understood the situation. But maybe we didn't *because we automatically knew that Brit must have gone down in the basement to hide, and she had a reason. Maybe we wanted to respect that.*

We found her sitting on the concrete floor next to the water heater, the whole bottom of her nightgown wet with amniotic fluid, her face red and streaked with tears. Instinctively the three of us dropped down to circle her.

"I'm all right," she said, wiping at her face. "I'm fine."

"Um, no, I don't think you're fine." I brushed her hair back from her face. "What are you doing?"

"I was curious about what was down here," she said.

"Okay," said Amber. "Well, what's down here is the water heater and the water softener and the furnace." She clapped her hands together. "So now we know. Let's all go upstairs."

"No," Brit said. "I want to stay here." Then a spasm passed through her and she made a rough, grinding sort of noise in her throat, and sat back, breathing hard.

"I'm fine," she said again, when she could talk.

This, X, is what we call a predicament.

"Your baby is coming," Teresa said gently. "You need to go to the hospital."

"No!" Brit cried with a vehemence that startled all of us. "She's not coming. She's not supposed to come for another week."

Oh man.

"I think babies make up their own minds about when they're supposed to come," I said. "Tricky little creatures."

"No," Brit insisted. "I still have another week."

We all looked at each other helplessly. What could we do? Then another contraction hit her, hard. Sweat popped up on her forehead. I could see the whites of her eyes rolling back a little. She grabbed my hand and squeezed it so tight I lost feeling in the tips of my fingers.

"Brit," I said slowly. "I think it's time, sweetie."

"No." She started to cry. "No. I don't want to go. I like it here."

"You can come back," Amber said. "We'll all be here, waiting for you."

"Yes, we'll be waiting," Teresa added.

"But I don't want to go." Brit shook her head, sending her tangled red hair back into her face. "I'm not ready."

"Brit," I said.

No answer.

"Brit, come on."

"No" was all she said. "No, no." And then she groaned again.

I didn't have a watch, but these contractions seemed pretty close together. I glanced at Amber. The last thing any of us wanted was to deliver a baby down here. We needed to wake Melly. We needed to call an ambulance. Now.

Amber nodded and then slipped up the stairs. Brit didn't seem to notice.

"Brit, look at me," I ordered her. "Look at me."

She shuddered and then met my eyes.

"Tell me about the baby," I said carefully. "Tell us what she's going be like."

I'd heard her talk about it a dozen times, maybe more. This fantasy she had. Which was so much easier for her than the reality.

"She's a girl," Brit panted. "She's going to have red hair, like me, and freckles."

"I have freckles, see?" I said, pointing at my cheek. This counts as the one time in my life my freckles might have ever been useful. "Maybe this baby will get them, too?" I glanced down at my belly—at you, X, and you shifted so hard I could see it through my shirt. Like you were agreeing or something.

A tear slipped down Brit's cheek. "I get one more week with her. One more week. I don't want to go now." She sniffled and wiped her nose on the sleeve of her nightgown. "She's going to be smart. And beautiful. And perfect. And when she's old enough, we'll find each other again. I'll tell her everything."

"That will be so great," I said.

"Yes," agreed Teresa faintly. "What a wonderful day that will be."

Another contraction hit Brit. She almost screamed with it this time.

I could hear the faint sound of sirens. St. Luke's was less than ten minutes away. If Amber had done her job, the ambulance would be here soon.

"Brit," I urged as gently as I could. "Brit, it's time to go."

"No," she said. "Please."

"I know you don't want to," I said. "But the baby is coming. You know she's coming. She wants out, and it wouldn't be good to try to stop her. You've got to think about what's best for her, Brit."

"What's best for her," she repeated. "Okay."

I got an arm under her, and Teresa came in on the other side, and we hoisted her up between us and started for the stairs. We went upstairs slowly, one step at a time. We had to stop in the middle for another contraction. When we reached the top, there was Melly, once again wearing her rumpled hair and pj's and perfectly calm expression.

"Hello, Brit," she said.

"Hello," Brit replied. Then she turned to me again and grabbed my arm. She looked like a little girl who'd swallowed a basketball. "Why can't I be what's best for her?"

I knew exactly what she meant. But I didn't know the answer.

We moved slowly through the kitchen and out into the front hall. Amber was there, holding Brit's flip-flops and a hairbrush. Teresa hurried to her room and got her robe, which she tucked around Brit's shoulders even though it wasn't cold. Red and blue lights started to blaze through the windows. The sirens were off now, but there was a squeak of brakes as the ambulance pulled up to the curb.

Brit seemed calmer. She walked without help to the bottom of the stairs. The paramedics were cheerful as they helped her into a gurney and loaded her into the ambulance, Melly climbing in beside her. They didn't turn the sirens back on as they drove away, only the lights.

We lingered on the front step—me and Amber and Teresa—the lights splashing us like fireworks, finally fireworks, and we watched the ambulance until it was out of sight.

Then we came back in and went off to our rooms without another word. I sat down at my desk and tried to think of how I would describe it all to you, what happened, what I feel now.

What do I feel?

I don't know. Sad. Scared. Tired. And like I'm not ready, either. It's weird, but I don't want our time to be over yet.

I guess I'm just not ready to let you go.

S

26

I'm not ready, I think as I watch my mom open her Christmas presents.

We're having Christmas at Thanksgiving break, because Christmas is too far away, and Christmas is my mom's favorite thing after cake. We have a little fake tree set up in the corner of her hospital room, and I've strung Christmas lights around the window, and Dad and I are both wearing ugly Christmas sweaters (Dad's features a polar bear with a puff-ball nose and mine has a gingerbread man with his legs broken off that says, "Oh, Snap!") along with oversized Santa hats. We're going all out. Christmas turkey. Christmas cookies. Christmas songs. The Blu-ray of *A Christmas Story*, Mom's favorite holiday movie, playing on the hospital television. The other patients in my mom's hall must think we've gone crazy. And maybe we have.

We've laughed a lot this week. Enjoyed each other. Savored every candy cane, so to speak. But all I keep thinking is that I'm not ready. I'm not ready for this to be the last Christmas I get with my mom.

"Oh, Bill," Mom breathes as she unwraps a little black velvet box. Inside, I already know, is a pair of pearl earrings that I helped Dad pick out for her. Mom's never liked diamonds. She prefers pearls. They're more beautiful, she always says, because they're formed by a living thing with a great deal of effort.

"These are gorgeous," she says, pushing her cannula up on her face a little. "Thank you."

I wait for her to say that he shouldn't have, that they're too expensive. Mom's always been frugal, even when we had money, but she doesn't say anything but that she loves them, and then she closes the box and puts it next to her bed. She can't wear them. You're not supposed to wear jewelry in the hospital.

Which means maybe she's not even going to wear them while she's alive.

"And for you, Boo." Dad hands me a box. "From your mother and me."

I open it. It's another box, a flat white box with different-colored columns along the bottom. *Welcome to you*, it reads.

I glance up. "What is this?"

"A DNA test," Dad explains. He seems a bit jumpy about it, like he's not sure I'm going to like this. Or he's not sure if he does.

But Mom's smiling. "We know that you have questions that we can't give you the answers to. So we thought—I thought, anyway—that this might help you with that."

"Okay," I say slowly. "Thank you."

It's been almost a month since I went to the Vital Records office, and I've heard nothing more about this mysterious letter that may or may not exist. Which is probably, I think now, a good thing.

"I'd like to get a DNA test myself," Mom says. "See if what your grandma's been telling me all my life about our ancestry is actually true. She says we're German, Swiss, and Welsh. She claims that's where we get our light hair but dark eyebrows from—the Welsh."

Grandma and Uncle Pete are supposed to be here later. I wonder what Grandma's going to say to the idea of this DNA test.

"I'm content not to know that stuff," Dad says. "No one defines me."

"You have red hair, freckles, green eyes, your middle name is Patrick, and you bear the last name McMurtrey. With you it's obvious." Mom has no problem defining him. "You're Scottish, sweetie. With a generous dollop of Irish thrown in there, I'm sure."

"I'm my own man," Dad says like he didn't hear her.

I open the kit. Inside is this weird little tube I'm supposed to spit in. Like, a lot of spit—up to a certain line that's printed on the vial. My heart's beating fast again, but if I think about it, this test is less scary than any of the other adoption-related stuff. I don't have to search for anything or try to find anyone. I can spit in a tube, and I'll get answers.

It's a nice gift. Thoughtful. "Thank you," I say again.

Mom squeezes my hand three times.

"So I've been meaning to ask you . . . ," she says.

Oh boy. "What?"

"What's going on between you and Nyla?"

"Nothing." And that's the truth, sort of. On the outside, everything looks the same. I go to school, and I have lunch with the same friends, at the same table. I see Nyla almost every single day, and we talk about the regular stuff, mostly: class, theater, rehearsal, repeat. We even laugh at each other's jokes. We act like nothing happened.

That's the worst part. I've apologized, like twice now, and Nyla's technically accepted my apology, so it feels like now we should be moving on. Only we're not, really. I can feel it. We can sit in the same spot in the lunchroom and talk about the same things, but there's a wall between us now. I've lost Nyla's trust. She can be the bigger person about it, and say it's okay, but she hasn't forgiven me.

If she were mad, I could handle that. I could apologize again. I could make her believe that I mean it. But there's nothing I can do now that I've said I'm sorry and she's said it's okay. It's like that topic is closed. Possibly forever.

It feels like the entire school is mad at me, too. Ever since I lost it in the cafeteria, no one has looked at me the same way. Everybody's still friendly. They smile at me. They ask about Mom. They make small talk. But they're keeping me at a distance, too. Even Ronnie and Alice and Bender.

In other words, I've ruined pretty much everything, but it kind of feels like it doesn't matter. Because my time with my mom is running out.

"Did you and Nyla have a fight?" Mom asks, and I look at Dad. He shakes his head. He didn't tell her.

"No," I outright lie to my mom. "Why, has she said something?"

"No," Mom says, frowning. "But lately you don't talk about her, and when she's here, she doesn't talk about you. Which is not normal behavior from either of you."

"We're busy, is all," I insist. "We're fine."

I feel bad for lying, but I want my mother's world to be like a frozen lake. Perfectly still. No ripples. No waves.

261

"Busy with the play," Mom says.

"Yes. The play."

We're still a couple weeks away from the performance. I've been dutifully keeping up with school and rehearsals, and slipping in to see Mom every other free minute, and Mom's still here. But even if she's still around two weeks from now, they wouldn't let her leave the hospital to go see the play. And it's not like the doctors gave us an exact date. They said six weeks. If that. I've decided those words—*if that*—are the worst thing, worse even than knowing she's dying. Because they mean anytime. At any moment, she could make her exit.

"And the boy?" Mom asks slyly. "How's Bastian?"

I hate to think about how Bastian was there, that day in the cafeteria. He got a front row seat to my moment of crazy. I keep remembering the way he said "Hey" and tried to take my hand, but I didn't let him. So I've probably ruined things with Bastian, too. Even if he's miraculously still interested in me, romance has been the last thing on my mind lately, but I'll play along for Mom's sake. "We're going to start practicing the make-out scene with real kissing soon."

Dad groans. "I don't want to hear this."

Mom grins. "I see. You'll have to report back."

"Yes, ma'am."

"Nyla seems to like him," Mom says.

I've noticed. Nyla and Bastian are becoming fast friends, it seems. They've got so many scenes together, after all, Cinderella and Cinderella's prince, and they're hanging out more now that Nyla and I are hanging out less. Maybe Bastian will end up as Nyla's boyfriend. I can't even call up the emotional energy to be jealous.

"So Nyla was here?" I ask Mom. "When?"

"Yesterday."

I try to keep my voice light. "What did she say?"

"She's been busy, too, making audition videos for all these colleges she's applying to. Do you need to do a video for College of Idaho?"

"No, I'm going to audition in person," I answer. "That's not until January."

"Oh, good," she says. "I know you're going to blow them away."

I hope so, because I obviously still need as much in the way of scholarships as I can get. But lately it's like my parents aren't worried about the money anymore. They both seem to have accepted that I'm going to C of I, even though I only applied a couple weeks ago, even though I haven't been accepted yet, even though I don't know how I'll pay for it. Mom especially keeps talking about what things will be like when I go to college. When I'm living at College of Idaho. When I'm gone.

Like I'm the one leaving her.

"Who wants alcohol-free eggnog?" Dad says suddenly.

"Um, yuck." I pretend to gag.

Mom raises her hand. "Me, definitely me!"

Dad goes out to the hall. I think he left the eggnog in the fridge in the nurse's lounge.

"I used to make an eggnog cupcake with spiced rum," Mom remembers mournfully.

I remember, too. I don't like eggnog, and I thought that cupcake was divine.

"Oh, go catch your father and tell him I'd like cinnamon. He always remembers the nutmeg but forgets the cinnamon. They should have some in the cafeteria."

I dash into the hall. Where I nearly run smack into Dad outside the nurse's lounge, leaning against the wall. Crying.

I've only seen him cry once since my mom had her heart attack. It was after the first surgery. We'd been up all night in the waiting room, waiting to find out if she was alive, and then the surgeon came out and told us that she'd made it, and Dad started to sob. I'd never seen him like that. This time it isn't the sobbing kind of crying. It's a quiet suffering. He's holding it all in, still. Trying to be brave.

He doesn't see me, so he's surprised when I throw my arms around him.

"Oh," he says. "Oh, hi. I'm sorry, Boo."

"Don't be sorry," I tell him. "You have to feel what you feel, right?"

"It's just, I'm not ready," he says, wiping at his eyes. "I'm not prepared to go on without her."

"I know," I whisper. "I know."

27

I'm not ready, I think again as I stand on the stage with Bastian.

Mama Jo claps her hands together. "Okay, everybody out but Bastian, Cass, Nyla, and Bender. We're going to give Bastian and Cass some privacy to actually practice the kissing scene. So Nyla and Bender, you have to stay, obviously, because you're going to need to be part of this scene in the middle, but don't gawk at them, okay? Let's be sensitive."

The rest of the cast files out of the theater. Then Bastian and I are essentially alone. Up on the stage. Under the lights.

Bastian exhales with a short "whew" sound and smiles at me nervously. "Oh, wait," he says, digging into his pocket. "I came prepared."

He produces two tubes of lip balm and gives me first choice at picking mine: orange or cherry flavored. I pick orange, because I loathe anything cherry. He nods and opens the cherry one and makes a big show of slathering his lips. I do the same.

I think we may slide right past each other.

"Also—" He goes for the other pocket and holds up a little container of orange Tic Tacs.

"I love those!" I gasp.

"I know."

"You know?"

"Nyla told me."

I glance over at Nyla, who's talking to Bender offstage. She meets my gaze over his shoulder, then looks away.

"Are you two ready?" Mama Jo asks.

No, I think. My stomach rolls. Don't puke, I tell myself sternly. That would not be sexy.

It's not like it's a big deal. It's just business, really. It's acting. That's all. It's silly that Mama Jo always makes a production out of the first kiss rehearsal. She thinks this is going to make it easier, but this is somehow worse than if we'd been kissing in rehearsals all along. It puts a false importance on what is, in the end, only a kiss.

"Cass?" Bastian's looking at me.

I didn't answer Mama Jo's question: Am I ready?

"Yeah," I say quickly. "Let's do it."

It's only a kiss, I tell myself.

"Be patient with me," Bastian whispers as the music starts. "I'm new at this."

"This?"

"I've never kissed a girl before," he admits, scratching his eyebrow.

I find this incomprehensible. Bastian is hot. He's funny. He's smart—he memorized his lines before any of the rest of us. He quotes Shakespeare at random times. He has a voice that could melt any heart into a puddle of butter. How is it possible that Bastian Banks has never kissed anyone?

"All right. Places," calls Mama Jo, and I don't have time to question Bastian about this, because we start on opposite ends of the stage. And we end up (breathe, Cass, breathe) kissing.

It goes okay. Bastian, as the confident, womanizing prince, sings, "May I kiss you?"

Then we kiss. It's that simple. His lips, my lips.

It's supposed to be a little awkward, actually, since the baker's wife is completely shocked that this handsome prince would be interested in kissing her.

"May I kiss you?" Bastian's hands are at my waist. Pulling me into him. His mouth touches mine, soft and supple and not at all slimy with cherry-flavored lip stuff. He smells good—I'd almost forgotten how amazing he smells, like the bar of Irish Spring at Grandma's house, and orange candy, and sandalwood, or whatever it is they put in guy's cologne.

"Keep your body stiff at first, because the baker's wife is shocked," Mama Jo directs me. "But then go limp. Give in to it. Put your hand up to his face."

I do as she says. This is so weird, I think, choreographing a kiss. His cheek under my palm is soft, as smooth as mine, and warm.

"Now break," Mama Jo says.

"No," I gasp, stumbling away from Bastian. "We can't. You have a princess. And I have . . . a baker."

Mama Jo chuckles. "Great," she says. "Let's stop there for a minute. How was that?"

I turn to Bastian. "How was it?"

It was . . . only a kiss.

He puts a hand to his chest. "I felt the earth move."

I laugh, but it comes out as a snort. I put my hand over my mouth.

"So that was the first kiss," Mama Jo says briskly, all business now. "Let's do the next one."

Right. There are *five* kisses.

It's going to be an interesting night.

28

"Hey you, come down to earth." Grandma jostles me.

"What?" I glance up at my mom and grandmother. I haven't been listening to what Mom's been saying for about five minutes, which makes me feel a stab of guilt. She only has a certain amount of words left. I shouldn't miss any.

"How was it?" Mom asks again, gently.

"It? The kissing scene?"

Her eyebrows lift. "Oh, the kissing scene? Was that today?"

Grandma scowls. "What kissing scene?"

Crap. "Yes. It went fine. He told me I was his first kiss."

Mom gasps. "Get out."

"I know!"

"Is this that boy you're going to have sex with?" Grandma asks.

"No, Grandma." I glance at the door for the nurse. "I'm not going to have sex."

"His first kiss, hmm," Mom says. "That's a big deal. How did it go?"

"It was . . . a kiss."

"No fireworks, huh?" Grandma says. "Too bad. That happens sometimes."

"Yeah, but this was stage kissing," I argue. "It's not like real kissing. It's a performance. You're not supposed to really feel anything. Usually."

"Did you feel something?"

"Don't answer that question." Grandma makes a face. "We do not need to know what you felt."

"Grandma! Geez!"

Mom's laughing. And then she's coughing. And coughing. We all sober up a bit.

"What did Nyla say?" Mom asks when she can talk again. "When you told her this was his first kiss?"

"Um . . ."

"What's going on with you and Nyla?" Grandma asks.

"Yes," Mom says. "What's going on?"

"I told you."

"You didn't tell me. You lied to me about it."

"I did not. I—"

"You're lying right now," Mom says, then sighs like she's too tired for this crap. "I'm your mother. I can tell when you're lying. Remember that time with your rubber duck in the bathtub?"

"Don't lie to your mother," Grandma says.

"Okay!" I burst out. "We had a fight. At the drama competition, Nyla got this amazing scholarship, and I didn't, and I was mad because I need that money, and she doesn't need it, and I said . . . I said . . ."

Mom's eyes are sad. "What did you say?"

"I said something . . . racist."

"Oh shit," says Grandma.

"What did you say?" Mom asks.

I tell her.

"Yep, that's racist," Grandma assesses.

Mom's mouth is a flat line. She actually looks mad, and (gulp) ashamed. "Do you think you're better than Nyla?"

"No!"

"Then why did you say what you said?"

"Because—" I have to stop and think about this for a minute. "Because I was hurt, and I was jealous, and I wanted to hurt her, too."

Mom nods silently. "Did you tell her you were sorry?"

"Yes, but things haven't been the same since then."

"Some wounds take time to heal," Mom says. "In the meantime, you have to decide whether or not it's okay to say something racist, for any reason. If that's who you want to be."

I swallow. "Right."

She touches my cheek. "Everything's going to be all right, sweetie. You'll mend things between you and Nyla—you've been friends for too long for it to end over a single sentence. You'll go to College of Idaho, and Nyla will go wherever Nyla decides to go, and you'll miss each other terribly, and you'll think about this horrible fight you had and shake your head about how wrong you were and how much growing up you still had to do."

"I miss her now," I admit.

Things are quiet for a while, with only the *beep beep beep* of her monitor.

"Mom," I say, because clearly it's a night for being honest, and maybe she'll be honest, too. "Why do you keep saying that I'm going to go to College of Idaho like it's a sure thing?"

"Well," she says.

"Don't say the universe. Even if I get in—"

"Oh, for heaven's sake, you'll get in," Grandma says.

"It's so much money. Money we still don't have. And yes, I'll get scholarships, maybe, but even if I get the highest possible theater scholarship and the highest possible academic scholarship, and even if I work full-time during the summers and part-time during the school year, I'll be short." Like ten thousand dollars a year short. I sat down and figured it out a few days ago.

Mom looks down at her hand with the IV. Curls and uncurls her fingers. Clears her throat lightly.

"Well," she begins softly, "when I . . ."

"There's life insurance money," Grandma says for her. "One smart thing your parents did—they got large life insurance policies when you came along, in case there was ever an accident. Or an illness, I suppose." Her lips tighten. "So when your mother . . ." Even she can't say it. "When she's not with us anymore, there'll be some extra money. Money for you to go to College of Idaho. Or wherever you'd like to go, honestly."

My eyes fill with stupid tears. It takes a minute for me to be able to talk again, and then I say what I've been thinking about ever since I didn't get the scholarship. Which is maybe I'm not meant to do all of this. Maybe my purpose right now is lying in a hospital bed in front of me, and I should focus on her.

"Thank you for telling me." I lean over to take Mom's hand. "But I'm not going to go."

She pulls back to look at me. "What?"

272

"I've decided not to go to college next year." I rush on before Mom can argue. "I'm going to stay home. Find a job. Save up. Because that's the responsible way to do things."

Grandma frowns. "Say that again—my hearing's not the best."

"Cass," Mom says, but then she flounders. "Honey, I—"

"College can wait."

She shakes her head. "You don't have to do that. College is months away. I won't be here."

"But Dad will be here. He'll be all alone." This isn't entirely true, either, I know. Dad has friends. And Uncle Pete. And Grandma, who's as much of a mother to him as my grandparents in Portland. But the thought of Dad sitting in our empty house when Mom's gone, with me four hours away, it feels wrong on a gut level.

Mom's shaking her head. "You can visit your father. You can call him, every day. You don't have to give up—"

"I'm not giving up," I tell her. "I'm only deciding what it is that I want. And this is what I want." I squeeze her hand three times. "This. Then after you—you get your heart, or whatever happens, after you . . ." I take a deep breath. "After you die . . ." My eyes flood with tears again, but I dash them away. "After everything's settled down, and I've had time to process it, too, you know? I'll go then. Will it make you feel better if I promise I'll go? Later?"

She's still shaking her head. "Baby, we can't let you—"

But then Grandma jumps in. "Yes, you can let her, Kitty Cat. She's asking for some time to grieve, and I don't think that's unreasonable. It's her decision, after all."

"Mama." Mom frowns.

"What? She's an adult. She can make the necessary decisions about her own life. Heaven knows you did when you were her age."

That shuts Mom up. Grandma's good at that.

"It's my life," I say softly.

"Okay," she murmurs.

For a minute we all sit here listening to her heart rate on the monitors, which is faster than I'd like it to be. I'm feeling perfectly calm, though. I feel better than I have in a long, long time.

It's the right thing. I've made the right decision. I feel it.

Grandma's smiling at me. She looks like Mom, or I should probably say that Mom looks like her. She's what Mom would end up looking like if she ever made it to old age.

"Shall we watch some television?" she asks. "I think we might still be able to catch *Wheel of Fortune*."

Mom and I both groan, but we indulge Grandma, who finds her show and starts shouting out the answers and calling the contestants morons when they don't instantly know the words on the board.

Mom looks sad, though. I wish she didn't look so sad. I hope that she'll come to understand that while this is a present I'm giving her, and Dad, too, I guess, it's also a gift for me.

The gift of time.

I only wish that time could be with her.

29

"Let the moment go!" I sing as hard as I can, lifting my face to the lights. "Don't forget it for a moment, though. Just remembering you've had an 'and' when you're back to 'or.' Makes the 'or' mean more than it did before. Now I understand . . . and it's time to leave the woods!"

This is still just a tech rehearsal, but from offstage I hear Bastian give a whoop of applause. I smile and turn a slow circle, getting my bearings among the large, fake trees that constitute our set. Then I (as the baker's wife) begin to count my steps again.

"Seventy-one, seventy-two, seventy-three . . ." I stop. There is the boom of a giant's footsteps. The caw of birds. Fake leaves rain down from above.

I look up in terror, and the lights change so a shadow seems to fall over me. There's the sound of a tree falling. I scream. And the lights go out.

Offstage again, I pull out my phone. I'm officially dead now, not on again until the end of the show, where I appear to give a pep talk to the baker. It's not so much time that I can go hang out in the green room, but enough time to mess around on my phone for a while.

Then I literally bump into Nyla.

"Sorry," I whisper.

"No problem." She's staring at me like she wants to say something. I wish she would *say something*. "Great job on your song."

"Thanks." I want to say *You too*, but she's headed to the stage to sing her big act two solo right now. I'm standing in the way. I take a few steps back and gesture at her to pass by.

"Thanks," she whispers.

You want to get something to eat, after? I want to ask her, but she's already past me.

I find a corner to hide in and turn my attention back to my phone. That's when I see the email. My eyes skim over the subject line: *You've Got A 100% Match!*

I reel myself back to the sender. Adoptedsearch.org.

My breath catches. I glance around, like I can feel the freak-out coming on, and I want to know if anyone's watching. No one is. I'm standing here in the dark, minding my own business, getting on with my life, and then, BAM.

Life-changing email.

My finger hovers over my phone, about to open it, but I stop myself. I'm in the middle of rehearsal here. It's probably not a good idea to read this email right now. I should wait until I get home. When I'm alone. And I can process.

But . . . it says a 100 percent match.

One hundred percent.

I click on the email.

Dear CassieintheRye,

We at adoptedsearch.org are pleased to inform you that there has been a perfect match to the profile you created on our site. When such a match occurs, we assign a member of our staff as a mediator to get in touch with both involved parties and verify the match. Later we also help arrange a meeting, if both parties desire a reunion.

Please respond promptly to this message with the dates and times that it would be most convenient for us to contact you, along with the best phone number where you can be reached.

Thank you for your patience. We'll be in touch soon.

Sincerely,

Jennifer Benway
Adoptedsearch.org

Time gets fuzzy. I read the email a bunch more times in rapid succession, and then I have to stuff the phone back in my pocket and hurry onto the stage, because I've almost missed my cue for the ghost scene.

I say my lines. I sing. I sing some more. We get to the curtain call song. My voice struggles on one of the high notes, when usually I reach it easily. I catch Nyla giving me a weird look when her back is turned to the audience, but I don't meet her eyes.

I shouldn't have opened the email, I think. I should have waited.

Then we're done for the night, and I hurry back to my phone to compose a reply.

Contact me anytime, I write. And give my number.

Dear X,

Okay, I'm ready, kid. Get out.

I'm only kind of kidding. I have about a month to go before my due date, but I'm already freaking enormous. I can't see my toes. I can't get up or down from a chair without major effort. I've got stretch marks. Swollen ankles. The works. I'm constipated, too. It's all your fault. You're almost fully baked in there. If you want to come early, that's fine by me.

School's back in session. The grounds are full of noise again. Babies crying. Girls laughing and gossiping like normal. Teachers droning away. I'm glad. It was too quiet this summer.

Teresa had her baby about three weeks ago. We were sitting around in the living room, each reading our own dog-eared copy of the What to Expect book, when Teresa sat up suddenly, made this little hmm noise, rubbed her back, and then went back to reading. This happened two more times before I caught on.

"Oh my God, are you having contractions?" I asked.

"I believe I am, yes." And she went back to reading.

"Braxton Hicks contractions, or the real kind?" I'd been having the Braxton Hicks myself, where I'll be minding my own business and suddenly all the muscles in my abdomen will lock up for a few seconds. It doesn't hurt, but it isn't exactly pleasant, either. Practice contractions, Melly calls them. My body is going over the exit strategy.

Anytime, X. Anytime.

"The real kind. It hurts," Teresa said.

"It hurts? How bad? On a scale of one to ten, one being like a stubbed toe—"

"Three," she answered. Then she frowned and rubbed her back again. "Four."

"So I should go get Melly?"

"Not yet," she said. "The book says it could be several hours, and the book says it's better to labor in the comfort of your own home for the first stage."

I squinted at her. "Are you thinking about hiding in the basement? Because I am not in the mood for stairs right now."

She smiled. "No. I will go when it's the right time."

"The right time for what?" We both looked up to see Amber with a plate of pickles and a peanut butter sandwich balanced on her giant belly. She's making us all look bad. She glanced from me to Teresa. "What's going on?"

"Teresa here is having contractions," I announced.

Amber's eyes widened. I always thought that Amber's eyes should be, well, amber in color. But they're dark brown. Her hair's not amber, either. There's nothing Amber about Amber.

"Should we get Melly?" she asked.

"No need yet," Teresa said.

"Melly told us she wants us to inform her immediately if we start having contractions."

"I know. But I don't want to bother her. She's dyeing her hair."

Little-known fact, X, but in the bottom floor of the old brick building that used to be the school that used to be the lying-in hospital there's a bunch of special sinks in a line, like the kind you'd find in an actual salon, because, back in the old days when the old brick building marked the very edge of town, and nobody in town was supposed to know about the pregnant girls who lived here, they had to do something about their hair. It was the sixties. Hair was a big deal. Now every six weeks or so, Melly goes over there to cover up her grays. So that's where she was.

"Are you going to hide in the basement?" Amber asked Teresa.

"That's what I said!" I exclaimed.

"No," Teresa said firmly, and also a little sadly. We haven't seen Brit. I mean, she's fine—she didn't die in childbirth or anything. She had her little girl, and that little girl did, indeed, as Melly reported to us, have red hair. Also according to Melly: Brit gave the baby up to the adoptive family without a hitch. But she didn't come back.

I guess that's not a surprise. What could she come back for?

"I'm going to miss you both." Teresa was obviously thinking the same thing.

So she sat there for a while, rubbing her back and frowning every seven to ten minutes, and then every five to seven minutes, and then she stood up.

"Does it even hurt?" Amber asked. "Or are you like the toughest chick on the planet?"

"It hurts. It's definitely a five now," Teresa answered.

"Are you going to get the epidural?" Amber said this like the epidural is the good-quality weed. "I can't wait for the epidural."

"God gave Eve pain in childbirth," Teresa said quietly. "To remind her of her sin."

"Bullshit," I said, which I probably shouldn't have, in retrospect. It's what Teresa believes. I should respect that, even if it's bullshit.

"I'm going to get my things," Teresa said, and waddled off down the hall toward her room.

Amber ran and got Melly, who drove Teresa to the hospital a few minutes later.

We haven't seen her since.

So then there were three weeks of just Amber and me, me and Amber, hanging out. I like her, but I kind of want to punch her again.

Anyway. Oh yeah, the point of this letter: I have good news. And I have bad news. Which do you want first?

I always pick the bad news first. So the good news can cheer me up from the bad news.

So bad news, it is.

Here goes: I called Dawson. College is back in business, too, and I called the number. But he wasn't there. Shocker, right? Ted answered. Also not a surprise.

I felt a little weird talking to Ted this time, because of the dreams. Yep. There's more than one now. The make-out-with-Ted dream is starting to be regularly scheduled programming in my brain.

"Is Dawson there?" I asked.

"He doesn't live here anymore," Ted said. "He moved to the Kappa house."

I'm sorry to inform you, X, but your biological father is apparently a frat boy now. I have faith you will overcome this flaw in your genetic makeup.

But unfortunately that's not the bad news I mentioned.

I found the number for the Kappa house in the phone book. I called. It took a few minutes for the guy who answered to locate him, and there was a lot of loud music in the background, but Dawson finally came to the phone.

"Hello?" he said.

"How are you?" I don't know why I asked this. I just hadn't heard his voice in a while. It brought back some feelings.

"Yeah, who is this?"

I was paralyzed for a few seconds. It'd been months since I'd sent him that letter about me being pregnant.

"Yeah, this is (whoops, almost wrote my name here, X, but I still don't think it's a good idea to do that)—this is (and I said my name). You know, from last year."

"Okay." His voice was immediately chilly. "Can I help you with something?"

"There's some paperwork you're going to need to fill out," I told him. "You might have to come in to sign some forms."

"What are you talking about?"

"For the baby."

Silence. You could have heard crickets chirping, X.

"You know, the one I'm having. The one you're the father of. That baby," I said. Okay, so I was a little irritated.

More silence.

"Hey," I said. "You don't have to be involved. I'm giving it—her, actually, it's a girl—I'm giving her up for adoption. You won't have to do or pay for anything, but it'd be nice if you filled out the forms, so that she could know something about you."

"Is this a joke?" he said. At least that's what I thought he said. The music was loud.

"What part of this strikes you as funny?" I asked.

Something did, though, because then he laughed. "Okay. A baby. You got me."

"That's right. A baby. She's due on September 26. So we don't have a lot of time."

"You dumped me," he said. "You disappeared. And now you call and tell me there's a baby?"

"Wait a second!" I protested. "I didn't dump you. I'm not the dumper here. I'm the dumpee. You're the dumper. I told you about the baby, and you ditched me."

"You never told me about a baby."

"I wrote you a . . ." I stop. I think about it. I left the letter in my dad's office, in the outgoing mail basket. I've done it a hundred times, no problem. But I didn't actually take it to the post office, which would have been the smart thing.

"Fucking Evelyn," I whispered.

"What?"

"Never mind. I'm sorry. God, I'm sorry. I wrote you a letter, and I thought you got it. I'm having a baby. Soon. I guess I should say, we're having a baby, you and me. We should meet and talk about it. I'm sorry to tell you this way. I really did think you already knew."

I mean, Ted knew. I told Ted. Why wouldn't Ted tell Dawson?

For all of three seconds I felt like maybe there was another path for me. Maybe Dawson would have another idea about what to do. Maybe he'd want to keep you. Maybe there was a way to work it out. Maybe—

"It's not mine," Dawson said then, and he hung up.

Sooooooooo.

Bad news, X. Your dad's out. I mean, not your dad. Your sperm donor, like I said in the beginning. And it's not like anything's changed. But now I guess it's official. No baby daddy.

On to the good news, though.

I know who your real daddy is. I picked him out. He's an elementary school teacher. He's also kind of crunchy—the Oregon hippie type, which makes sense, because he's from Portland. He spent a few years volunteering for some organization like Greenpeace, but I don't think it was Greenpeace. I can't remember now. He was a national park ranger for a while. Then he got his teaching degree at Boise State, which is where he met your mom (I don't know that story—but you probably do, don't you?). Then he taught at some inner-city schools in the Los Angeles area for a couple years. He must have liked Idaho, though, because then they moved back and he started teaching at an elementary school. He has kind eyes. Green eyes. That's the thing that I noticed first about him.

I like him. I know I'd want him to be my dad.

It wasn't the dad, though, that got your parents into the YES pile. It was the mom. She owns a cake shop. She makes cupcakes for a living. I mean, could you ask for anything better than that? There was something so cool about her, like she's Martha Stewart if Martha Stewart was warm and loving and sweet. I wanted to hug her. She looks like she'd give good hugs.

So, I didn't find any real cons to your new family. And trust me, I was being picky. But here are the pros:

They aren't super rich. But they're not poor, either. They're solidly middle, maybe upper middle, but regular people, you know? They can afford to give you what you need. But they don't seem like they'd give you so much that you'd think money grows on trees. Or think that you were entitled to everything. Or misunderstand, the way my folks do, that money equals love.

They know how to handle kids. The dad especially, right? I mean, he's handling kids every day. By choice. He must know how to do it. He must be a boss at it. Elementary schools are like jungles, so this guy must be like Tarzan.

And your mom can cook. I can almost smell the chocolate chip cookies. It makes me smile to imagine the kind of birthday cakes you'll have.

On the form they talked a lot about family—not just the family they want to have, but the family they do have. So you're going to be surrounded by grandparents and uncles and aunts and cousins and friends. You might be an only child, but you won't be lonely.

They're solid, X. I loved the pictures they included in the file. There's one that must have been a photo for a Christmas card or an engagement photo, where they are standing in a field in front of a fence, their arms around each other. They're looking into each other's eyes. And they're laughing. And in the next photo, she's feeding him a cupcake. Still laughing. And in the next one, they're all dressed up in formal wear, and she's pretending to choke him with his tie. Maybe not the best choice for a photo to send to the person who's deciding whether or not to give you a baby, I'll admit. But they're funny. I could tell in the way they filled out the forms. I mean, not too funny, as this is supposed to be serious business, a *transaction ending with a child, but I could tell they know how to laugh at themselves.*

> *You're not going to be their fixer baby. Or their pet.*
> *I could feel their happiness.*
> *I can feel it in my uterus: you belong with them.*
> *So that's the good news. That's what I want to leave you with today.*
> *S*

30

I get the call from the adoptedsearch.org representative the morning after I got the email. I've been up since like five, without really sleeping. Dad isn't awake yet. I contemplated telling him, last night after I got home from rehearsal, but he was at the hospital anyway, and then I thought, I should wait. See if this is real. I remind myself that I already got a match on this site once, and it wasn't me. It wasn't her.

When I see the strange area code come up, I get so nervous I feel light-headed. I can't breathe properly. I don't know what I'm more afraid of—that I might have actually located my birth mother, that she searched for me, too, that it's happening and now we're going to have to hurry and get her over to meet my mom, and what will that be like? I wonder—or that this must all be some kind of cruel joke the universe is playing on me.

"Hello?" I can't keep the tremble out of my voice.

"Hello, is this Cassandra McMurtrey?"

"This is her. I mean, this is she."

"My name is Jennifer Benway. I'm calling from adoptedsearch .org?"

"Yes. I've been expecting your call."

"So as you know, yesterday there was a match to your profile. A perfect match."

"What does that mean," I ask, "perfect?"

"A woman who is currently searching for the infant she gave up for adoption eighteen years ago created a profile on the site. The details match yours perfectly. That's what it means."

I struggle to remember the details I put on the website. Just my birthday and my place of birth, I think.

Jennifer Benway clears her throat. "Now I need to gather some more information from you so that we can make sure that this is an actual match."

"Okay."

"Do you know what hospital you were born in?" she asks.

"St. Luke's."

"You're sure?"

"Yes." That's on the form my parents gave me.

"And was your adoption private?" Jennifer Benway asks.

"It was through the state."

"And do you know your birth mother's age at the time of your birth?"

"She was sixteen."

"Excellent." She sounds excited. I must be giving her the right answers. I feel like I'm passing the most important pop quiz in history. "Do you have any additional information that could be helpful?"

"Yeah." I rummage in my desk drawer for the worn, yellowed envelope. "I have the form of non-identifying information."

"That's great. We should be able to confirm everything with that. Would you mind scanning those papers and emailing them to me? Then I'll check it against the information we have from the birth mother and call you back later today."

That's it? She'll call back? "Okay."

"Great. I'll call soon."

"Wait," I say before she can hang up. "But the other stuff I told you, that I was born at St. Luke's, that I was adopted through the state—does that information match?"

"Yes," she says, and I can almost hear her smiling. "It does. We have to cover all the bases, but it's likely that this woman is your birth mother. It's very exciting. Congratulations."

"Yeah." I'm light-headed again. "Thanks."

I scan the forms and email them right away. Then I wait for Dad to wake up.

"What's the matter?" he asks the moment he comes into the kitchen and sees my face. "Your mom? Did the hospital call? I'll get dressed."

"It's not Mom. It's something else." I tell him everything that's transpired in the past twelve hours, and then I start to pace back and forth across the kitchen. "Do you think I should tell Mom? She said she wants to meet my birth mother. I should tell her, right?"

He sits at the kitchen table with a cup of coffee and blinks a lot before he says, "Not until you know for sure."

"Right. This might not even be my birth mother," I say lightly.

"I don't know. How many sixteen-year-olds do you suppose

had a baby girl at St. Luke's on the same day you were born?" Dad says. "It sounds like you, Boo."

That's what I've been thinking since the phone call. It must be me. It's a perfect match. How could it not be?

Dad sets down his coffee and scratches his chin. "But we should wait. I don't know how your mom will react. She's so fragile right now. I don't want her to get overly excited."

"Yeah," I agree. "I think you're right. We'll wait until we're sure."

He stares out the window at the falling snow.

"Dad?" I ask him. "Are you okay? I know you hated the idea."

He snaps out of it. "Yes. If it's what you want, I'm okay. Yes."

"I love you." I stretch out my arms. I'm in this hyper mood all of a sudden. "This much."

He stretches out his arms, too, that are so much longer than mine. "But I love you this much."

"It's not a competition, Dad," I remind him.

"But if it were, I'd totally win. I've got much longer arms. Want to hear a dad joke?"

"No."

"You're American when you go into the bathroom, and you're American when you come out, but do you know what you are when you're in there?"

"Dad, stop."

"European."

I bust out laughing. I hate myself for it, but I can't help it. "That's awful."

"I know," he says, grinning. "Want to hear a joke about a piece of paper? Never mind. It's tearable."

My phone rings. We both freeze mid-laugh. I pick up my phone and check the number.

"It's her," I say.

"Sit down," Dad suggests, and I do. I answer the phone.

"Hello?" There's that quiver in my voice again.

"Cassandra?"

"That's me."

"This is Jennifer Benway from adoptedsearch.org."

"I know. Hi."

"I hate to be the bearer of bad news, but . . ." She sighs. "I'm afraid this isn't your birth mother after all. I've been going over the details, both yours and the other profile's, and they don't line up."

All the air goes out of my lungs. "What? But how could—"

"This woman has brown eyes," Jennifer Benway says. "And she's tall: five eleven, not five three like what's recorded on your form. And this woman was the youngest child of four. I think she might have attended the same school that your birth mother did, which also served as a home for pregnant young ladies, but this is not your birth mother, Cassandra."

"Oh" is all I can think to say.

"I'm so sorry," says Jennifer Benway.

Dad's watching me. I try to keep my face neutral.

"We'll keep your profile open, of course," she rambles on. "There could be a match out there anytime. And I'll talk to this woman and see if there's anything she can add that might help your search."

"Okay." I'm spacing now. Numb.

"I'll let you know," she says, and hangs up.

I put my phone on the table and stare at it. After a while I look at my dad. It wakes me up a little, seeing the sorrow in his eyes. He wants to protect me from this, I think, but he doesn't know how.

I swallow. "It's not her," I tell him, attempting to keep my voice casual like it doesn't matter, but it wavers slightly.

"Oh, honey," he says, reaching across the table to take my hand. "I'm so sorry."

"Let's not tell Mom," I say. "Let's never tell her."

31

I have a dress rehearsal that night. I try to put the last twenty-four hours out of my mind, act like it didn't happen, but it really is starting to feel like the universe is playing a cruel joke on me. That's the worst part of this whole adoption thing: this sense of helplessness. Someone else has been making these decisions for me my entire life. Who my parents would be. How much I'd be allowed to know about the circumstances of my birth. It's all completely outside of my control.

I gaze down the long dressing room table at Nyla. I haven't even started on my highlights and shadows yet, but Nyla's got her costume on already, her Cinderella rags, her hair tied up. She's ready. She looks focused. I sigh.

My phone buzzes. A text.

From Nyla.

Nyla: What's the matter?

I glance over again. She's looking at her phone, not me.

Me: How do you know something's the matter?

Nyla: I know you. Is Mama Cat okay? Do you need to go? I can drive you.

Reading that feels good, because she still cares, obviously.

Me: My mom's fine. I mean, not fine, really. But it's not about my mom.

Nyla: Oh. Whew.

Me: But thanks.

Nyla: What is it about, then?

I bite my lip. Nyla and me, we're broken, our friendship fractured, and it's my fault, and she's being nice—maybe she wants to fix it even—but our relationship can't always be about my drama and her trying to make me feel better.

I have to have something to give her, too. Something I owe her.

I stare down at my phone. I mean, I did tell her I was sorry right after it happened, and again later, but both times it was a generic apology, the "I didn't mean to say something that hurt you" kind of apology, which didn't ring true, of course, because I *did* mean to hurt her that day. I understand that now. So it was really a non-apology that I gave her.

Now my thumbs peck out the words I should have said.

Me: What I said that day about them giving you the scholarship—it was racist, and it was wrong of me to say that, and I'm sorry. You got the scholarship because you are the most singularly talented actor I know. Period. You deserve that scholarship. I was upset because I wanted it, too, and I was only thinking about my own issues, but that's no excuse. I know that. I've been so ashamed since then. I am disappointed in myself. I didn't think I had that in me, to say something like that, to anybody, ever. Ever, ever. Especially to you. I know it must have hurt you so much to have that kind of thing come from me, when I'm supposed to be the one who's got your back. I'm so sorry, Nyles.

I send the text and then watch her out of the corner of my eye as she reads it. She bows her head for a minute, then gives a little weird laugh that I don't know how to interpret, then sits up again and lifts her phone. I see the ellipses that mean she's writing something back.

But then it stops. Then nothing.

She doesn't look over at me. She's staring at her phone.

I'm flooded with shame all over again. God, I'm such a coward. I should have said all this in person. It's so gutless, sending it in a text.

Me: I should have told you this weeks ago.

Nyla:

Me: I miss you.

Nyla:

Me: I love you. You're my best best friend in the whole world. You know that, right?

Nyla:

Me: But I'll understand if you can never forgive me.

Nyla:

Me: I just wanted you to know how sorry I am.

Nyla: Shut up a minute, will you? I'm trying to compose a response and you keep texting me.

Me:

Nyla: I accept your apology.

Me:

Nyla: It did hurt my feelings.

Me:

Nyla: But I miss you, too. I love you, too. You were having an epically crappy day that day. So I'll give you a pass.

Me:

Nyla: This one time.

Me: There won't be a next time. I promise.

She pushes back from her chair and comes to stand next to me.

"Can I sit here for a minute?" she asks Alice, who's putting on her makeup in the next seat. "I have to have a word or two with Cass."

Alice smiles radiantly like she knows we're making up finally, gathers her stuff, and moves to Nyla's place down the table.

Nyla sits.

"Thank you for apologizing," she says. "I think we can get past it now."

"Okay." I look at her all teary and then laugh.

"What?" she asks.

"I want to hug you, but I don't want to mess up your hair."

She laughs, too, pats her updo. "You think the world is ready for a black Cinderella?"

"Doesn't Brandy get to claim black Cinderella, though?" I point out. Nyla and I only watched that movie fifteen thousand times when we were younger.

Nyla nods solemnly. "Yes. Brandy will always and forever be black Cinderella. But you know what I mean."

"Yeah, I know," I say. "And you're going to be the best Cinderella, period, that this town has ever seen." I hope she can tell I mean it.

She hugs me. "So," she says when she pulls back. "What's the matter? What's got your face like that?"

I don't want to get into it now.

"Come sleep over at my house, after the show," I say. "Then I'll tell you everything."

We're snuggled up under a blanket on my couch about four hours later, eating popcorn by the handful, watching but not really watching the Disney version of *Into the Woods*, and I tell Nyla everything. I tell her about today's false alarm with the less-than-perfect match. The whiplash of the whole experience. The weird little ache it filled me with, like really bad heartburn.

"Wow," she says when I'm done talking. "That's intense."

"I know, right?"

"It's all so . . . complicated."

"Look up complicated in the dictionary," I sigh. "That's me. My life was high drama even before I was born."

"So what are you going to do?" Nyla asks.

"I don't think there's anything else to do. I applied to get the letter, but I haven't heard anything. I filled out that waiver. Same story. I did the internet thing, and I think we can both agree that turned out badly." I choke back a laugh. "I even searched the high school yearbooks, didn't I, Ny? I think I've done it all." Tears spring to my eyes, and I laugh again. "And I keep freaking crying. I don't get why. I'm not sorry I was adopted. I'm not sad about it. I'm not yearning to reconnect with my biological parents. I'm not trying to find a family—I have my grandma and my grandparents on my dad's side and Uncle Pete and . . . you."

She puts her arms around my shoulder and squeezes.

I let out a shuddery breath. "I have the best support system I can imagine. The thing with my mom dying is hard, but I'm okay. Really. I'm fine. I'm curious about my birth mother, is all. I want to know what happened, because I feel like . . . I should be able to know my own story. It's mine. It's about me."

"I get it," she says.

I know she does.

I dab at my eyes. "So why the waterworks? I'm sitting here, boohooing over a stranger, because—"

Because why? Do I even know?

My eyes well up with tears all over again.

"Because . . . she's out there. But she's not searching for me. Even though I have a great life, and she gave me that life, this better life that she sacrificed so much for, the idea that she's not looking for me, it . . ."

"It hurts your feelings," Nyla says.

"Yeah." I nod and wipe at my face. "Yeah. It hurts to think she would forget about me."

"She didn't forget," Nyla says.

I blow my nose. "Okay, so right now, I want to watch something really stupid to get my mind off all of this, like this mockumentary about vampires I keep hearing about, but I didn't want to watch without you."

We start the movie, which is both hilarious and dumb. We're there giggling when I suddenly remember: "Oh, I need to tell you about Bastian."

She tucks her legs up on the couch and swivels to face me immediately. "Yes?"

"When we kissed, the first time."

She leans forward, eyes wide. "You kissed Bastian?"

"No, for the play, silly. The first time we kissed for the play. Catch up."

"Okay, the first time you kissed for the play," she says.

"He said I was the first girl he ever kissed."

"Shut up."

"No. He said that."

She makes a confused face. "Wow."

"I know, right?"

"Uh-huh. Maybe he's LDS," she muses.

I scoff. "He can't be Mormon. We'd know if he were Mormon, right?"

"We've been hanging out a lot," Nyla says. "I think I would have figured it out, if he was LDS."

"Yeah. He'd talk about his ward, and his mission. And he'd go to seminary." The Mormons have a church building right on the campus of the high school where all the Mormon students (which is like 80 percent of BHS) take religion classes every week. Okay, so it's technically not "on campus," because the church owns the land it sits on, apparently, but it's like fifty feet from the common room door. And I've never seen Bastian head that way for class. "And he drinks coffee. And he swears."

"News flash, Cass," Nyla says matter-of-factly. "We're all individual people. Some Mormons drink coffee. And some swear. And some don't go to seminary."

"But not the good kind, right?"

She closes her eyes like she's embarrassed to be having this conversation. "Cass, I swear—"

I snicker. "No, you don't."

She punches me. But then she laughs.

"Hey!" I protest. "Back to Bastian. The type of Mormon who swears and drinks coffee is probably the type who kisses girls before he's married, right?"

She sighs. "We can kiss all we—"

"I don't think Bastian's Mormon," I say.

"I agree. So it must be something else, for him not to have kissed a girl. I always thought there was something about Bastian that he wasn't telling us. Maybe something to do with his dad."

"His dad does sound a little extreme."

Right then my phone rings. A familiar number.

"Shit," I burst out.

"Hey. I've got you," says Nyla.

"Hello?" I say wearily into the phone.

"Can I speak to Cassandra?" says the voice I now recognize as Jennifer Benway's.

"Speaking."

"This is Jennifer Benway, from adoptedsearch.org. I hope it's not too late to call."

I stare at Nyla. "It's fine, Jennifer. What do you need?"

"I was just following up," she says. "I spoke with the other party, the woman who . . ."

"Who's not my birth mother," I say sharply.

"No," she says. "I mean, yes, she's not your birth mother, but she gave me permission to tell you some of the things she remembers."

"What's going on?" whispers Nyla.

"What things?" I ask.

Jennifer clears her throat. "About your mother—excuse me, your biological mother. This person believes she was with your birth mother at Booth Memorial, or that's what it was called then. She thinks the details on your form match the description of another sixteen-year-old girl she went to school with there, who gave birth the same night that she gave birth to her daughter."

I don't know what to say.

"Are you there?" Jennifer asks.

I find my voice. "Yes. Sorry. I'm here."

"She doesn't remember the girl's name, unfortunately, which would of course be useful," she continues. "It was almost twenty years ago, you understand. And she said she only lived there a few weeks. Or maybe she's trying to protect your birth mother's identity. But she did tell me that the other girl's name started with an *S*. Sally or Sarah or something similar."

I think about all the names that start with *S* on my list of yearbook girls. "An *S*. Did she remember anything else?"

Nyla disappears for a minute and comes back with a notepad and a pencil. She hands them to me.

"She said your birth mother was kind to her," Jennifer says. "And she said, if you ever find her, tell her thank you."

"What's her name?" I ask.

"She thinks it starts with an *S*," Jennifer says again.

I shake my head even though she can't see me. "No, I mean *this* woman's name. Who's not my birth mother. What's her name? Can you maybe give me her number? Can I talk to her myself?"

She doesn't answer for a few seconds. "I can't release that information. I'm sorry."

I can feel my jaw tightening. "So how am I supposed to tell my birth mother thank you, if I ever find her, if I don't even know this person's name?"

Another pause. "Well," Jennifer says slowly, "I can't tell you her name. But I can mention that she has a profile on our site. You should even be able to see her, as a match."

I understand immediately. "Okay, thanks."

"Thank you, Cassandra. Again, I'm so sorry this didn't work out the way you'd hoped. I wish you all the best in your search. Good night, then."

I hang up and Nyla and I go straight to my laptop and call up the website. Jennifer's right; it's still showing a 100 percent match with someone.

I force down the wave of disappointment and click on the link to the lady's profile.

Amber84

I am searching for my daughter.

She was born on September 17, 2000, in Boise, Idaho.

She was adopted in Idaho six weeks after her birth.

We have not been in contact since the time of the adoption.

Personal message: I want her to know she's loved.

Nyla puts her arms around me, and I literally cry onto her shoulder.

"So my birth mother's name might start with an *S*." I wipe my eyes.

Nyla nods. "You should write that down."

32

"Cassandra McMurtrey to the front office, please. Cassandra McMurtrey to the front office."

I'm in choir this time. I look over at Nyla in the alto section. She shrugs.

"You can go, Cass," the teacher says.

So I go. But then I come around a corner and there's Dad standing in front of the office door with his brave face on.

My legs fail me. I sink down onto the floor like I'm made of cooked spaghetti.

Dad runs over to me. "It's okay. It's okay, honey."

No, it's not, I think. No, it's not. It's not ever going to be okay again. I should be crying. Why aren't I crying? I wonder. I always thought I would cry when it happened.

Dad's talking. I can't understand what he's really saying.

Something like, "Oh, God, I'm so sorry. I screwed this up royally. I just thought you'd want to be told in person."

And *then* I'm crying. Hooray, I'm not broken. My mother has died, and I'm crying. I start to sob. It's the scene where Cass loses her mother. The one that has everyone in the audience bawling.

Dad has me by the shoulders. He even gives me a little shake. "Cass. Look at me. Look at me."

I meet his eyes.

"She's not gone. She's alive."

I'm dazed. I'm confused. My tongue feels thick in my mouth for some reason. My heart is thumping strangely in my chest. "What? She's not dead?"

"No." He smiles. It's the happiest smile I've ever seen on him. It's like their wedding photos smile. "It's happened, Boo."

"What?" I say again.

"Is she all right?" This is the front office lady, leaning over us both, looking worried.

"She's fine." Dad looks at my face. "Well, she's going to be fine."

"Dad?" I don't know what's happening. My mom was dead, but now she's not. "I don't understand."

"Your mother got a heart."

We make it to the hospital right before she goes into surgery. She's glowing when we see her, luminous in a way that's hard to look at, her hope is so bright.

She squeezes my hand three times. "No matter what happens. Remember."

I squeeze three times back.

Then they're wheeling her away to some brightly lit room where they're going to cut open her chest, take out her faulty, messed-up heart, and give her a better one.

Grandma starts sobbing in the waiting room. I've never seen her cry like that before, even on the worst days. Then she wipes her eyes and laughs.

"I can't believe it," she says. "I didn't really think he'd come through."

She's talking about God now, I think, which is not a normal topic of conversation in our family.

"She's going to be all right now," Dad says.

I sling my arm around Grandma. "Amen to that."

The old heart goes out. The new comes in. There's a chance Mom's body will reject it, so they have to put her on a bunch of meds to try to keep that from happening. But even in her room after the surgery, even before she wakes up, there's a pinkness to her cheeks that I haven't seen in a long time.

After she wakes up, she's full of dreams again. They've told her that she can go home in ten days. Of course she's going to have to keep coming back for months. The new heart has to be constantly checked. She has to do rehab, rebuild all the muscle mass she lost while she was in the hospital, get strong again, but she can come home in ten days.

Ten freaking days.

I'm with Grandma. I can't believe it.

Mom keeps talking, too. Laughing. I worry that she's laughing too much. "I can't buy back the shop," she says. "But maybe Jodi would give me a job there. That'd be funny, wouldn't it? Or I could get another job at a different bakery."

"Whoa there, champ," Dad says. "You won't be ready to go back to work for months. Maybe even a year."

"Yes, yes, I know." She waves her hand at him. "But after that. When I can, I'll work. I've been lying in a bed way too long."

"Okay, dear," Grandma says. "You can work."

We're all quiet for a minute, soaking in the idea of Mom getting to have her life back. Mom squeezes my hand again. I compose a text to Nyla. It's picture night for the play—when Mama Jo invites all the parents to come see the final rehearsal and come up onto the stage with their cameras. It's kind of fun—at any time during the performance a parent can shout, "Freeze!" and all of the actors have to freeze in place and have their picture taken. Mama Jo says if we can stay in character and keep moving through the play smoothly with all of these interruptions, it means we're truly ready for the performance. It's always been one of my favorite rehearsals for any show.

I'm not even a little bit sorry to miss it.

Mama Cat has a new heart, I write. *It's working fine.*

Dear X,

Brace yourself: this one's going to be a doozy. But it's relevant, X, or at least it's a part of my story, which is your story, so hang in there.

I went to see Dawson today. I know, I know, I'm a glutton for punishment. But again, I keep thinking about you, X, and how you'll want to know the things about him that only he could tell you. I hate to admit, but I didn't get to know him that well when we were dating. (Or whatever it was that we were doing.) I also wanted to make him look me in the eye and tell me, face-to-face, that you aren't his, when he knows you are. He knows it, and I know it. I want to hear him say it.

Plus I was feeling cooped up at Booth. I feel like everyone's staring at me, waiting for me to pop. I needed to get out for a while, so I asked Melly to take me to the Kappa house to give the birth father the forms.

"And you're sure this boy's the father?" she had the gall to ask me as

we were driving over there. Melly always uses these occasions to try to talk things through with me. Like apparently what a promiscuous teenager I am.

"I know this might totally shock you," I answered, "but he's the only guy I've ever slept with. So yeah, I'm pretty sure."

"Hey, I'm not judging. I was just asking." She glanced in the rearview mirror. "It does make a certain amount of sense for him to deny it."

I stared at her, not knowing if I should be wildly offended or not. "How does that make sense?"

"He's in college. You're in high school. Having a sexual relationship with you was technically illegal."

I was fully aware of this—it occurred to me back when my dad asked me about the father that first day we knew about you. It was unsettling, thinking about how some people might put the word rape on what had happened between Dawson and me, when it was absolutely consensual. Melly saying this stuff made me want to reconsider the entire trip. "You won't report him, will you?"

"No. That's not my business. My job is to help you."

Whew. I mean, I want you to know as much as you can about your birth father, X. But I don't want him to be arrested. I'm mad at him—sure—but I don't want to see him get punished. Not for this.

"We should also probably talk about contraception," Melly said.

I was drinking from a bottle of water when she dropped this little gem on me, and I choked a little.

"I think it's too late for the sex talk, Melly." I coughed. "It's safe to say that I know all about the birds and the bees."

"You're be surprised at what some of the girls have asked me over the years, considering that they're pregnant. But you're not going to be pregnant much longer. You'll be out there in the world again. I like you—you're actually one of my favorites, kid, if I'm allowed to say that—but I don't want to see you come back to Booth."

"I don't want that, either. No offense."

"None taken," she said. "So let's talk about how to prevent this situation in the future."

"I know all about it. Pills. Condoms. Diaphragms. Some weird little thing they can stick up in your uterus that will keep you from getting pregnant for five years. I like that option. I might go with that."

"But the IUD won't keep you from getting sexually transmitted diseases," she said so casually, like we were discussing the stock market. "So it's safest to use condoms, too."

"Condoms fail," I pointed out by motioning toward my belly. "Case in point."

"Let's talk about that," she said. "How did it happen?"

I tell her about the missing condom.

"Hmm" is all she said. "Well, they can come off. But you never . . . located it?"

"Nope."

"Hmm," she says again.

I felt stupid then. Like I was one of those girls she'd been referring to. The clueless type.

"Nice weather we're having today, huh?" I said to change the subject. A joke, since it's so hot out still you'd burn your feet on the sidewalk if you walked barefoot. It was over a hundred degrees out. I was enjoying sitting in front of the air conditioner in the car and having it blast me in the face. "I hear hell is nice and moderate this time of year."

"It'll cool off," Melly said. "Just give it time."

We drove the rest of the way in relative silence. When we pulled up to the Kappa house, which was located across the street from the college

310

campus, I told Melly I wanted her to wait in the car.

"All right," she said. "But if you have a problem, let me know."

"I'm going to drop these off and maybe have a little chat with him," I said, grabbing the forms.

"He'll need to come in later and sign the adoption papers with a lawyer and a notary," she reminded me.

"I'll tell him."

The problem was, Dawson wasn't at the Kappa house. And the one half-drunk guy at the Kappa house who finally answered the door had no idea where he was.

"Does he have class?" I asked.

"I have no idea," he said.

"When does he usually come home?"

"No idea."

I told Melly that I was going to take a walk and see if I could find him. She offered to come with me, of course, but I said no. I crossed the street and the parking lot and made my way into the heart of campus. Then I stopped and turned in a circle. There were so many buildings. So many places for Dawson to be. I didn't know where to look.

I did know where the SUB was, though. It seemed as good a place as any to start.

I walked slowly down a big tree-lined sidewalk for a while, and then turned off toward the only building I recognized, not counting the dorm where Dawson used to live. The students parted around me like I was Moses before the Red Sea, staring at my protruding belly, whispering to each other.

It was like being back at high school would have been, if I'd stayed the year there. I was getting noticed for all the wrong reasons.

"Hey!" Someone was calling me. I stopped.

311

Ted came jogging up.

"Hi," he said. "I thought that was you."

"You thought right. Hi."

"How are you?" he asked, making an effort to look at my face and not my baby bump. Ted's a nice guy. Every time I see him or talk him, he proves it more and more.

"I've been better," I murmured. I could feel a blush coming on, just seeing Ted. "I'm, uh, looking for Dawson. As usual, I guess."

"Of course," he said.

"I have no idea where he might be."

"Well, I don't know his schedule," Ted said, "but whenever I wanted to find Dawson last year, I started with the theater. Usually he hangs out at the studio." He actually offered me his arm, like we'd gone back in time a hundred years. "Come on, I'll take you over there."

We waddled along—or, I should say, I waddled, and Ted kept his pace slow to match mine—back down the sidewalk to a large building I'd been in before, but couldn't remember when. Ted held the door open for me and led me through the lobby, which was all white and marble and tall pillars, to a door marked "Studio Theater."

There was a group of students standing in the middle of the stage holding little paper books. Scripts, I guess. An older guy sitting in the front row turned to look at me.

His gaze went straight to my stomach. "Can I help you? Are you lost?"

"I'm—" Maybe this was a bad idea, I thought. It might look bad for Dawson, to have me in the state I was in wandering around campus search- ing for him. I didn't want to humiliate him, not really. Everybody didn't have to know that he'd gotten a girl pregnant. I couldn't prevent people knowing, in my own case, since you, X, are super obvious to everybody who lays eyes on me at this stage. But it didn't have to be that way for Dawson.

This was a mistake, I thought.

"Yeah, I'm lost," I said.

Ted shook his head. "She's looking for Dawson."

"Oh," said the older man. He checked his watch. "I'm afraid Dawson's not here at the moment, but he'll be here for a rehearsal in about an hour. If you'd like to come back."

"Thank you," I said. "I will."

Ted and I went back out into the lobby and stood there for a minute. Then Ted said, "Hey, I know where we can wait," and he walked down a hallway where there were a bunch of doors. He tried one of them and found it locked, and then tried another, which opened.

It was a small room with an upright piano in the corner, a bunch of folding chairs, and a couple of music stands.

"This is a practice room," Ted explained. "For when you want to suck at your music in private."

"Do you play an instrument?" I asked.

Ted got adorably red in the face. "I play violin. My mother thought because I'm part Asian, I was going to be a musical prodigy by the age of five. So she made me play. I was not a prodigy."

"Your mother? Are you adopted?" I asked.

"No. My mom is white. My dad's Japanese," he explained. "They're both great, but even she had to work through some preconceived notions about race, and I didn't help by being good at math and science and enjoying the occasional game of chess, but I did my part to break down her assumptions by sucking at music."

"Oh." I couldn't think of anything else to say.

He unfolded a chair for me, and I sat. He grabbed another chair and straddled it backward across from me. He seemed different than he was last year, taller, even. Not as shy. I wonder what happened over the summer to *give him this boost of confidence. I wanted to ask him, but we're not friends.*

I'm just a girl who got knocked up by his roommate, who he was being

inexplicably nice to, because I needed help and he's a nice guy.

"So why did you tell the director in there that you were lost?" he

asked. "What happened?"

"I don't want to embarrass Dawson," I confessed.

Ted gave a short, sarcastic laugh. "Why do girls always do that? Why

do they try to protect the guy? I don't get it."

It was a valid question, but it got my hackles up.

"It's not like you didn't do the same thing," I shot back.

"Me? What did I do?"

"It's more about what you didn't do," I said. "Or say."

"You've lost me."

"You didn't tell Dawson about . . ." I gestured to my belly. ". . . this."

He stood up. "Why didn't you tell him? That's why you were there

that night, right? Did you chicken out then, too?"

You know the answer to that, X, which is yes. I totally chickened out.

But I said, "No, I wrote him a letter, explaining the situation. I thought

he received it, but it must have gotten lost. . . . So all this time I thought he

knew, and he didn't want to deal with it."

Ted sat down again. "Oh. No, he thought you dumped him for no

reason. He really liked you. He was actually a little heartbroken, if you

ask me. And pissed."

My stomach gave a guilty twist, or it could have just been you doing

one of your backflips in there. "I got that same impression when I called

him last week. But you knew all along, and you didn't tell him. Why?"

"I didn't think it was my place," Ted said. "That's a pretty serious

bomb to drop on a guy. He probably wouldn't have believed me, even if

I had told him."

I nodded. That made sense. Sort of.

"So what's going to happen now?" he asked. "Are you . . . I mean, obviously you're going to have the . . ."

"Baby." I can say it now. You're a baby, X. You're a real live human baby. I guess that's progress from how I thought of you in the beginning. "I'm going to have her."

"So it's a her."

"I'm going to give her up for adoption. I've already chosen the parents and everything." I tried to smile. "I need Dawson to fill out some of this paperwork, and come in and sign the documents, and it will be a done deal."

"Good for you," Ted said.

"Except when I told Dawson, he said the baby isn't his, and he hung up on me."

"Oh, dude." Ted dragged his hand down the front of his face. "Oh man. What an asshat."

"Yeah."

"No wonder you're nervous about seeing him."

"Yeah."

"Well. I do not know what to tell you."

"It's okay. I don't know what to say, either."

"Dawson's not a bad guy. I mean, he can be a little . . . vain, maybe? A bit obsessed with himself. I used to make fun of him for the way he kept looking in the mirror and practicing all these dramatic expressions." Ted laughed, but then got serious again. "He's had kind of a crapshoot life, but he turned out okay. He's not really an asshat, so . . . I think he'll come around."

"I think you know him better than I do," I said.

"I know him well enough to bet he does the right thing here." Ted

315

stood up and walked over to the piano. "In the meantime," he said more cheerfully. "Do you know 'Heart and Soul'?"

"Everyone knows that song."

"All righty, then." He cracked his knuckles. "Let's play."

We fooled around on the piano for a bit, which effectively got my mind off the situation for a few minutes, and then we went back out into the lobby to wait for Dawson. The director guy was right—around four o'clock Dawson came ambling into the building. His arm around some redhead.

I don't own him, I told myself. It's fine.

When he saw me, his arm dropped away from the new girl. "What are you doing here?"

"I need to talk to you," I said as quietly as I could.

He looked at Ted. "What are <u>you</u> doing here?"

"I'm moral support," Ted said.

"Who is she?" asked the redhead.

"Nobody important, don't worry."

I met Dawson's eyes again. "We need to talk."

"I told you before, it's not my—"

"Dude, don't be that guy," Ted said. "Hear what she has to say. Step up."

"Who is she?" asked the redhead again.

"Hey, can you go tell Joe I'm going to be a few minutes late?" Dawson asked the redhead. She didn't look happy about it, but she went.

Other actors were also entering the building, giving us curious stares.

"Do you want to go somewhere more private? I only need a minute," I suggested.

"Okay. This way," he said.

"I'll wait for you here," Ted said.

Dawson led me down another hallway to a small room, but this was a kind of dressing room with a big plaid couch along one wall.

I didn't sit because a) I wasn't sure I could get up again without help, and I didn't want Dawson to see me flounder around like that, b) I suddenly had to pee, and c) at this point I wanted to get this conversation over with.

The door closed behind us.

"You're the father," I said. "I can get a paternity test, if you want, but you are the only guy I ever slept with. Or not slept with, to be more accurate."

He opened his mouth to protest, and I put my hand on his lips. God, I used to love his lips. They were one of his best parts.

"I'm not asking anything from you. Not really. I intend to give this baby up for adoption. It's all arranged. Like I said on the phone, you won't have to be involved, or pay any money, or do anything. I just want you to fill out this form, so she—"

He pulled my hand away from his mouth. "She?"

"Didn't I tell you? It's a girl. She loves to kick me in the spleen, but otherwise she's pretty awesome. She's probably going to want to know about you. Who you are. Some of your health history. Illnesses that run in your family."

His Adam's apple jerked, and something tightened in his jaw.

I held out the form. "Please. Not for me. For her."

"Okay." He took the papers. His hands, I noticed, were shaking a little. I felt bad for him. I wanted to hug him and tell him it would all be okay. I believe that, now. I really do think it will all be okay.

"Thank you," I said.

"I was a jerk. I'm sorry."

"I surprised you in the worst possible way," I said. "I'm sorry, too."

"When is she—"

317

"About three weeks." I rubbed my belly. "Although, seriously, if she wants to come early, I'd be all over it. It's getting pretty uncomfortable." I shifted from foot to foot. I still had to pee. "I've been writing her letters. I don't know if she's ever going to get them, but I keep writing them. Telling her about things. About us."

"Can I?" His hand hovered above my stomach.

My heart started beating faster. I mean, I wanted Dawson to be okay with the adoption. I wanted him to be glad, the way I am, that you're alive. But what if he wanted more? What if he wanted a different plan? You're his kid, too, X. What if he wanted to know you?

I'm not sure I can handle that. I have a plan now, one I've given a lot of thought to. I don't want it to get all messed up.

"Sure," I squeaked.

He put his hand on my belly, right at the top. "Whoa, it's really solid."

"Yeah, I didn't expect that, either," I said. "I thought it might be like a big water balloon in there, but it's so hard. Sometimes I feel like it's full of cement." I pressed down until I felt you under the layers of muscle. You shifted slightly. "I can never tell what part is what." I took his other hand and guided it to the spot. "But this . . . is either an elbow or a knee."

He left his hand there for a minute. Then he gasped like he'd been burned, because you moved, like you pushed back, and he felt it.

I got teary, I confess. I hadn't ever let anyone else touch my belly. No one except me had ever felt you move before. So now you were real to both of us.

Dawson took his hand away. I wiped at my cheek. "I'll call you about the paperwork—there's something you need to sign before she can be adopted. And I'll have someone call you when she's born. I'm sure they'll let you see her, if you want to."

"I don't know," he said. "I don't think—"

318

"Right, it's okay. I understand." I took a deep breath. "Goodbye, Dawson."

"Bye," he said.

He stayed in the room after I left. I went back out to the lobby and there, true to his word, was Ted, sitting at the bottom of the big marble staircase.

"I'll walk you back across campus," he said. "Did you . . . drive? How did you drive like that?"

"Oh my God, Melly!" I gasped. "I've been gone for hours. She must be freaking out."

Melly was, indeed, freaking out. She was about an eyelash from calling the police when Ted and I huffed up to the car. She stared at Ted intently.

"Is this the guy?" she asked.

"Uh . . . ," said Ted.

"No. This is Ted. He's a friend."

Ted smiled. He nodded. "I'm a friend."

"You did what you came here to do?" Melly asked.

"Mission accomplished," I said.

"Okay," said Melly briskly, still eyeing Ted a bit strangely. "Let's go."

So now I'm back at Booth, letting it all soak in. What did we learn today? I ask myself. What can I pass along?

We learned, I think, that Ted was right. Your sperm donor is not a total asshat.

I'm glad I was wrong.

S

33

"She's here!" Nyla exclaims, peering through the tiny space in the curtains. "I can't believe she's actually here."

"I know." I peek out into the house, too, where I see my parents—my dad *and* my mom—slowly making their way into the seats I reserved for them in the center section.

"Oh my gosh, your dad's so funny. He's acting like she's a porcelain doll," Nyla observes. He has his hand on the center of Mom's back, guiding her gently, on the lookout for anything that might become an obstacle or a hazard of any kind.

"Well, in a way she is." My heart squeezes as I watch Mom interact with a friend of hers who stops her to say hello. Mom's wearing a surgical mask to keep any germs at bay—a condition of the doctors letting her come tonight, but I know the smile that's under that mask so well. It's this fragile, shy little smile, like she's embarrassed at how thrilled everyone is to see her out and about after she's basically been a ghost in our community for more than a year. "She's not allowed to come home yet," I point out to Nyla. "She's got two more days."

I take a deep breath and smile, nervous, of course, but in the best way imaginable. All week we've been doing this, Thursday, Friday, and Saturday nights, a Sunday matinee last week, so this is the seventh time I'm about to perform this, but tonight feels like the singularly most important show of my life. "You think they're ready to see their only daughter make out with a prince?" I ask Ny.

"Oh, they're ready," Ny laughs.

Right on cue, Bastian appears from the boys' dressing room, straightening the royal-blue sash that crosses his chest. He makes a beeline right for us.

"Hello," he says in the deep prince voice, arching an eyebrow at me. Then he breaks character and grins that little-boy smile he has. "Hi."

"Hi."

"Hey," says Nyla.

He glances at the curtains. "Who are we spying on?"

"Mama Cat," Nyla answers.

"My mom," I clarify.

Bastian's brown eyes widen. "Your mom? But didn't she have heart surgery a few days ago?"

"Eight days ago, to be exact. But the doctors said she could come for tonight."

"That's a huge deal," he says. "Wow."

I get misty all of a sudden, which is bad because I can't smear my makeup. "Yeah. It kind of is."

Mama Jo bustles up to us, wearing the black velvet dress she always wears on closing night and these perfect sequined shoes that sparkle when the stage lights strike them. She looks us all up and down the way she does before every performance and seems generally satisfied with our costumes and painted faces. "Are you ready to do this one last time?" she asks breathlessly. All these years in the theater, and she still gets nervous for every performance.

If I do ever become a drama teacher—and right now I'm not decided about what I want to do, but I haven't ruled teaching out, either—I want to be like Mama Jo, and then I, too, will wear sparkly shoes on closing night. "We're ready," I say.

"Ready to kick butt and take names," Nyla agrees.

We do our fist bump.

"All right," Mama Jo laughs. "Break a leg, you three."

She moves on to check in with the other actors.

"This is sad," sighs Bastian. "Closing nights are so depressing. It's over. We're never going to get to do this, ever again."

"I know, but isn't that kind of how life works?" I say.

"After this we're on to the next thing," says Nyla. "And it will be even better."

Bastian sticks his lip out. "Promise we'll still be friends, though. Even without the play."

Friends, again. "Of course," I promise.

"Ladies and gentlemen, please take your seats. The curtain will rise in five minutes," says a voice over the loudspeaker.

We hear rustling from the orchestra pit. The musicians are getting into their places. They start to tune their instruments, and the house goes quiet. All of a sudden there's that current of electricity in the air, running from an actor to a violinist, from the violinist to a stagehand, back to an actor, to me, to the conductor of the music, to Nyla, to my parents in the audience. It's like we're a single organism, breathing together, waiting. Waiting for the lights.

I feel my shoulders relax. I'm home.

"Break a leg, Cass," Bastian says, giving me a quick hug. "Only don't, really, because that would ruin our performance."

"Break a leg," I whisper.

"See you in a minute, Cindy," he says to Nyla, back to being Cinderella's Prince. He disappears into the wings.

I stare after him, smiling faintly.

"Are you ever going to go out with Bastian?" Nyla asks.

I frown at her. Blush. "Um, well . . . I've been kind of preoccupied," I point out.

"True. But now you're not preoccupied," she says innocently. "Now you're free."

She's right. Now my mom's going to be okay. Now my life doesn't seem like I'm wandering through the fun house at the county fair. Now I can actually focus on me. I can have a normal life. I can have (gulp) a boyfriend. And I happen to know the perfect boy.

"I'm just saying, maybe you should think about asking him out. . . ." Nyla rolls her head to one side, stretching, and then the other.

"Okay, fine." I say like this would be a chore, but now I'm definitely thinking about it. I help Nyla with the kerchief that's over her hair, making sure it's pinned down tight, then turn around for her to tie the back of my apron into a neat bow.

The music starts. We exchange glances.

"Here we go," Nyla says.

Here we go.

34

That night, the last night of *Into the Woods* at Bonneville High School, feels like the first night of the rest of my life. I sing my heart out. I make people laugh. I make people cry. I soar to the stars and back, all in the space of three hours, and when the three hours are done and I'm standing in front of the cheering audience, my parents come into sharp focus. My mother, smiling and crying, my dad, on his feet and clapping so hard it must be hurting his hands. And I am happy, as happy as I've ever been, and I think, finally, that Mom was right about the universe.

After we've taken our final bows and the curtain has closed, we go out into the hall, where our friends and family are waiting to congratulate us in person. Nyla's parents are there, too, along with her brother and two sisters, all dressed up and looking so proud. They sweep Nyla into one giant embrace, and then off they all go in a noisy crowd.

I locate Mom at the end of the hall, sitting on a bench by the gymnasium. She stands up to hug me. She's still crying, dabbing at her mascara. It's so great to see her wearing mascara, even if it's smeared.

"That was beautiful," she gasps from behind her mask. "I'm so glad I got to see it."

She's wearing gloves, too. The doctors are being nice, letting her come out tonight, but they're not messing around. I squeeze her hand three times through the latex. "Me too."

"You were simply amazing, Boo." Dad gives me a bouquet of a dozen pink roses from Uncle Pete's shop, but Uncle Pete came to the show on opening night. And Grandma came for Friday night. And Dad's parents drove up from Oregon last weekend. Everybody showed up to support me—and to see Mom. It was nice.

Dad sighs wistfully. "I remember when I was your prince." Because when I was like four or five years old, my parents used to do plays with me, like *Snow White* or *The Little Mermaid* or whatever other movie I'd been watching. Dad always played the prince. Mom was the witch, because somebody had to be the villain. I think she secretly loved it. And I obviously had to be the heroine of the story.

"You're still my prince," I tell Dad now, and he grins goofily.

The rush of the evening is starting to fade. The electricity's dimming. The actors are going back into the dressing rooms to take off their makeup and their costumes and resume life in the real world. But I don't want to return to earth yet.

Speaking of princes, I spot Bastian slipping toward the side door.

"Bastian!" I call, lifting my hand up like he wouldn't otherwise see me. "Bastian, wait. Come meet my mom."

He ambles over. "Hi, Cass's mom! I've heard so much about you."

"Oh, you have no idea," Mom laughs.

"And it's good to see you again, sir," he says to Dad.

"Great show. The agony songs were hilarious!" Dad claps him on the back. "I love that the two princes are the princes from every fairy tale. It's so twisted."

"And the wolf song was so good, too," Mom adds. "You've got some voice there, don't you?"

"Thanks so much," he says a bit shyly, which I think is funny.

"What about your parents?" I ask, looking around. "Were they here tonight, or did they come earlier?" I don't remember him ever mentioning that his parents were in the house for any of our other shows.

He shakes his head. "My parents like those big booming musicals from the olden days. *Annie Get Your Gun. Seven Brides for Seven Brothers.* Meet me in St. Louis," he sings, then sighs. "They'd be okay with the first act of *Into the Woods*, the one where everyone is happily ever after, but the second act, when happily ever after falls apart—" He grimaces and shakes him head. "Plus I play a roving adulterous prince and a sexy wolf. They wouldn't understand. It's for the best, them not coming."

"Right." I wonder again if Bastian is Mormon. Or if his parents are.

"I like act one better, too, though," Mom muses. "Act two is kind of dark."

"Anyway, great show tonight, Cass. Your daughter is a rock star," Bastian tells my parents. "I should—" He looks toward the door.

"Do you have somewhere you have to be?" Usually, there's a cast party on closing night, but this time Mama Jo decided we'd combine it with a strike-the-set party tomorrow afternoon.

"No," Bastian says. "Not really. But I should—"

"Do you want to get pie with us?" I ask. "We could go to Perkins. They're open all night."

"Well, you know I loathe pie," he drawls with a half smile.

My mom's eyes widen. "Who hates pie?"

"He's kidding. He loves pie," I say. "Chocolate cream pie, if I remember correctly."

"Guilty as charged," Bastian says.

"Stay where you are," I say, moving backward toward the dressing rooms. "I'll meet you right here in five minutes."

I've never gotten dressed so fast in my life. When I return to the hallway, my parents and Bastian are deep in a conversation about the best books to get fifth-grade boys into reading, and Mom's smiling up at him from behind her mask, stars in her eyes, and Dad, too, is clearly getting a little crush on Bastian himself, I can tell. Not that I can blame them.

We walk out together to the parking lot.

"I'll ride with you?" I ask Bastian.

"Actually," Mom says slowly, "I have to get back to the hospital."

"But the hospital's right by Perkins," I point out.

"Yes, but I'm the Cinderella now," she says. "The ball is over, and midnight has struck, and I'd better get back before I turn into a pumpkin."

Dad nods. "Doctor's orders."

"Oh." I frown and turn to Bastian. "Sorry. I guess I can't have pie."

"Oh, no, you two should go," Mom says. "Don't let me spoil the evening. You should celebrate your pitch-perfect performance to end this show you've worked so hard on. Go." She nudges Dad, and he gives me a twenty-dollar bill.

"But—"

"Can you drive her home, then?" Dad asks.

"Sure," Bastian says. "I'll get her home."

Off go my parents. This seems suspiciously like they have set me up on a date, but it's with Bastian, so . . .

I smile. "All righty, then. Here we go."

"So tell me the truth: Are you a Mormon?" I ask him later.

He pretends to choke on his bite of pie. "You think I'm *Mormon*?"

I shrug. "I don't know. You're still kind of a mystery to me. Conservative parents. Never kissed a girl before you kissed me. Lover of all things musical theater. . . ."

"I'm not Mormon," he says with a laugh. "My parents aren't, either. They're just a little traditional about the world."

"I see. Well, parents will be that way, I guess."

He raises his eyebrows. "Your parents seem great."

"They are great."

He sighs. "I think you're great, too."

I'm blushing. God. It's so bizarre that almost every night for the last three weeks or so, I've been kissing this guy, getting carried off by him, rolling around with him, literally, but it's tonight that feels like a kind of beginning. Maybe because it's the first time we've actually been alone together.

Thank you, universe, I think.

"I'm so glad I met you." He lifts his cup of coffee. "To us."

"To us."

We clink and drink. He gives a little moan at how good his coffee is. "I couldn't survive without coffee. How could you have ever thought I was Mormon?"

I don't know. I really don't know.

* * *

He drives me home. He's quiet on the way, like he has something on his mind. I guess I can't blame him. I have something on my mind, too.

I want to tell him that I like him. That I've always liked him. That he's my version of the perfect boy. I want to ask him on another date, a real date where he picks me up and we go see a movie or something.

We pull up to my house. The windows are dark. My dad's not home from the hospital yet.

Bastian stares out the windshield. "I didn't tell you when I was here before, but . . ." He turns to me, smiles, and my breath catches. "I love your house. It's got character."

Oh. My house. "The blue window boxes were my idea, but the rest is my mother. She's the decorator in the family."

"I'm so happy for you, that she got a new heart."

"She deserved it." I smile. "She's the best."

"Right. But I mean I'm happy for *you*. There were some days when you looked so sad at school and rehearsal. And other days where you seemed . . ."

"Pissed off?" I answer for him.

He nods. "You were a cute pissed off, but yeah. And then there was the fight with Nyla."

My stomach gets all twisty. "I wasn't myself that day. You believe that, right?"

"Yeah, you were going through something," he says so easily I could sing. "Everybody freaks out from time to time, don't they? But now things are fine again with Nyla, right? You two are back to being like peas in a pod. Or, like, joined at the hip. Birds of a feather."

"Did Nyla ever say anything about our fight?" I wonder if she told him about the other thing I said to her that day. The racist thing. I don't know if I could look him in the eye if he knew.

"She said you were having a bad day because your mom was sick, and we all have bad days."

Because Nyla really is the best bestie.

"Anyway," he says.

"Anyway." I wonder if he'll lean over now and kiss me. A real kiss this time, with no one else gawking at us. I wet my lips nervously.

"I better get going," Bastian says. "I have a pretty strict curfew, and I desperately need to sleep. We've got to take down the set tomorrow."

He walks me to the door. We stand for a minute under the porch light. Then he says, "Good night, fair maiden!" in the prince voice and drops into a courtly bow.

I giggle and attempt a curtsy. "See you tomorrow. Good night."

That's when I lunge forward and press my lips to his.

Bastian steps back, his dark eyes wide. "Whoa. What was that?"

"Me, trying to be brave," I explain. "Make the first move. Own my feelings."

"Yeah, but Cass—"

"I like you," I say finally. "Hasn't that been obvious? I think I've been pretty obvious. I like you so much."

He frowns. "Yes. I like you, too, but . . ."

He's upset for some reason. I don't know what the problem could be.

"Cass," he groans. "Oh, Cass."

"Bastian." My stomach suddenly feels like it's on the sidewalk.

He doesn't like me back.

"Is it Nyla?" I ask hoarsely.

"Nyla? What?"

"Are you in love with Nyla? I would understand if you were. I know you two are close now. I mean, Nyla's beautiful and talented and smart."

He shakes his head like he's trying to wake himself up from a bad dream. "Yeah, Nyla's great—I love Nyla—but Cass . . ."

He loves Nyla. God. "I'm sorry. I'm really sorry. I shouldn't have— I should—"

"I'm gay," he says.

I'm floored. "Huh?"

He drags a hand through his hair. "I thought you knew. Nyla knows, doesn't she?"

"No, Nyla doesn't know you're gay," I gasp. "How would we know?"

"Well, doesn't everybody know about . . . and I told Alice months ago. I thought she would have . . ." He shrugs. "I thought you knew."

"But you've been flirting with me."

He looks stricken. "Oh my God. That's how I make friends, Cass. That's not how I flirt. I am so sorry. I didn't know you were—"

"But you said I have great lips."

"Because you do," he says. "I'm gay. I'm not blind."

"But you kept staring at me when you didn't think I was looking. Like you were crushing on me."

"You reminded me of someone I know," he says.

"Oh." I stagger back a few steps. "Oh . . . boy. I'm a total fool."

He shakes his head urgently. "You're not. You're brilliant. You're like the most amazing girl I've ever met. If I liked girls, you'd be the perfect girl for me."

I give him a sharp look.

"Okay, I get that that's not helping." He holds his hands out like he's trying to give me some invisible something that will make this all less humiliating. "What can I do?"

"I think I need to . . ." I open the door to my house and stiffly step inside. "Good night, Bastian."

"Good night, Cass."

"I'll see you . . . tomorrow." Oh flip, how can I possibly see him tomorrow?

"Okay. Tomorrow. We'll talk then, right?"

"Good night." I slam the door and lean against it for a minute. "I'm a fool."

"You're not a fool," he says through the door.

"Go away, Bastian!" I yell.

"I'm going away now!"

I fumble for my phone. I can't call Nyla fast enough.

I unlock my phone, and the first thing I see is the notification for a missed call. A voicemail in my inbox from a number labeled IDAHO HEALTH AND WELF— And then it's like my world freezes for a second. Everything stops.

I click on the message.

"Hello," the lady's cheerful voice says into my ear. "This is Linda, calling from the Bureau of Vital Records and Health Statistics regarding your request to receive any letter that might have been written to you in the Birth Mother Correspondence Program. Well, we've got some letters for you. We'll need you to come and pick them up in person. Please bring two forms of identification—your driver's license and social security card would do. Our office hours this week are Monday through Friday, eight a.m. to five p.m. Call me if you have any questions, but I hope to see you soon."

All thoughts of Bastian and my utter humiliation fade in an instant. I put the phone down, then pick it up and listen to the message one more time.

"Wait," I say to my empty house. "Letters, as in more than one?"

Then I call Nyla for an entirely different reason than I was going to sixty seconds ago.

"Ny, wake up," I say when she answers.

"What's happening?" she asks blearily. "Hey, did you leave tonight with Bastian? Your mom said something yesterday about how she might try to use her mom powers or the universe or something."

"Bastian's gay. But I don't care about that."

"*What?*"

"It doesn't matter. I've got bigger stuff to deal with. As usual." My hands are shaking so hard I almost drop the phone.

"Bigger stuff than Bastian being gay?"

"I need you," I gasp. "Can you come over now?"

Dear X,

I keep telling myself that at some point I'm going to stop writing these letters. You know all about me by now. You're probably even sick of me. I can imagine you opening this one thinking, God, just give birth to me already! Get it over with! Stop talking!

Sorry, X.

Of course it's possible that in the next few days all that I'll be capable of writing is UGHHHHHHHHHHHH.

It's been a rough day.

Which brings me back to why I am writing this particular letter. My dad came to visit me today. I was genuinely surprised when Melly knocked on my door and said he was waiting for me downstairs. He never wanted to really talk to me, ever, even when I lived with him. For a guy who's supposed to make his living relating to people, he doesn't know how to talk to them.

I went downstairs to the living room and there he was, sitting awkwardly on the couch, his hands folded in his lap.

"Hey, Dad," I said a little shyly. "Long time, no see."

He stared at my belly. "You look—"

"I know."

He shook his head, as if he couldn't believe I could get myself in this situation. As if the thought of me having sex still shocked him to the core. "How are you feeling?" he managed.

I came right out with it. "Why are you here?"

He cleared his throat. "I wanted to see how you were."

"You did? Why?"

"You're my daughter."

"Oh, okay. So why did you want to see me now? You weren't so concerned before."

"I've called," he said.

"Once. In the five months I've been here."

He looked down at his hands. "Evelyn and I are getting a divorce."

I couldn't help it—an incredulous laugh slipped out. "Oh my God. Why?"

"It's complicated."

"I think Evelyn's a total she-demon, so it doesn't seem that complicated to me." I lowered myself carefully onto the couch next to him. "Are you going to be okay?"

"I'm fine."

It struck me then that, in so many ways, he and I are exactly alike. "Are you sad?" I asked.

"I'm sorry about Evelyn," he said. "How she treated you."

"Which time?"

He gave a miserable, humorless laugh. "Do you want to come home? You asked me if you could come home, before. Did you mean it?"

My breath caught. Of course I'd said that. But did I mean it? Would I want to go home, if Evelyn was gone?

Dad glanced around the room, like he finally cared and was figuring out if this place I've been living in was good enough for his little girl. I was instantly aware of the shabby carpet, the dinosaur television straight out of the eighties, the faint stain on the couch cushion right under my leg.

Dad sighed. "If you feel like I pushed you into this—being here, giving up this baby, any of it, you don't have to do it, honey."

"You didn't push me," I said automatically. "I made the decision on my own."

"But if you want to come home. If you want to bring the baby home, too, you can. I'll help you. We could hire a nanny."

I started laughing that self-defense laugh where I can't stop. I laughed and laughed until I peed a little. Then I stood up.

"What about your constituents? It would look bad for you. You'd come off as a hypocrite. It'd hurt your career."

"I could handle it," he said.

I felt like I was going to throw up. I haven't vomited in a while, I realized. Almost nine months in, and I'm finally past the morning sickness. Hooray for the small favors.

Dad stood up, too. He had come to tell me something, and he had. He could now check that errand off the list. It was time to flee. "Think about it," he said.

"I will."

I was thinking about it as I walked him outside and down the sidewalk to where he'd parked his car on the street. I was thinking about it hard.

"I'll be in touch," he said, which I thought was a strange thing to say to your daughter. It must have been habit—what he tells people at the end of a meeting. In touch. But that doesn't mean he actually wants to touch me.

"Bye, Dad." I went to hug him, but my belly got in the way.

I tried to imagine the life he'd just offered me: the big brick house on the hill, with him and me and no Evelyn and possibly a nanny. And you.

You. Who currently has the hiccups.

You could be mine again. I could hold you and talk to you and play you all my records and push you around in a stroller and actually be your mother.

The word felt like it got stuck in my throat.

Mother.

And then I thought, having access to a nanny doesn't suddenly turn me into a suitable mother. The problem was never that I wouldn't have childcare. It wasn't Evelyn. Or my dad's career. Or that I wouldn't have money to feed and clothe you, like so many of the girls here at Booth have to struggle so hard to do.

The problem was that I'm not mother material. Not yet, anyway. Maybe not ever.

"Who's that?" Dad said, and a car door slammed, and I looked up to see Ted ambling up the sidewalk toward us.

It was a full day of visitors here at Booth.

"Hi," I said. "Long time, no see." I meant this to be funny, since I'd only seen Ted a week ago.

337

"Hi." He handed me something small and disc-shaped wrapped in brown paper. "They have these great chocolate chip cookies at the SUB today. I brought you one."

"Thanks." I stared at him, charmed and suddenly hungry and wildly confused. I like Ted. I think about him, probably more than I should. I mean, what pregnant girl gets a crush on her baby daddy's former roommate who she hardly knows?

But, and I think this is an equally important question, who visits a pregnant girl at a home for unwed mothers to bring her a cookie?

"Oh. And I brought you this." He handed me an envelope.

I peeked inside. It was the non-identifying information form I'd given Dawson last week, all filled out, it looked like, in Dawson's messy scrawl.

"Thank you," I said.

You shifted inside me. I instinctively put my hand on my belly and rubbed. It's getting crowded in there.

It was getting pretty crowded out here, too.

"Don't tell me this is the father," Dad said then in this hard voice that made me turn to look at him. He seemed like a different person than he had ten minutes before, staring down Ted with this furious expression like he was considering taking a swing at him.

Ted looked genuinely alarmed and embarrassed, which didn't help matters. "Um, sir, I—"

Dad kept going. "Where are you from?"

Oh, NOW he gets protective, I thought, now he cares. But then I watched his lip actually curl back, and I realized, he wasn't acting like this because he was trying to protect me, his poor pregnant daughter.

Ted said the name of the college.

Dad shook his head. "No. Before that. Where's your family from?"

Ted's jaw tightened. "Uh, Homedale? I also have some family in Jerome. But my parents live in Homedale."

"You should be ashamed," Dad snarled. "You know you don't belong with my daughter."

Right. So this was because Ted doesn't look white. Or white enough, anyway.

This was because, apparently, my dad's a racist.

Excuse me, X, but I lost it for a minute.

"He is the father," I blurted out. "So can he move in with us, too, Dad? Help raise our daughter? I could even marry him, if you wanted." I tried not to notice the way Ted's face went pale and slack with amazement. I kept on talking. "We'd be one big happy family then, wouldn't we? That'd be nice. I can picture our Christmas card."

"I don't think that's a good idea." Dad cleared his throat again. "You're doing the right thing with the adoption."

At that moment I hated him, because I knew. It wasn't only Ted my dad was rejecting here. It was you too, X, if he thought Ted was your father. Just like that, he'd decided he couldn't love you.

But I pretended not to understand. "What, now I can't come to live with you again, either? Why not? What's wrong, Dad?"

He turned and unlocked his car. "We'll talk about it later."

"Will we?"

He didn't answer. He got into his car and drove away.

So that's a no.

I turned to Ted, who was still standing in the middle of the sidewalk with his shoulders kind of caved in, looking at me.

"I'm sorry," I said. "There's no excuse for him."

"What about you?"

"I don't know why I said you were the father."

"I do. You wanted to stick it to him."

"Maybe."

"I should go," Ted said.

I tried to fix it. "Ted, I'm sorry. I didn't mean to—"

"It's okay," he said. "I just don't really like being used. Enjoy the cookie."

"Wait, can I at least call you?"

"Uh, sure," he said, but I could tell he meant no. Then he got back in his car and drove away.

It's been a lonesome afternoon. But today has been illuminating. It's made me face two big truths that I've been dancing around lately:

I am doing the right thing with the adoption. I need to get you out of here, X, get you somewhere you'll have a chance to grow up around decent people.

I can't go back to living with my dad, not even after you're born. I can't go home. I'm not even sure, at this point, where my home is.

Now I only have to figure out where I'm going to go.

S

35

"I will sail my vessel," Nyla's singing really loud, "till the river runs dry. Like a bird before the wind, these waters are my sky . . ."

It's a fine Sunday morning, cold but with clear blue skies. There's snow on the ground today, and the sun is shining. Mom and Dad think I'm at the strike-the-set party and then staying over at Nyla's tonight, but instead we're taking a little drive with Garth Brooks.

I didn't tell my parents about the letter. Not yet. I didn't want to excite my mother, is how I explained this decision to Nyla. There's only so much that her new heart can take. But the real reason for not telling Mom is a question that's been bugging me since last night.

What if she doesn't want me to get this letter anymore, now that she's not dying?

And now that I know for certain that there *is* a letter from my birth mother, and all I have to do is show up to get it, it hasn't felt like a choice.

I have to see this letter.

Or letters, plural. That part was a bit unclear.

So it's just Nyla and me, cruising along in Bernice with the heater on high, singing country songs, driving west, again. To Boise, again. Cutting school tomorrow, again. Paying a visit to the Bureau of Vital Records and Health Statistics. Again.

But this time it's different.

"You okay over there?" Nyla asks, glancing at me.

"Yeah," I say tensely. My stomach rolls. I try to focus on the far-away horizon and not the stuff we're zooming past.

"Well, I know I'm freaking out a little," she says. "So I can't imagine how you're feeling."

I'm trying to manage my expectations. I've been burned so many times with this adoption thing in the past few months that the truth about my birth mother has started to feel like a myth, something that doesn't exist in reality. Like a fairy tale.

"What if this is opening up a can of worms, like you said?" I ask suddenly. "What if I shouldn't do this?"

She grips the steering wheel more tightly. "It's just a letter, Cass. You can decide what to do about it after you read it."

"Right, but what if reading it really messes me up? I can't unread it."

"I don't know. But if there was a letter from my mother, I would want to read it," Nyla says quietly. "No matter what."

I readjust my seat belt along my collarbone. I can't get comfortable. "It's just a letter," I say again.

The next morning we show up at the Bureau of Vital Records and Health Statistics the moment they open. This time I am issued number E05, and the current number is E03. Nyla and I take a seat in the waiting room.

"What makes a record *vital*, exactly?" Nyla asks, cocking her head to one side.

I don't know. This place feels pretty vital to me.

She takes out a ball of fuzzy, bright yellow yarn.

"What is *that*?" I ask her.

"It will be a hat for your mom. She told me once that yellow is the color of happiness. Of sunshine and daisies and baby ducks. So I'm making her a happiness hat."

I sigh and twist the star ring on my finger guiltily.

"Your mom is going to be fine." Nyla arranges the yarn and the needles and starts to knit, a mesmerizing, repetitive motion that instantly makes me feel calmer. "It was her idea, remember?"

"I know. But what if she changes her mind?"

"What if she doesn't?"

My phone buzzes. A text from Bastian. I've received a barrage of texts from him over the last twenty-four hours, but I haven't answered him yet.

Bastian: You and Nyla skipped the cast party. Now I'm at school and you're both not here. This is getting ridiculous. Where are you? Please, you can't avoid me forever. We need to talk.

I can practically hear the hurt in his voice.

I sigh. He deserves some kind of answer.

Me: I'm not avoiding you. Something came up, and I had to skip the cast party and go to Boise to take care of it.

Bastian: Boise? What's in Boise?

Nyla glances at my phone. "Bastian? Oh boy. Here we go."

Of course I've already told her everything. Here's how she responded:

"Well, that makes sense."

And I said, "Sense? What kind of sense does that make?"

"He said kissing you was the first time he'd ever kissed *a girl*. Not the first time he'd ever been kissed."

"Oh. *Oh*."

"We should have known. He loves *Hello, Dolly!* And he has excellent taste in shoes."

"Nyla," I explained. "Not every gay man loves musicals and has good shoes. They're all individual people. Like my uncle Pete. He's a florist, but he also has a scraggly beard and rides a Harley."

"Oh, right, your uncle Pete."

And now she seems to think the entire thing with Bastian is kind of sweet and also vastly amusing.

"Tell Bastian hello from me," she says now.

Bastian: Look, I'm sorry. Please forgive me. I want us to be friends, Cass.

That's what he always wanted, wasn't it? That's the word he used. *Friends.* Why didn't I listen to his words?

Bastian: I'm sorry I'm sorry I'm sorry.

Me: Don't be sorry! I'm the one who should be apologizing. It was me who misinterpreted everything. I completely misread your signals. But it really is fine. I'm over it.

It's true, I find as I type the words. I'm fine. I mean, I'm still wildly embarrassed, especially when I think of how it must have looked when I flung myself into Bastian's unsuspecting arms. Or how I screamed "go

344

away" at him through the front door. But my heart didn't get broken over Bastian Banks. My heart is still very much intact.

Bastian: Wait, you're OVER it?

Me: I want to be friends, too. I already have a best friend, obviously, but let's be second-best friends. Okay?

Bastian: Sure. Second-best friends.

Me: Oh, and Nyla says hello.

"Want me to teach you to knit again?" Nyla asks, dangling the will-be-a-hat at me. "It might get your mind off things."

I shake my head. The last thing I need is to get tangled up in a mess of yarn right now.

Nyla sighs and throws the hat back into her bag. "You're killing me here, Smalls. I can't knit when there's so much tension in the air. I keep messing up." She grabs a magazine and flips through it. I don't know who's more nervous right now, her or me.

Someone calls number E05.

I thrust my phone into my pocket and stand up.

"Hello, my name is Cassandra McMurtrey," I tell the woman at the counter. "I got a call on Friday regarding some letters that are being held for me?"

"Oh, yes," says the woman, smiling warmly. She turns and calls into the back. "Linda!"

I get that surreal feeling again as Linda steps up to the counter. Maybe it's because Linda is wearing the same pink sweater she had on last time. In fact, she looks exactly the same as she did the last time I saw her—the same pearl earrings, the same perfectly manicured pink fingernails, the same hair. Only this time she doesn't look annoyed. In fact, she seems happy to see me.

"I came for the—"

"Letters," she says. "I know. Sign here."

I sign a paper and show her my various forms of ID, which she hardly glances at, because she knows I'm me.

"I have to say, I've never seen anything quite like this," she says as we're filling out the paperwork. "It's unusual, to say the least."

I stare at her. I'm floating somewhere above my body again, like my head is a balloon full of helium bobbing near the ceiling and I'm holding on to it by the string.

"Here you go." She reaches down and pulls out a large stack of yellowed envelopes, held together by a red rubber band. She plops them onto the counter in front of me. "All yours."

"All of them?" It seems impossible that these could all be for me.

Linda beams. "All of them. Good luck."

I fall back into my body for a second so I can draw the stack to my chest and lift it off the counter. It's not as heavy as Linda made it look. I turn and float over to Nyla, who glances up at me.

"Ready to—whoa," she says. "What the *what?*"

I sink into the chair beside her. I should wait until I get somewhere private, but I'm not exactly in control of my body right now. I don't wait. I pull the top letter free from the rubber band and open it. Inside is a piece of yellow paper, and when I unfold that, there's the weird handwriting I recognize from the non-identifying information form. Half cursive, half print.

It's her. She wrote this. My birth mother wrote this.

Dear X,

Today Melly has us writing letters to our babies. . . .

I fold the letter up again quickly, stuff it back into the envelope

346

and the envelope back into the pile. I snap the rubber band around them.

"Hey." Nyla touches my shoulder. "Just breathe."

I look up at her. A tear trickles down my cheek.

She reaches up and brushes it away. "It's going to be okay, Cass."

"I know." I take a deep, shuddering breath.

She stares at the pile in my lap. "So all of these are letters from your birth mother?"

"I think so."

"Holy crap," she murmurs.

Yeah. Once again, that about sums it up.

36

Back in the car, as we're driving to Idaho Falls, I read the letters—all seventeen of them—in the space of an hour. At one point Nyla has to pull over so I can throw up at the side of the road, because reading in the car really exacerbates my car sickness, but I can't stop. I keep reading, one letter after another, in a rush, like I'm at the birth-mother buffet and it's all you can eat. I gobble the letters up. Then I read them aloud to Nyla, and we spend the rest of the ride in silence, mostly, digesting the letters. These words, written for me.

When Nyla finally drops me off, I stagger back into my house and lock myself in my room and read each letter again slowly, taking it sentence by sentence, line by line, until they all start to bleed together into a single conversation.

Dear X,

Me again. Who else? . . . I'm just going to lean into this letter thing. . . . I'm sitting here all knocked up and there's no Prince Charm-ing in sight. . . . Your sperm donor is not a total asshat. . . . I was going in one direction, and then something happened to cause me to go the other way. . . . I'm so sorry about the weird feet. . . . You belong with them. . . . I want you to have THESE PARENTS, the teacher and the cake maker and the laughing. . . . I'm not ready to be a mother. . . . I guess I'm not ready to let you go. I'll see you on the other side.

S

She writes like she's speaking, pages and pages of her talking with me—at me, directly to me—and I feel irrationally guilty that I have no memory of her or of any of the moments she describes when I was with her. But her letters make me laugh my head off and cry my eyes out. I stare and stare at the picture of myself, the grainy black-and-white sonogram, and I try to imagine what it must have been like to hear her voice, to feel her touch, to drift off to sleep to the beating of her heart.

Then, when I've fallen apart a few times and put myself back together again, I get Nyla to pick me up and drop me at the hospital. My mom is officially being released in about three hours.

My parents are kissing when I come through the door to Mom's room. Kissing. Like old times when I used to catch them kissing when they thought I wasn't looking. In the hallway. Kissing. In the bathroom right after they brushed their teeth. Kissing. Folding laundry. Kissing. Making dinner. Kissing. Like, well, teenagers. I used to think they were excessive and gross. But now the sight of them kissing again like normal, healthy people fills me with joy.

I try for a joke. "Hey, is that good for your heart?"

"Oh, hello, sweetie," Mom says, and she's smiling, and she's not

349

wearing a cannula or an IV anymore, not hooked up to anything. It's a sight I never thought I'd see again. "I was hoping you'd come by," she says. "How was your day?"

"Fine," I croak.

"No more rehearsals. You're a free agent." Dad grins. "Want to all go to a movie?"

"Bill." Mom frowns. "Not a movie."

"Well, why not?" he says. "Okay, so we had one epically bad movie experience. But does that mean we should never see a movie again?"

"I think it might mean that, Dad."

"No," he says. "No, we have to get back on the horse. I used to love movies. I miss movies. We should go."

"All right," Mom laughs. "What's playing?"

"The new Star Wars movie," I inform them.

Dad groans. "Okay, it's too soon. How about dinner? What's close to here?"

He's joking; at least I think he is. Mom's supposed to go home tonight, not out on the town. She's supposed to go straight home and straight into bed, where she's supposed to rest and rehabilitate for weeks. Months. Years, who knows? But that's fine by me, so long as she's home.

"Perkins," Mom says, playing along. "Oh, I do miss pie." She turns to me. "How was Perkins, by the way? You've kind of clammed up on us since Saturday. Somehow I never got the details about your date with Bastian."

"Bastian's gay." I feel weird about telling them this, this thing that is so personal about Bastian, but if I don't tell them they'll continue to build it up.

"He *is*?" Mom is shocked. "But I thought you liked him."

"I did."

"So when did you find out he was gay?"

"Right after I kissed him, on Saturday night, after our date at Perkins."

"Oh, Boo," Dad says, in sympathy. "Bummer."

I shrug. "We discussed it, Bastian and me. I'm okay, and he's okay."

"Obviously it wasn't meant to be," Mom says.

"You don't seem too broken up about it," Dad observes.

"I'm fine. I'm better than fine. You're coming home."

"Home," Mom sighs, smiling. She turns to Dad. "Let's go home, Bill."

He checks his watch. "We've got a couple more hours. What will we do to pass the time?"

That's my cue. "I need to tell you something," I blurt out. Because if I'm going to shock my mother with this news, it should probably be at the hospital. Just in case.

"Uh-oh," Dad says. "Tell us what?"

"I need you to be calm, all right? Both of you. Don't freak out."

"Cass . . . ," Dad says like a warning. "What are you doing?"

"I can be calm." Mom grabs Dad's hand. "We can be calm, can't we, honey?"

I just spit it out. "I went to Boise today. Well, yesterday and today. I just got back."

My parents look at each other. "What? Why?" Dad asks.

"They found the letters from my birth mother." I sling my back-pack off my shoulder. "They called and left me a message on Saturday, saying I had to pick them up in person. So I went to get them."

Silence. They're both staring at me in shock.

"Letters?" Mom asks after a minute. "As in, more than one?"

I take the bundle out of my backpack and hold them up.

"There are seventeen of them," I report with a giddy laugh. "Some of them are really long, too, like ten pages front and back. She's long-winded. But she's honest and whip-smart and hilarious, Mom, and I feel like I know her, reading what she wrote."

"What do they say?" There's a tremor of fear in her voice.

"They're amazing. Some of them are about my birth father, who was an actor—an *actor*, right?—and some of them are about her life at the school, like she's writing in a diary. She was living in a home for pregnant girls. I don't know if you knew that. And some are about her dad and her evil stepmother and her mom in Colorado and this guy Ted she had a crush on." I stop myself. I can't tell them everything right now. There's too much.

"Did she give . . . names?" Mom asks.

"No. She made up names, like aliases, for everybody in her life. And she always signed what she wrote with the letter *S*. So I guess that Amber lady was right, after all."

Dad's expression freezes. He's been looking kind of frozen this entire time, actually. Like my news has turned him to stone.

"What Amber lady?" Mom asks.

I'd forgotten that I never told Mom about the false alarm with the adoption registry website. My bad.

"I'll tell you everything later," I say quickly. "I promise. But you can read the letters yourself. When you get home. Or . . . now. If you want."

I hold the bundle out to her.

She's calm. But she gazes at the stack of letters like she's not sure what to do.

"You're my mother," I say like it's a disclaimer. "Nothing will ever,

ever change that. Do you still want to know about her, even though you're not dying anymore?"

She looks up at me, and her eyes are uncertain, and sad, and understanding, all at the same time. "I don't know," she admits softly. "Everything's happening so fast."

"Cat, we don't have to—" Dad starts.

"I want to know," I say firmly. "And I want to share this with you."

Mom takes the letters carefully out of my hands. "Thank you, honey," she says.

"Okay. Good." I go out and close the door behind me. I want to give them time, alone, to read and process it all.

Then we have a lot to talk about.

Dear X,

I've been thinking, actually, that I don't need to write this letter. If you're reading this, you've been adopted, so it doesn't matter, right? I should write about something else. The weather (still hot). Sports (ugh, not sports). Something. Not this. But then I got thinking about how I want you to know as much as possible about me, and about Dawson, so that by knowing about the two of us you'll also know more about yourself; a little more, anyway. It all comes back to: if I were you, I'd want to know.

In my last letter you'll recall that Ted brought me the form—the non-identifying information form, filled out by Dawson. I thought I'd pass it along to Melly, and she could put it in the official file along with my form (the boring version of my form, that is) and you'd have a more or less complete picture of the two of us.

But then I read Dawson's form.

It's messed up, X. I remember now that Ted said Dawson had a kind of crapshoot life, and you can totally read between the lines and see that crapshoot life when you read the form. It's not great, is what I'm saying. It brings up a lot of potential problems. I worried for you when I read that form, and then I worried about your parents.

What if they see what's in there and decide that they don't want you after all? What if they're turned off by his baggage? Not that any of it is his fault. I want to stress that Dawson's smart and talented at everything he tries and funny and sexy and cool. But what if all your parents see is the word jail and the word drugs and they want a different baby, a new and improved baby?

I'm two weeks away from having you, X, if that.

I can't find new parents for you now. I don't want to. I want you to have THESE PARENTS, the teacher and the cake maker and the laughing.

So this morning, I made up my mind. I decided not to turn in Dawson's form. It wouldn't be out of the ordinary for the birth father not to fill out the form. No one would ask me about it. No one would go to Dawson and demand that he fill it out again. I could throw it away, or keep it, put it in a drawer somewhere and forget about it. That would be the smart thing to do.

But I never have been that smart, now have I?

So I asked myself, then, why? Why would I hide Dawson's form from you and from your parents? Why not simply let the truth be the truth? Let the chips fall. Keep it real.

And the answer was an easy one: because I'm scared, DUH.

This whole pregnancy deal is all about fear lately. When my mom was pregnant with me, they might have told her something vague about not getting drunk when you're pregnant and maybe not smoking. I don't

355

know. It was the eighties. This was probably the gist of the pregnancy advice: "Don't drink too much and/or don't do too many drugs. Now push."

But these days there's this huge list of don'ts. I shouldn't drink at all, or smoke, obviously. I shouldn't eat a ham sandwich, because there could be listeria in the deli meat, and pregnant women are susceptible to listeriosis. I could literally die from eating a ham sandwich. You could die. Also, no sushi—although I'm not a big fan of raw fish anyway—and no soft cheese or anything unpasteurized, and no black licorice, which I happen to love. No hot baths—I could cook you inside of me if the water is hotter than 99 degrees. No roller coasters (okay, this one makes sense) and no lying on my back when I sleep—I should lie on my left side, because you get more blood flow that way or something. I shouldn't eat too much, because then I might inadvertently imprint obesity into your DNA, but I shouldn't eat too little, because you need to grow quality eyeballs and such. I shouldn't eat too many peanuts, because you might develop a peanut allergy. But I shouldn't avoid peanuts, either, because you . . . might develop a peanut allergy.

I mean, what the hell?

The point is, I'm supposed to be afraid now, very, very afraid. And sometimes I am. Sometimes you sleep inside of me for a long time, unmoving, and I feel this fear bubbling up in my brain, that maybe you got tangled up in the cord and you're strangling in there and how would I even know? My body starts to feel like a hazardous place for you. So I drink cold water to wake you up, although I'm not sure how that's supposed to work. And if you don't start moving around after that, I poke you. That's right. You're a baby, simply trying to take a nap, and I'm out here poking you in the back because I'm scared I'm not keeping you safe enough.

Ugh, right? And it's not really better out here. If you were born already, your parents would have a lot to be afraid of, too. SIDS. Autism. The things you'll grab and put in your mouth. Whether vaccinations are actually safe, which they are, but there's a bunch of people out there screaming about how they're not, so then you have to be afraid of vaccinations or afraid of your baby getting sick and dying because someone else didn't vaccinate their kid. Then there are kidnappings and your face on milk cartons. Kids coming to school with guns and killing people, like at Columbine last year. Date rape. Drug overdoses. STDs and teenage pregnancy—ha! And on and on it goes, a never-ending list of things to be terrified of when it comes to you.

It's society, I guess. We're always being told that we should be afraid.

But I'm sick of being ruled by fear. I refuse to be. Don't you deserve to at least know both the good and the bad? Don't your parents deserve to know? And if they do reject you because of things in Dawson's background, they probably shouldn't be your parents, no matter how great that woman's cupcakes are.

So I've now decided to be honest with you and not hold anything back. If I were you, and this form had all this information about my biological father, I'd want to read it.

I'd still want to know.

Okay, I turned in the form at lunch break. And yeah, it's not flattering, X. Your parents can throw it in a drawer, too, if that's what they think is best. I'm going to leave that up to them to decide. But if you're reading this now, like I said, it doesn't really matter. They adopted you anyway. You've probably read the form by now, and maybe you're not thrilled about it. But that's okay.

I just want to say: your genes don't define you. Dawson actually wrote that on the form himself, or something similar to it, and he would know. Your genetic makeup is only a small part of the person you'll become. I'm counting on that, X. I'm taking the side of nurture over nature here.

You're going to be fine, X. You're going to be great.

S

37

I return to the hospital. It's been two hours since I dropped the letter bomb on my parents. It feels too soon, and I'm not sure what I expect to find when I go back into that room, but Mom's about to be discharged. We're out of time. I should have waited until she was home, I chide myself as I shuffle down the hallway toward her wing. I should have waited like a week or two. Maybe more. But it felt . . . impossible not to tell them. It had to come out.

My parents are both sitting on the bed when I slip back into the room. The letters are scattered between them, and they're talking earnestly, but when they see me they stop and both kind of open their arms, and I go over, and we all hold each other for a while. And then they let me go, and I stand back and look at them. Assessing for damage.

Mom's eyes and nose are red.

Dad clears his throat. "Before we talk about this, before we go any further, we—I—need to tell *you* something."

"This is about Dawson's form, right?" I swallow, hard. That letter did make me stop and wonder what I might be getting myself into. Do I really want to know this stuff? "It's bad, isn't it?"

"It's not bad." Mom shakes her head like she's baffled at the idea. "I don't remember it being so bad. It was a long time ago when we received that form. Of course we had to wait until you were older before we could share it with you. Honestly, I'd forgotten about it."

I put a hand on my hip and give her a "Yeah, right. Nice try" kind of look, which is an expression, by the way, that I picked up from her. "But it was bad enough that you didn't give it to me when you gave me the one from my birth mother this year. Right? You kind of edited that part out."

"That was my choice," Dad sighs through his lips. He shakes his head sorrowfully. "It was the wrong call. I should have given them both to you. I see that now very clearly."

"Yeah, well, what do they say about hindsight?"

He meets my eyes steadily. "I'm sorry."

I'm not mad at him, even though I probably should be. The thing is, I trust my dad. He's always done his best to look out for me, to keep me safe, to do what he thinks is best, so it must be bad if he thought that what was best was for me not to know about it. Dad's always been an all-cards-on-the-table sort of father.

"It's okay," I say. "I hid some things from you, too."

"I didn't want you to get hurt," Dad says. "That's all."

"I know."

"But then your mother had to go and remind me of how totally capable you are at handling everything that's thrown at you."

"No," I protest. "I am not."

"Yes, you are," Mom says. "You're our little rock."

"You see, we know. We were there, Boo," Dad continues. "I was right there next to you for the worst moments of my life and your life, too. And I think we must have done a bang-up job raising you, and I'm trying not to get a big head about it," he adds. "Because you're the strongest person I know."

And . . . I'm crying. Gah.

Dad stands up and hugs me that way he does where he puts his arms around me tight and rocks me from side to side. Then he pulls away. "Anyway. I'll give you the form in question as soon as we get back to the house, if you want. It's in the filing cabinet."

"All right." I glance at Mom. "But let's get it all out in the open when we get back, okay? We'll tell each other everything now. Everything we've been afraid to say. Everything we've left out."

"After we get home," Dad agrees. "Yes. Full disclosure."

"Speaking of home," Mom says, and gestures to the nurse who's appeared in the doorway. "It's check-out time."

"Let's get you out of here, Cat," says the nurse. "I'm sick of you."

"I'm ready," Mom says in practically a cheer. "Let's go, let's go."

We drive extra slowly all the way back to the house, with me riding shotgun and Mom in the back seat wrapped in a blanket, a strange reversal of roles. Then we walk her carefully up to the house, where Nyla has pinned up a sign across the front door that reads, "WEL-COME HOME, MAMA CAT" and through the living room and down the hall and into my parents' bedroom, where we arrange Mom on the bed and prop her up with pillows and ask her if she needs anything about a million times.

361

"No," she keeps saying. "This is all I need, right here."

Then she's asleep.

"I have to go fill some prescriptions," Dad announces when I come in from unpacking the car. "But first . . ."

He holds out a little bundle of folded paper. My breath catches.

"Maybe I don't want to read this," I say as I take it out of his hand anyway.

"Your mom's right. It's not so bad. Remember how I said your birth mother was a human being? The same goes for your birth father. Just read it. Or not. You can put it in a drawer, too. But it's yours now."

He leaves to get Mom's pills from the pharmacy. I sit at the kitchen table and unfold the papers. I don't want to be—how did S put it?—ruled by fear.

My phone pings. Nyla.

Nyla: How'd they take it?

Me: Like champions. As usual.

Nyla: Good. You mom's home now?

Me: Yes. She's sleeping. She loved the sign.

Nyla: Good.

Me: Dad gave me non-identifying information form.

Nyla: I thought you already had that.

Me: For my birth father.

Nyla: Oh. I was wondering about that. What does it say?

Me: I haven't read it yet. Dad literally gave it to me two minutes ago.

Nyla: Oh, sorry. I'll let you read.

(Like one minute later.)

Nyla: Do you need me to come over and read it with you? Remember I got you.

Me: Thanks. No. I got this myself.

I mute my phone and pick up the paper again. I feel like it should be labeled, "Caution. Proceed at your own risk." But I won't be ruled by fear. So I read on.

NON-IDENTIFYING INFORMATION
FOR ADOPTION REGISTRY

SOCIAL AND HEALTH HISTORY   ☐ Birth mother ☒ Birth father

The information in this report has been provided by the birth parent.
The Bureau of Vital Records is not responsible for the accuracy of this information.

DESCRIPTION OF SELF

Marital status: ☒ Single ☐ Married ☐ Separated

☐ Divorced ☐ Widowed

If married or separated: ☐ Civil marriage ☐ Religious ceremony

Are you an enrolled member of a Native American tribe, Alaskan village,

or affiliated with a tribe? ☐ Yes ☒ No If yes, what tribe?

Religion:

Catholic

Ethnic background (e.g., English, German, etc.):

I don't know. My grandma used to claim that her mother was half
Cherokee.

Country or state of birth:

Idaho

Race (e.g., Black, White, American Indian, Japanese, etc.):

White

Height:

5'11"

Weight:

150

Hair color and texture:

blond, curly

Eye color:

green

Unique physical features (e.g., freckles, moles, etc.):

Complexion: ☐ Fair ☒ Medium ☐ Olive ☐ Dark

☒ Right-handed ☐ Left-handed

Physical build (e.g., big/small boned, long/short limbed, muscular, etc.):

Slender, a little muscular—I work out.

Talents, hobbies, and other interests:

Theater, listening to music, playing guitar, painting and sculpting, writing songs, going to movies.

Which of the following describe your personality (check all that apply):

☐ Aggressive ☐ Emotional ☐ Happy ☐ Rebellious ☐ Shy

☐ Serious ☐ Calm ☒ Friendly ☒ Irresponsible ☒ Fun

☐ Temperamental ☐ Critical ☒ Outgoing ☐ Stubborn ☐ Unhappy

Comments:

I'm depressed sometimes. I handle it.

EDUCATION

Last grade level completed:

12

Average grade received or GPA:

B student

Presently in school: ☒ Yes ☐ No

Future plans for schooling:

I'm a theater major—going to graduate with my BA and then move to New York and be an actor full-time.

Subjects you are interested in:

Theater, music, art, history, literature.

Any school-related problems or challenges (tutoring, Special Ed, etc.):

None

EMPLOYMENT HISTORY

Current occupation:

Military service: ☐ Yes ☒ No If yes, branch of service:

Vocational training:

Work history:

gas station attendant, worked at a drive-in, fast food

FAMILY HISTORY

Was anyone in your family adopted? ☒ Yes ☐ No If yes, who?

I was adopted by my grandmother when I was 10.

Your order of birth (e.g., 1st of 4):

1st of 4

Personal relationships with parents, siblings, or extended family members:

Before I went to college I lived with my grandma and my brothers and sisters. She's strict but we are all pretty close. My mom's in jail for drugs. My dad split before I was born. So it's just my grandma and my siblings.

Summarize adjustment to pregnancy. Include how you and your parents adjusted to the pregnancy, and if you had peer support:

I told my grandma about this yesterday. She thinks I should keep the baby. But I think this is better.

YOUR BIRTH PARENTS (child's grandparents)
FATHER

Age (if deceased, state age at time of death):

?

Health problems:

?

Height/weight:

?

Hair/eye color:

?

Build: ☐ Small ☐ Medium ☐ Large ☐ Extra large

Complexion: ☐ Fair ☐ Medium ☐ Olive ☐ Dark

Right-/left-handed:

?

Description of personality (e.g., happy, shy, stubborn, etc.):

No idea. My grandma doesn't like to talk about him.

Talents, hobbies, interests:

Taking a walk.

Education:

?

Occupation:

?

Number of siblings:

?

Race (Black, White, American Indian, etc.):

?

Ethnic background (e.g., German, English, etc.):

?

Now I wish I knew.

Religion:

Probably not.

Marital status: ☐ Single ☐ Married ☐ Separated

                    ☐ Divorced ☐ Widowed

Aware of this pregnancy? ☐ Yes ☒ No

MOTHER

Age (if deceased, state age at time of death):

37

Health problems:

Her teeth and skin and hair are all bad because of the meth.

Height/weight:

5'9"? Always skinny.

Hair/eye color:

blond, green

Build: ☐ Small ☒ Medium ☐ Large ☐ Extra large

Complexion: ☐ Fair ☒ Medium ☐ Olive ☐ Dark

Right-/left-handed:

right

Description of personality (e.g., happy, shy, stubborn, etc.):

She's also bipolar so it depends on the day. I remember that sometimes she was really happy and sometimes she cried a lot.

Talents, hobbies, interests:

I don't know. She could play the piano a little.

Education:

?

Occupation:

incarcerated

Number of siblings:

1

Race (Black, White, American Indian, etc.):

white

Ethnic background (e.g., German, English, etc.):

German, Grandma says, and a little Native American.

Religion:

She used to go to the Calvary church sometimes when she was trying to get clean.

Marital status: ☒ Single ☐ Married ☐ Separated

☐ Divorced ☐ Widowed

Aware of this pregnancy? ☐ Yes ☒ No

YOUR BIRTH BROTHERS AND SISTERS (child's uncles and aunts)
1) ☒ BROTHER ☐ SISTER

Age (if deceased, state age at time of death):

17

Health problems:

Height/weight:

5'11"

Hair/eye color:

blond, green

Build: ☐ Small ☒ Medium ☐ Large ☐ Extra large

Complexion: ☐ Fair ☒ Medium ☐ Olive ☐ Dark

Right-/left-handed:

right

Talents, hobbies, interests:

smoking pot

Education:

11th

Occupation:

student

Religion:

none

Marital status: ☒ Single ☐ Married ☐ Separated
☐ Divorced ☐ Widowed

Aware of this pregnancy? ☐ Yes ☒ No

2) ☐ BROTHER ☒ SISTER

Age (if deceased, state age at time of death):

15

Health problems:

Height/weight:

5'6"

Hair/eye color:

black, brown

Build: ☒ Small ☐ Medium ☐ Large ☐ Extra large

Complexion: ☐ Fair ☐ Medium ☒ Olive ☐ Dark

Right-/left-handed:

right

Talents, hobbies, interests:

movies, music, drawing

Education:

9th

Occupation:

student

Religion:

none

Marital status: ☒ Single ☐ Married ☐ Separated
☐ Divorced ☐ Widowed

Aware of this pregnancy? ☐ Yes ☒ No

MEDICAL HISTORY

Please indicate "None" or "You" if you or any genetic relatives (i.e., your mother, father, sisters, brothers, grandparents, uncles, aunts, or any other children you have had) ever had or now has any of the medical conditions listed below. Please explain in the comments section.

Baldness:

Grandma says Grandpa was bald.

Birth defects: *None*

Clubfoot: *None*

Cleft palate: *None*

Congenital heart disease: *None*

Cancer:

Grandpa, lung cancer.

Other: *None*

ALLERGIES

Animals:

My younger sister is allergic to everything.

Asthma:

My younger sister.

Eczema:

Grandma

Food:

Younger sister

Hay fever/plants:

Sister

Hives:

Sister

Medications:

Sister

Other allergies:

Sister

Other (specify):

VISUAL IMPAIRMENT

Astigmatism:

I wear glasses/contacts.

Blindness: *None*

Color blindness: *None*

EMOTIONAL/MENTAL ILLNESS

Bipolar (manic depressive):

My mom. It came on when she was 22.

Schizophrenia:

Grandma says an aunt has that.

Severe depression:

My mom, my brother and sister.

Suicide:

One of my little sisters tried to kill herself last year. I was like that, too, when I was her age.

Obsessive-compulsive disorder: *None*

Personality disorder: *None*

Alcoholism/drug addiction:

My father, when he lived with us, and obviously my mom.

Other (specify): *None*

HEREDITARY DISEASES

Cystic fibrosis: *None*

Galactosemia: *None*

Hemophilia: *None*

Huntington's disease: *None*

Hypothyroidism or hyperthyroidism: *None*

CARDIOVASCULAR DISEASE

Heart attack:

My great-grandpa, before I was born.

Heart murmur: *None*

High blood pressure:

Grandma

Diabetes:

Grandma and my aunt.

SEXUALLY TRANSMITTED DISEASES

Chlamydia: *None*

Gonorrhea: *None*

Herpes:

My brother gets cold sores.

Syphilis: *None*

HIV/AIDS: *None*

Other (specify): *None*

NEUROLOGICAL DISORDERS

Cerebral palsy: *None*

Muscular dystrophy: *None*

Multiple sclerosis: *None*

Epilepsy: *None*

Stroke:

My great-grandma had a stroke but she was pretty old.

Rheumatic fever: *None*

Other (specify): *None*

DEVELOPMENTAL DISORDERS

Learning disability / ADHD:

My brother and I both have this.

Mental retardation (specify type): *None*

Down syndrome: *None*

Speech or hearing problems: *None*

Low birth weight:

    My younger sister.

Other (specify): *None*

HISTORY OF DRUG USE

PRESCRIPTION:

Specify type (e.g., Prozac, Accutane, etc.)

    Paxil

Date of last use:

    today

☒ Before conception   ☒ After conception

OVER-THE-COUNTER:

Specify type (e.g., diet pills, antihistamine, etc.)

☐ Before conception   ☐ After conception

OTHER TYPES OF DRUGS USED:

Alcohol

    Some

Specify type:

    Beer and hard stuff sometimes.

Date of last use:

    yesterday

☒ Before conception   ☒ After conception

Downers (i.e., sleeping pills, barbiturates, etc.)

Specify type:

Date of last use:

☐ Before conception   ☐ After conception

Cocaine ("Crack")

By injection? ☐ Yes ☐ No

Date of last use:

☐ Before conception ☐ After conception

Heroin/pain killers

By injection? ☐ Yes ☐ No

Date of last use:

☐ Before conception ☐ After conception

Hallucinogens (i.e., LSD, Ecstasy, PCP, etc.)

Specify type:

Date of last use:

☐ Before conception ☐ After conception

Cigarettes

I smoked in high school.

Specify type:

Marlboro

Date of last use:

☒ Before conception ☐ After conception

Marijuana

Yes

Date of last use:

Last week

☒ Before conception ☒ After conception

Other

Specify type:

Date of last use:

☐ Before conception ☐ After conception

SOCIAL AND HEALTH HISTORY   ☐ Birth mother ☒ Birth father

If you wish, please add any additional information that will further describe you and your situation. (Consider your schooling, health, work, goals and hopes for the future, relationship history, religious or spiritual beliefs, challenges, strengths, etc.)

I don't know what to say, because I just found out about this baby. My grandma raised me the best she could and she did a pretty good job. I am the first person in my family to go to college. I have messed-up genes, too, and I'm doing great. Okay, maybe not great, but fine. I'm going to make something of myself.

38

The first thing that sticks out to me is that my birth father was adopted, too. I mean, I know it's a totally different situation from my own. He was adopted by his grandmother, along with his siblings, but it's also true that he, like me, was raised by people who were not his biological parents. We have that much in common.

Oh, and then there's the part where he wants to be an actor in New York City. My birth father had the same love of the stage and the lights and the adrenaline of the show. So I may have inherited my birth mother's duck feet. But I inherited my birth father's dreams.

Reading the letters made me feel like I knew S, really knew her, understood the way she thought and how she felt about the world. Reading this form makes me feel like I know my birth father, who I like to imagine as D—D for Dawson, but I know that's not his name. And D's life wasn't perfect by any stretch of the imagination. I knew that going in. Yes, there's some stuff on that form that's less than ideal. But if I were Mom and Dad's biological child, I'd be worried about heart disease and MS, which is what my dad's sister died of a few years ago. Everybody's got baggage. And everyone has skeletons hidden somewhere in their family tree.

I'm just profoundly grateful that my parents didn't ask for a refund when they read the form. Say the words *jail* and *drugs* and *bipolar disorder*, throw in a few suicide attempts and an alcoholic deadbeat dad, and a lot of people would tap out. Instead they took a chance on me. They picked me. They loved me. They gave me a beautiful life.

After a couple of days, when things calm down a bit, my parents and I have the full-disclosure conversation. They tell me a different kind of story from the one I grew up hearing, the one about the desperate couple and the brave young girl. They recount everything they remember about my adoption, the stuff I already know and the stuff I didn't—every person they talked to during the process, lawyers and social workers, doctors, friends, every detail of their journey into acquiring me as their kid. And I, in turn, tell them about all the little steps of my search up to now, the stuff they already know and the stuff I kept to myself up to now: the birth certificate, the internet registry, the yearbooks, the letters. And when we're all finally on the exact same page of this story, we talk about what we want now.

"I want to find her," I say, looking back and forth between them. "I hope that's okay."

This goes beyond simple curiosity for me now. I'm becoming achingly aware of an S-shaped hole inside of me, an empty space that was always there, but I can feel it more keenly now that I've read the letters. I can hear S's voice in the back of my head. Her funny, sarcastic way of talking. I can hear myself, is the thing. In her voice, I can hear part of me. Or maybe I've got that backward.

She's part of me. I'm a part of her.

"We want to help you find her," Dad says, and I believe him this time.

"But can you wait for a little while, so we can all do it together?" Mom asks tremulously. "Maybe this is selfish, but . . . I don't want you to do it without me."

"Yes," I agree, because it feels like I owe her that much. "Yes, I'll wait."

Dear X,

I feel like an elephant, like you've been in there for two years and you're never coming out. Like a stuffed turkey in the oven. Or a beached whale. I'm bloated and ready to pop.

I want to do all the things that are listed in the What to Expect book you can do to bring on labor. I'm taking long walks through the neighborhood. It's cooled down a little, like Melly said it would, so the walks would be so nice, except I can't walk properly. I duck walk, though, and I manage to get where I need to go. I'm also eating spicy food, drinking a bunch of water to stay hydrated, doing the pelvic rocks, which is a move Melly taught me where you get on your hands and knees on the floor and move your pelvis back and forth to strengthen those muscles and get the baby moved into the right position. There's something about castor oil you can try if you get desperate, which as far as I can tell brings on labor by making you have the worst diarrhea of your life, so no thank you. And you can have sex. Orgasms, according to my trusty book, can stimulate your body into going into labor.

I'm sorry, X, but ha ha ha. Orgasms. I'd laugh, but then I'd start to cry.

I shouldn't complain—I realize this. You're healthy. You'll come out when you're ready. And I probably shouldn't be in a hurry to get to that part, because you coming out is not going to be so fun for me.

I hope you're not too big. The doctor says you're about seven pounds. Which seems like a lot.

When I was kid, we had a dog who had puppies. This was before Evelyn, obviously. My parents got her as a fixer dog, as opposed to a new fixer baby. Actually she was a distraction dog, to attempt to distract my brother and me with a puppy so we wouldn't notice how bad things had gotten between my parents. Anyway. The dog's name was Noodle. I don't know why that was her name, because she was a yellow Lab and in no way resembled a noodle. I suspect that it was me who named her, though, since I was like six. Noodle sounds like a name a six-year-old would give a dog.

And Noodle was awesome. She loved to play fetch and run around everywhere I went and sleep snuggled up next to me, and she was, honestly speaking, the perfect distraction from my horrible, fighting parents.

When she was about a year old, my dad decided to breed Noodle. She'd cost him more than a thousand dollars to buy, because she was a purebred with champion bloodlines, because if we had a dog it had to be the very best dog, so he thought he'd breed her and sell the puppies and get a return on his investment. She had a visit with another purebred Labrador across town, and returned properly knocked up.

I didn't notice anything different about her until this one day she was sitting next to my bed and instead of her usual happy self she looked completely miserable. She was panting. Her belly was all distended and her little dog breasts were swollen, and she kept looking up at me like, make it stop.

That's me, about now. Make it stop.

My mom got a big cardboard box for Noodle to lie in on a pile of towels, and late one night, she woke me to tell me that Noodle was having her puppies. I was right there when it happened. I saw the first one come out. It was in a little slimy sac, and Noodle twisted around to look at it, all confused, like, "Hey, did that thing come out of me? How embarrassing."

Then the thing moved, and Noodle yelped, like, "Oh my God! It's alive! What is that? Get it away from me!"

She would have crawled away, terrified, but my mom reached in there and broke the sac from around the puppy and then lifted it and put it next to Noodle's head. Noodle sniffed it. It whimpered. She started licking it. And then the next puppy came out, and the next one, and the next, until there were seven puppies lined up against Noodle's side, whimpering and whining, and Noodle licked all of them thoroughly and then looked up at me again, her tail thumping against the towels. I guess she was happy. She finally understood what she had to do.

That was my experience with birth, until I got to Booth, that is. I've been through two of the other girls' labors while I've been here, and they were night and day different, Brit in the basement and Teresa with her hmms. Neither one makes me feel excited to go through it myself.

Noodle the dog, I should add, was never quite the same after having puppies. Before she had this smooth little belly she'd turn over for me to rub, and afterward she was all lumpy and saggy and sad. I thought that maybe she'd go back to the way she was before, but she never did.

"She looks old now," I told my mom, and my mom laughed and shook her head and said, "She looks like a dog who's had puppies. That's all."

I'm going to be that way, too, I know it. It might not be as obvious, my stretch marks hidden away under layers of clothes, but they'll still be there. I like the idea. It will be something to remember you by, like an epically bad tattoo. There will be a story behind those marks. Our story. Yours and mine.

S

39

"Hey, Cass, wait up!" I turn to see Bastian dashing toward me in the hall. The bell has just rung to let school out for the day. I'm on my way to find Nyla, who should be coming from AP Government, which Nyla loves because, while my backup plan if I don't become a Broadway star is to be a drama teacher, what Nyla's decided to do if the whole Hollywood actor thing doesn't pan out is to go to law school and become a judge.

I can totally picture it: Judge Henderson.

"Hey, beautiful!" Bastian reaches me and twirls me around like we're dancing.

"What's up?" I laugh.

"Do you and Nyles want to get food? With me? Later?" He gets down on one knee, and the students part around him, staring and giggling. "Please say yes."

It's been about a month since I made a fool of myself with Bastian on closing night. After we established that I was going to wait for Mom to get back on her feet before we do any further digging into my birth-mother situation, things have settled down. I auditioned for theater scholarships at C of I, although I still don't know if I've been accepted there. We had Christmas, a real Christmas, on the real day. Mom wore the pearl earrings out on a date with Dad. We all went to a movie and survived. We've been taking it day by day.

Through it all I've gone to school and hung out with my friends, with Nyla, of course, and Alice and Ronnie and Bender, too, and Bastian, and with Bastian it feels like he's been my good friend for a lifetime now—we can practically finish each other's sentences. But Bastian and I never talked seriously about what happened the night I kissed him, outside of the "You okay?" "I'm okay" text exchange we had right after. I didn't want Bastian to think I had any hard feelings, so I've been extra super overboard friendly every time we've been together. And he's been the same way with me. We're overcompensating, but I guess that's okay.

I pull him to his feet. "You don't know what to do with yourself if you're not in a play, do you?"

He shakes his head. "Thank God there's an audition for another one on Saturday. You are auditioning?"

"Of course."

He claps his hands together. "*Peter and the Starcatcher*! I still can't believe it. That was my favorite book when I was a kid."

"And you want to be Peter, I suppose."

"Well, I mean, Peter's the star of the starcatchers," he says, grinning. "Or Black Stache." He wiggles his eyebrows. "I could grow a mustache," he says in the low, grown-up version of his voice.

"Could you, though?"

"You offend me, woman," he scoffs. "And you probably want to be Molly Aster?"

"It's either Molly or Mrs. Bumbrake," I point out. There are only two female characters in this show, and Mrs. Bumbrake is an old grouchy lady who's only in like two scenes. What was Mama Jo thinking? But we'll handle it, like we always do. "Anyway, the answer is yes, I will go eat with you, but first I'm going to retrieve Nyla, and we'll meet you by the entrance."

But it turns out Nyla can't come. "I've got twin duty," she says with a sigh when I locate her at her locker. "Alexei's got the flu, so I have to take the girls to dance class. For, like, hours."

"Oh, boo hoo, you have brothers and sisters," I fake moan.

"Shut up."

"You know I love you," I sing sweetly.

"I do." She pouts. "Have fun with Bastian. Without me."

Bastian's not by the school entrance, though, when I get there. It takes me a little while to find him. He's sitting outside on the concrete steps by the gym. And he seems like an entirely different person now from the happy-go-lucky boy who danced me around five minutes ago. His eyebrows are all screwed up.

"What happened to you?" I ask.

He lifts his phone. "I got the early-acceptance email from College of Idaho."

A mix of terror and hope zings through my entire nervous system. I sink down on the steps next to Bastian. "So you were accepted?"

He nods.

"Isn't that supposed to be a good thing?"

He nods again.

I can't get my phone out fast enough, and miraculously, there's an email for me, too, from College of Idaho. I read it in like a millisecond, and what it says makes me put down my phone and hold back a girly squeal. "I got in," I gasp. "I got in I got in I got in!"

But getting in wasn't the part I was worried about, now was it?

"Congratulations," Bastian says, beside me. "I knew you'd get there."

"Give me a minute." I click on the file they've attached with my awards letter.

"Show me the money," I whisper.

I scan down the list of funding I've been given. I received the highest possible theater scholarship. The highest academic scholarship. A separate little side scholarship I didn't know about. And a grant.

I'm holding my breath, but I can't help it. What's listed here is not enough without taking loans, or it wouldn't be enough, if that was all there was. But there's more.

There's what I like to call flower money.

A couple weeks ago, Grandma and Uncle Pete were over at the house, and when Uncle Pete and I were alone setting the dinner table, he started trying to tell me something, but he couldn't seem to spit it out.

"I never had kids" is what he said at first, his face getting all red and splotchy under his scraggly beard.

I didn't understand what he was getting at. "I know," I said slowly. "Did you want kids?"

"I don't have any kids, so you're like my kid."

"Oh. Well, thanks, Uncle Pete. I love you, too."

"I'm not exactly rich," he said as he placed the circle of plates on the table. "But I do all right. It's been a good year for flowers."

This was getting awkward. "Good for you. I'm . . . glad."

"So I could afford to give you something."

I stopped and stared at him, my hands full of forks. "What?"

"I can give you some money to go to College of Idaho."

I was totally surprised. I never expected to get help from Uncle Pete. I never would have even considered it. Then later that same night, after the dessert had been eaten and the dishes were done, Grandma took me aside.

"I've been selling some of my crafty-type things on Etsy," she told me. "I make paper roses, mostly, out of the pages of old books. Gives me and my glue gun something to do while I watch *Wheel of Fortune*. And it turns out young people desperately want to buy these roses, for proms and weddings and such. I'm making a killing."

"That's awesome, Grandma. You'll have to teach me."

"Sure, but my point is," she said, taking me by the arm and leading me farther away from the rest of my family. "I've got some extra money lying around from all these flowers, and I want to give it to you."

"To me?" Once again, I was totally surprised.

"To go to College of Idaho."

So. I have flower money.

Now, sitting there on the steps, I do the math quickly, adding in the flower money to the total of my financial aid statement. It's close. I'm still going to have to work full-time in the summers, and probably at least part-time during the school year, but it's doable. It's workable, without taking loans, even. So, yes. Yes yes.

I'm going to College of Idaho.

"I'm actually going," I breathe, and then I'm laughing, until I start crying a little, because I'm so overwhelmed and relieved and thrilled and humbled by the willingness of my fricking amazing family to help me and I feel so . . . loved. That's the word. Loved. I'm bursting with it. I can't wait to tell my parents.

"I guess it's good news," Bastian says. "I'm so happy for you." But his face is still drawn, his eyes missing their usual sparkle.

I sober up a bit. "What's wrong? Can you not afford it?"

"Money's not the problem," he says. "My uncle's going to pay for my college."

I gasp. "Mine offered to chip in, too, actually. Yay for uncles, right?"

He smiles a sad little smile. "My uncle's the best."

"So what *is* the problem?"

"Nothing, I guess. I should be happy. I should be jumping up and down. I should have"—he points at my face—"*that* expression right now. And I did. I saw the email, I opened it, I was excited, and then . . ."

"And then?"

He sighs. "And then I wanted to call my parents. I wanted to cheer with my mom, and for my dad to, I don't know, say he's proud of me. But that's not going to happen."

"I'm sorry." I put my arm around him. He lays his head on my shoulder. "But you are going to College of Idaho?"

"Yes. I'm going," he says in a determined voice. "No matter what they think."

I pat his cheek. "Well, then I'm cheering for you. *I'm* proud of you, and I will be there with you, and we will have the best time."

He lifts his head. His eyes are suspiciously shiny. "Thanks, Cass."

"Now let's get off these steps, because my butt is freaking cold. Let's go eat."

"I'm not actually hungry," he admits as we get to our feet.

"Then let's go somewhere else. Somewhere we can talk. I think we're overdue for a heart-to-heart conversation, don't you? Do you have your car?"

40

We end up at Thunder Ridge, of all places. It's quiet, and it has a nice view.

Bastian thinks this is hilarious. "This is the town make-out spot?" he asks incredulously after he parks his car on the edge of the hill facing out. Below us it's starting to get dark. Idaho Falls feels bigger from up here, spread out onto the whole valley, surrounded by a patchwork of potato farms. It's kind of beautiful.

"You want to make out?" I turn to him and lift an eyebrow suggestively.

He lifts an eyebrow, too. "I thought we established why this would not be a good idea."

"I am sorry about that. It's so embarrassing," I groan.

He shakes his head. "It's not your fault. You were blinded by my debilitating hotness. It could happen to anybody."

I stifle a laugh. This isn't too far from the truth, actually. "You really do rock a pair of tights."

"You know it. But seriously, I should have paid more attention to your signals, too, Cass. I didn't mean to hurt your feelings."

"I know. I'm okay now, but how silly is it that I actually believed for the longest time that you were going to be my boyfriend? You're the perfect guy."

He makes a sound that's half laugh, half snort. "Right. Me, perfect. That's a good one."

"No, really," I insist. "You are. That much is still true. I was just wrong about the part where the universe had destined us to be together."

He's quiet for a minute, and then he says, "I spent a long time wishing I was straight. A long, long time. It would have been so much easier."

"It would have been easier for me, too," I agree. "You've ruined me."

He stares at me. "What?"

"After our brief time together, primarily as the baker's wife and the prince, but still, you set the bar so incredibly high that no one else can measure up," I say mournfully.

Bastian nods. "Oh. Well, that's the plight of straight women everywhere, I'm afraid."

"You're probably right."

"I did date a girl once," he says. "I don't want to brag, but I was the best boyfriend ever."

"What girl?"

"Her name was Katie. We were in ninth grade, and I took her to the winter formal. I do think I kind of broke her heart."

He looks sad.

"Sounds like maybe she broke yours, too," I say.

He shakes his head. "No, it's not that. It's just, that was a hard time for me. I knew who I was, the real me, deep down, but I was afraid nobody else would care about that person. I was so far in the closet I found like Narnia back there."

I laugh and nod. I think I get it, at least in part. Idaho Falls is a tough place to grow up if you're not the same as everyone else. Like anywhere, I suppose.

"So when did you come out?" I ask.

"Last year." He sighs. "At my birthday party. I got caught kissing a guy from school. I thought he was gay . . . and I still think he is, actually, but he was not ready to come out, so he kind of threw me under the bus. Said *I* was trying to corrupt *him*, or something. And that is basically why I had to change schools."

I grab his hand. "I, for one, am glad you changed schools."

He smiles, but it doesn't last on his face. "That was the last time my dad spoke to me. Literally. That was the last time."

My heart squeezes for him. "I'm sorry. I'm just . . . sorry."

"Oh, he'll come around," he says lightly, like it doesn't hurt. "But it might take him a decade or so. He's religious. I mean, both of my parents are very religious. It's a hard thing to let go when you think the God rulebook says your son is going to burn in hell. I know not everybody who's religious thinks that. But my dad does." He coughs. "So what about you? You're not without drama."

"I'm all about the drama. Trust me." I consider telling him about being adopted. I'm working out where I should start, how I even bring up the subject, but before I get a chance, Bastian says, "I mean, your drama's mostly over now, right? Your mom's okay."

"My mom's okay," I agree.

He nods. "I love hanging out at your house when we're all over there, watching you and your mom interact."

"You watch us? You mean, like zebras at the zoo?"

"You're really classy zebras. It's so obvious that she's your mom. She tilts her head the same way you do when she asks a question. And she uses her hands to talk exactly like you. And she bites her lip when she's thinking, and you do that all the time."

"You've been paying attention," I murmur.

"Well, that and you look just like her," he says.

I glance away, out the window, smiling. It's fully dark now, and the lights of Idaho Falls have blinked on and it feels like I'm staring down into a field of stars. And then I look back at Bastian. "I guess I do."

"So, see? You've had a lot of drama lately, but you're at the happy ending."

I laugh. "The happy ending."

"You end up here," he says, gesturing out to the pretty view. "Right now. With me."

That's right, I think.

I end up here.

Dear X,

I keep imagining your parents right now, preparing themselves, set-ting up your room, building the crib and putting up a painting of a rabbit or a sheep or something equally cute on the wall they painted in soft colors just for you. I want your mom to have a rocking chair. I want her to sing to you. My mom used to sing to me, I think. When I was little.

I called my mom today. She asked me how I was, and I said I was ready.

"Can I move in with you?" I asked her. "After she's born?"

"You want to move to Colorado?" she asked me, surprised. I always wanted to stay in Idaho before, with Dad and his quiet instead of Mom and her yelling.

"I don't want to go back with Dad," I told her, and I didn't tell her why—God knows she's already fully aware that Dad has his problems. I

didn't want to bring up the way he looked at Ted, and how every time I think about Dad now, I see Ted's face trying to be nice to this guy who's obviously a racist asshole.

"I'm sure we can work something out," Mom said. "I'll ask Brett, but I think he'll be okay with it."

"Thanks."

"Then you can really put it behind you, once this is all over. You can start fresh," she said.

"Right," I agreed with her. "I'll have a clean slate."

I really am ready now, X.

It makes me think about something Heather said once, back when she was about as pregnant as I am now. Her grandmother was in the process of dying of cancer, and Heather said she felt like they were both having a similar experience—her grandmother and her. They were about to go through something inevitable and terrifying, something that they couldn't control and didn't know exactly when or how it would happen. But eventually they'd both just have to get it over with—to die, to give birth—and come out on the other side.

I guess I'll see you on the other side.

S

41

We're here. Mom and Nyla and I are finally standing in the middle of Twenty-Fourth Street, in Boise, Idaho, looking up at a large brick building with the Salvation Army symbol over the doorway. It's called the Marion Pritchett School now, and it's still meant for pregnant girls, but the girls don't live here anymore. Behind the brick building there's another long, tan-colored building, and a van that says "Giraffe Laugh Early Learning Center" on the side. School's not in session, because it's spring break, so everything's perfectly quiet.

We're still standing in the street when a woman comes out the front door. She's wearing a plaid shirt and glasses and comfortable shoes, and when she sees us she pushes her glasses up on her nose and asks, "Can I help you, ladies?"

I wish she were wearing a name tag, so I could tell if she's Melly, but then I guess Melly is not Melly's real name. S said she changed all the names, so Ted and Dawson and Evelyn—the whole cast of the characters that made up her life—are all going about their business in the world being called something else.

Except for Amber. I think S kept Amber's name, because that's also the name of the woman on adoptedsearch.org who was looking for her daughter, and that can't be a coincidence. So maybe she didn't change Melly's name, either, or the other people from the school. I mean, why would she need to?

"No, we're just walking around," I say to maybe-Melly.

The woman looks both me and Nyla up and down to see if we're uniquely qualified to go to the school. Neither of us looks pregnant, but maybe we're not showing yet.

"If you're interested in becoming students here, I'd be glad to give you a tour," she says.

"That'd be gr—" begins Nyla.

"No," I say firmly. There is a part of me that wants to see the room where S slept and the living area where she did her homework and the basement where Brit was hiding on the Fourth of July. But the dorms have all been converted to offices, from what I could tell by using the powers of the internet. I also don't want to sneak around pretending to be someone I'm not. I only wanted to see the school. To stand on the same sidewalk where S stood, if only for a few minutes. To see what she saw.

But from the outside.

"Okay, well, if you change your mind, here's my card." The woman pulls a little piece of cardstock out of her pocket and hands it to me.

"Thanks."

She smiles and passes us and goes down the street to her car, and then gets in and drives away.

"Do you think that was Melly?" Nyla whispers.

"I don't know. Melly worked here like nineteen years ago. Did that lady look like she'd been here nineteen years?"

"I'm going to choose to believe that was Melly," Mom says.

I turn to her and smile. "Me too."

She takes my hand and squeezes three times. I squeeze back.

I glance at the card. *Carmella Lopez*, it reads.

"So what do you want to do now?" Mom asks me.

"I want to find S."

Finally, we're ready. Mom is stronger. Her body has accepted the new heart. The doctors don't even seem worried anymore. She's got pink in her cheeks, a little spring in her step. She's a beast in her physical therapy. The medical professionals have okayed her for a short trip to Boise. So we're here.

Mom laughs. "I meant for lunch."

"Oh. I have no idea." I meet my mom's eyes. "But I do want to find her, Mom. Not just take a tour of the letters, but actually find her. That's really okay with you? You're not saying that because you know it's what I want to hear?"

She smiles, and it's a real smile and not one she's putting on to make me feel better.

"I want you to find her," she says. "It's what I want, too."

"Okay. If you're sure."

"I'm sure if you're sure." She swings my hand between us the way she used to when I was little and she was trying to make even walking down a sidewalk something fun, like a dance.

"I'm sure."

"Good."

"Well, come on, then," Nyla says from up ahead of us. "Let's go find S."

We meet Dad for lunch, and then we stop by an office supply store, where Dad buys a big whiteboard like the ones he uses at school, because he's a nerdy teacher and thinks all of life's puzzles can be solved by mapping things out in dry erase marker. Then we go over to the BSU library and make copies of the letters for each of us and spend a few hours poring over them, reacquainting ourselves with S's world. Taking notes. Looking for the little details that might turn out to be clues.

"What a pretty campus," Dad says as we're bumming around Boise State.

"Dad."

"I'm just saying."

He's more open to the find-the-birth-mother quest than I expected him to be. Things changed the night he read the letters. He's officially on board now.

"Okay," he says when we're settled into one of the study rooms at BSU. He sticks the whiteboard to the wall with Fun-Tak putty. "Let's write what we know."

At the end of the next hour, the board looks like this:

First name starts with S.
Lived at Booth.
Could have come from another city or state, but it's unlikely, since her father visits her.
S mentions that her old high school was BHS (Boise? Borah?

Possibly Bishop Kelly High school, but it would then have a BK).
Mother in Colorado.
Brother a football "star?" at college across the country.
Amber mentions that S's father is "big politician," and S talks about
his constituents. The NII form says he's a lawyer.
Check out potential colleges that Dawson could have attended.

I step back, taking it all in. It seems like a lot, what's written up there. We know so much more now, about S, about her life.

"So what's the plan?" Dad asks, because if there's one thing Dad loves, it's a plan. "What's next for today?"

"I think we should head over to the Boise Public Library." I've already given this a lot of thought. "Check out the yearbooks again. Maybe look at some microfilm for the local newspaper for the high school football 'stars' who were playing at the time S's brother would have been. Make a list of all the state and US congressmen for the year in question, especially those who were newly elected. We should also look into city council members and any other elected office."

Dad raises his hand. "I get football."

"Yearbooks," Mom laughs. "Maybe I could recognize your chin." I've already tried that and totally failed, but okay.

I turn to Nyla. "I guess that leaves us with the rotten politicians." She cringes. "Yay."

42

"I'm ready to call it a day," Dad sighs about three hours later.

I rub my eyes. "Yeah, me too."

"Me three," says Nyla. "Plus the library's about to close."

I glance over at Mom, who's still buried in yearbooks, but she doesn't look up.

"Hey, Mom. Mom?"

The librarian gives me a "shh" look. I get up and go over to touch Mom lightly on the shoulder.

"Yes, honey," she says, her voice kind of dreamy.

"We're tapped out over here."

"All right." She closes the current yearbook.

"Any luck?"

The tiniest frown appears behind her eyes. "No. I mean, maybe. There are a lot of sixteen-year-old girls at these schools with a first name that starts with the letter *S*. But no, nobody who's obviously the one we're looking for. How about you?"

I sigh. Nyla and I made a list of congressmen and tried to cross-check those names with what we know about S and her family, and we were able to eliminate several men who were in office at the time, but there was no clear candidate.

"We did okay," I say. "But like you say, no one obvious."

We gather up our stuff and leave the library. We're quiet on the drive back to the hotel.

"We did good today," Dad says. "We made progress."

But it doesn't feel like we have anything more to go on than when we started. It seems like all this information provides us with leads, but the leads don't go anywhere.

Maybe that's on purpose, whispers a tiny warning voice in the back of my head, one I've been trying to ignore. *Maybe S didn't give you any real clues because this isn't a scavenger hunt for her. This is her life. If she wanted to make contact, she could do it in a heartbeat.*

Shut up, voice. I know. I *know*. But it's like Mom said in the beginning. It's been almost twenty years. Things change.

"What about my birth father?" I say.

My dad's smile dims a little. He might be on board with me finding S, but I don't think he's as sure about D. Still, he's determined to be supportive and let it be my choice.

"Let's focus on one thing at a time," Mom says brightly. "We have so much on your birth mother, and if we locate her, she can give us Dawson's real name. It shouldn't be too difficult from there."

"Exactly," Dad says. "Let's stick with S."

At the hotel, Mom takes a nap. Dad goes for a walk. He says he needs to get some air, even though the air quality in Boise's pretty bad—what people won't tell you about Boise is that it's shaped like a bowl, and sometimes there's an inversion, and all the city's pollution hangs out in the bowl. The sky is a gritty mix of brown and gray. The snow's all melted off, and the grass is dead. The air is cold and wet and this strange kind of heavy.

Boise is a pretty good reflection of my mood, I find.

Nyla and I go out on the balcony of the hotel room to talk.

"Okay, tell me straight," she says. "How are you doing?"

She's been quiet today, mostly, tagging along, offering her opinion only when called upon. It's not like her.

"Fine," I report. "How about you?"

"Today wasn't quite the episode of *Cold Case Files* that I expected, but that's okay." That's how this search thing sounded, when we were talking about it earlier this month. We were all going to go back to Boise, where my story started, and we were going to put all the jigsaw pieces together to form a picture. But we didn't. We're not any closer to finding my birth mother than we were yesterday. Or last month. Or last year.

I was trying to put on an "oh well, at least we tried" face for my parents, because they don't want to see me get hurt. But it hurts.

I say all of this to Nyla, in not so many words.

"That bites," she says. "I'm sorry. Maybe it's not the right time, you know?"

"The right time? When's the right time?"

"Maybe you're not supposed to find her now. What's that your mom always says? Things happen when they're supposed to happen?"

"Something like that."

"It'll happen if it's supposed to happen," she says.

"What if it's not supposed to happen?"

"I guess by this logic, that would mean it won't happen."

"Like ever."

She's not exactly cheering me up.

"I just want to know," I murmur. The hotel balcony has a magnificent view of the parking lot, and below me I watch a woman trying to get her screaming toddler into her car.

"Oh come on!" I hear her say in frustration. "Let's go!"

This woman might also be a good reflection of my mood. Or the toddler. I'm not sure which.

"What do you want to know?" Nyla asks.

"Who she is."

"You know who she is. You know the important stuff, anyway."

I sigh. She's right. "Then I guess I want to know who I am."

"What, and you want to meet her so she can tell you? How would she know who you are?"

"Well . . ." Gosh, Nyla, I think, way to be rude about it. "She's a part of me, a part of who I am that I've never had access to."

"Yeah, you said that, once. But the thing is, Cass," Nyla gently points out, "we all wonder who we are, whether we know who gave birth to us or not. We all ask the same questions, right? *Who am I? Why am I here?* And even if we know the simple answers, the question never goes away. It never gets easier. It never gets solved."

I get the sense that she's not talking about my life so much anymore, but hers.

"I know my first parents' names, and my brother's name. I know the place I was born. I know why I ended up in the orphanage. I don't *want* to remember some things, but I do. Like the smell of rotting food. My mother hid me in a trash can when the bad men came to our house. It's in the file my mom has."

She's never told me that. I hug her, but it doesn't feel like enough.

"I can't really remember her face," she says. "I wish there was a picture, or a letter, but I don't think she even spoke English. Bindu, that was her name. Did I ever tell you?"

"Yeah. I'm sorry. I'm so sorry, Nyles."

She sighs. "No, I'm sorry. I just made this about me. Wow."

"It's about both of us, I think."

"My point is, I know everything. I know what picture my second parents looked at when they picked me out of a pile of photographs of these sad parentless children who were available to be rescued. I know that part of my story, but none of that defines who I am now. I am who I am. Full stop."

"You're right."

"Dang right, I'm right. But it still sucks, what happened—or I guess *didn't* happen, today. Maybe you'll find your birth mom someday, but don't build up your identity on that. On her. Because that's not on her. It's on you."

"Oh, Ny, tell me what you really think."

She laughs. "Sorry. A little tough love, there."

"Thank you. And thanks for coming over with me. Again. I know it's not easy for you."

She turns to give me a full hug. "No worries. I got you, babe."

"I got you, too."

She starts humming "Bless the Broken Road" by Rascal Flatts.

Through the sliding glass door I can see that my mom's awake. She waves at me. "Hey, let's go in."

"I'm going to go scrounge up some candy from the vending machine," Nyla says after we come back inside.

Mom pats the bed next to her, the most familiar of gestures. I sit. She puts an arm around me.

"So today didn't go the way you thought."

"No, but that's okay."

She leans back to look at me. "It is?"

"I'm not going to find all the answers in one day," I say.

She makes a little hmm noise. "Yes, that's probably true."

"It'll happen if it's supposed to happen, when it's supposed to happen."

"Well, look at you," she says, squeezing me. "How'd you get so very wise and grown up?"

"It's a mystery," I say.

43

I wake up later that night to Nyla jerking upright in bed.

"The picture!" she says loudly, and I want to tell her to keep it down—my parents are sleeping in the next bed over—but then she throws back the covers and jumps out of bed. She runs over to the little table in the corner of the hotel room and turns on the lamp.

I'm blinded and annoyed. "Hey. Ny. What are you doing?"

"Where did we put the picture?" she says, still way too loudly.

I swing my legs over the side of the bed. "The picture. What picture?"

"The . . ." Nyla closes her eyes and her face scrunches up. "I can't think of the word. The picture, you know?"

Dad sits up. His hair is a tangled red mess, and he looks somewhat freaked out.

"Hey, uh, girls?" He rubs his hand down his face and glances at the clock on the bedside table. "It's two in the morning. Time for sleep?"

"Is everything okay?" comes my mother's bleary voice from the covers next to him.

"I don't know." I turn back to watch Nyla dig through all of our papers—the notes and forms we've been working on today, S's letters. She keeps grabbing a pile and rifling through the papers, then throwing them down with an exasperated sigh. "She's making a mess. Something about a picture?"

"What picture?" Dad asks.

"Not a *picture* picture!" Nyla says. "The picture of the baby."

"The sonogram?" Mom sits up.

Nyla looks up and points at her. "Sonogram! Gosh, I could not remember that word."

Dad scratches his head. "Because it's two in the morning. Maybe this could wait until the actual morning."

"No." Nyla crosses to the other side of the room and starts searching through some stuff there, moving like she's made of liquid energy. She's clearly wired, muttering to herself, but I can't understand what she's saying.

She can't find the sonogram. She slumps against the wall. "Maybe I should have waited until morning," she says. "But I can't go back to sleep now. I remembered seeing . . ."

"Seeing what?" I demand to know. "What's going on?"

She looks at me. "You don't know your birth mother's name."

"Right. Except that it starts with S."

"You don't know, because it's not in the letters," she babbles on. "She's careful not to give the real names of people in the letters. Remember that one where she almost writes her name, but then she catches herself?"

"Of course I remember. Look, Ny. You're freaking out my parents. And I was having a nice dream."

"I think her name *is* in there."

I'm fully awake now. "What? No, it isn't," I say with absolute certainty. I've read the letters a thousand times by now. I could recite whole passages by heart. I would have noticed a name. "S never tells me her name."

"She never tells you," Nyla insists. "But she did give it to you. She probably didn't realize. Or who knows, maybe she did."

Now I'm really confused. "What?"

She slaps her hand down on the table in frustration. "Goshdangit, I need the flipping sonogram!"

"It's here." I grab my backpack and retrieve my wallet. I keep the sonogram in my wallet, because it's the only picture, like S said, of her and me together. It's right next to a photo my parents and I took when I was a kid at a photo booth. I hand the sonogram to Nyla, and she lays it on the table and puts her finger near the top of the grainy black-and-white picture. I really do look like an alien here. Then my eyes focus on the faded white print by Nyla's finger. But it's just a bunch of letters and numbers that don't make sense.

"It's medical jargon, I think," says Nyla, moving her finger down the picture. "But here, below where it says, PROFILE 1. Here, Cass. You had it all this time."

S. WHIT, it says.

"S," I murmur.

"Yes, but 'Whit,'" Nyla says impatiently. "That must be her last name."

"S. Whit," I repeat again. "S. Whit."

409

"As in, Governor Whit," Dad says from behind me. He's fully awake now, too. "S's father was in politics, right?"

"Governor Whit? I . . . I've met him. He can't be my—"

"It makes sense, though," Nyla says. "It fits."

It does.

"My notes," I whisper. "I need my notes. They're in a yellow notebook." We all get up, Dad in his boxers, Mom in the white hotel bathrobe, Nyla in her pj's, and dig around trying to locate my yellow notebook. Mom finds it and brings it to the table like she's about to read from the Dead Sea Scrolls or something. The hair on the back of my neck is standing up, goose bumps prickling up and down my arms.

Mom lays the notebook down on my desk and starts flipping through it for the page where I listed the politicians.

"Here." Dad, from over my shoulder, points to a list. *State senators*, it says in my handwriting.

It's the third name down.

"Michael Whit, junior senator," Dad reads. "It's got to be him, right?"

"Governor Whit," I say.

"Ew," Nyla exclaimed. "Your grandfather is Governor Whit?"

"He's not my grandfather," I say hotly. "I don't know him."

Nyla sobers. "I'm sorry. You're right. You're absolutely right."

"This is pretty flimsy," I say. "It's, what . . . circumstantial? Just because the name Whit is on the ultrasound doesn't mean it's . . . Whit could be the doctor's name. Or the sonogram technician's name. Or something."

But the wheels of my brain are still turning, turning, turning, ever so slowly, until they arrive at the destination they'd started toward the second I saw the word *Whit*.

"Wait." I pull the notebook toward me and flip back a bunch of pages, to the yearbook notes I took last year with Nyla.

Boise High School Newspaper Staff
Kristi Henscheid
Melissa Bollinger
Melissa Stockham
Sandra Whit
Sarah Averett
Sonia Rutz
Amy Yowell

"Sandra Whit," Mom breathes from beside me.

I look around wildly and start rustling through the stacks of papers again, until find the photocopies Mom made today of some of the yearbook pages from the high schools that start with *B*. "It was in the red one, I think. Boise High School."

IN SEARCH OF THE STORY, I remember the page was called. I hope Mom made a copy of it. And yes—then I find it. A copy of the school newspaper page. The first one I looked at when I was going through the yearbooks with Nyla the day of the drama competition.

This time, the name leaps out at me.

SANDRA WHIT.

I put my finger on the name, then follow the order that the students are standing in to figure out which girl in the picture is Sandra. It's not a great photo, and the one who's supposed to be Sandra isn't looking at the camera. She's looking off to one side, like she's laughing at something. Her long straight hair is falling directly across her face.

I can't see her at all. "I wish there was a better picture."

"They keep the yearbook archives online now," Mom says quietly. "The librarian told me."

She hands me my laptop.

I open it and do a search for Boise High School yearbooks. And it's there. The right year and everything. I click on the yearbook. I type "Sandra Whit" into the search bar, and it informs me that this particular student appears on two pages: the yearbook page and the individual student pictures. I click on the individual one.

The photo is in black and white. She's smiling, but not with her eyes. She looks bored, like there's someplace she'd rather be.

"Cass, she's got your teeth," Nyla says.

"My teeth?"

Dad leans closer to the screen. "Yep. Those are your teeth. They're small, pretty close together. Hers are straighter, but they look basically the same. You also have the same chin, but different lips."

I stare at the girl's chin. It is vaguely familiar. I'm not the spitting image of Sandra Whit, but there is something of me in there. If I'm not imagining things. I mean, I did look at this picture once before, and Mom looked at it, too, only a few hours ago, and neither of us saw anything to make us believe that this girl is the one who gave birth to me.

Nyla cocks her head to one side. "God, what is she wearing?"

She's got on not one tank top but two, layered one on top of the other, both dark in color. Her hair is straight, long, and pulled over one shoulder. A beaded choker is hanging tightly around her neck. It's the choker, I think, that Nyla is referring to. It's pretty nineties.

I sit back. Mom leans over to take a look.

"She has your eyes," she murmurs. "If this picture was in color, they'd be blue."

412

I wonder. I also wonder if I'm in this photo, too, invisible, but there. Just out of the frame. I can't stop staring at her face, like I'm gazing into the eyes of her former self, and I'm able to see her in real life, wherever she is.

"Nice to meet you, Sandra," I whisper. "If it's you."

Dear X,

We did it. I'm lying in a hospital bed right now, wearing that basic pale blue horribly unflattering hospital gown, and you're not in my belly anymore, X. You're out. You've arrived. You're here.

I feel empty and full, at the same time.

I'm trying to sort it out now, to tell you about last night.

It basically started out like every other night lately. Yesterday was a Sunday, so we didn't have much to do all day, Amber and me. We don't go to church or anything resembling a brunch or an afternoon stroll. We laze around and watch television and, according to Melly, "eat her out of house and home."

So that's what we did yesterday. We sat around eating the proverbial bonbons, and I worked on a paper I'm writing for English class on Romeo and Juliet. We watched The Simpsons and I wrote my paper during the commercials, and I thought about how messed up even Juliet's life was, a simple teenage girl back in the day who only wants to know what love is, and she can't catch a break. Amber started in on like a pint of peanut butter cup ice cream, because she said she was so hot she could die, even though it's cooler out now, and then she and I went out on the front porch to get some air. It was late evening by then, and the moon was up and full, as bright and big as I'd ever seen the moon, casting the whole street in a sheet of silvery white.

It was so beautiful it kind of hurt. Or maybe that was just my back.

"Give me some of that," I said to Amber.

She passed me the ice cream.

"Did you ever consider," I said around a mouthful of peanut-buttery goodness, "how the moon is shining on everybody, all over the world, and how it's the same for all of us?" Right then I was thinking about how this very moon was also shining down on my mom, in Colorado, and my dad, in his lonely house on the hill, and on Heather and Brit and Teresa. And Dawson, wherever he was. And Ted. And it was like in that moment the moon connected us all together, into one space.

It's shining on us now, X. On me, in here in this room, alone, and on you, in the nursery.

But Amber, of course, didn't look at it that way.

"No," she said flatly. "It's just the moon."

"Hey, I'm trying to have a moment here," I said.

"You're trying to be romantic. But you can't be romantic about the moon. It's a hunk of cold lifeless rock circling around our planet. Big whoop."

"Lots of people are romantic when it comes to the moon," I argued.

"Well, I'm not."

"Obviously."

415

"It's just the moon," she said again.

"You know what you should be when you grow up?" I said. "An accountant. That's the perfect non-romantic job for you. That's still the plan, isn't it? Because people will always need accountants. Will you do my taxes someday?"

She frowned. Amber didn't talk about her plans anymore. She didn't talk about her baby or cloth diapers or the support system that's going to help her raise her kid while she goes back to school. That was bullshit that she told us back in the day to make us think she had it all together. That all ended the night she showed up here with the bruises on her neck.

"Shut up," she said to me. "What are you going to be, like a waitress? Or one of those women who cleans hotel rooms?"

"Don't make me punch you in the nose again."

"Maybe I'll punch back this time."

Neither of us really wanted to get in a fight. We were both just irritable and lonesome, in spite of the fact that we were together. It was the moon's fault, I think.

I gave her back the container of ice cream. "On that note," I said, "I am going to bed."

I waddled back to my room and got into my nightgown (I don't wear pajamas anymore because they can't keep up with my expanding waistline) and washed my face. Then as I was brushing my teeth I noticed something.

Three drops of blood.

Right below where I was standing, there were three bright red drops of blood.

Now I can look back at it and think, cool. Three drops of blood against the white linoleum of my bedroom floor. Like in the Grimms' fairy tale of Snow White, where Snow White's mother pricks her finger when she's sewing and three drops of blood fall to the snow. And afterward she gives birth to a daughter that's red as blood and white as snow. It's a good omen, those three drops of blood.

But right then as I was standing there at the sink I thought, well, apparently I'm bleeding. That can't be good.

So I wiped up the blood and put on my slippers and went to wake Melly right away. You weren't moving around right then, and I couldn't remember the last time I'd felt you move—I mean, I was sure you'd moved lately, but I couldn't remember, and I wasn't like gushing blood but I was bleeding a little and I'd seen way too many movies where the woman starts bleeding and then in the next scene the doctors are telling her that her baby has died. So I booked it to Melly's room.

She wasn't asleep. For once. She was sitting in her bed reading a book. Something about Ophelia.

"What's the matter?" she asked, and I told her.

"Are you feeling any pain?" she asked, and I said I wasn't.

"It's probably fine," she said, but she told me to wait for her outside the door while she got dressed and then she'd take me in to St. Luke's to be sure.

I was out there waiting in the dark hallway when Amber came shuffling up.

"My water broke," she said like she was reporting on the weather.

I knocked on Melly's door.

"I'll be out in a minute," she called through the wood. "Can you go tell Amber that we're going to the hospital, so if we're not back in the morning, she'll know where we went?"

"Amber's here. Her water broke," I say.

The door opened. Melly peered out.

"Your water broke?"

Amber would have answered, but by then she was bent over having a contraction. Then one hit me, too, a real contraction that started under my ribs and vibrated down through my entire body.

"Ow," I said. "OW."

Melly looked from Amber to me and back again. "Both of you? Oh my God, is it a full moon?"

"As a matter of fact . . . ," I gasped.

"Come on," Melly said, all business now. "Let's get you girls in the car."

She looked up as we were making our way down the sidewalk to where her car was parked.

"Goddamn moon," she muttered to herself.

So the pain. The pain was pretty bad, X. I won't lie. On a scale of one to ten, one being stubbing your toe, this was like twelve point five. At least at the end there, when I actually thought I might die. At the beginning, I didn't think it was so bad, like period cramps, maybe a little worse.

I got to the hospital and they checked me out and said the blood was probably just a little of my mucus plug, but you were fine. I was fine. But I was having contractions, small ones that I didn't really feel, every five minutes.

They hooked me up to a monitor and had me walk around a little, which was supposed to make things move along more quickly. I was only at like two centimeters when I came in, so not very far. That was at about nine p.m. We had a long night ahead, the nurse told me.

But by 9:45 I was at nine centimeters.

"I have to poop," I informed the nurse.

"What?" She checked my chart. "No way."

But she checked, and yes, I'd gone from two to nine in less than an hour. And I was ready to push.

That's when the pain got bad. Before that, I thought people were being overly dramatic about the pain. It hurt, but not too much. But now, now the pain crashed over me. I stopped talking and tried to remember how they taught us to breathe in those classes they'd made us take at Booth, because breathing suddenly became a difficult task.

"Isn't there some kind of position that's supposed to make it better?" I asked the nurse.

"No," she said. "There's no magic position. Put your feet here."

She guided my feet into the stirrups. It felt wrong. What my body wanted to do was to stand up, or maybe squat or get on all fours. With my feet in the stirrups I felt like a turtle who'd been kicked over onto its back. Everything felt pointed in the wrong direction.

"No, stay like that," said the nurse as I moved to get down again.

"What about the epidural?" I gasped. "You know what I'm in the mood for right now? A good old-fashioned epidural. I'm not one of those hippie-dippie girls who think it's a right of passage to feel the pain or I want to be all-natural or anything like that. Bring on the epidural. Now, please."

"It's too late for that," the nurse said.

"No, no, it can't be!" I may or may not have started to cry. "I can't do this tonight. Maybe if I go home and rest up a little. Come back tomorrow."

Melly grabbed my hand. "You can do this," she said. "I'll be right here with you."

Then we both heard Amber scream from the room across the hall.

"She's crowning," we heard the doctor shout.

"Go on," I said to Melly.

She let go of my hand and moved toward the door. "Goddamn moon," I heard her say as she went out.

Now I was really on my own. My doctor wasn't even there—he was delivering Amber's baby, apparently, but I was okay. It hurt. A lot. But I could take it.

Then my entire body started to bear down without my say-so. I made this weird animal sound that I never knew I could produce.

"Don't push!" ordered the nurse. "Wait for the doctor! He'll be here in a minute."

"Okay," I agreed, and my body pushed again. I couldn't stop it.

"I'm sorry," I panted. "I'm sorry."

"Just breathe," the nurse told me. "Pretend like you're blowing out birthday candles. Like this."

She got right into my face and started to blow out these little breaths. Whew. Whew. Whew. I tried to do it with her. I could feel everything stretching, the watermelon versus the lemon, and then my body heaved again.

"Don't push!" ordered the nurse.

"Can't you just catch her or something!" I screamed, and then I made another animal noise.

I heard a baby crying. It was confusing, since my baby still seemed to be trying to rip me in half.

"Dr. Rutledge!" called the nurse. She was now down on her knees between my legs, preparing to catch you, X.

I felt like I was on fire down there. And the watermelon was definitely stuck.

"Dr. Rutledge, in here!" the nurse yelled again.

My body pushed again.

The doctor literally slid into the room, snapping on a fresh pair of gloves, mask already in place. He basically skidded in there right as you were making your grand entrance into the world.

I screamed.

Something gave way inside of me.

And then there you were. A baby.

Your face was purple, and your body was an alabaster white. The cord was around your neck, and in a flash the doctor cut it and gave you to the nurses, who wrapped you in a towel and started rubbing you all over.

You didn't cry.

It was me who started crying. "Is she okay? What's happening?"

Three people were working on you by that time, and the doctor returned to his spot to deliver the afterbirth stuff (gross) and started sewing me up. Apparently you came out so quick that I tore. You owe me, X. I'm going to be like Noodle after this, I know it.

"Somebody talk to me!" I yelled.

That's when you cried. It was the best noise in the whole world. You cried, and everyone in the room gave a sigh of relief. Your body got pink instead of purple and white. The nurse held you up.

"It's a girl," she said.

"Yeah, I know."

"A beautiful, healthy girl."

"She's healthy?"

"She's fine. Gave us a little scare, is all. Would you like to hold her?"

I'd been thinking about whether I'd hold you ever since Heather. I wanted to. There was something about the skin-to-skin contact, and something about the special milk, and more than that, you were right there. I could see your little fist waving in the air, like you were reaching for me. I could smell you. I wanted to count your fingers and toes, to kiss the top of your head, to whisper hello in your tiny ear.

But then I wouldn't have let you go.

I couldn't have.

In that way, maybe Amber was right.

I couldn't hold you and then give you up again.

"No," I whispered. "I can't hold her."

The nurse nodded without judgment and snuggled you closer to her body, like she was going to play the part of your mother now. Then she wrapped you in a blanket and took you away.

The next bit was hard. They moved me to another room, and they gave me a big shot in the hip because of my blood type or something and made me pee before they'd take the IV out of my arm. When I'd done all that, when I could walk a little, they gave me a rubber glove full of ice to stick between my legs and left me alone.

In that hospital, every time there's a baby born they play part of a lullaby over the loudspeakers. So I lay there, drifting in and out of sleep, crying a little, and listening to the song. It played three times. It reminded me of how many babies there are in the world. Five last night in this hospital alone, you and Amber's baby, who arrived right before you.

In the morning Melly came to see me.

"You did good, kid," she said. "I'm proud of you. I'm sorry I wasn't there."

"How's Amber?"

"She had a girl, too."

"And what's going to happen with her?" I asked.

Melly looked sad. "I don't think she knows yet."

"Did you see my baby?"

She smiled. "I did. She's a beauty. I'm obligated to tell you that your baby is cute, but most newborns look like they've been in a boxing match and lost it, if you know what I mean. But your baby is beautiful. She's already got everyone wrapped around her little finger."

"What about her parents?" I asked.

"She'll go to a foster family for six weeks, and then they can come and get her."

"Why six weeks?"

"That's how long the state gives you to change your mind."

"Oh." I swallowed. "Well. I'm not going to change my mind."

"Good for you," she said. "I think you're doing the right thing. The best thing for her."

"I know."

She left, and I used the hospital phone to call Dawson at the Kappa house. He didn't say much, but he seemed happy that you're alive and well.

"And how about you?" he asked me.

"I've been better," I said. "It's hard."

"I'm sorry."

"Don't be sorry," I told him. "Be happy for her."

"Okay," he said. "I will."

After a while I got up and made my way down the hall to Amber's room. She was lying there all alone, like me, staring toward the window where the light was streaming in. It was nice outside, sun shining, the leaves starting to turn against the foothills. A pretty fall day.

Amber looked surprised to see me. "Oh, hi."

"Hi. How are you feeling?" I asked.

She wiped at her face. Tears tears tears.

"Me too," I said, handing her a tissue.

She blew her nose. "There's so much I can't give her, and I want to give her the world."

"I know."

"I've been a brat to you."

423

"Yes, you have."

She smiled. "But I admire you. You always knew what you were going to do, and you stuck to it. You're so sure of yourself. You make the rest of us look bad."

"Yeah, well, I'm thinking about sneaking down to the nursery and grabbing my kid and making a break for the parking lot, if that makes you feel any better."

"It does," she said. "You won't, though."

"I won't." I sighed.

"I won't, either."

"You're going to give her up?" After the way she talked, I didn't think there was any way she'd choose adoption, no matter what.

"She deserves more," Amber said.

I nodded. "If you want to talk, I'm right down the hall. I swear I won't punch you."

She laughed. "Promise?"

"As long as you're not too annoying."

After I left Amber's room, I made my way to the nursery. Not because I intended to steal you back, but because I wanted to see you again. I couldn't help myself any more than I could yesterday when I couldn't stop pushing. My body took me to you. My feet had a mind of their own.

The nursery was set up with a bunch of plastic bassinets in a big room in front of a window, just like you see in the movies. It took me no time at all to find you, a little bundle right in the middle, still waving your fist.

The other babies had their last names already, written on a card on the back of the bassinet. Baby Holmes. Baby Marushia. Baby Payne.

They didn't put my name on you. Your card was labeled, "Baby Star."

I liked the idea—like you were born as more than a mere infant. You were a star, fallen to earth. You were shining so bright.

You were wrapped in a white blanket with a pink-and-blue stripe along one edge, and you were wearing a knitted pink cap, so I don't know if you had any hair, and I can't remember from yesterday. But your eyes, X. Your eyes were darker than mine, but maybe that's a baby thing. They were a deep, ocean blue.

I stood there for almost an hour staring at you, while other people came and went, mothers and fathers who were there to visit or pick up their babies, grandparents and aunts and uncles who wanted a look at the new member of the family, that sort of thing. The nurses fed and changed and rocked whoever cried.

You didn't cry. You stared up toward the ceiling, waving your hand.

I took a deep breath. I waved back.

"Nice to meet you, Baby Star," I said. Then I blew you a kiss and went back to my room, and now that I've said hello, I started writing this letter to tell you goodbye.

S

44

Sandra Whit. The name is like a magic spell I've memorized, and I find myself saying it even when I'm thinking about something else. I'll be in the grocery store buying apples, and I'll think about that bit she wrote about Heather in the grocery store, and I'll think, "That's right, Sandra Whit. I could be here with Heather, too. She could be that lady right over there, and we would never know."

When I found her face on the yearbook webpage, Mom started to cry, and that made me cry. Again. Still. It's like the name makes my birth mother real. It makes her actually attainable. It was all kind of an exercise in existentialism until then.

"I wonder if it's short for Cassandra," Mom sniffled out when she recovered herself enough to talk, which had not occurred to me until that moment. "Wouldn't that be strange and wonderful, if you had the same name? Or is it possible that some part of me knew about her, to name you something that included Sandra?"

I don't know. Before my parents always told me they simply liked the name. I looked up what it meant once on some baby naming site, and it referred me to either a Greek woman who could see the future (but no one ever believed what she predicted), or Batgirl. I preferred Batgirl.

Mom started crying again. Dad made her sit down on the little sofa in the hotel room and drink tea.

"You have to be careful now, Boo" was all he said. "Tread lightly. These are people's lives."

I took what he said to heart and have spent the last week only doing some light virtual stalking of Sandra Whit. Fortunately for me, the name Whit (as opposed to White) isn't as common as you'd think. There's Governor Whit, of course (it still blows my mind that I met him, that there's a picture of him and Nyla and me framed in the display case in the hallway of Bonneville High School). And Jeremy Whit, who was indeed very good at football and graduated from Notre Dame, who ended up in New York State in an architectural firm. And Beverly Olsen, who was formerly married to Michael Whit, aka Evelyn, a literal beauty queen turned real estate tycoon up in McCall. The internet offered them all to me, and I ate them up eagerly.

But Sandra is harder. Sandra doesn't live in Idaho anymore, for one thing, and she's quiet, not the sort of person to seek the spotlight for herself. She doesn't even have a Facebook profile. The pictures I find always come from other sources: a news article where she was mentioned, a party she attended, a book club photo. Her social media is always designated private. But little by little I find out what I can.

Sandra Whit currently lives in San Francisco.

She's married. In one of the pictures I see a ring on that finger and a tattoo of an Asian symbol on her wrist.

She's a music producer and software developer in the video game industry. It's so perfect, my birth mother who loves music ending up turning music into her career. It makes me want to cheer and hug her and tell her I'm proud, like her victories, in some small way, are my victories.

Mom was right that Sandra Whit has my eyes. Or I have hers, anyway. They're the same shape, the same exact color, with the same eyelashes, even. My eyebrows are a bit lighter. My hair, I think, if I can even remember my natural hair color before I started dyeing it all the time for theater, is also lighter than hers. But she has my eyes. My smile—my teeth. My ears. She's shorter than I am, and slightly skinnier. She seems so young compared to my mom.

She is young, I remind myself. She's only thirty-four.

The more I see her, the more I know, the more I want to find out more. I want to know where she went to college. How she met her husband. Why she chose the career path she did, and how she made it happen. So I start making a plan. I discover an email address that might work. I begin to mentally compose the message I would send.

Hello, Sandra, you don't know me, but . . .

God, that's awful. So cliché.

Hi Sandra, I hope this message finds you well. I recently discovered that you are my birth mother. I just wanted to say thank you.

It's not much better, and it's not entirely true. Saying thank you is not all I want to do. But Dad's right in that I have to be careful. Go with baby steps. Introduce myself first. Figure out if we should meet later. When we should meet. How. I can imagine that, too: knocking on her door. The hug. The tears. Introducing her to my parents (my mom!), which would involve more hugging and more tears. Talking about the letters. Telling her about my life, and hearing about hers. I can see it all, a pretty daydream I've secretly been having for months.

I try again.

> Dear S,
>
> You would know me as Star, but the name my parents gave me is Cassandra McMurtrey. I got your letters a few weeks ago. Thank you so much for writing them. I loved every single one. They make me feel like I know you (or the sixteen-year-old version of you, anyway), and that makes me feel like I should know you—I would like to meet you—if you'd like to know me, too. . . .

I write the message carefully, agonizing over every sentence, and it feels like I'm making some progress with it.

Until the day I stumble over a picture online that stops me cold.

It's a normal photo, like a million others posted by a million other women, but this one somehow slipped by Sandra's strict privacy practices. It shows two little girls standing on the street in front of a school bus. They're different ages—one is probably six and the other eight or nine. They both have shiny long dark hair and dark eyes, not blue, but . . . they also have her smile—the teeth and everything. They are wearing school uniforms, blue-and-green plaid with white ballet-collared blouses. They both have pink backpacks and little Mary Janes. Their arms are wrapped around each other, their cheeks pressed together, smiling wide.

First day with both the munchkins at school, Sandra captions the photo. *Brb I've got something in my eye.*

It's such an S thing to say that tears spring to my eyes. I stare and stare at the picture, seeing my smile, my earlobes, the subtle layer of baby fat I used to have around my neck at that age. I wonder if they even have the duck feet.

They're my sisters. My biological half sisters, anyway.

The thing is, they look happy. They look like everything in their world is as it should be.

I can't help but think then about how this message I'm writing to their mother could upset that world. It leads to a lot of questions I haven't wanted to ask myself before.

What if Sandra Whit's husband doesn't know about me?

What would it do to their relationship to find out she had a baby she gave up for adoption? A baby who is now grown up and wants— no, is freaking demanding—a relationship she didn't ask for?

How would those little girls feel then? How could Sandra Whit possibly explain it to them?

And what if Sandra doesn't *want* to know me?

This life—these two little girls and their dad—is the life that Sandra Whit meant to have. It's what she chose for herself.

Who am I to break that life wide open and insert myself in there again?

She works in the computer industry. She definitely knows how to google. She knows, and she hasn't made that choice. Because she's happy with the way things are now. She's happy.

I'm happy.

It all comes back to this hard truth: if she wanted to find me, she could.

45

"You were quiet at dinner," Mom says. "What's going on in that head of yours?"

She's still too darn perceptive.

I shrug. I'm sitting hunched over the kitchen counter, watching my mother frost a cake. "Sandra Whit," I confess as she smooths the frosting with an expert hand over the surface of the cake. The whole kitchen is filled with the heady smell of vanilla and my mother's dreams come alive again.

But my dreams, well. I don't know.

"What about S?" Mom asks. She still calls her S, while the rest of us have taken to calling her Sandra Whit like that's all one name. And who knows? Maybe Sandra Whit doesn't go by Sandra, any more than I go by Cassandra. Maybe she's something else.

"I don't think I should contact her," I say.

Weirdly, Mom doesn't seem surprised by this. "That's a tough decision," she says.

"What do you think?"

She sighs. "I can see it both ways."

"Would you still like to meet her?" I ask.

She dips her knife into a small glass of milk, then keeps frosting, smoothing the wrinkles, perfecting it. "Yes. Of course. I would still like to thank her. But only if I knew that my presence—our presence—wasn't going to be any big disturbance to her life."

"Exactly," I agree glumly. "That happens to be exactly what I think."

"Good," Mom says. "Maybe I raised you well. You're thinking of her, instead of yourself."

"But you know, on one of those adoption registry websites it said that ninety percent of the women who give their babies up for adoption are open to being reunited with them at some point. That's a pretty high percentage."

"Yes, it is. So I guess that means it's likely that she's open to it, too." She sets the knife down and turns the cake, eyeing it from all angles. "Like I said, it's a tough decision."

I nod. I go to stick my finger in her big bowl of frosting, and she smacks my hand. We both laugh.

"But you told me to find her. You were up for disturbing her life back then," I argue.

"I was thinking of what you needed."

"What, you thought I needed a mother?"

"I thought you needed an answer."

"Oh. Well, now I have lots of answers."

"Yes, you do." She picks up an envelope she's created out of wax

432

paper and spoons some of the frosting into it. Then she folds it closed and squeezes it until a little bit of frosting comes out of the end. She takes a toothpick from a box and holds it up, then starts to make petals on it, from the center on out. A rose out of frosting, which is something she often tried to teach me, but never could. My roses always ended up looking like pine cones.

"When I was dying, I used to think about my heart," she says, and my breath catches. I've never heard her say it like that. *When I was dying.*

"People would tell me that I'd get a new heart. Someday, when I'd given up hope for it, they'd say, a new heart was going to come along, like magic. I tried to believe that, to have faith in the idea, to visualize it happening to me. But I knew that this heart wouldn't actually be magic. It belonged to someone else. It was being carried around, even in the moment I was thinking about it, in someone else's chest, beating for them, keeping them alive. I used to think about that heart so much, even in the dark moments when I wasn't sure it really existed or if I'd ever receive it. What was the heart doing, I wondered, out there in the world? Was the woman jogging, and so her heart was racing as she sprinted around some track? Was she in love, and her heart fluttered when she saw the person she was in love with? Was she a mother, too? Did she love her child the way that I love you—so fiercely she'd easily give up her life on her kid's behalf, so completely, so truly?"

I bite my lip. I don't know where she's going with this, but I know it's important to listen.

"And then one day, out of the blue, in the nick of time, I got the heart. Now I carry it inside of me, and I feel responsible for both of us, this woman and me. I have her heart. I have to take care of it, and love my life because of it, and never take it for granted, not even for a moment."

I nod. "I think I'd feel that way, too."

My mom closes her eyes for a second. "That's also how I feel about your birth mother. She carried you inside of her, and loved you, and looked out for you, until the day that you came to be mine instead. It's like . . ." Her voice wavers. "I know that I have her heart. And I have to take care of it. And I have to honor her choice, her sacrifice."

We're both in tears by this point. She's still making the rose out of frosting, so I can't hug her. I want to hug her. Finally, she finishes with the last petals. "Hold out your hand," she says, and I do. She places the rose gently into the palm of my hand.

"For you, my Cassandra Rose."

"I love you, Mom."

"I love you, too."

We would probably have started crying again, but then Dad comes through the door. He stops in his tracks, and lifts his head and smells the air.

"Cake," he whispers.

Mom laughs and wipes her eyes. "We're almost ready to eat it."

I put the rose in my mouth. It tastes fragile and sweet and like a perfect representation of what my mother is.

"Hey, you got some mail," Dad says, and holds up a large, official-looking envelope.

"What is it this time?" I groan.

It turns out to be the log-in information for the DNA test I did last year, the Christmas gift from my parents. The results are available for me to see.

Mom cuts the cake, and then she and Dad and I sit at the table and eat the entire thing. We're so stuffed by the end I can hardly move. Then I take the DNA test stuff down the hall to my room and sit down at my desk and open my laptop. I intend to simply read the results, but something stops me.

There's something I should do first.

I locate the draft of the email I was composing to Sandra Whit, and I delete it.

I've decided: I'm not going to contact her. I'm not going to cyberstalk her anymore. She deserves her privacy.

I'll let her go.

I know what I need to know, I tell myself. I know my medical history. I know the story of how I came to be a person. I know Sandra Whit loved me. She loved me. That will have to be enough.

You go your way, I think. I'll go mine.

Dear Star,

This is the last letter I'm going to write you. I don't know if it will be included with the others, since you were adopted today, and I know the people who started the letter program with the state really only meant for me to write one letter, and this is so many, and I can't go on writing them now that you're not mine. You belong to your parents and not to me. I mean, I don't think you've ever really belonged to me. I just got to lug you around with me for a while.

I'm doing okay since the hospital. My dad came to pick me up, which was not ideal, but he insisted. He drove me back to his place, which, again, is not what I wanted.

"I'm going to live with Mom," I told him. "I told you."

"I know," he said gruffly. "I have your stuff all packed. She'll be here tomorrow. But I wanted to give you something."

It turned out that something was a car.

I'd like to say I refused, out of principle, or because I will not be bribed into making nice with him. But I took the car. It was a moment of weakness that I can't make myself regret.

The first thing I did was drive over to the college to apologize to Ted. He lives in the same dorm room as last year, the dorm room where you were conceived, Baby Star, and yeah, that was a little weird, waiting outside in the hall again for some boy to come along.

Ted smiled when he saw me, this fleeting little smile, but then he tried to act like he didn't care. "Hi."

"Hi."

"What are you doing here? Do you need me to help you find Dawson?"

"No," I said. "I was looking for you. I owe you an apology."

"No, you don't."

"I do. I used you. Like you said. That was wrong, and I'm sorry."

"Okay."

"Okay?" I couldn't help but smile. "Just like that?"

"Okay."

"Good. Thank you." I turned to go.

"Wait, do you want to come in?" he asked. "I have tea."

"All right."

I went in and sat on the bed opposite his—he must have had another roommate, but I didn't ask about it—and he made me a cup of tea. With sugar, this time. And milk.

"No Pop-Tarts," I said preemptively.

"You're not pregnant anymore," he pointed out.

"Nope."

"So she's okay?"

"She's perfect. She's with her parents now."

"And what are you going to do?"

"I'm going to move in with my mom in Colorado."

"Oh." His face fell. I have to admit I liked how disappointed he seemed.

"But after I graduate, I might come back here. To school, I mean."

"Now you want to go to college?"

"I like it here." I stood up again and looked around as if I'd never been in there before. "So maybe. I'm going to play things by ear for a while. See where I end up."

"Well, for my sake, I hope you end up here," he said.

I arched an eyebrow at him. "For your sake?"

"I like you. Maybe that's weird."

"Why is that weird?"

He blushed. "This is the first time we've had a real conversation where you weren't pregnant with my roommate's baby. I mean, who makes a move on a pregnant girl?"

"Did you make a move? Did I miss that?"

"I'm thinking about making a move. Sometime in the future."

"When?"

"In about ten seconds," he said.

"Oh."

"Nine, eight, seven," he counted, stepping toward me.

I counted along, too. "Six, five, four."

I kissed him on three.

"Thank you for being a nice guy," I said when I pulled away.

"Um, you're welcome," he breathed.

"You helped me so much. You made me believe that I might have some kind of future."

"The future is whatever you make it," he said. "That's from, well, Back to the Future."

"You glorious nerd," I giggled.

That was all that happened, Star, I promise. A kiss. A joke. Then I had to go. But I meant it when I said I believed in the future now, and whatever it holds.

It's easy for me to imagine your future. You grow up to be beautiful and smart and strong and good. Someone is there to pick you up when you fall down, to kiss your scraped knee, to make your birthday cakes and sing songs to you and teach you about the world. You're loved, every minute of your life. You're so loved, and you never doubt that, even when things get tough. You're loved.

That's the future, Baby Star. That's what I know to be true, because I'll be there, too, even if you don't know me, even if you can't see the ties that bind us. I'm under the same sun as you, the same moon, walking the same earth, and I'll be thinking about you every day, every step. I'll be hoping for the best.

I'll be loving you.

S

Epilogue
Six months later

"Happy birthday, Cass," says Bastian.

"Thanks," I say, smiling. Nineteen feels older this time, a little more weathered than who I was last year. Wiser. More aware of myself. More comfortable with who I am.

Bastian holds up a bag. "Chocolate chip cookie? The cafeteria makes these insanely good ones. Like, the-freshman-fifteen-might-be-worth-it good."

"Okay. Yum."

"Wait. There's more." He unwraps the cookie and sets it on a napkin in the middle of the stage, then pulls a little white candle and a lighter out of his back pocket, sticks it in the cookie, and sets it on fire. He starts to sing, and the other people in the cast notice and turn to us and start to sing along.

I clap with them at the end and blow out the candle.

"And many more," Bastian sings.

We share the cookie and then get back to work painting the set of the new fall play at College of Idaho: *The Marriage of Bette and Boo*. We both have small parts, Bastian and I, because we're freshmen. We're still little fish at this school, it turns out, but we'll get there. We'll grow.

My phone buzzes. A text from Nyla, who I miss terribly, like an amputated limb. I get phantom pains for Nyla all the time.

Nyla: Happy birthday, Cass! I wish I were there to celebrate!

Me: How's USC?

Nyla: I have sand in my pants.

Me: Sorry if my heart doesn't exactly bleed for you right now. How'd the audition go?

Nyla: You think the world is ready for a black Sandy in "Grease"?

Me: The world is definitely ready.

Nyla: How's the new bestie?

Me: He's only my second-best bestie. He's still unfairly pretty.

"Tell Nyla I said hi," says Bastian. He's not really second best. He's just second in the bestie line.

Me: Bastian says hi.

Nyla: Is he taking you out for a birthday dinner?

Me: Better. It's homecoming week. There's a big ceremony, and my parents are coming.

Nyla: Awesome! Give Mama Cat a hug from me.

Me: I will.

Nyla: 🖤 🎉 🎂 🖤

Me: 🖤 😌 ☺

My phone buzzes again. Mom this time.

Mom: We're here. We're at the SUB.

Me: I'll be right out.

* * *

My parents are standing at the foot of the steps at the student union building when I get there, both grinning. They've been here before, of course, when they dropped me off in August, and we all went around on the campus tour back then (and Dad had been on the campus tour before, that time we went college shopping), but today when I show them around it feels more official, somehow. I am showing them *my* college. My favorite table in the cafeteria. My spot under my tree in the quad, where I like to read. The desk I always sit at in the library. That pretty classroom on the third floor of Strahorn Hall, where yesterday I learned all about Christopher Marlowe from Dr. Spencer. My dorm room, all decked out now with my stuff. My new roommate, Lindsey, who's hilarious and helpfully tidy and who can do the harmony with her violin to any song I play for her: country, R & B, pop. And the theater, of course.

My theater.

We while away the afternoon wandering around campus and hanging out with my roomie in the dorm. And when it's almost time to leave for the homecoming ceremony, Dad suddenly says, "I get it now, why this is where you wanted to come. It's very you."

"It is," I agree happily. "It's where I was supposed to end up. I always, like, knew it somehow. I'm meant to be here. I don't know why, but . . ."

"The universe unfolds as it should," Mom says sagely.

"Exactly."

"And right now the universe is telling us it's time to eat," Dad chimes in. "I'm starved."

I run us back to the caf. We have to hurry with our meals because it's almost time for the ceremony, which is held in the big auditorium.

When we get there Mom and Dad go sit with the other proud parents. I find Bastian and we walk together with the incoming freshmen through something called the alumni walk, where the people who graduated from C of I stand along the edges of the aisles as we go in and hand us the tassels that we'll wear four years from now, when we graduate.

"My uncle gave me my tassel," Bastian says as we're sitting down.

"Your uncle is here?"

He doesn't have time to tell me about that, though, because then the ceremony gets started. We sit back and listen to speaker after speaker talk to us about the future, about the opportunities we're going to have here at C of I, about how we are free now to figure out our purpose in life, and about how much fun we're going to have and all of the lasting relationships we're going to build here.

"Like you, second bestie," whispers Bastian, bumping his shoulder into mine.

I smile. I know it's true.

Afterward there's a reception in the lobby where we meet up with my parents again. There are tea cakes and cookies and punch.

"Hello," Mom says to Bastian. "Fancy meeting you here."

"Hi, there!" he greets her. "You're Cass's older sister, right? You look just like her."

He's still doesn't know I'm adopted. I'll tell him soon, I think, but for now I am enjoying the way he thinks I look exactly like my mom.

"Oh, you," she giggles. It's good to see her this way, all dressed up, her body filled out again, stronger, her cheeks flushed with color, her hair shiny and her eyes bright. "You're a flatterer, you are."

"And flattery will get you everywhere with her," I add. Snerk.

"It was a great ceremony," Dad says. "I feel so inspired."

"Me too," Bastian agrees. "I know I'm on the brink of figuring out my purpose in life."

We laugh. Then Bastian spots somebody across the room.

"There's my uncle," he says. "Come and meet him."

"Where are we going?" my mom asks as Bastian grabs my hand and I grab hers and we start to weave through the throng of people. She grabs my dad at the last minute. We're like a silly people train chugging through the crowd.

"How come I've never met this mysterious uncle before?" I ask as we make our way over there. "I mean, you've met Uncle Pete."

Bastian grins. "My uncle doesn't live in Idaho. But he's the reason I wanted to come here, actually. He went here. He's always talked about C of I like it's the best place on earth. He develops video games now—have I told you that? He's like a millionaire, but you'd never know it to look at him."

"He develops video games? How cool is that?" This makes me think of Sandra Whit, and my throat tightens. I swallow and push past it. I'm trying not to think about her so much.

"It's pretty awesome," Bastian says. "Growing up I also had the best video game collection out of all my friends."

"I would never have pegged you as a gamer."

"I became a theater nerd. I don't have the time," he explains. "Hey, Uncle Theo!" He raises his hand, and a dark-haired man turns and waves at us.

"He and his wife came all the way out from California," Bastian says. "Because my dad still . . ."

His dad still isn't speaking to him. His parents aren't here with all the other parents, so his uncle is filling in.

We finally get to the other side of the room and pull up in front of Bastian's uncle: Bastian, me, my mom and dad all in a line.

"Hey, buddy," his uncle says, clapping Bastian on the shoulder. "Great ceremony, wasn't it? Isn't this place the absolute best? And who's this?"

"This is Cass McMurtrey, the bestie I'm always talking about," Bastian says.

"Hi," I say awkwardly.

"And this is Cass's mom and dad, Cat and Bill McMurtrey," Bastian continues. "Meet Theo Takamoto, my infamous uncle."

"Wait," I say. "Takamoto?"

"It's Japanese," Bastian says. "I'm one-quarter Japanese, didn't you know?"

"Video game developer," I murmur.

"Are you okay, honey?" Mom touches my arm.

"Yeah, it's just . . ." I have goose bumps.

Bastian doesn't notice that anything's weird. He hugs his uncle and glances around. "And my aunt's around here somewhere, I assume, also very cool, also graduated from here."

"She's at the punch bowl," Uncle Theo says.

We all turn. There's a woman over there carefully pouring herself a glass of punch. She has brown hair, which is falling in a curtain across her face as she looks down at her cup.

"Aunt Sandy!" Bastian calls. He turns to me. "I'm the only one who calls her Sandy. Her name is actually—" He sees my face. "Are you okay? You look like you're about to pass out. Maybe you should get some punch, too."

"Her name is Sandra," I breathe.

"I'm confused," Bastian says. "Do you know my aunt?"

445

"She went here," I whisper. "She married Ted. Theo is Ted."

"What's this?" Theo asks. "Who am I, now?"

My mom's been listening all along. She suddenly squeezes my hand so tight I lose the feeling in the tips of my fingers.

"What's going on?" Dad wants to know.

"Aunt Sandy!" Bastian calls again.

The woman looks up. She sees Bastian, smiles.

"Her eyes," Mom says. "Look at her eyes."

Even from here I can tell: her eyes are blue. She's looking at me, and then at my mom and my dad, who are both staring at her with their mouths open. Her forehead creases slightly. She starts to walk toward us.

"Cat," Dad says breathlessly, taking Mom's other hand.

Here we go, I think.

Here we go.

Note from the Author

In so many ways, this book is the book of my heart.

I was adopted when I was only six weeks old. My adoption was something that felt like a fairy tale told to me by my parents from the time I was old enough to understand stories—the one about the loving but lonely couple who desperately desired to have a child, and the brave sixteen-year-old girl who was determined to find a better life for her baby. I was the happy ending of that story, like Cass, and like so many other adoptees I've always been curious to know how that story began. When I was eighteen, with my parents' blessing, I embarked on a journey to try to find my birth mother, or, at the very least, to find out who she was. It was a heart-wrenching and often frustrating quest that spanned more than twenty years, and I never did find her. I still don't even know her name.

In some ways I wrote this book to explore my wishful feelings about that elusive sixteen-year-old girl. Still, I want to clarify that this novel is a work of fiction. When I write I try to escape myself and find new characters and, hopefully, follow them home. Cass and Sandra both came to life for me in that magical way that characters do, and went off in directions I never expected. And so, dear Reader, *The How & the Why* is not *my* story, although I will confess that three major details are lifted from real life:

1. I did go to College of Idaho, one of the best and most formative periods of my life. This book is my love song to this amazing school, where I learned so much and where I also, all these years later, sat in the gorgeous new library and composed this book. I also went to Boise State for graduate school, where I really committed myself to becoming a writer.

2. There really did used to be a letter-writing program in Idaho in which birth mothers could leave letters for their unborn babies.

3. There was indeed a home for pregnant girls in Boise, which is now called the Marian Pritchett School, and is still helping pregnant teens today. The people who work in this place are, in my eyes, nothing short of educational rock stars. They make a difference in the lives of young people in such a huge and tangible way that it truly is changing the world one life at a time.

On that note, the first person I'd like to thank is Lindsey Klein, for her enormous help when I was researching this novel. Lindsey gave me a thorough tour of the school and patiently answered all my seemingly inane questions about the history and daily operation of Booth Memorial. I also want to thank Amber Young, who worked in the dorms in the final years that the school operated as a home, and who gave me so much valuable insight into what life would have been like for Sandra Whit.

I'd also like to thank one of my oldest and dearest friends, Amy Yowell, who drove with me over to Booth to be my moral support because she knew that it would be emotional for me to be there. She read the first draft like a cheerleader, but also as a kind of expert, because she's a high school teacher, she grew up in Idaho Falls, she's my former roommate at College of Idaho, and, in a weird coincidence, she just happened to be at the exact same Pearl Jam concert I randomly chose for how Sandra and Dawson met. Amy is the best bestie I could ask for, and I can't adequately express how glad I am to have her in my life. To Ben, her husband, and her amazing and funny daughters, Katie and Gwen; I am also immensely happy to call them my friends.

As usual, I owe an enormous thank-you to Katherine Fausset, my agent. She has seen me through all the ups and downs, not just with this book, but over the past ten years of guiding me through my life as an author. So much more than fifteen percent of any success I've had in this business is due to her hard work and perseverance.

I also want to thank Erica Sussman, my editor. This was an emotionally challenging book for Erica, too, as an adoptive parent, and I'm so grateful for her good humor and her patience as this story evolved through so many different drafts. The entire team at Harper-Teen has been so amazing to work with: Stephanie Stein, Louisa Currigan, Gina Rizzo, Jenna Stempel-Lobell, Alison Donalty, Alison Klapthor, Alexandra Rakaczki, and Michael D'Angelo. I'd also like to give a shout-out to my new out-of-house publicist, Sarah Kershaw.

This time around I was fortunate to have people who read this book to help me to better convey the experience of those in my story who had backgrounds so different from my own: Francina Simone, especially—thank you.

As always, I'm grateful for my friends: Wendy Johnston, Lindsey Hunt, my fellow stooges Brodi Ashton and Jodi Meadows, Tahereh Mafi and Ransom Riggs, my book club: Melissa Bollinger, Heather Ramey, Heather Westover, Rani Child, Danaka Stanger, Amber

Woolner, Breya Fujimoto, Krista Cromar, Krissy Swallow, Jami Harris, Claire Boyd, and Kerry Ramey.

I'd also like to thank my family: my parents, Rod and Julie Hand / Carol and Jack Ware; my brothers, Allan and Rob Follett; my kids, Will and Maddie; my stepkids, Wilfred and Grady; and my utterly sweet, funny, and supportive husband, Daniel Rutledge. That line Ted says about S being "hot for a while" came straight from him, and it still makes me smile.

And you, Dear Reader, *you*. Thank you for reading this book of my heart.

Keep reading for a sneak peek at
WITH YOU ALL THE WAY

1

"My mom isn't home," Leo says as he opens the door.

That's when I know that he wants to have sex.

"Oh" is all I can think to say.

"She's out of town until Tuesday." It's Friday afternoon. He definitely wants to have sex. We've been dating since February (this being mid-June), kissing a lot, making out whenever we can find somewhere private to hide away. Sex is the obvious next step.

"So we've got your place all to ourselves," I say giddily. I've been thinking about Leo all day, wondering when I would get to see him, daydreaming about the smooth warm feel of his lips against mine. When he texted that he wanted to hang out this afternoon, it was the best kind of surprise. And this, well, it feels like I'm having a sexy dream about Leo.

Only this is real.

Leo smiles, a little-kid-about-to-open-his-birthday-present type smile. "You could even—I don't know—stay the night?"

I laugh, that giggle I hate, the one I do so often around Leo. Stay the night. Wow. How can I even pull off being gone all night? My parents will notice if I don't come home. Pop will notice, anyway. Mom probably wouldn't notice if I went missing for a week.

"You could tell them you're sleeping over at a friend's house," Leo suggests. That's the obvious play. My best friend, Lucy, will go for it, too; she's so excited that I—quiet, nerdy Ada—finally have a verifiable love interest. At first they teased me that I made Leo up, this perfect boy I kept talking about. I had to practically beg Leo—who hates high school dances—to take me to prom, just to prove he was real. Ever since then my friends have been referring to Leo—popular, non-nerdy Leo—as "The Miracle." And this—him wanting to have sex with me, not just once, apparently, but all night long—seems miraculous, too.

I nod. Laugh again. "Okay."

His smile grows wider, kid-on-Christmas-morning level excited. "Okay? Really?"

I try to act like my heart isn't thudding in my chest. "I mean, Friday's family night, which is seriously sacred to my stepdad, but I can miss it. We're going out of town next week, so we're going to have a lot of family time, so—"

"I'm going to miss you," he says, "when you're in Hawaii."

I smile. "I'm going to miss you, too." Stupid compulsory family trip to Hawaii. "So yeah, I guess, I can stay the n—"

"So you really want to?" he asks.

"I do," I say breathlessly. I get out my phone and text Lucy, who

2

enthusiastically agrees to be my alibi, and text Pop that I'm having a sleepover at Lucy's.

Have fun! Pop texts back.

Then Leo takes my hand and leads me toward what I'm guessing is his bedroom.

His house is in Santa Clara, a few train stops before San Jose. It isn't a large house. Three bedrooms, two baths. From the street it looks tiny, especially if I'm comparing it to my own house in Redwood City. If I'm being nice—and my default setting is nice, I can't seem to help it—I'd say it was "refreshingly minimal." When I picture myself as an artist (like Leo's mom, who's a famous local sculptor) I can imagine living in a house like this.

I've never seen Leo's room before. He's invited me over a few times since we started going out, but his mom was always home. There was some unspoken understanding between them that we wouldn't hang out in his bedroom, so we stayed in the kitchen or streamed movies on the living room sofa. Now, as we move down the hallway toward the inevitable (!!!) sex we're about to have, I pause to look at the framed photographs hanging on the wall. Most of them are of Leo and Diana with various people I assume are relatives. I point at the photo of a toddler with something bright red—beets? tomato sauce?—smeared all over his face. "Aw. Look at you."

He cringes. "My mom won't take it down. She loves to humiliate me."

"I think it's cute," I say.

"You're cute," he counters.

We come to a room crammed with tables and sculptures in various states of progression: his mom's studio. She works with wax and clay in there and then takes it to a place in the city to cast it into bronze. I barely resist the urge to go inside and attempt to absorb some of her genius.

Leo, however, is not impressed. He tugs on my hand to get me moving again, toward a smaller bedroom at the end of the hall. His.

"Welcome." He ushers me inside. Closes the door. "Make yourself at home."

There's nowhere to sit but on his bed. I perch on the edge and fold my hands into my lap, gazing around at the various posters on the walls. Most of them are of swimmers. Leo's captain of the swim team at his school. By the look of it, he's obsessed with Michael Phelps, and this other guy with a huge tattoo that covers most of his left arm.

I wouldn't have pegged Leo for a posters-all-over-the-walls kind of guy.

"That's Caeleb Dressel," he explains almost shyly. "Two gold medals. Holds the world record in the hundred-meter butterfly."

"Nice." I try to seem appreciative, but it's weird to be admiring these spandex-clad older men. I can't imagine sleeping in here with their eyes on me. Or sleeping in here, period.

"So," says Leo.

"So," I say. My heart is skittering again. *I'm okay*, I tell myself. I'm sixteen, which I consider old enough to make a mature decision about it. Leo's seventeen. We've been dating for almost five months. I like Leo, really like him. I'm curious about what sex will be like. With Leo, like everything has been with Leo so far, it will probably be great.

"Do you want to listen to some music?" He reaches around me to turn on a speaker on the bedside table. Then he thumbs through his phone to find a soundtrack for the business at hand. The first song is about (you guessed it) having sex. It's a little cringey, how Leo obviously googled the best songs to have sex to. I hope there's not an entire playlist of sex songs.

Leo sits down next to me. We kiss. He buries one hand in the hair at the base of my neck, cradling my head. Kissing him is always so good. Delicious. I can't define what he tastes like, exactly, but it's not similar to any food or drink I know. Not sweet, but spicy isn't right, either. He tastes like Leo. Which I like.

After a few minutes he pushes me gently back onto the bed. I hang on to his shoulders. Leo has broad, muscly shoulders, from the swimming. He's a big guy—six three, solid, which is one other reason I like him. Leo being so big makes me feel smaller, in a good way.

His mouth is on my neck now. Goose bumps jump up along my arms. I tilt my head to give him better access. He moves to my ear. I predict he's going to stick his tongue in there. He's done that before, and I wasn't really a fan. I turn so he won't. Touch his face so I can pivot him back to my mouth. Kiss him again. Again. Exploring. Trying the different angles.

He moves on top of me, his large body stretching over mine. For a few seconds I feel smothered; he's too heavy, squashing me, but then he shifts his weight onto his arms and I can breathe again. His body against mine is familiar, but the way he's moving is new. The bulge—that solid bump that I know is his, uh, junk, what my mom would insist on calling his penis, because Mom refuses to be anything but technical and precise about naming things—presses against my thigh.

Oh god, I'm thinking about my mother. I squirm, and Leo pulls back. His face is so red it makes his eyebrows stand out against his

5

skin, like furry caterpillars clinging to his forehead. It's distracting.

"You're beautiful," he mumbles.

"You too," I say automatically, and blush so hard it feels like my cheeks and neck have been scalded. Leo keeps kissing me and touching me, and I'm totally into it. At least my body is. My lower half seems to be transforming into hot liquid. There's a knot of sensation building between my legs. But the further along we get, the closer to the actual sex that's going to be happening any minute now, the more weirdly disconnected I feel. To the point where I can almost slip out of my body and float over us. See myself from the outside.

I'm wearing a red Harry Potter shirt from last year's trip to Orlando. It reads "9 ¾" on the front. It's childish—I can see that so clearly now—and unflattering, a size too big for me, because I prefer loose-fitting clothes. Leo is pulling this shirt up, exposing my very white, not-very-flat belly, and underneath he discovers a gray sports bra, which confounds him because it doesn't have any kind of hook or clasp. My mind whirls trying to remember what panties I'm wearing. Hopefully not the plain white cotton with the hole in the butt, which I should have thrown away months ago, but they're the most comfortable pair I own. Shit. It's probably those. My hair is tangled around my head. My chest heaves behind the sports bra, which is dark in places, because I'm so sweaty.

From this vantage point, the one in my imagination—seeing as how my eyes are actually squeezed shut—I know I'm not beautiful. Leo only said that to try to make me feel sexy. So I would want to have sex.

I do want to have sex, don't I?

Yes, I tell myself. *Relax. This is fine.*

But then Leo's hand is on the button of my shorts, and my upper half turns to ice. *Wait*, I think. *Wait*, and then I almost knock heads with him as I try to sit up.

He examines my face. "Hey. Are you okay?"

I swipe at a strand of hair that's clinging damply to my cheek. "I'm good. Sorry. Can we just take it slower?"

He nods. "Of course. Whatever you want."

"Okay." I lean in to kiss him again. We do that for a while, and the tension in my shoulders eases. He's very good at kissing, and I'm not so bad at it, either. It's not sloppy or teeth-banging. There's just the right amount of tongue involved. His arms feel solid around me. His hand squeezing my breast is good. I try to touch him, too, running my hands along his back, his swimmer's chest. Then lower.

"I love you," he says then, softly.

My hand stills. He's never said that before, the L-word. Neither of us have.

He says, "I should, uh, get some protection."

I blink up at him. Somehow I'm lying down again, although I don't know when that happened. "What?"

He spells it out for me. "A condom."

"Oh. Right. Yes." How responsible of us.

He gets up and goes out of the room. I wonder where he's going for this condom. Is he ransacking his mom's bedside table? Or the bathroom, where he has a stash for situations such as these? Has he done this before? We haven't talked about it. We really should have talked about it. At least then I would know what to expect.

I smooth my clothes back down over myself and take a steadying breath. The gray jersey sheets beneath me smell like fresh laundry detergent. I sit up. I'm surprised, actually, by how clean Leo's room is. There are no piles of dirty laundry like you'd find on the floor of my room. The carpet even has vacuum lines in it.

How long has he been planning this? Did he wake up this morning thinking *tonight's the night*? Did he tidy up and wash his sheets and hug his mom goodbye with a secret smile because he knew he was going to get laid? When all that time I was thinking that we were simply going to a movie this afternoon, then maybe we'd go back to his house, have dinner and talk art with Leo's mom, stream a show. Most of our relationship consists of watching various things together. And making out while his mom isn't looking.

But this.

It's unfair of him, springing this on me. I would have dressed better if I'd known, done something with my hair. Picked different underwear, at least. Shaved my legs.

Oh *god*. I haven't shaved my legs in days.

I glance around wildly like a razor is just going to magically materialize. Michael Phelps glares down at me from the walls. One of the posters reads, *FEARLESS. If you want to be the best, you have to do things other people aren't willing to do.*

And Leo just said he *loved* me. Was he being serious? Did he mean *love* the way you can say, *I love peanut butter cups*? Or the real way? Was I supposed to say it back? I like him, yes, so much, but could I say I love him? I mouth the words "I love you," and it feels fake. Maybe I could mean it in the peanut-butter-cup sense. But it's too late to respond now, anyway. He said he loved me, and I didn't say anything, and now we're on to the sex.

This is happening. I'm about to have sex.

Leo returns. He holds up a foil packet triumphantly. "Okay, let's do this."

That's when I know I can't do this.

"Actually, let's not." I stand up, eager to get off the bed.

His smile fades. "What? What happened?"

"Nothing. I . . ." I choose my next words very carefully. "I just don't want to go all the way. Not tonight. Okay?"

Now he looks like a little kid who's opened his Christmas present to discover a sweater. "But why not?"

"I'm not ready. I thought I was, but I'm not. Sorry," I tack on, and then hate myself for apologizing. I'm not supposed to be sorry. But I am.

Leo's frowning, but he says, "All right. I don't want to do it if you don't want to do it, obviously."

I smile. "Thanks."

Silence builds between us. A new song starts pouring out of the speaker, a song I know this time, a slow song by The Weeknd called "Earned It." Over Leo's shoulder I read another inspirational Michael Phelps poster. *You can't put a limit on anything. The more you dream, the farther you get.*

Leo puts the condom on the bedside table. "So what *do* you want to do?"

I wouldn't mind making out some more, but that could send a mixed message. Besides, my lower half is starting to ache, a tight but heavy, decidedly unpleasant feeling, like period cramps. I try to smile at him. "I don't know. Maybe we could watch something?"

"Sure," he says dully. "Whatever you want."

2

"I thought you were staying at Lucy's tonight," Pop says when I come into the kitchen later.

"I just wanted to be home." Things were awkward with Leo, so awkward that I finally said I wasn't feeling well—which wasn't really a lie—and he insisted on walking me to the train station.

"You're my little homebody," Pop says now with a smile. Like that's cute.

My five-year-old sister, Abby, is sitting at the counter coloring while Pop makes dinner. "What's a homebody?" Abby asks.

Pop continues dicing a stalk of celery. "A homebody is someone who loves to be home more than anywhere else."

"I like to be home," Abby announces. "But I also like to go places. Today we went on an African safari. I made a batik."

It takes me a second to realize that Abby is talking about the day camp she goes to during the summer, since Pop works nights at El

Camino Hospital in Mountain View, and Mom works days at Stanford Hospital in Palo Alto. Although to say that Mom works days is inaccurate. Mom works all the time.

Speaking of which: "Where's Mom?"

Pop keeps chopping vegetables. "She said she'd be home in time for dinner. It's family night, you know."

"I know." Normally I would stay and help him finish making the salad, but that could lead to conversations like "How was your day?" and I don't want to go there. So I grab a carrot and flee upstairs to my room. I close the door and go straight to my desk, where I take out my journal and art pencils and begin to sketch Leo.

I can still see him clearly in my mind's eye. That expression on his face when I said I didn't want to go all the way. The way his eyelids lowered, not squeezing into a squint or a glare, but dropping like protective shutters over his eyes. His eyebrows angled up at the inner edges, pressing together, causing two small bumps to appear in the space between them. The discontented downturn of his mouth.

My pencil practically dances over the paper, capturing that look. It takes me ten minutes, and the moment I finish I know it's one of the best sketches I've ever done. It illustrates the moment perfectly—the feeling in it, the tension. Strange how the worst experiences can lead to the best art. But that's life, I guess. Beauty in the pain.

I pick up the carrot I stole from Pop and crunch on it miserably. Clearly I've made a huge mistake here. Why didn't I want to have sex? Was it the *I love you* bit? Do I believe, deep down somewhere, that to "make love" you need to be *in love*, and I don't love Leo enough for that? Do I love Leo? I've never considered my feelings like that before: either love or not love. I like Leo. I love being with him. I'm attracted to him. Shouldn't that be enough?

Or was it the unshaved legs thing? The holey underwear? The sports bra? Am I so uncomfortable in my own skin that the idea of Leo seeing me naked is more than I can handle? I know I have body issues, but am I really that self-conscious?

Or maybe it was Michael Phelps.

Whatever the reason, it was the wrong call. Leo was offended. He might say it's all right and that he respects me and that he can wait, but he got instantly distant with me after I wanted to stop. He couldn't help it. He was disappointed.

Yeah, well. I'm disappointed, too.

I sign and date the sketch. It needs a title. I scrawl a word I like: *crestfallen*. That's what Leo was. His crest had definitely fallen. I snort, then erase the word carefully. *Not ready*, I write instead.

Not ready. I sigh. I flip back through the journal, past the pages and pages of sketches like this one, documenting the moments of my life as intimately as any diary would. There are so many drawings of Leo. Leo on the beach at Santa Cruz, the sea breeze ruffling his hair. Leo tying his shoe. Leo in swim trunks that one time we swam in his aboveground backyard pool, his back to me as he stood at the edge of the water, the muscles tightened as he prepared to dive in. He's beautiful. Built. Sexy. What is wrong with me?

I flip back a few more pages, to February and the first sketch I ever did of Leo, at his mother's show.

He was slumped in a chair to one side of the gallery, a modern teenage boy as Rodin's *Thinker*, rumpled hoodie, holes in his jeans, elbow propped on his knee and his chin in his hand. I knew after two seconds of seeing him that he was Diana Robinson's son. For a minute I just stood there, looking, internalizing his shapes and shading for this sketch, the one I'd do of him later. Then I actually went over and talked to him, a move so unlike my introverted self that thinking back on it surprises me every time. How was I so inexplicably brave that day?

"It must be weird" is what I said to him.

He looked up, startled. "Weird?"

"To be your mom's, like, muse." Almost all of Diana Robinson's sculptures featured a little boy doing something strangely adult: reading Proust, driving a car, shaving, fastening a cuff link to his sleeve. I'd recognized Leo from the back—that cowlick he has on the right side of his head. It's in every sculpture, that uncooperative swirl of hair.

"How did you . . ." Leo seemed confused at how I knew who he was, but then he glanced around and realized. "Uh, yeah. It's weird. Little bit."

We struck up a conversation, and at the end of it he asked me out. This still feels like the most improbable thing ever. A guy asking me out doesn't seem like something that is possible in my world, which consists of Notre Dame High School (Catholic, all girls), babysitting my little sister, hanging out with my big sister, and my art stuff (a largely solitary obsession). I'd never been asked out before. And then suddenly—bam—there was Leo. Athletic, affable Leo. Who likes me, maybe even *loves* me. Who wants to kiss me.

And other things.

God, I think. *What have I done?*

There's a single sharp rap on my bedroom door. Pop's voice. "Dinner."

"Okay," I call back faintly. "I'll be right down."

YOU MAY THINK YOU KNOW THEIR STORIES . . .

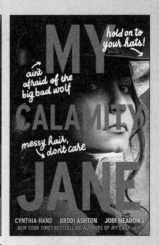

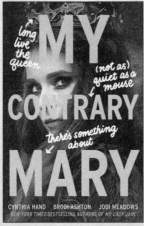

Go on these fantastical and romantical adventures through the past with these stories you won't find in any textbook.

ALSO FROM
CYNTHIA HAND

Insightful standalone novels about love, life, and family.

READ EVERY NOVEL
IN THE CAPTIVATING
UNEARTHLY SERIES
by CYNTHIA HAND

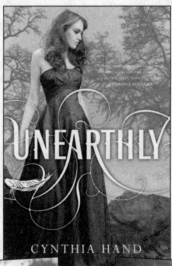

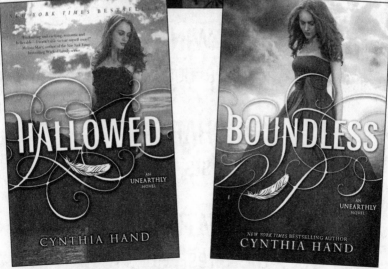

JOIN THE

Epic Reads
COMMUNITY